THE GREEN WITCH

WITCHES OF PALMETTO POINT BOOK 12

WENDY WANG

Copyright © 2021 by Wendy Wang

All rights reserved.

No part of this book may be reproduced in any form or by any electronic or mechanical means, including information storage and retrieval systems, without written permission from the author, except for the use of brief quotations in a book review.

Cover Design by Dark Imaginarium Designs

V10.10.21

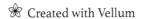 Created with Vellum

CONNECT WITH ME

One of the things I love most about writing is building a relationship with my readers. We can connect in several different ways.

Join my reader's newsletter.

By signing up for my newsletter, you will get information on preorders, new releases and exclusive content just for my reader's newsletter. You can join by clicking here: http://wendy-wang-books.ck.page/482af1c7a3

You can also follow me on my Amazon page if you prefer not to get another email in your inbox. Follow me here.

Connect with me on Facebook

Want to comment on your favorite scene? Or make suggestions for a funny ghostly encounter for Charlie? Or

CONNECT WITH ME

tell me what sort of magic you'd like to see Jen, Daphne and Lisa perform? Like my Facebook page and let me know. I post content there regularly and talk with my readers every day.

Facebook: https://www.facebook.com/wendywangauthor

Let's talk about our favorite books in my readers group on Facebook.

Readers Group: https://www.facebook.com/groups/1287348628022940/

You can always drop me an email. I love to hear from my readers

Email: wendy@wendywangbooks.com

Thank you again for reading!

CHAPTER 1

Lisa Holloway parked her white BMW close to the entrance of the Palmetto Point Florist and Garden Center. This was the last step in her grand purchase. A purchase that still filled her with doubts. The deal she had brokered with Peter Gannon felt almost as if she were taking advantage of him. He'd priced the business well below market value, and try as she may, he wouldn't hear of taking a penny more.

Lisa had to constantly quiet the voice inside her head that said this was too good to be true. She'd pored over the financials, and nothing seemed out of line. Both the garden center and the boutique florist reported healthy sales in all four quarters last year. She'd met the staff, and they seemed to love the company. She was delighted to hear they all wanted to stay on even after the purchase.

Lisa found new things most difficult when her intuition argued with her logic. She had even asked her cousin Charlie, the psychic in her family, to meet her this morning and walk through both businesses. Just to make sure she cleansed the place of spirits or any other supernatural issues.

Lisa took a deep breath and told herself, "You got this," and stepped out of her car just as Charlie emerged from her blue Honda Civic and waved hello. Lisa waved back.

She walked up to her cousin, shielding her eyes from the bright morning sun. "Hey, Charlie."

"Hey, yourself." Charlie grinned and threw her arm to Lisa's new business beyond the parking lot. "This place looks fantastic. I got here early and couldn't resist walking along the fence and peering inside just to get a feel for it. I can't wait to get in there and look at all the statuary. I'd love to have a little birdbath that I can see out my kitchen window. I also noticed those old-fashioned gazing balls. Bunny used to have one in her flower bed. I love those."

Lisa laughed nervously. "Me too. I'm sure Daddy would be happy to help you make a flower bed. And, of course, there'll be a family discount."

"I appreciate that. I didn't realize the florist was this close to us. I thought it was on Market Street."

Lisa shrugged. "Nope. It's always been here, according to Peter. He told me his family used to have a farm where they grew the flowers themselves and sold cut bunches at the nursery. It was so popular his wife opened a florist."

"Do they still have the farm?" Charlie strolled toward the entrance next to Lisa.

"No, not anymore. They contract with a local farmer now for the fresh-cut bunches." Lisa thought for a minute. "I guess I'll be the one contracting with the farm now."

"I guess so." Charlie grinned. "So when do you take possession of this place?"

"We sign the papers next Friday, and then it's all mine. Unless you sense something bad. There's still time to pull out of the contract." Lisa pressed her hand against her belly.

"You worry too much. So far, all I sense is a cheerful place. There're emotions of all sorts. Especially coming from there." Charlie pointed to the small square box of a building with a wide front window and an artfully painted sign that read Florist. Even with twenty-five yards and a shared parking lot between them, Lisa felt the different energies of the two parts of the business, and no doubt Charlie had too. "Maybe it's the root of all your nerves."

"What do you mean?" Lisa asked, giving her cousin a wary glance.

Charlie hemmed and hawed for a moment, stuttering through her words. Finally, she looked her cousin straight in the eye and answered. "Now, don't get mad. Sometimes, when there are big emotions involved, you withdraw into your shell and put out spikes. Just keep that in mind. You know, the people who come to a florist usually come in for love, comfort, or grief. We all know emotions are just not your thing."

"That's not true," Lisa snapped. "I do fine with people's emotions."

"Okay, okay." Charlie held up her hands, surrendering before the battle could even begin. "You're right, and I'm wrong."

"And anyway, it's not like I'm going to be managing them every day myself. Both places have managers and staff already. I might get my hands dirty in the beginning, and after that occasionally, like the holidays, Valentine's or Mother's Day."

"You're right." Charlie tipped her head and shrugged. "You probably won't have to deal with anything at all."

Lisa stared for what seemed like a long time at her cousin, wishing she had Charlie's ability to snatch thoughts out of people's heads. "If you see something, please tell me."

"I think what you mean is, please talk me out of buying this place."

And she was right. As usual. Charlie had picked up on her buyer's fear. Lisa rolled her eyes at her cousin and gestured toward the front gate. "Come on. Let's go look at those birdbaths."

"Great," Charlie said and followed Lisa inside.

CHAPTER 2

With a quick flourish of her pen, it was finally done. Despite Lisa's typical worrying about taking on the new business, on Friday afternoon, she signed the last of the papers that made her the new owner of Palmetto Point Florist and Garden Center.

She texted her fiancé, Jason Tate, the news then headed from her law office to meet Mr. Gannon so he could introduce her around.

Lisa approached the entrance of the nursery and found Mr. Gannon waiting with a wide smile on his face, raising a hand in a wave. His silver-white hair glowed like a halo in the scorching August sun, and gray-tinted glasses hid his warm brown eyes. His friendly, wrinkled face welcomed her, and all her lingering doubts melted away.

"Hello there, young lady," he called.

She gave him a friendly smile, her excitement building. "Hello, Mr. Gannon. Looks like business is booming." She looked past him into the garden center.

"Yes, ma'am. And this isn't even our best month. Wait till you see what happens in the spring and early summer."

"That definitely makes me feel good." She joined him in front of a square trellis that opened into rows of long wooden tables holding plants for sale.

He grinned. "You ready for this?"

"Ready as I'll ever be, I guess."

"Fantastic." He nodded at her t-shirt, shorts, and trail shoes. "I was worried you were going to show up in one of your pretty, pinstriped suits."

"No, sir," she said. She pulled a pair of garden gloves from the pocket of her cargo shorts. "I came prepared to work."

"That's the best way to learn this business." He gestured for her to follow him. "Come on back. Let's you and I pitch in and help Maria take care of some of these people."

"Yes, sir."

* * *

Lisa hovered her hand over a flat of Portulaca, and the brightly colored blooms of the mossy succulent shifted their double-petaled faces toward her fingers. She could feel their radiant energy, and it sent a thrill through her.

"Now, if you're looking for ground cover." Lisa turned to the customer that had followed her across the garden center, and continued her riff on one of her favorite plants. "You can't go wrong with Portulaca. It's beautiful, it spreads like wildfire, and it will reseed. In fact, you might find it in places you'd never expect after the first year. So you may want to monitor it. But it's also drought-tolerant, and it likes hot weather. So, if you don't have a watering system in place, it's perfect."

The woman tapped her pointed chin. "Is pink the only color it comes in?"

"No, ma'am, we have many colors here." Lisa gestured across the table like a game show hostess. "You could buy several flats and mix-and-match."

The woman pursed her thin lips, and the bright orange lipstick she wore bled into the lines around her mouth. "I like yellow."

"We have about four flats here. If that's not enough, we can order more. It will take about a week to get them in." Lisa hoped she remembered the correct order schedule Maria had told her about earlier.

"I don't have an enormous area to cover at the moment, so I'll take the four flats that you have."

"Wonderful. Is there anything else you need today?" Lisa lifted the first flat from the table and placed it on the large flatbed cart the woman had dragged behind her.

"I could use some mulch. Is there any way you could help me load it into my car?"

"Of course." Lisa grinned and finished loading the other three flats of Portulaca. "How many bags do you need?"

"You know, I'm not sure. I need to re-mulch all my flowerbeds. Do you give discounts on large quantities?"

"I believe we do. Although if you have a large area, we can sell to you by the cubic yard, which will be cheaper. We can even deliver to your house."

"Oh my, that's wonderful. Let's do that then."

"Yes, ma'am. Have you ever thought about putting in a birdbath? All our statuary and birdbaths are on sale this weekend. And I don't know about you, but I love watching the birds."

"I do, too. In fact, I had my husband put up a bird feeder this past spring. Of course, it's become more of a squirrel feeder." The woman chuckled.

"Just so you know, we have bird feeders that are squirrel-proof. I got one for my daddy last year, and he loves it. Although he felt so bad for the squirrels, he had to put out a corn holder for them." Lisa grinned but didn't meet the woman's eyes. It wasn't a lie exactly. She bought a bird feeder for her father, but Jack Holloway had never felt sorry for a squirrel in his life. It took Charlie, Jen, and

Lisa shaming him to keep him from shooting the poor little critters with a pellet gun.

"Well, I suppose it couldn't hurt to look."

"Of course. Let me show you where they are."

After she finished ringing up the woman's order for mulch, six more flats of flowers besides the Portulaca, a birdbath, and a brand new squirrel-proof feeder, Lisa looked around the garden center, her nerves thrumming with excitement.

"I had no idea you were going to be so good at this," Maria said, joining her in the kiosk. "I swear, girl, our sales are through the roof today, and it's you that's done all the selling."

"Oh, it's just beginner's luck." Lisa chuckled. "Plus, it's been really fun. I didn't expect to like it so much."

"It is fun. You know, I'd love to talk to you about ways we can improve the business if you're interested." Maria lowered her voice and glanced around. Her gaze settled on Peter standing across the garden center in front of an extensive selection of pavers available for special order.

"I love Peter Gannon to death, but he is not a man who likes change. You know his whole attitude is, if it ain't broke, don't fix it."

Lisa perked up. "I would love to hear your ideas." An excited thrum radiated through her chest. "As much as I'd like to quit my job and do this full time, I don't see that happening anytime soon. Not unless I win the lottery."

"I hear you."

Lisa leaned in toward Maria to keep their conversation private from customers' ears. "But growing this business could go a long way to making it happen, and I'm so glad you're here to help me navigate and run things."

Maria's face lit up with an enthusiastic smile. "I'm really excited about the opportunity. I think we should do more than just offering plants and mulch and hardscape to DIYers. You know they can get that stuff at a big box garden center."

"It's the expertise people come for at places like this. And the customer service, of course. What are you thinking?"

"I don't know if Peter told you this, but I have a degree in landscape design. I've tried a couple times to hang out a shingle, but it's difficult if you don't have the money to back it up."

At that news, Lisa felt the thrill of new ideas and possibilities, exactly why she wanted to try this new venture. "Maria, that's amazing. I didn't know. Landscape and garden design would be a wonderful addition to the business. We'll need to make alliances with some contractors."

Maria's voice rose to an excited vibration. "My brother's a contractor. He does a lot of sprinkler systems and hardscape building right now, but he's open to anything."

"Really? That's fantastic." An energy Lisa had never

felt before filled her from head to toe. "Not only are we going to rock this business, but we're going to grow it."

"Really?" Maria's face lit up.

Her faint green aura, which Lisa had noticed when they first began talking, grew brighter. A strange thought flitted through Lisa's head. Was Maria a potential green witch? Her energy made it seem so. It was possible to have an affinity for nature, a spiritual bond with it, and not realize how much power she could channel from it.

So many witches didn't recognize their own magic in the beginning, especially if they had no one to guide them. Lisa thanked the goddesses every day she'd been born into her family of witches. For now, she'd keep an eye out for any other signs from Maria. It was too early in their relationship to ask her if she had a spiritual practice. She'd keep her remarks businesslike for the time being.

"I mean, I need to run some numbers and see exactly what it's gonna cost and that sort of thing. And then I'll have to come up with the money, of course, but I think that's very doable."

Maria made a squeeing sound and danced on her tiptoes.

"Looks like you two are hatching some sort of plan for world domination." Peter Gannon approached the kiosk with a customer in tow wearing a denim jumpsuit that had seen better days. "Maria, could you help this gentleman order some of those flagstone pavers?"

"Of course." Maria traded glances with Lisa and

reached for a clipboard from the cubby beneath the counter.

Lisa touched her arm. "We can talk later."

"Sure thing." Maria nodded and turned her attention to the customer. "How can I help you, sir?"

CHAPTER 3

By the time 6 o'clock came, Lisa's back ached a little, and she felt tired down to her bones, but it was the best kind of tired, the kind that came from hard work. When the last customer left the center, Maria shut the chain-link gate and hung the closed sign. She signaled for Lisa to follow her to the office near the back of the garden center.

Inside the small building, Lisa found a showroom with an array of tools, fertilizers, seeds, houseplants, and specialty items for orchid and koi pond care. A large lattice screen separated the office and bathroom from the larger space. Somehow, Peter Gannon had managed to squeeze an L-shaped desk into the small office, and he barely looked away from the computer when they entered.

"So, what do you think?" Maria asked, settling into

one of the folding chairs. Her shoulder-length dark wavy hair lifted when they walked through the air conditioner blowing just over the door.

Lisa took another chair and let out a satisfied breath before answering. "I think you and the team here do an outstanding job. I'm really impressed."

"Thank you," Maria said.

Mr. Gannon took a break from going through the day's receipts and smiled at Lisa. "Looks like the lucky streak is holding. This was one of the best days we've had all summer. And we've had some good days."

"I don't know about luck," Lisa said. "Y'all are pretty skilled at getting people what they want."

Gannon grinned widely. "Oh, I don't disagree; everybody here is dedicated and skilled, but don't discount lady luck."

Maria rolled her eyes. "All right, Peter. You should at least tell her about the lucky plant."

Lisa's cheeks hardened when she clenched her jaw, and her eyes widened. "What lucky plant?"

"I'm going to show you, young lady." He smiled at Maria as if they had a secret.

"Okay, but I tell you what, you're making me nervous."

"Oh, there's nothing to be nervous about. You told me the whole reason you wanted this place is because you love plants, and you love the idea of making people happy. Which is what we do here. But I can't do it all on my own."

THE GREEN WITCH

"You know, Mr. Gannon, we have a full-disclosure clause in our contract. If you haven't been forthcoming on everything…"

"Oh, it's nothing like that." He waved off her anxiety. "Allow me to introduce you to the one thing that makes this place run so well."

"All right," Lisa said warily.

"Come with me." He rose from his chair, and Lisa followed him. The three of them walked out of the small office toward the vine-covered trellis shielding the cash registers. A large pot sat on a shelf near the top of the kiosk, the vines overflowing it on all sides. Lisa looked at the silvery, heart-shaped leaves. "Isn't this a pothos?"

"Yep, she's a silver satin pothos."

"I know they're used in Feng Shui, but I didn't know they were lucky."

Lisa brushed a hand over a leaf. The plant trembled at her touch at first before the leaves expanded, opening as if breathing her in. A long tendril reached for her hand, and she watched in wonder. A spark of magical energy connected with her fingertips and wound itself around her forearm. She cast a furtive glance at Peter and Maria to see if they'd noticed it.

Peter's dark eyes flattened to slits. "Huh. Never seen it do that before."

Lisa pulled her hand away and turned her attention back to the conversation. The magic of the plant retreated.

"Do what?" Lisa kept her face neutral and pretended the plant hadn't reached for her. Hadn't just curled magic around her hand and arm. She'd learned to love plants at her mother's feet, learned they responded to her touch and learned some plants held magical properties of their own. It reminded her so much of her mother and all the times she spent helping her mother care for her plants. A pebble formed in her throat. Why was she getting so emotional over a plant?

Peter Gannon stared for a moment more before he shook his head. "Nothing, I guess." His friendly grin returned.

"So tell me more about the pothos. Where did you get it?" Lisa dropped her hand to her side and leaned her back against the counter. Another vine brushed against the back of her shoulder and she fought the urge to jump as if it had goosed her. Maybe before she left today, she'd take a cutting and add it to the dozens of plants scattered throughout her condo and balcony.

"It was a gift to me from a Filipino woman when I was in the Navy. This was long before I married my wife. We had stopped at port, and I had a relationship with this woman. She gave me a cutting and told me that if I kept it alive, it would bring me nothing but prosperity and happiness. And so I did. I snuck it back on board my ship and kept it alive for months before we finally reached port. I planted it properly when I got home, and ever since, I've had nothing but luck. I met my wife soon after, and we married and started this business together. She ran the florist and I ran the gardening business. We raised three sons who have their own successful careers. Every single one of them has taken a cutting from this plant and nurtured it and made their own lives prosperous."

"Kind of like lucky bamboo?"

He chuckled and shook his head. "I never had much luck with lucky bamboo."

Lisa nodded. She loved the popular house plant and had several of the thin bamboo-like stalks growing in trays of pebbles in her condo. "They can be tricky. They're fussy about chemicals in the water."

"We've sold our fair share of it, but it never thrived for me. This plant, however, has always brought me prosperity."

Peter held his hand out but didn't seem to notice the tendril shrinking away from his palm. He roughly grabbed hold of a leaf between his thumb and forefinger. Lisa's breath caught. She feared he might tear the poor thing. She opened her mouth to say something, but Peter let go of the plant.

"I can attest to that," Maria chimed in. "After I'd been here about a year, Peter gave me a cutting, and I took it home and nurtured it. It has done nothing except bring me good luck."

"Money?" Lisa fully brought her attention back to the conversation.

Maria shrugged and shook her head. "Not exactly. I

think it listens to your desires and gives you what you want. I had a string of bad luck with boyfriends, then within two months after I planted the cutting, I met my husband, and we now have a four-year-old son. They're the best thing in my life."

"That's wonderful." Lisa smiled, genuinely happy for Maria. She turned her gaze to Peter. "Are you taking it with you?"

"No, you bought this place, and all the plants come with it, but I'm going to take several cuttings from it if you don't mind."

"Of course not. Take however much you need." Lisa glanced up at the plant but didn't touch it just in case it moved toward her again. "We'll water and feed it to make sure it stays healthy."

"You don't believe me." Peter cocked his head.

"Oh no, it's not that…" Lisa crossed her arms and gave him a reassuring smile. "It's not that at all."

"It's okay. I know how it sounds." He chuckled. "But if you take care of the plant, the plant will take care of you. It's like anything in life, I guess. You reap what you sow."

"Yes, I suppose you do." A pang of anxiety filled Lisa's chest again. Just like before she had signed the papers. She glanced around the empty garden center. What if she couldn't handle it? What if she couldn't make the numbers work? What if she failed? Her employees were counting on her to keep things going. *Too late now, Lisa*

Marie. Failure isn't an option. One of the plant's long shoots dropped softly onto her shoulder as if to reassure her.

Peter gave her a cheery grin. "I'll be around town for another month if you need some advice. After that, Carla and I are hitting the road in our RV. It's always been our dream to travel across the country and visit all those places we've wanted to see."

"What a wonderful adventure." Lisa breathed a little easier, taking in the positive energy of all the plants surrounding them. The force she connected with the most. "I plan to spend my evenings and weekends here and at the florist while I learn the businesses. Please be sure to stop in and say goodbye before you leave town."

"I sure will." Peter nodded and smiled.

CHAPTER 4

"Hi, Maria." Lisa arrived a little before 4:30 pm on Wednesday afternoon and stowed her purse in the garden center kiosk. For the next couple of weeks, she'd lightened her schedule at her law practice so she could work at the garden center or the florist in the late afternoons, or early mornings, to get a better feel for the businesses. She stepped back and looked at Maria's handiwork. "You're giving the lucky plant a trim?"

Maria gathered up the trimmings on the counter into an empty cardboard box. "Yeah, it's getting a little crazy. This thing grows like a weed."

Lisa reached into the box and grabbed a couple of cuttings. Even separated from its mother plant, the energy from the leaves and stem flowed into Lisa's hand, and her fingertips prickled. The temptation to snap her fingers just to see if they would emit green sparks entered her head, but she pushed it away. "You mind if I take a few?"

Maria chuckled. "Of course not. Technically they're yours."

Lisa gathered a few more cuttings in case some of them didn't root when she put them in water

"How are sales today?"

"It's been a decent day for a Wednesday. I scheduled a couple of ads last month to run for the Labor Day sale. I got a mockup today from the paper if you want to look at it."

"Great. Can you email it to me?"

"Sure."

"Excuse me," a man approached the kiosk. Lisa didn't know if it was his hulking size or the dark energy emanating from him, but something made her want to shrink away. She shook off the feeling and painted a smile across her face.

"Hi, how can we help you?" Lisa asked.

"I was wondering if you could sell me that plant?" He pointed to the lucky plant.

Lisa opened her mouth to answer, but Maria was faster.

"I'm sorry, it's not for sale."

"Okay," he said, clearly miffed. "What kind of plant store is this if you don't sell the plants that are here?"

"We sell plenty of plants." Maria stood her ground. "It's just this one is the personal property of the owner."

"Who's the owner?" He put his hands on his narrow hips. The muscles in his arms rippled.

"I am." Lisa raised her hand. "And I'm sorry, but it's not for sale."

His lips curled into a snarl, and his jaw flexed. He raised his voice louder. "I can't believe you won't sell me a plant."

Lisa's gaze flitted around the garden center. People milling around the aisles of plants and gardening gear stopped and stared at the spectacle. Her cheeks flamed with heat, but she didn't back down.

"Again, I'm sorry, sir, but it is not for sale."

His face turned almost purple, the color stretching from his forehead to his chest. Why was he so angry? Did he really think pitching a fit like a two-year-old would make her give in? He pressed his lips together as if to keep his fury inside his mouth, then reached for the lattice. A couple of long vines hung down, and he snatched them, yanking so hard the pot fell to the ground. The terra-cotta container shattered into pieces against the concrete. Dirt spewed outward over their shoes. A look of surprised glee crossed his face when he glanced at the broken vine in his hand.

A high-pitched keening filtered through Lisa's mind. A wave of nausea overcame her, and she suddenly felt the urge to vomit.

"Hey!" Maria said. A wicked grin spread across his lips, and he took off running. It shocked Lisa when Maria lit out after him.

"Adam!" Maria shouted, "We've got a runner!"

Adam Lane, the other full-time employee, stopped in the middle of watering the row of hanging geraniums and scanned the garden center. Maria pointed to the man. Adam dropped the watering wand in his hand and took off after him. The man raced through the open chain-link gate, slammed it closed behind him, then scrambled over the tailgate of a black pickup truck parked in front of the entrance with the engine running. He banged his hand against the truck bed and shouted, "Go, go, go."

Adam opened the gate and chased the truck across the parking lot until it screeched into traffic and sped away. The man gave Adam a little wave and flipped the bird at him before the truck disappeared around the curve.

Adam gulped in air and bent over with his hands on his knees.

Lisa and Maria caught up to him.

"Oh my God, I didn't expect you to chase the truck." Maria put her hand in the center of his back. "Are you okay?"

"Yeah, I'm fine. What an asshole." Adam pushed up straight and pressed his hand to his gut. "Did you see him flip the bird at me?"

"I missed that part. Sorry," Maria said.

Lisa stared worriedly at the path the disappearing truck had taken, then turned to Adam. "I'm glad you're all right. He could've been a nut job, you know. It's just a plant. It wouldn't have been worth dying over if he had a gun or something like that." She flashed on Jason Tate. Her fiancé was a sheriff's deputy. Should she tell him about this? She never planned to draw him into her business.

"The license plate had one of those covers that makes it harder to read, but I think I got part of the number. If you want to report it," Adam said.

"I do," Lisa said. Of course, Jason should know about this. The guy committed a crime.

Adam nodded. "PBU. Or it might've been BBU. Like I said, it was dark."

"No worries." Lisa whipped her phone from the front pocket of her cargo shorts and typed the partial plate info into her notes app. Then quickly texted it to Jason.

"Yep." Adam rubbed his side as if he had a stitch. "Dang, I need to take up running again. You'd think with all the lifting I do around here, I'd be in better shape."

"Maybe you're just getting old." Maria poked him in the ribs.

Adam didn't look a day over twenty-five. His short brown hair and bright gray eyes sparkled. "Yep. Getting to be an old man for sure. So what was that all about, anyway?"

"He wanted to buy the plant we keep at the kiosk," Maria said.

"The lucky plant?" Adam snickered.

"You laugh, but it's true. If you'd take a cutting, you'd find out." Maria grinned. "He grabbed it, tried to take it but just ended up making a big mess."

"Yeah." Lisa threw a glance over her shoulder at the garden center. Most people had ignored the excitement and gone back to shopping. "We should get back in there and clean it up, check on the customers."

"Yes, ma'am." Adam nodded.

After they returned to the kiosk, Lisa gingerly lifted the poor broken plant. "The root ball seems to be okay."

Maria swept much of the mess into a dustpan. "I'll geta new pot and some soil. Be right back."

"Thanks." Lisa inspected the longer tendrils Maria had spared. Now broken, most would have to be cut off. She felt a connection with the plant, and when she touched it, its energy flowed into her fingertips, up her arms, and into her chest.

"I'm so sorry that happened to you, but I promise I'll take good care of you. You're going to be all right." She took the trimming shears from the counter and carefully sliced away any broken tendrils and leaves, and dropped them in the cardboard box. The plant shuddered in her hands.

Maria put a ten-inch terra-cotta pot with a tray and

half-full bag of potting soil on the counter next to Lisa. "I'll get a watering can."

"Thank you." Lisa filled half the pot with soil and set the root ball on top. "Set your roots to grow, through which your lifeblood flows," she whispered over the plant and added handfuls of potting soil. She spotted Maria on her way back to the kiosk and added more soil till she covered the plant's roots. Before Maria returned, Lisa quickly tamped the dirt in place and uttered an incantation. "Earth, air, water, and fire, I call all the elements to heal you from this blow."

Lisa shielded the plant from Maria's view as the light from her energy flowed from her fingertips into the soil.

Maria set the watering can down on the counter, seemingly unaware of Lisa's special ministrations. "Here you go."

"Thanks." Lisa lifted the can and soaked the soil, watering it thoroughly. "That should do it."

"Poor thing. You really had to cut it back."

"I know. It'll rebound, though. These guys are resilient."

"Yeah. They sure are," Maria mused. "What did you do with the cuttings?"

"I put them in there with the others you cut earlier." Lisa pointed to a box on the ground. "It's for composting, I assumed."

"Cool. I'll take care of it. I'll get this all swept up, too, if you want to head back to your office and catch up on the books. I've already put in all the entries through yesterday."

"Thanks." Lisa lifted the plant in its new pot and placed it onto the shelf. "Maybe we should find some way to strap that pot in place. Just so something like this doesn't happen again."

"That's a great idea. I'll ask Adam to do it. He's really handy that way."

"Great." Lisa flipped up the pass-through. She paused before closing it. "Have you worked on that thing we talked about last week?"

Maria stopped sweeping up the dirt and broken shards of the pot. "I have. But I'm not done yet."

"Cool. I can't wait to read it."

"I've never really written a business plan before. So, it's not like it's going to be perfect or anything."

"Don't worry. Perfection isn't the point. We just need to get our intention for expanding the business on paper. You're the one with the numbers for that."

Maria grinned. "You have no idea how excited I am about this."

"Me too. Stop in before you leave for the day, okay?"

"I will." Maria nodded and knelt to sweep up the rest of the broken pot.

CHAPTER 5

Friday morning, Lisa took a seat at her breakfast bar and poured herself a bowl of raisin bran cereal. She added a splash of almond milk and sliced up half a banana. Jason called it her old lady food. But it was her favorite breakfast, stretching all the way back to her childhood. She could remember her mother pulling down three bowls and filling them with cold cereal on busy mornings before she and Jen left for school. Jen wouldn't touch the raisin bran cereal with a ten-foot pole, and her mother often ended up making instant oatmeal for her sister. They'd been so young when their mother died. Sometimes the memories seemed dreamy and glowing as if they had happened during a long, heavy sleep. She scooped a spoonful of the raisin bran into her mouth, catching a piece of banana. A cool breeze wafted across the back of her neck, and the smell of gardenia filled her senses. Lisa closed her eyes and breathed in the out-of-place aroma before she glanced around her condo to find the source.

The two-bedroom, two-bath condo she'd gotten for a steal overlooked the river. On days when she got home before sunset, she loved to sit on the balcony with Jason. They'd drink a beer while they talked about their day, unwind among the hanging plants and planters she had attached to the banister. It was her own little haven. And the view of the marsh turning golden in the sun's setting rays always relaxed her. But she had no gardenias on her balcony. And none in the hanging planters near the sliding glass door. Everything in her living room appeared normal, from the white couch to the large, green modern-style armchairs that flanked it. She checked the dark cherry coffee table, arranged artfully with candles and spiky plants in the center. Undisturbed as well.

Gardenia was her mother's favorite flower.

"Mama?" she whispered to the living room. Of course, no answer came. She wasn't Charlie. It wasn't like she could see or hear spirits. Still, she couldn't shake the feeling that her mother's presence was with her, although not in an ominous sort of way. It comforted her to think of her mother walking through life with her, watching over her.

She went back to taking a bite of her raisin bran cereal. Jason had left at the crack of dawn to file some paperwork that he had put off too long already. When she finished, she rinsed the bowl and retrieved her tarot cards from her altar. She had time for a quick reading before she headed into her office for an early morning appointment with a client about making changes to her estate. Lisa's law practice covered estate planning and probate law.

She closed her eyes and shuffled the cards, then spread them out in a half-moon shape in front of her. Her hand hovered from one side to the other, and she waited for a familiar tingle in her fingers before drawing the first of three cards. She repeated the process two more times. She laid the cards in a straight line, the three-card spread representing past, present, and future. She had so many decisions to make about their wedding, and the resistance from Jason seemed stronger than ever. He would've been perfectly happy to just elope. She didn't even know why she wanted a big wedding; it just seemed like the thing she should do.

She turned over the first card, revealing The Lovers. She smiled because it represented her past with Jason, how they had chosen each other. It may have started out as some fun brief fling, but it became so much deeper. Never had she expected him to feel so much like home. Especially after he had mooned over Charlie when he first met her cousin.

Next, Lisa flipped over The Sun card, representing contentment and happiness, a good marriage, and children. She touched her finger to the child sitting on a horse in the center of the card. Children. She and Jason had certainly discussed it. He wanted to be a dad; she still had reservations about motherhood, though. And they hadn't even started their marriage yet. It was too soon to think about kids.

You're not getting any younger, Lisa Marie.

She pushed the thought away and turned over the third card, The Empress.

"What the hell?" she muttered. When she looked at the spread overall, it showed something that she wasn't ready for. Not yet. Marriage, pregnancy, motherhood. They came with the territory but seemed more like abstract concepts to her. She blew out a heavy breath and reshuffled the cards. They had to be wrong. She wasn't ready to be a mother.

When was the last time she had her period? She'd have to check her calendar. She cut the cards and dealt three in a row again. She breathed a little easier when she turned the Three of Cups. Sure, it could represent birth, but it was in the past position, and she took it to mean the birth of her new project, her new businesses.

She flipped the next card. The Sun again. Her stomach flip-flopped. Carefully, she took a deep breath and turned the last card. The Empress. The card of motherhood.

"Shut up." She snapped at the deck and scowled. "I will not get pregnant anytime soon. Jason and I still have to get married, and I just took on these businesses." She argued with the deck as if it somehow understood her, then stopped herself. Had she lost her mind?

The alarm on her wristwatch went off, announcing it was time to leave for work. She glanced down at the fancy smartwatch and dismissed the notification. She didn't have time to worry over a tarot spread right now. She'd drawn cards plenty of times that turned out to be wrong.

She gathered all the cards into a neat pile and put them back on her altar. And pushed the thought of motherhood out of her head for now. She had a client in an hour, and she needed to get to her office to prepare.

CHAPTER 6

Somewhere a witch was going to die today.

Charlie Payne had dreamed it, and more often than not, her dreams came true. Once upon a time, she thought her dreams a curse. She was beginning to think so again, ever since she started having reaper dreams as well as prophetic ones. She could help the people hurting in her prophetic dreams, if the dang universe gave her enough information. There was nothing she could do to prevent the deaths in her reaper dreams. She was powerless.

Charlie spun the quartz obelisk on the corner of her desk and fought with the images from last night's dream. If it were a reaper dream, she could no more stop the death of the witch from happening than she could stop her own eventual fate of becoming a reaper.

Maybe, she thought, if she let the dream flow through

her, she would finally be free, and she could get back to work.

The scene unfolded in her head like a movie, starting with Charlie finding herself walking across the tiny living room in the home of a young woman, then kneeling in front of a two-tiered coffee table.

Little things stood out in the room—a bookshelf full of books on herbs, potions, and magic, An abstract painting hung above an antique-looking sideboard, an array of photos on the wall near the door leading to a hallway. Charlie's focus caught on a picture of the woman in a field of wildflowers with her arms flung up and an unbridled grin on her face.

The woman herself knelt on a white, shaggy rug, the pink bottoms of her bare feet shining clean and fresh. Charlie noticed the woman's black ripped jeans hugging her curves and the way she tugged at the matching black tank top she wore. The woman retrieved a wicker basket with a hinged top from the bottom tier of the coffee table and opened the flap.

Charlie recognized familiar items inside the basket, telling her the woman was a witch—a black altar cloth, candles with holders, matches, a bowl of crystals, an incense burner, and several boxes of different types of incense. The witch quickly went about setting up her altar and lit three white candles with a wooden match.

The crystals sparkled in the warm light of the flames. The woman placed a picture of a man in front of the candles, and then she lit two cones of incense. Smoke coiled up from the incense in long, pale gray ribbons. Charlie could almost smell the heady aromas of frankincense and myrrh mixed with sandalwood.

The witch's choice of incense set boundaries to make her place free of negativity and to give her some peace. Had the man in the photo robbed the woman of her peace? Broken her heart? Charlie wished she could stop the scene from happening, wished she could sit down and talk with the woman, but all she could do was watch her perform her ritual.

The woman's dark curly hair reached the center of her back when she raised her face skyward and closed her eyes to commune with the goddess. The silver glint of the knife caught Charlie's attention. Her heart thudded in her ears. She wanted to scream at the woman to run, but only a garbled croaking escaped Charlie's mouth when he plunged the blade through the woman's neck, severing her spinal cord, ending her life.

Charlie opened her eyes, and her big empty office came into focus, her desk solid under her fingers. Reality flooded in, chasing away the replay of the dream that had haunted her during the night. But she couldn't stop the sour bile filling her mouth from the sickening scene she'd witnessed, even if it had just been a dream. She fought the urge to vomit. She grabbed the crystal again on her desk and tightly wrapped her hand around the quartz. The cold stone grounded her to the here and now.

She glanced at the desk across from hers. Her boss Ben—with whom she shared the office space—was at the Defenders of Light headquarters in Charlotte all week. The office felt huge and lonely without him. Her hand tightened around the obelisk again before she released it and returned it to its spot on the desk.

Her computer dinged. A message from the DOL's messaging app appeared, settling on an open chat window.

Good morning. Athena Whitley's words appeared in the window. *I hope you don't have a busy week planned. We've got a new case.*

Charlie began typing in the thread:

I figured it was coming.

You did?

Yes. Reaper dreams, remember?

Okay. What did you see?

I saw a witch get stabbed to death.

Did you also see him paint her blood on the wall?

No, I woke up screaming before then.

I'm sorry to hear that. Did you see his face at all?

No. It was as if I were watching from a corner of the room. All I saw was him holding a knife by the hilt. He plunged it into her neck.

Wow. It's like a death party in your head all the time.

Pretty much. Where'd the crime happen? And were we officially called in?

Yes, officially. The sheriff evidently knows you.

Really? Where am I going that I already know the sheriff?

Charleston County, South Carolina. Mclellanville.

Are you joking?

Nope.

That's Jason's territory. I'm surprised he hasn't called.

Would he work that far north?

I don't know. Any chance you want to come down and help me with the investigation? Since Ben is in Charlotte this week.

I'd love to. I'm not sure that I'm up to dealing with real criminals face-to-face, though.

I think you are. The only way to learn some things is to just do them.

Okay. I'll talk to Ben and make sure it's okay with him. Then I'll be on my way.

Great. Send me the information and I'll head that way.

Sure thing.

CHARLIE LET HER MIND DRIFT AS SHE DROVE UP HIGHWAY 17 toward McClellanville. She couldn't get the dream out of her mind, and dread settled into her stomach. How close would the crime scene be to her vision of the woman's death?

A little more than an hour later, she pulled onto the street Athena had given her and found it partially blocked. The police had set a perimeter around the duplex. Neighbors stood on porches or in their yards, gathered in groups, chatting and pointing at the woman's house.

Charlie parked in front of a house down the street, grabbed her credentials, and hopped out. She braced herself for the pushback that usually came with these sorts of cases. Those involving witches.

A uniformed deputy stopped her a few feet away from the yellow tape that extended from the driveway to the other side of the yard. He looked her up and down, his expression stony. "Ma'am, you can't come this way."

Charlie flashed her badge. "Hi, I'm here from the DOL. The sheriff requested me. I'd like to talk to the detective in charge, please." She gave him a smile, but his hard face didn't change as he studied her credentials.

"What is the DOL? I've never heard of it."

"I know. Most people haven't. We're a small agency."

He eyed her suspiciously before he said, "Wait here," and absconded with her credentials. She scowled but didn't put up a fuss. There wouldn't be any point. She tracked his movement through the deputies, combing the lawn for clues.

A woman wearing a dark gray suit and bright pink blouse took the credentials from the deputy and examined them before she gave Charlie a cautious glance. Charlie watched the woman pull her phone from her pocket and call someone.

Charlie gritted her teeth. The sheriff had invited her. Why hadn't he communicated that to the detective? As an outsider, she expected some doubt. But even at this distance, she could feel the woman's suspicion. Charlie folded her arms across her chest and stared at the woman.

For a second, she thought about using one of Evangeline's spells to make the woman more compliant. Her aunt had used that spell on them when she and her cousins were little kids. Charlie paused a moment to think—she couldn't count how many times. But since she would probably need to work with this detective, she decided against it. Better to start out on an even footing than to resort to witchcraft, for now.

The detective nodded to the person on the other end of her phone call. She glanced at Charlie again, clearly frustrated with how the call ended. An irritated frown formed on the woman's lips, matched by the one in the lines on her forehead. The detective clipped her phone to her belt and headed toward Charlie.

"Hi." The woman handed Charlie her credentials. "I'm Detective Billie Taggart. My boss evidently called you in to consult on this case?"

"Yes."

"What the hell is DOL?" She didn't hold back her annoyance.

Charlie scanned the scene. Too many curious eyes cast her way, and a sense of possessiveness spread across the scene like a thick, unwelcome fog.

"Is there someplace private we can talk?"

"Sure." Detective Taggart lifted the tape, and the two of them walked a comfortable distance from the crime scene, stopping close to Charlie's Honda Civic.

Charlie turned to face Detective Taggart. The woman stood all of 5'4", and her short dark hair curled around her ears. Her large brown eyes studied Charlie. Two silver hoops twinkled in the morning sunlight. A moon charm dangling from one earring caught Charlie's eye.

"DOL is Defenders of Light. We deal in things most police agencies don't want to admit exist," Charlie said nonchalantly. "That's a nice charm on your earring."

Billie Taggart tightened her full lips. Her cheeks sank in as if she'd sucked them in, making her angular face appear sharper, harder. She gave Charlie a hard stare. "Thanks. What sort of things?"

"Supernatural things. Witches, mainly. But we handle the odd creature case now and then."

Billie tucked her head back and narrowed her eyes. "You're kidding me, right?"

"No. I know this is difficult to accept. But I've worked with the sheriff before, and he's totally aware of my organization and what we do. I'd really prefer if we can work together on this."

"Or what? You'll come in and take my case?"

Charlie considered her words. The last thing she wanted was to step on anyone's toes. It could make investigating the witch's death more difficult.

"If he's a witch or some other creature, we get the

arrest. If this is a run-of-the-mill guy with a fetish for killing witches, we both get to close our cases, but you can have the arrest."

"What else would it be besides some guy with a fetish for killing witches? If it's not the boyfriend or somebody who had it out for her."

"You and I both know there are monsters in the world. Most of them wear a human face. But some of them don't. That's where I come in."

Billie Taggart narrowed her eyes.

Charlie didn't flinch. "You know, I have a feeling about you."

"Oh, please don't keep me waiting about your feelings." Billie didn't hold back her disdain. Something inside Charlie told her it was an act. The strange thing was, she couldn't seem to get a read on the detective's thoughts. Everything about Billie Taggart screamed 'guarded,' which made Charlie even more curious.

Charlie took a stab in the dark. "I think you're intrigued. And I think you want all the help you can get. You've never seen anything so horrendous as this crime scene."

Billie stared at her for a moment, her dark eyes unwavering before she rolled them. "I will work with you because my boss says I have to. Not because I'm intrigued by anything you have to say. If it were up to me, I would kick you off my crime scene, and if you tried to get back on, I'd arrest you."

"Good to know," Charlie said. "And for the record, I would do the same to you. Only it would involve a spell that left you with no memory of this place or this crime." A flicker of something that Charlie couldn't read flashed across Billie's face. "Just so long as we understand each other."

"We do," Billie said.

"Great," Charlie smiled. "Why don't you get me signed in, and we can walk through the scene together."

"Fine," Billie said, but it didn't sound fine.

If Charlie didn't make peace soon, she might have trouble. She really didn't want to take the case away from the detective. She'd much rather build a relationship with the Sheriff's Department than tear one down. She'd give Jason a call later to get more information on the detective. Maybe he'd give her some pointers on dealing with Billie Taggart. A deputy brought Charlie a pair of gloves and she snapped them over her hands. "Okay, I'm ready."

CHAPTER 7

Jason Tate stood back and watched as the coroner and his assistant inspected the body of a twenty-seven-year-old female slumped forward on a large round table. The enclosed carport where the woman died appeared to have served as her place of business.

The ancient aluminum windows let light into the room. And bugs. A dense cloud of flies buzzed around the body. The grimy, mildewed window unit at the back of the place still pumped cold, damp air into the room, but it wasn't enough to keep the stench of death from filling Jason's nostrils, even with mentholated rub smeared across his upper lip. Jason swiped at the flies landing on the victim's arms to get a better look at the cards spread out in front of her.

A black velvet tablecloth covered the pedestal table, and decorative cards formed a V-like pattern. Two cards were missing, and the others displaced. It seemed when she fell forward, the force of her torso hitting the table had scattered them. He recognized the tarot cards right away. Lisa consulted them regularly to make many decisions about her life.

One time he teased her after she'd changed her clothes three times for a meeting, and said, "didn't your cards tell you what to wear?" She'd cut her eyes at him in a way that made his balls shrivel a little. Afterward, he thought she might have hexed him for it. For a few days after his careless remark, everything seemed to go wrong. When he complained to her, his luck changed. He never teased her about her cards again.

The victim's blood soaked the tablecloth just under her upper body, and another puddle gathered on the floor near her feet and saturated the black jeans she wore.

The coroner brushed away a fly and pointed to her neck. "Her throat's been slashed." As if Jason couldn't see that. "She's out of rigor, bloat's set in, and based on lividity and her liver temp, she's been here at least a couple of days. The M.E. might give you a more precise time of death. But it's hot in here." Sonny Hodges wiped at his brow. "The temperature in here's going to affect TOD accuracy."

Jason nodded and watched the coroner lift her head

to point out the dark purple lividity coloring half her face where her blood had pooled in her body after death. The rest of her face had gone gray with purplish undertones, and her half-open eyes revealed cloudy irises.

"Also, I don't think he was very skilled." The coroner bent over and studied the woman's neck. The bald spot on the top of his head shone with sweat.

"Why do you say that?" Jason moved in closer so he could take a better look. The sight of the maggots in the wound made his stomach turn, and he grimaced.

"The wound is kind of jagged. He nicked the artery enough for her to die, but it was slow and probably painful. Maybe he hesitated." The coroner wiped his glove on his gray baggy coveralls as he stood up, then placed his hand on his lower back, stretching. His slight paunch jutted out.

"Lordy, my back is giving me fits today."

"Jesus H. Christ," Marshall Beck, Jason's longtime partner, and sometimes pain-in-the-ass, dropped his inspection of the victim's kitchen and joined Jason's conversation. "And you think he didn't know what he was doing? Sounds to me like he wanted her to die slow."

The coroner shrugged, and his long, wrinkled face soured. "That'll be y'all's call. I'm just telling you my opinion. You'll want to get the complete report from the M.E., of course."

Jason nodded. "Sure."

Jason and Beck stepped back so the coroner and his assistants could insert the corpse into a body bag and transport it to the county morgue. Jason scanned the room.

"We should check to see if she had an appointment book." Jason pointed to the table where she'd lain.

"Yeah. Could've been someone didn't like their fortune." Beck cocked his head and studied the array of cards. "What do you think this means?"

"I don't know." Jason pulled out his phone and snapped a quick picture, trying to crop out as much blood as he could.

Beck rolled his eyes. "You calling Charlie in already? We've barely started."

"Nope. Tarot cards aren't her thing. I'm sending this to an expert." Jason attached the photos to a text and pressed send.

Beck's forehead wrinkled, and he scowled. "Who?"

"Lisa." Jason jotted off a quick note and then gave Beck a sly grin.

"Um, detectives? Y'all are going to want to look at this." The coroner appeared to be moving something back and forth in the woman's mouth. Jason's lips twisted with disgust when the coroner drew out a folded tarot card.

"Well, shit," Beck said.

"I'll take that." Jason reached for the card with his gloved hand. "Hey, I need an evidence bag." A deputy handed a plastic zippered bag to Jason. He opened it up and slid the card inside.

Beck moved in so close Jason could feel his fiery breath against his ear.

"The Emperor," Beck said. "What do you think it means?"

"Do you mind? You're in my personal space." Jason elbowed his partner lightly.

Beck rolled his eyes and took a step back. "You know, you're getting awfully woo-woo."

Jason chuckled. "Says the man who won't walk under a ladder." Beck didn't respond. Jason stared him down. "We still have a scene to finish processing and interviews to do. Why don't you go see if you can find an appointment book or something?"

"Fine." Beck sniffed and headed back through the kitchen into what used to be a dining room and now served as the woman's office.

Jason turned in a circle, trying to imagine what had happened to the woman. A bright red neon sign glowed in the window. He could make out the word "psychic." A list of her services painted on a piece of plywood included things like tarot reading and aura cleansing. Was the woman a witch? Or just a charlatan trying to make a buck? Just a few years ago, he wouldn't have even asked himself those questions. Wouldn't have believed witches were real. Now, he knew better.

He took his phone out again and snapped a photo of

the card in the baggy, and pressed send. Less than a minute later, his phone rang. He grinned down at the caller ID. Lisa Holloway. "Hey."

"What did you just send me?" she asked, sounding both curious and disgusted at the same time.

"I'm working a case. It's a tarot spread."

"Are the cards covered in blood?" Lisa asked.

"I was kind of hoping you wouldn't notice that."

"How could I not notice that?"

She sounded irritated. She'd been moodier than usual lately. He almost asked if it was that time of the month, but thought better of it. The last thing he wanted was to be cast out onto the couch for the week, or worse, jinxed.

"You're right. I should've warned you. My bad."

"What happened?"

"A psychic out near Rantowles was killed last night. The spread was on the table where it happened. That last picture I sent you? That was stuffed in her mouth."

"Oh, my, goddess. Do you think the spread had something to do with her death?"

"Maybe." He looked at the cards. "It's a shot in the dark, I guess, but I'm thinking maybe she had a client who was not happy with the outcome."

"You think somebody killed her over a tarot reading?"

"Don't know yet. We're canvassing the neighborhood to see if anybody heard anything. I know this is a stab in the dark, but is there anything particularly wrong with the spread?"

Lisa grew quiet. "Give me a few minutes to look it over. I'll call you right back."

"Sure thing. Thanks." The line went dead, and he stuck his phone in the holder on his belt and went to find Beck.

Beck stood behind a desk with a book open in his hands. His reading glasses perched on the end of his long, thin nose. "I think I've got something. She had an appointment two nights ago at 6:45 with a B. Drake. There's a phone number."

Jason perked up. "Excellent."

"Yeah, from what I found in her book, she had a pretty full afternoon. We'll interview them all. You never know what somebody saw."

"Yep." The phone on Jason's hip rang. "That'll be Lisa and all her woo-woo."

Beck snorted and rolled his eyes.

Jason answered, "Hey, babe."

"Hey. I have a couple of questions."

"Sure, hang on a second." Jason left Beck to sort through the woman's desk and headed back to the table where she'd been killed. "So what do you think?"

"Can you tell where the last card was placed? The one that's on the floor."

Jason glanced down at the card. "Um, I'm just

guessing here, but it's on the right-hand side of the table, so maybe it was the last card of the V near the top. She fell forward when her assailant slit her throat, so it probably got knocked sideways then."

"Well, that's an image I didn't need in my head today. Thanks, honey."

"Sorry. I forget you're not used to this stuff like Charlie is."

"No, I'm sorry. Didn't mean to snap. I'm just a little on edge these days."

"You've got a lot going on. I mean, you just bought a new business for crying out loud."

"Thank you for recognizing that."

To say nothing of a weirdo smashing plants in the center, but he didn't remind her of that scary incident. Especially since he had no clue as to the assailant yet.

Her voice softened. He could almost hear her smile. "So can you tell where the card you found in her mouth was in the spread?"

"I don't know." He studied the spread again. "There's a card missing on the left side, so maybe it's that one."

"Okay, that was fourth from the top."

He could almost hear her brain whirring. "Um. What does it mean?"

"The Emperor card alone usually means someone who is in authority or control. It can also mean fatherhood, but if it's the missing card on the left, it represents the client. So he's evidently someone in control or authority. I wish I knew if it was laid out reversed or not."

"Would that make a difference?" Jason asked.

"Maybe. What's interesting from the pictures is the Moon card in the third position. It's reversed. That's hidden influences, and the card in that position shows secrets. This guy is hiding something. Maybe his real motive isn't as cut and dried as it might look on the surface."

Jason glanced at the spread. "At the moment. I don't have a motive, so I'll keep that in mind."

"No suspects yet?"

"No. Too early. Beck and I have some people to interview, though."

"At least you have a place to start. Have you called Charlie?"

"I hadn't planned on calling her. Why?"

"I think this woman is a witch."

"Just because she reads tarot cards?"

"No. I remember something about a witch from one of the local covens opening a business a couple of years ago in Rantowles. Hang on, let me check something. I seem to recall the woman gave Evangeline some business cards to hand out for her. I think I still have one."

He heard some shuffling in the background when she put the phone down. A moment later, she returned.

"Yep, here it is. Madame Turberville, for all your psychic needs," Lisa read the card aloud. "Charlie can check the witch registry for you through the DOL. Although there are plenty of witches who don't register, so it's not always the most reliable source."

"Good to know. Thank you. I appreciate your help with the cards. I'm going to trust since you're an officer of the court and all, you won't share any of this, as it is an ongoing investigation."

"Of course I won't. Consider me a consultant, just like Charlie." Her tone softened. "There's one other thing I should mention. The eight of swords card in the fifth position is interesting. That's the influences of others."

"Okay. Why's that so interesting?"

"Because it represents imprisonment or being trapped. And everything that he's doing in the spread seems to lead him to jail or a situation that he can't get himself out of."

"If the cards say I'm going to arrest him, I don't have any reason not to believe them, right?" Jason said, half-joking.

"It's something to consider. Will you be home for dinner?"

"Yes, and you?"

"I'll probably be a little late," she admitted, sounding sheepish. "I went by the florist this morning and worked for a bit, so I've got things to catch up on here."

"Why don't I get takeout and meet you at your office when I'm done with my shift?"

"Sounds good. Text me when you're on the way."

"Sure thing. Love you."

"Love you, too."

Beck waved him over from the door of the office. "Um, if you're finished loving up your phone, I've got something you should see."

"Sure." Jason clipped his phone to his belt. Beck led him through the dining room, down a short hallway to a room that, Jason guessed, might have been a small bedroom once. The large stainless steel table centered in the space seemed out of place in the avocado green room. A gray marble mortar and pestle and several jars of various dried flowers covered part of the tabletop.

Shelves made of two-by-fours stretched from floor to ceiling on one wall, full of ingredients in jars of all sizes. On the adjacent wall, a short, wider shelf was empty. Only a few torn leaves and some heavy-duty grow lights remained. Jason picked up a piece of leaf litter.

"What the hell do you think she was growing?" Beck asked.

"I don't know." Jason flipped over a broken half of a leaf. The spacing on the bottom two shelves made Jason pause. "Is it just me, or does it look like this shelf might have been crammed full, and now stuff is missing?"

"Could be." Beck scrubbed his narrow chin.

"I've seen this kind of stuff before." Jason picked up a jar with some small bones in it.

"Weird stuff? Yeah, me too." Beck joked, but there was no humor in his tone. Only weariness.

"No. Witchy stuff." Jason met Beck's gaze.

"Fuck. I was afraid you were going to say that."

"I'll call the sheriff and let him know." Jason reached for his phone. "Then I'll call Charlie."

"Yep."

CHAPTER 8

Charlie's stomach churned a little when she walked into the living room and found the victim's body slumped over her altar. The scene looked identical to her dream. She turned to Billie. "When's the coroner arriving?"

"He's working on another case now. It'll be at least another hour before he gets here," Billie said.

"Another murder case?"

"Yeah. You weren't called out for that one, too, were you?"

"No." Charlie shook her head. "Do you know who's on point?"

"Um, no. Why do you care?"

Charlie shrugged. "It's just I'm friends with another detective in the Sheriff's Department. Jason Tate. Do you know him?"

"Yeah, of course, I do."

"I've helped him on other cases. And he's engaged to my cousin," Charlie said.

"I guess no one can ever say that Charleston County isn't a small world," Billie said.

"Very true." Charlie leaned in to get a closer look at the objects on the table. "So, what do we know?"

"Don't touch the body," Billie warned.

Charlie held her gloved hands up in surrender. "I know. This isn't my first rodeo. Just fill me in, please."

"Twenty-nine-year-old female. Apparently stabbed to death."

"Do we have an ID on her?" Charlie picked up a crystal obelisk on the table in front of the corpse and set it back in place. Something was missing from the altar. She knelt next to the coffee table and searched beneath it.

"Yeah, we do. What are you looking for?" Billie snapped.

"Was there a photo on her altar?"

"I don't know. Please stop touching stuff until we get it all documented."

Charlie scowled at the detective. "We're on the same side, you know. I'm just trying to get a feel for what happened here and what type of witch she was."

"There are different types of witches?" Billie asked.

"Yeah, of course. What was her name? Looks like she was communing with The Morrigan." Charlie picked up a metal raven sculpture sitting on top of the table. The white candle in the center of the altar had a painted triskelion symbol on one side.

"What's The Morrigan?" Billie gave her a skeptical look.

"A goddess. I wonder if she has a coven."

"Her name is Nicole Brewer, and the coven thing is more your department."

Charlie glared at the detective. "Did we recover a cell phone?"

"No, *we* didn't," Billie said, scowling. "It looks like he took her electronics. There's a laptop cord on the desk where a computer must've been, but we found no sign of a phone or a tablet."

"So he has all her contacts," Charlie muttered. "That's not good."

"Why? What are you thinking?" Billie asked.

"I have an ongoing case involving a group of organized criminals. Although they're not usually so blatant. Until now, they've tried covering up their murders as suicides or accidental poisonings. This is just out-and-out murder."

"What kind of group?" Billie asked.

"They call themselves Witch Finders. They target witches all over the country. Although I've only done investigations here in the South. It looks like they're recruiting more brutal killers."

"You can say that again." Billie grimaced. She pointed to the wound on the back of the victim's neck but didn't touch the body. "Looks like he stabbed her. The coroner will have to confirm that, of course."

"He didn't just stab her; he executed her." Charlie moved in closer to the victim, and the image of the woman's death flashed through her head. She swallowed hard. "With a big ass hunting knife."

Billie eyed her with disbelief, a half-sneer twisting her lips. "There's no way you can know that."

"Oh, I guess I forgot to mention it. I dreamed about her death last night."

"You dreamed about her death?" Billie narrowed her eyes, and the disbelief on her face morphed into contempt.

"Yes. It's one of my specialties." Charlie met the detective's steady glare.

"Oh, I'm sure you're special, all right," Billie said.

"Listen." Charlie put her hands on her hips and squared her body to face the detective. "The sheriff called me here because technically, this witch's death falls under the jurisdiction of the DOL. I would prefer we work together on this case. You know this area better than I do, and I'm going to need a space to interview witnesses. But if you're going to be a snarky bitch and impede my investigation, I will call the sheriff and ask him to remove you. Now, are you here to help, or are you here to make my life harder? If it's the latter, you should just go now. I have a job to do."

"Fine." Billie straightened her shoulders and jutted

her chin. Dark pink striped across her sharp cheekbones. But she stopped arguing. Charlie could feel the detective's anger and distrust, but there was something else there, too. Curiosity. Maybe her shot in the dark earlier had been right. Billie rolled her eyes.

"Sorry," Billie muttered. "We'll work it together."

"Great." Charlie let out a relieved breath. "Let's go through the house while we wait for the coroner."

"So, what do you think this is about?" Billie pointed to circles of smeared blood stretched across part of a wall.

"I don't know. I woke up before I saw him write this." Charlie moved in front of the blood spatter and tried to make out whether there was writing beneath the smears. "It must mean something, though. The Witch Finders are all about messages. I'm just not sure what."

"Maybe it means nothing. Maybe he did it just to screw with us." Billie stepped up next to Charlie and stared at the wall.

"Maybe. I'd have to spend a little more time alone in here to figure it out, and I'd like for you to finish with your forensic gathering before I set up crystals and burn incense." Charlie gave Billie a side-eyed glance and fought the grin tugging at the corners of her mouth.

"Is that a real investigative technique? Or are you just pulling my leg?" Billie glanced up at her.

Charlie's lips curved into a wry grin, and she shrugged. "Maybe a little of both."

Something soft brushed up against Charlie's forearm,

and she glanced down to find a wilted silvery-green plant with heart-shaped leaves rubbing against her hand. A large spider plant perched next to it almost hid the small plant. A pale green light emitted from its leaves, and Charlie cocked her head, unsure of what she was seeing. She held her finger out to touch it, and her breath caught in her throat.

The plant lifted a leaf to touch her. She cast a furtive glance toward Billie to see if she'd noticed. A deputy drew Billie away to ask a question, and Charlie let out a breath of relief. She brushed a knuckle against the leaf, and it quivered. Plants rarely responded to her, and there was no denying this one had some magical properties based on the energy it put off. She retrieved her phone from her bag to snap a photo.

"You're photographing the plant life around here now?" Billie said, rejoining her.

"No. I'm curious. Witches often keep plants for a variety of reasons." She gestured to the large array of houseplants near the front window of the living room, some small, some almost reaching the ceiling. Most were ornamental, but Charlie spotted a few medicinal herbs in a tray, along with some culinary herbs. "I'm just wondering if she might have been a green witch. That's all."

"What the hell is a green witch?"

"A witch that has a knack for growing things and using plants in potions and certain types of spells."

"I don't see what that has to do with anything," Billie said.

"It may not mean a thing, but I'd appreciate it if you'd indulge my curiosity." Charlie also took a quick picture of the wall with the smeared blood.

"We're documenting the scene." Billie gave her a cross look. "You don't have to take cell phone pictures. Wouldn't want them to end up in the wrong hands, would you?"

"Don't worry. I'll enter any photos I take into the chain of custody." Charlie tucked her phone into the front pocket of her bag. "I'm going to check out the rest of the house since the coroner is taking his sweet time. You're welcome to join me."

"The forensics team is already checking everything out. What do you think you're going to find that they won't?" the detective asked.

Charlie dropped her voice to a whisper. "Oh, they won't find what I'm looking for."

"Which is what exactly?" Billie didn't hold back her exasperation.

"Nicole's ghost."

Billie quirked a brow. A shadow crossed the detective's face, and Charlie felt the tug of war going on inside the woman. Billie's instinct was to make a snappy retort. But somewhere deep inside Billie, Charlie also sensed a burning curiosity. And it was stronger than her doubt. Even stronger than her smart-ass defenses. Maybe that's why Billie had become a detective. It was her first actual glimpse of the woman's interior thoughts. Charlie knew that if she made fun or even an observation out loud, Billie's wall would go right back up.

"So, do you want to go ghost hunting or not?" Charlie gave the detective a welcoming grin.

Billie scoffed a little before a strange smile crossed her face. "Okay. May as well cover every base, I suppose."

"Let's check her bedroom first," Charlie said.

"It's upstairs." Billie pointed to the ceiling.

"Lead the way."

CHARLIE WALKED THROUGH THE WOMAN'S BEDROOM, letting her hands graze across the surfaces. The room looked as if the woman had thrown her bedroom together with finds from flea markets and side-of-the-road cast-offs.

The full-sized iron bed had been spray-painted dark purple and adorned with hand-painted gold stars and moons. A mosquito net hung from the ceiling and draped around the headboard and both sides of the bed. A patchwork quilt reminded Charlie of a stained-glass window with its vivid hues and borders of black sashing.

The antique dresser, an oak tallboy with tarnished brass pulls, the finish worn away in places, filled the space across from the bed. A red leather jewelry box drew

Charlie, and she opened it, finding an array of silver jewelry set with beads made mostly of, Moonstone, Amethyst, Agate, and Black Tourmaline.

"She was definitely a witch," Charlie said.

"Yeah? You can tell all of that just from her jewelry?"

"Yes, I can." Charlie pulled an address book from inside the jewelry box with a gold-leafed pentacle inscribed on the cover. She held it up for Billie to see.

"Okay," Billie said. "You have my attention. What's inside?"

Charlie thumbed through it. "Looks like a list of her coven. Names and phone numbers. Potential suspects, witnesses, at least people who knew her."

"I'll get an evidence bag."

"Thanks," Charlie said. She waited until Billie left the room before she put the address book on the dresser, closed her eyes, and took a deep breath. The faint odor of sage still hung in the air. Had Nicole cleansed her space regularly? Or was it for a specific reason?

"If you can hear me, Nicole. I'm here to help you. My name is Charlie Payne, and if you show yourself to me, I will see you."

Charlie waited a beat, her heart thrumming in her throat. Her fingers twitched, and a chill settled over her skin, causing goosebumps to rise.

"It's okay, Nicole. You may be confused about what happened. And I'm so sorry you had to pass that way."

A faint mist appeared in front of the mirror, hanging

on the wall over a makeshift vanity table. Charlie touched the pentacle pendant hanging at her throat before she leaned in and peered at the mirror.

"Nicole Brewer, is that you?" Charlie asked. The frosty mist spread across the whole of the round mirror. When it had covered the entire surface, Charlie watched, mesmerized, as an invisible finger scratched through the icy coating.

Bdbbhbbbb scrawled across the mirror.

"I don't know what that means," Charlie said. "What are you trying to tell me?"

"What the hell?" Billie walked up behind Charlie. "Where did that come from?"

"From our spirit. Nicole."

Another line appeared beneath the first. Bddbbbhbb.

"Looks like gibberish." Billie reached her hand out to touch the mirror, but Charlie stopped her.

"Don't. Mirrors can be portals. The last thing you want is for whoever this is to get attached to you and follow you home."

Billie pulled her hand to her body, and her expression changed from curiosity to trepidation. "That could happen?"

"Yeah. It could." Charlie glanced around and sighed. The ambient temperature returned to normal. "Whoever it was, they're gone now."

"That's good, I guess." Billie returned to the dresser and stuffed the address book into the evidence baggy.

"Let's finish processing the scene, and then, this afternoon, we can start calling some of these folks."

"Sounds like a good plan." Charlie took her phone from her purse and snapped a photo of the spirit's message just before it faded away.

CHAPTER 9

Jason stepped onto the front porch to call Charlie. The phone rang three times while he watched the coroner and his assistants load the body into the back of the coroner's van.

"Hey." Charlie sounded surprised to hear from him. "What's going on?"

"I'm at a crime scene. Lisa suggested I call you."

"Well, that's interesting. Because I'm at a crime scene too."

"You are? Where?" he asked.

"McClellanville. Someone killed a witch last night. The sheriff actually requested me."

"Really? Who are you working with?"

"Hold on just a second," Charlie said. Her voice became breathy as if she were walking fast. "I just wanted to step outside. I'm working with Detective Billie Taggart. You know her?"

"Oh, really? Yeah, I know her. I'm surprised that she let you in her crime scene."

"She didn't have much choice. The sheriff intervened."

"I see. So, I guess there's no chance of you being able to help me with my case?"

"Maybe. If you can convince your boss you need me. What's going on?"

"I have a psychic who was murdered a couple of days ago. Lisa said she's a witch but told me to check with you. Y'all have some sort of witch registry?"

Charlie chuckled. "We do. I didn't know you were consulting with Lisa on cases now."

"I had a tarot question. My victim was a tarot reader, and it looks like someone killed her during an appointment."

"How did she die?" Charlie asked.

"Apparently, her throat was cut."

"And it happened a couple of days ago?"

"Based on the condition of the body, it looks that way. You think you can help me, or are you too busy?"

"I'm happy to help you, Jason. I just have to figure out the best way to coordinate the two cases. Ben's in Charlotte this week. Athena's coming down to help."

"We can set up in a conference room at my station if you can convince Billie," Jason offered.

"Technically, I've already taken the case from her, but I still need her help. Just like I'll need your help if I end up taking your case."

"Of course."

"We're still waiting on the coroner. Let me finish up here, and then I'll text you so we can work out next steps. Y'all are still processing your scene, right?"

"Yeah. We'll probably be here a while, but if you can't make it here before we're finished, we can always come back later."

"That sounds great. See you soon."

"Yep," he said and ended the call.

* * *

A DEPUTY STUCK HIS HEAD INTO THE LIVING ROOM AND announced, "The coroner's here."

"'Bout damn time," Billie muttered.

"Thank you, deputy." Charlie gave him a smile. "Please show him in."

Dr. Sonny Hodges walked into the crime scene in clean gray coveralls. A serious expression molded the features of his thin, wrinkled face until he laid eyes on Charlie. His countenance brightened.

"Hello there, Ms. Payne." Sonny's tone turned upbeat. "I should've known I'd find you here at this crime scene."

"You know any time it gets weird, you'll find me there," Charlie teased. "How's Doris?"

"She's doing pretty well. She's going to retire at the end of this year."

"That'll be nice for her. And for you too, I'm sure," Charlie said.

"Yeah, twenty-two years is long enough." He tugged one of his gloves. "After my term is up as coroner, we're going to retire to sunny Florida."

"That sounds wonderful," Charlie said.

"Now that we've established that it's old home week and we're all acquainted here," Billie said, not hiding her annoyance, "can you please look at this body and tell me if there's anything I need to know before you ship her off to the Medical Examiner's Office?"

"Oh, yes, of course. I'm sorry. Let me look." Sonny stopped for a moment and put his hands on his hips. His head tipped to the right. "You know this is the weirdest thing."

"What is?" Charlie moved to his side.

"I took care of another body this morning that was posed almost identically."

"For Jason Tate?" A flutter of nerves filled Charlie's chest. She had her doubts when Jason had called her earlier. But maybe the cases were related, after all.

"Yep."

"Really?" She tried to keep her face neutral and bit back the dozens of questions flooding her head.

"Yeah, it surprised me you weren't there." He smiled,

and the wrinkles around his eyes spread down to his cheeks.

Charlie shrugged. "They called me here first."

"Lucky you." He winked and started his examination. Charlie stepped back and, as she had done in several other cases, watched the coroner work.

Sonny bent over the body. Charlie cringed when he attempted to lift her head and it resisted. Her neck joint was locked. Blood had settled in her cheek, forearms, and palms.

"She's in full rigor. Sorry detective, this may take a while."

"Great," Billie muttered.

Charlie's phone rang, and she retrieved it from the front pocket of her bag. "Sorry, I have to take this." She stepped out onto the front porch and pressed the green answer icon. "Hey Athena, everything okay?"

"Yeah, everything's fine. I'm almost to Charleston."

"Great."

"I also just got word from Ben that they have asked us to take on another case in Charleston. Near Rantowles, to be exact."

"Yeah, I was kind of expecting this. Jason Tate called me."

"Are the cases related?" Athena asked.

Charlie suddenly felt as if someone was watching her. She glanced over her shoulder and found Billie Taggart staring at her through the open front door. Charlie waved at the detective and forced a smile. "I think there's a distinct possibility."

Athena lowered her voice. "Do you think it's a Witch Finder?"

"I don't know yet. But we've got two dead witches killed in a ritualistic way."

"Wow," Athena whispered. "Where should I go first?"

"You can head to the one in Rantowles, and I'll meet you there. You've got the address, right?"

"Great. I sure do. See you soon," Athena chirped and hung up the phone.

"There's another witch murder?" Billie stepped out onto the porch.

"Looks that way. The sheriff has asked us in on that case, too." Charlie met Billie's steady gaze. "I know this is a weird situation, but I need you."

Billie's dark brows knit together, and her forehead wrinkled as if she were thinking hard about Charlie's words. After a moment, she nodded. "All right."

"Great. Thank you. I'm going to leave you and your team to continue gathering evidence. I'll be setting up a command post at the Sheriff's Station out near John's Island."

"That's a bit of a drive."

"I know. If it's too much…"

"It's not. I'll gather everything I have and bring it with me," Billie said.

"Thank you," Charlie said.

CHAPTER 10

An hour and twenty minutes after leaving Billie Taggart with the Brewer crime scene, Charlie pulled into the uneven cement driveway of a ranch-style house. The pinkish brick veneer and white siding looked clean, and a picket fence surrounded the front yard. Through the windows of the enclosed carport, Charlie noticed a shadow hovering in midair. It seemed to undulate. What was that? She drew closer to get a better look. A swarm of flies lit down on the blood-soaked table. Others broke away and slammed against the window as if they were trying to escape. Charlie grimaced and turned away, heading back to the gate.

Rambling vines of dark purple clematis and bright pink climbing roses covered the fence. Charlie spotted vegetables mixed with herbs and flowers in the garden beds. A hodgepodge of large potted plants, including a small lemon tree lined a crushed gravel path running to the front steps. A tall plant stake with tiny bells attached to metal branches jingled in the wind. A deputy in his brown shirt and khaki pants stood guard at the picket fence gate. Charlie recognized him and gave him a slight wave.

"Hey, Deputy Alvin," Charlie said. "How are you doing?"

"Hey, Ms. Payne, I'm doing all right. Lieutenant Tate said you'd be along. I just need you to sign in here for me."

He held out a clipboard with a sign-in sheet, and she quickly jotted down her name and signature. He pointed to a box of gloves and booties resting on a folding metal table. She helped herself to a pair of each.

"I have my partner coming today. She's about fifteen minutes out. Her name's Athena Whitley."

"No problem. I'll sign her in and get her through to you."

"I really appreciate that. So when's your wedding?"

A look of surprise crossed his face. "October 5th. Thank you for asking."

"I think it's wonderful. I'm sure you'll be very happy together." Charlie gave him a friendly smile.

"Thanks. We're excited." His head bobbed up and down. "Ms. Payne, do you mind if I ask how you knew about my wedding?"

"Lieutenant Tate mentioned it," she lied. The deputies

already talked about her special abilities, and Charlie didn't want him to know that the first thought she sensed from him when she approached was about his future bride and how much the wedding was costing.

"Oh, right." He gave her a smile, then opened the gate.

Charlie ambled up the few steps to a covered front porch that had a white rocking chair and a small matching table. Plants covered almost every inch of the porch. Potted houseplants and common cooking herbs like parsley and sage lined the floor. Flowers filled the boxes affixed to the wooden porch railing.

"Charlie?" Jason met her at the door, then stepped out onto the porch. "Great to see you."

"It's great to see you, too. But it's not like I haven't seen you recently," she teased.

"I know. It's just been a while since we've worked on a case together." Jason smiled.

"That's true. Athena's on her way and should join us soon."

"Good. We could use her brain on this one too."

"So, you ready to show me around the crime scene?"

"Sure thing. Right this way." Jason stood back and let her pass into the house. The sickly sweet odor of decay struck her nostrils, and she quickly covered her nose and mouth.

"Oh, sorry." He pulled a small jar of mentholated chest rub out of his pocket and handed it to her.

Charlie scooped a small amount of the gel on her

finger and smeared it beneath both of her nostrils. It didn't block out the odor completely, but it helped. "Thanks."

Jason led her through the house to the table where the victim had lain. Tarot cards lay scattered on the table. It looked like they had been in a V-spread.

"So, you called Lisa. What did she say?" Charlie pointed to the cards.

"She gave me some insight. But I don't know what it means." Jason moved beside her and stared down at the table as if interpreting the layout of the cards.

"Well, it probably means something. I know these guys. They're heavy into symbolism." Charlie took a step back as a cloud of flies rose from the table and swarmed around them. She brushed them away from her head. "Can we go back into the other room?"

"Of course." Jason held out his hand, and they headed back into the cramped, dark kitchen, where there were no flies, at least. A dish drainer next to the sink held two clean coffee mugs.

"You're assuming it's one of your Witch Finders. I'm not completely sold on that."

"Right," Charlie said absently. "These cups haven't been printed yet."

"The CSU techs are working the entire scene. They'll get to it."

"So, tell me why you think it's not a Witch Finder."

Charlie folded her arms across her chest and cocked one eyebrow.

"Her stuff's missing. Her wallet. Cell phone. We found cell phone bills on the desk in her bedroom, so we know she had one. Why do you think one of these Witch Finders did it?"

"Because I have a case that is eerily like this one. Witch stabbed through the throat. From the back, though. So a little different."

"Well, shit." Jason scrubbed his face with his hand. "We could be looking at two perps."

Charlie nodded. "Could be. Did you ID her?"

"Her business cards identify her as Madame Turberville." Jason handed Charlie a card. The simple script of her name and the crystal ball image were enough to show what the woman did for a living. There was no mention of psychic. No mention of tarot cards. Although when she'd driven up, Charlie had noticed the glowing red neon sign in the window that read *Psychic*.

"What do the bills say?" Charlie handed the card back to him.

"Her name's Evelyn Turberville," Jason said. "Which also matches the registration of the car in the driveway."

"Great," Charlie said. "That helps a lot. Just for the record, the victim's wallet and cell phone were stolen from the other crime scene I visited this morning. It could be their way of trying to make it look like a robbery.

A business like hers is pretty cash-heavy. I wonder where she kept it."

"I don't know. We haven't found any money," Jason said.

"I wonder if they knew each other." Charlie said.

"Why would they?" Jason asked.

Charlie shrugged. "The witch community in Charleston County isn't huge. It's something worth exploring."

"All right. We can look at that angle."

"It could also be another witch who, for whatever reason, has a grudge against these two women."

"Sure. Or they could be totally unrelated, and it's just some client who didn't like the card reading."

Charlie nodded. "That's possible too."

"Hello there, young lady," a familiar voice said. Charlie turned and found Sheriff Rex Bedford standing in the doorway. "I appreciate your coming."

"I'm happy to help however I can, Sheriff."

"Detective Taggart told me you've already visited her crime scene."

"I have. Although, I'm afraid she wasn't happy about it at first."

"Yeah, I gathered that. Don't worry, she's on board, now."

"I appreciate that. If you wouldn't mind, it would be great if we could set up a central location where I could work with the two detectives on both cases."

"I've already booked a conference room for us, Charlie," Jason said.

The sheriff gave her a wry grin. "See? Already done."

"Great," Charlie said. "And I know I can count on you if we need additional personnel."

"Of course."

Understanding the constraints of the Sheriff's budget, Charlie added, "The DOL can help with any overtime if necessary."

"I will take you up on that."

"Wonderful. Sounds like we're on the same page."

"Yes, it does. I won't keep y'all from doing your jobs. Just keep me apprised of the situation, Lieutenant."

"Yes, sir." Jason gave the sheriff a nod.

Athena Whitley arrived at the door, a little breathless. Bright red streaked her usually pale cheeks, and her red curls clung to her sweaty face. She gave the sheriff a smile and a hello as they passed each other. As soon as she walked into the living room, she immediately covered her nose and mouth, and her cheerful expression disappeared.

She grimaced, trying to hide her gag reflex. "Oh, my goddess."

"Jason." Charlie held out her hand, and Jason gave her the little pot of menthol ointment. She removed the top and held it out for Athena.

"Rub a little under each of your nostrils. That'll help."

"Thanks." Athena grimaced, but did as she was told.

She looked around as if she were trying to get her bearings.

"We were just running theories," Charlie said.

"Great," Athena said, still a little paler than normal.

"Jason, why don't you walk us through the rest of the scene. I'd like to see if I can contact anyone," Charlie said.

"Sure. Where do you want to start?"

Charlie shrugged one shoulder. "May as well start in her bedroom."

"Good idea," Jason said. "It's right through here."

CHARLIE STOOD IN THE CENTER OF THE SPACE BETWEEN THE simple platform bed and the black melamine dresser. A black-framed mirror hung on the wall above the dresser, with several photographs tucked into the frame on each side. Two silver candlesticks with black candles and a glass dish full of variously colored crystal beads were the only items on top of the dresser. Charlie held her hand above the flat surface. A tingle traveled across her fingertips, like little electric sparks.

She held her hand up in the air as if it were an antenna and slowly circled the room. A large abstract painting hung over the bed. It featured splashes of blues, ranging from electric to navy, with purples and dark green splashes mixed in. Charlie pictured a young man deftly moving a wide, square brush across the canvas with speed and purpose. A soft gray comforter covered the bed along with matching gray shams. Dark purple throw pillows formed an artful line across the bed.

The prickle in her fingertips continued. "The protections in this room are heavy. I felt it as soon as I came in here."

"Me, too." Athena dropped her bag on the floor and dug through it until she retrieved a small silver digital recorder.

"What's that?" Jason asked.

"It's an old ghost hunter's trick. I don't speak to spirits directly the way Charlie does. But I've found sometimes you can ask questions and hear a spirit's reply on the recorder." Athena held up the small box and waggled it back and forth. "It's pretty cool."

"Do you have an EMF meter in there, too?" Charlie asked, referring to another tool paranormal investigators often used to measure spirit activity. The device measured the electro-magnetic fields in a space, and sometimes helped determine ghostly presences.

"I do." Athena returned to mining for gadgets in her purse until she retrieved a black gauge about the same size as an old-style cell phone. "Here you go."

"Great." Charlie took the meter and turned on the power button. "I feel her here, but it's like she's hiding."

"Probably this room is safe, and she's scared. I mean, imagine dying the way she did? It was pretty traumatic."

Athena closed her bag and fiddled with the digital recorder.

"So you don't just see her, Charlie?" Jason asked.

"No. Sometimes that happens. It could be her fear, or since she just passed recently, she may not have enough energy to manifest."

"Or she may not want to." Athena looked around as if she expected the spirit to jump out at her. "We're all set to record. Where should we start?"

"Let me check the room for EMF first. Make sure there's no wiring or anything that would give us false readings." Charlie scanned up and down the walls for any apparent energy signatures.

Jason sidestepped Charlie to get out of her way. "How do we get her to come out?"

"That's easy." Athena shrugged. "We talk to her."

"Athena's right." Charlie finished up with her scans. "Looks like we're ready. There's some EMF energy around the plugs and light switches, but I'd expect that. Would you mind if Athena and I had some alone time with her, Jason?"

"Sure. Have at it." Jason jerked his thumb toward the door. "I'll be down the hall if you need me."

Athena let out a breathy laugh. "Okay, what do you want to do?"

"You brought the recorder. Why don't you start? I'll monitor the EMF to see if we have any spirit activity." Charlie gave Athena a *you first* gesture.

Athena blinked several times and cleared her throat. Her cheeks turned bright pink. Finally, she nodded. "Okay. I can do this."

"Of course you can." Charlie gave her a reassuring smile.

"Um... hi," Athena began. "I understand your name is Evelyn. It's probably been a hard day. But, I just want to assure you we want to help. Can you tell us if you're here with us right now?"

She glanced at Charlie as if looking for approval. Charlie gave her an encouraging nod and waved for her to keep going.

"My name is Athena. This is my friend, Charlie. We're both psychics. And if you talk to us, Charlie can definitely hear you." Athena shifted her gaze to Charlie, her green eyes wide. "Now you," she whispered.

"Sure." Charlie turned in a circle, trying to get some feel for the spirit.

"Evelyn, this is Charlie. Thank you for any help you can give us. We want to catch whoever did this to you. Did you see your killer?" The meter jumped, and Charlie held completely still. *I think she's here. Go ahead*, Charlie mouthed.

Athena nodded. "Evelyn, I know you're scared. I can feel your fear. Can you tell us who did this to you?"

Athena stared at the digital recorder in her hand as if it contained magic.

"Evelyn," Charlie said, so quietly it came out on a

breath. "If you tell us who did this to you, if you can *show* us who did this to you, I promise you, we will find him, and we will make him pay."

The air sizzled and popped suddenly, and Charlie's hair stood up on end as if she had just touched an electrostatically charged orb. A strange light darted past her face. Charlie tried to look everywhere at once to follow its path. She spotted the tiny ball close to the mirror. It hovered for a moment, then rushed toward the glass. A light trail filled Charlie's vision for only a second before the ball disappeared. A loud cracking resounded through the room, and a fracture spread across the mirror in an uneven pattern.

"Holy goddess. Was that her?" Athena gasped.

A piece of the glass splintered into tiny shards and flew across the room. Charlie grabbed Athena by the arm and dragged her out of the path of the flying shards.

"I think she's done with us," Athena said.

"Yep," Charlie agreed. "Let's give her some time to settle down."

"Good idea," Athena agreed, and the two of them hurried out of the room.

CHAPTER 11

After leaving the location of Evelyn's murder, allowing the forensics team to continue working the crime scene, Jason set them up in one of the conference rooms in the sheriff's station, several miles away.

Charlie made herself comfortable in a chair at a large wooden table, opened her laptop, and took a yellow legal pad out of her bag so she could take notes.

A long whiteboard took up half of one wall, and Jason taped up the driver's license photo of Evelyn Turberville he'd pulled from the DMV database. Below the photo, he wrote the pertinent information they'd gathered so far.

Athena had set up at the end of the table with her laptop, where she listened to the digital recordings of their encounter in Evelyn's bedroom.

"I called Detective Taggart, but she didn't answer." Charlie frowned and placed her phone down on the table next to her laptop. "I'm really hoping she'll decide to work with us."

"Yep. We need to determine how much overlap we have in our cases." Jason capped the dry-erase marker and put it on the tray attached to the whiteboard.

"Sure, that will make it much easier for us to coordinate our efforts."

"I just don't want you to get your hopes up," Jason said.

"Get my hopes up?" Charlie tipped her head. "About what?"

"About combining cases. There may not be as much similarity as you think."

"Oh yeah? You want to lay money on it?" Charlie teased.

"Sure." Jason gave her a cocky grin.

"Fine. I'll bet you a double date at that new Spanish seafood place downtown. Paella, I think it's called. Tom's been wanting to try it out."

"Just hold on a second. How expensive is that place?"

"I don't know. But if you're right, I'll buy, and if I'm right, you buy. It doesn't matter how much it costs. Unless you think you're wrong."

"I'm not wrong, but I can't drop two hundred bucks on dinner these days. Lisa and I are saving for the wedding."

"Right." Charlie gave him a skeptical grin. "Maybe you're just chicken."

Athena snorted at the end of the table, clearly amused by their banter.

"I'm not chicken," Jason grumbled. "I'll take your bet because you're the one that's going to have to buy dinner for me and Lisa."

"You're on."

Jason stuck his hand out. "Deal."

"You sure you want to do that?" Athena piped up. "Did you forget she's psychic?"

Jason pulled his hand back. "Are you jerking me around? Do you already know something?"

Charlie snickered and shook her head. "I know what you know." She gave Athena a pointed look. "Which isn't much at this point."

"All right then." Jason eyed her. "Let's go over what we know."

"Sure," Charlie said.

"Her last client appointment was at 6:45 PM with someone named B. Drake. There's a phone number."

"Did you call it?" Charlie asked.

"I did. It just goes straight to voicemail, which is full. I'm running a check on the number now, but it may take a while."

"I wonder if it's a burner?" Charlie asked.

"Could be. We'll run it and find out," Jason said.

"Give me the number. I'll run a check on it," Athena said. "I can get results back much faster."

"Really?" Jason reached for the notebook he kept in the breast pocket of his black polo shirt.

"Yep." Athena nodded.

Jason didn't hesitate or argue. He wrote the number on a piece of paper for her. A moment later, Athena's hands flew over her keyboard.

"So, did we get any information on the street canvas?" Charlie asked.

"Evelyn's neighbors were mostly businesses, but those who knew her said she was really sweet, a little strange but always seemed to know when somebody needed something and often showed up with just the right thing," Jason said.

"Like what?"

"Like…" Jason flipped through his notebook and read. "… at the insurance agency down the street, the receptionist said she'd had Evelyn do a reading for her, and they'd become friendly. One time, her babysitter flaked. She couldn't leave her job again without serious repercussions, and she didn't have anyone who could watch the kids. Evelyn showed up with a plate of cookies and said she was just thinking about her and asked if she needed someone to help her with her kids. She jumped on Evelyn's offer so she could keep her job."

"She must've been psychic," Charlie said.

"Yeah, that'd be my guess, too," Jason said.

Charlie couldn't help herself from grinning. Just a short three years ago, that thought would never have even entered Jason Tate's mind. He had been so skeptical of her when they first met; he threatened to prove she was a fraud.

"Hey, Charlie..." Athena said, taking her earbuds out of her ears. "I think I found something interesting."

"On the phone number search?" Jason asked, his tone hopeful.

"No, on the EVP recordings. Sorry." Athena gave him a sheepish smile.

"What'd you find?" Charlie moved closer to Athena's chair. Jason stepped behind her and peered over her shoulder. On the screen was a program that Charlie had never seen before. The window looked like the screen of a heart monitor with a thin blue line bisecting a gray background. The line suddenly spiked as if a heartbeat, a complicated heartbeat, had just started. Charlie assumed the vertical motion represented all the noises Athena had captured with her digital recorder. Athena unplugged her earbuds and clicked play.

Charlie's voice resonated through the laptop speaker, sounding like she was talking inside a tin-can. "Evelyn, did you see your killer?"

In a faint scratchy voice, Charlie heard the word, "Hurt." Charlie scooted her chair closer to Athena and stared at the screen, fascinated.

"Can you play that back again?"

"Sure." Athena scrolled back a minute and replayed it.

"Hurt," Charlie repeated. "Okay."

Athena cringed at the tinny sound of her own voice. "Evelyn, I know you're scared. I can feel your fear. Can you tell us who did this to you?"

A gravelly voice said, "No."

"No!" Charlie sat up straight. "She sounded pretty defiant, didn't she?"

"She sure did," Athena agreed.

Charlie heard herself speak again. "Evelyn, if you tell us who did this to you, if you can *show* us who did this to you, I promise you, we will find him, and we will make him pay."

"Make him paaaaay." The voice hissed, and then there was nothing but sounds of electrical popping and static.

Athena clicked the stop button on the screen. "Not super helpful."

"No. But, she sounded pretty pissed off to me," Charlie said. A chill skittered across Charlie's skin. "We may have to go back to the scene and talk to her again. See if she'll tell us who she's so angry with."

"And in the meantime, we have other leads we can explore," Jason said. "Her last appointment, for example. I need to check with Beck and see if he's found her next of kin. That's who we need to talk to next." He leaned forward and pointed to the screen. "So, is there anything else on the tape?"

"Not really. Just some odd screeching and popping noises. No more discernible words," Athena said.

"Maybe we should see where Beck is. Her family deserves to be notified," Charlie said.

Jason nodded, his expression solemn. "Yep. Let me go see what he's found."

"Great. I'm going to keep documenting." Charlie got to her feet, grabbed a dry-erase pen, and started writing.

"Evelyn Turberville. Twenty-seven. Single. Psychic. Witch?" Charlie pivoted to face Athena. "We should check to see if she's registered."

Athena nodded. "Sure thing." The sound of her typing filled the space between them. Charlie fidgeted with the pen while she waited.

"Yep. She registered as a witch, and so did her mother." Athena cocked her head as if she'd discovered something interesting. "Her father's dead. He died during a carjacking."

"How awful."

"Yeah," Athena said.

"Do you have a current address for her mother?"

"Yes, I do. She lives in North Charleston. Crenshaw Avenue? Do you know it?"

Charlie shook her head and capped the pen in her hand. "No, but my GPS will. We should head over there and talk to her."

"What about Jason?"

"We'll grab him from his desk on the way out. We need to ward this room, though. I don't want just anybody poking around."

Athena closed her laptop and stood up. "Sure thing, partner. No one's coming in here unless we allow it."

CHAPTER 12

When Jason parked in Delilah Turberville's driveway, Charlie didn't get out right away. Jason and Athena sat quietly while Charlie assessed the energy of the house. The simple white clapboard building had a tiny gabled front porch with scrolled wrought iron columns and a cement porch. The dusky gray cinderblock foundation peeked through the branches of the round, sculpted azaleas lining the front of the house and the porch. Mismatched planters hung over the metal banisters, and plastic window boxes filled with even more plants perched beneath the two windows facing the street. One lone crepe myrtle, choked with Spanish moss, stood like a tired sentry at the entrance of the cracked cement walkway.

"What is it?" Jason asked.

"Nothing, really. I'm sort of dreading this one," Charlie said.

"I'll do the notification if you'd like. I mean, technically, I should be the one doing it."

"Will you think I'm chicken if I don't do it?"

"Of course not. I hate this part of my job, but I've done it a lot more than you have."

"Thank you," Charlie said with a sigh of relief.

The three of them got out of the car and strode up to the house. There were even more plants on the front porch and pots arranged around a plastic Adirondack-style chair that took up half of the space. Charlie pictured the woman on a happier day sitting on the front porch sipping iced tea and waving to her neighbors. Jason rang the bell and took a deep breath.

A moment later, the door opened and a petite woman with salt-and-pepper shoulder-length hair appeared. Dressed in a pair of denim capris and a sleeveless purple blouse, she looked to be around fifty. Her black, painted fingernails matched her toes, and she smiled as her curious gaze circled the three strangers at her door.

"Hi, can I help y'all?"

"Are you Delilah Turberville?" Jason asked.

"It depends on who's asking?" The woman glanced down at the badge clipped to his waistband.

"I'm here about Evelyn Turberville," Jason said. "Are you her mother?"

"Yes, I am. Is Evelyn in trouble?" The curiosity in her eyes disappeared, replaced with concern.

Jason's expression became solemn. "I'm so sorry to have to tell you this, but we found your daughter's body today."

The woman's face crumpled. She shook her head and held up her hands as if to defend herself from the news. She stepped back into the tiny foyer, and her eyes rolled back into her head before she collapsed onto the floor. Jason reached for the two-way radio clipped to his belt and put it to his mouth.

"Wait," Charlie said. "She's coming around, look."

The woman's eyes fluttered open. Then she arched her back and let out a terrible wail. Charlie cringed and knelt beside her. She could not imagine the woman's pain. If something like that had happened to her son Evan... Charlie couldn't even bear the thought. The woman curled up on her side and wept into her arm. Jason gave Charlie a horrified look and awkwardly patted the woman's hand.

"I'm so sorry, ma'am," Jason said.

Athena dug through her shoulder bag and retrieved a small package of tissues. She pulled several out and thrust them toward Jason. He took them and held them out for the woman. After another moment of crying, she opened her eyes and took the tissues, and pushed herself up.

"I knew something like this was going to happen." She sobbed again and blew her nose.

"How did you know that?" Jason asked. He stood up and offered the woman his hand. She waved him off and got to her feet without his help.

"She said someone had been watching her. I told her to go to the police. I think it was that ex-boyfriend of hers. He was always such a jerk to her." The woman's eyes filled with tears again.

"I'm so sorry," Charlie said. "My name is Charlie Payne, and I work for the Defenders of Light. I'm here investigating your daughter's death. This is my colleague, Athena Whitley."

"The Defenders of Light?" The woman gave Charlie a surprised look.

"Yes, ma'am, are you familiar with us?" Charlie asked.

Athena added a sympathetic smile.

"Of course, I am. I'm a registered witch. So was Evelyn."

"Yes, ma'am. That's how we found you. I know this is a terrible time, but if you could answer some questions for us, we would be most grateful. It could lead us to who did this to your daughter."

"Yes," Delilah said, her voice full of emotion. "I'll answer what I can. Please come in." She gestured to the dark green velvet couch in the living room. "May I get you something?"

"No, thank you," Jason said. A pair of black leather

mid-century-style chairs flanked either side of the couch, and Charlie noticed more plants hanging from the ceiling in front of the picture window overlooking the front yard.

"You certainly have a green thumb," Charlie said.

"Lovely," Athena said, scanning the room with an appreciative glance.

"I consider myself a green witch." Delilah took a seat in one of the black leather chairs and gestured to the couch. Charlie sat close to her, with Athena on her other side. Jason perched uneasily on the edge of the leather chair across from her.

"My cousin is a green witch. I have a brown thumb."

The woman managed a polite smile. Charlie glanced at Athena. "Would you mind taking notes now?"

"Sure." Athena reached in her bag and pulled out a yellow legal pad and a pen.

Charlie leaned forward with her elbows on her knees. "So, can you tell me more about this boyfriend? Was he stalking her?"

"I don't know. But, he sent her a few texts that were ugly."

"I see. And what was his name?" Charlie said.

"Brett Travis. He lives in West Ashley." Delilah sniffled and reached for the box of tissues sitting on the end table next to the chair. "There is something else."

Charlie gave her an encouraging nod. "Please go on."

"I had a dream about this. I even warned her she should be very careful."

"You had a dream that your daughter died?" Charlie asked.

"She never died in my dream. I always woke up when he attacked her. I must've called her a dozen times about that dream. But, she just said, 'Don't worry, Mom.'"

Delilah sniffled and dabbed the tears from her cheeks.

"You dreamed this a dozen times?" Charlie asked.

Delilah nodded. "Yes. I'm a little psychic."

"Do you know any of your daughter's clients?" Jason asked.

"No, not really. Although I know she has several regulars that come to see her, sometimes weekly. Which isn't a bad thing." She shrugged her slim shoulders. "Their readings pay her bills." Delilah's eyes got watery again. "Do you think I could see her?"

Charlie glanced at Jason and noted the alarm in Athena's eyes.

"We've already made the ID on your daughter, and honestly, ma'am, I would recommend against it. You don't want to see your daughter the way she is right now," he said.

"I guess I'll have to have a funeral." Delilah pressed one hand against her heart and slumped forward. She rested her head in her other hand as if the finality of the situation hit her squarely in the chest. "I don't even know where to begin. Where do people begin with this sort of thing?"

"I hope this is not inappropriate..." Charlie patted the woman's arm. "... but I have a friend who's a funeral director. You certainly don't need to use his funeral home, but he would be happy to answer questions for you about the process."

Delilah grabbed one of Charlie's hands and held onto it as if her life depended on it. "That is so kind of you. Thank you."

Charlie placed her palm over the woman's hand. "Can you tell me more about why she felt she was being watched?"

Delilah let Charlie's hand go and sat up straight. "She said sometimes, when she was alone at work, she felt like someone was peeping at her through the bushes. I told her she should get a security camera. Maybe she could catch the creep. But she said she also sometimes got that feeling when she went home to her apartment."

"She has an apartment?" Jason sat forward on the edge of his seat. "Can we get the address?"

"Yes, of course." Delilah rattled off the address, and Jason scribbled it down into the little notepad he always kept with him.

"Thank you, ma'am. We thought she might live in the house where we found her. "

"The house belonged to her grandmother, and she left it to Evelyn when she died. Evelyn always had plans to renovate it someday and move into it permanently, but it needs so much work. The heat pump needs to be replaced. It doesn't work half the time. But, sometimes she stays the night. It's quieter than her apartment. Noisy neighbors, if you know what I mean." Delilah's lips twisted into a deep frown, and she sniffled. "And she's psychic like me and picks up on people's emotions. There's a couple that lives upstairs, and they fight all the time."

"So, she only felt watched when she was at work?" Jason leaned forward in his chair.

Delilah cocked her head as if she were thinking hard about the question. "No, sometimes she said she felt watched when she walked from the parking lot to her apartment, but she was too scared to check it out. I told her she was right to just keep on walking. I even bought her some pepper spray."

"That was excellent advice." Charlie gave her a reassuring smile. "Do you know if her apartment complex has security cameras?"

"I'm not sure, but she has one of those video doorbells."

Charlie and Athena exchanged a hopeful glance.

"I'll get the footage." Athena jotted the information on the pad in her lap.

Charlie cast her gaze to Jason and found him scribbling in his notebook. "Is there anyone else you can think of that might want to hurt her?"

"Maybe a client with a beef about a reading?" Jason chimed in.

"No. Her clients loved her." Delilah's voice broke. She reached for another tissue and quietly cried into it.

Charlie leaned forward and pressed a hand against Delilah's elbow to remind her she wasn't alone. "Ms. Turberville, I want to assure you that we will do everything we can to find the person who hurt your daughter."

"Thank you," Delilah said.

Charlie reached into her bag and pulled out one of Tom Sharon's business cards. She'd stuffed a few into her purse when she'd worked for him a while back. Then she added one of her own and handed both to Delilah.

"This one is my friend. Again, you are under no obligation to use his funeral home, but he is a kind man and will be happy to answer your questions. If you think of anything else, please call me." She pointed to her own card. "That's my cell number."

Delilah glanced down at the cards. "Thank you."

"We appreciate your time." Jason put his notebook and pen in his breast pocket and got to his feet.

"Of course."

Jason handed her one of his own cards. "If you think of anything, please give me or Charlie a call."

Delilah looked over the cards and ran her thumb over Charlie's name. "I will. And like I said, give her ex-boyfriend a long, hard look."

"Don't you worry. We will," Charlie said.

CHAPTER 13

Athena followed the long road to the bed-and-breakfast Jason's mother owned, Talmadge House. When Athena had mentioned she still needed to find someplace to lay her head for the night, Jason had been kind enough to call his mother. On the drive to Delilah Turberville's house, Charlie told her the story of how she'd met Jason when his mother, Susan, hired her to clear the house of ghosts before she turned it into a business.

"Jason hated me from the first moment he met me," Charlie had teased from the passenger's seat of Jason's Dodge Charger. Tension in the car had been building during the drive. None of the friends looked forward to breaking the sad news to Evelyn Turberville's mother. Charlie's story briefly distracted the trio and lifted the mood.

"I think hate is a little strong." Jason had frowned. "Skeptical is more like it. I just didn't believe Mom's place was actually haunted."

Charlie chuckled. "Man, were you wrong."

"Did you clear the house?" Athena asked.

"Mostly," Charlie had shrugged. "There are a couple of hangers-on."

"My mother swears there's an old butler that still sometimes opens the front door and closes it, usually in the middle of the afternoon." Jason shook his head. "But, I've never seen anything."

"Like that's a surprise. You're going to turn right up ahead," Charlie said, interrupting her tale to give directions to the Turberville residence. Charlie glanced at her phone and pointed to the light ahead. Then, she jumped back into storyteller mode. "I asked her if she wanted me to clear it out, but…"

"But, turns out having a haunted bed-and-breakfast is lucrative. Evidently, there's some sort of ghost registry," Jason said, his eyes peeled for road signs.

"It's a haunted house registry," Charlie corrected him. "And places that are haunted get rated based on people's experiences there," Charlie said, sounding amused.

"How many stars does your mother's property get?" Athena asked from the back seat.

"Oh, not stars. Mom got four and a half ghosts out of five," Jason said. "The butler comes in and messes around with people's stuff sometimes. Most guests like it. A few don't."

"Good to know. I'll ward my room to keep him out," Athena had said.

"You have arrived," the female voice of Athena's GPS announced, bringing her back to the present. She pulled into the gravel lot on the side of Susan Tate's large old mansion and parked away from the two other vehicles; a fancy red Dodge truck that looked expensive, and a silver Mercedes sedan.

The sun hung low, and soon it would dip completely below the trees, leaving a trail of dark pink and red splashed across the sky.

The events of the afternoon kept playing through Athena's head. She'd never taken part in a notification before, and it didn't surprise her how horrible it was, but watching Charlie in action, how she'd empathized with the woman's loss and got the information they needed, had been amazing.

Tomorrow they'd follow up on the leads they'd gotten from Evelyn's mother, and it both thrilled her and frightened her to think about talking to potential suspects.

Participating in investigations wasn't usually in her purview. Mostly she stuck to being the information keeper. If there was a search to be done, a database to find, she was your girl. Dealing with people that weren't witches—that was something completely different, something she was kind of longing for. Charlie was so good at it. Maybe if she just studied Charlie, the same way she had studied every subject in school, with unbridled determination, she could become good at it too. At least she hoped she could.

She popped the trunk and retrieved her small suitcase and computer bag. Then she locked the car and headed toward the entrance.

A slim woman with a dark, chin-length bob stepped out onto the expansive front porch. She looked like the perfect hostess in a pair of white capri pants and a sleeveless blouse with a brightly colored fruit pattern. Her silver sandals set off the outfit, and a gold bracelet twinkled in the late afternoon light when she raised her hand to wave.

The woman smiled. "You must be Athena?"

"Yes, ma'am." She adjusted her laptop bag on her shoulder. "You must be Mrs. Tate."

"Please, call me Susan. Jason called and told me you were on your way. Did you have supper already?" Susan asked.

"I picked up take out on my way here. Thank you." Athena stopped at the bottom of the steps and admired the beautiful Doric- columns. "This house is amazing."

"Thank you. It's taken a lot to get it back into good shape, but I think the old girl can hold her own." Susan patted a column. "Can I help you with your bag?"

"Thanks, but I've got it." Athena carried the wheeled suitcase up the steps and then grabbed it by the handle and followed Susan inside. "I should've asked, but you have wi-fi out here, right?"

"Oh, yes." Susan chuckled. "Jason would never come to visit me if I didn't."

"You actually live here?" Athena asked.

"I sure do. I'm on the third floor, so if there's anything you need, ring the bell. There's one in every room."

"Thank you." Athena stopped in the oversized foyer and looked up the grand staircase. "This is beautiful."

"It's been in my family a long time." Susan folded her arms across her chest. A wistful expression spread across her face. Athena noticed that Susan's hazel eyes reminded her of Jason.

"Why don't we get you settled, and then I'll show you to the dining room so you can eat your dinner. I hope you don't mind, but I'd prefer you not eat in the room."

"No problem." Athena leaned forward and tipped her head to peer into the formal living room to the right of the foyer. A silver-haired man and a woman with short white hair stood near an ornate fireplace with martini glasses in their hands.

"We have a happy hour every evening from five to seven. You're welcome to join us if you'd like." Susan gestured toward the living room.

"Thanks. I'm not much of a drinker, though. Jason told me you have a ghost."

"I do. His name is Henry Sheffield." Susan beamed

and guided Athena to the bottom of the stairs. "I used to be terrified of ghosts."

"And now?"

"And now, it's kinda fun. He leaves candy on my pillow sometimes. He's harmless, I promise." Susan put her hand over her heart.

"Cool." Athena kept her plan to ward the room to herself. Jason hadn't mentioned if his mother knew that she was a witch.

"I have your room all laid out for you. Jason said you drove down from Charlotte today. I'm sure you're just exhausted."

"I'm getting there." Athena gave Susan a weary smile and followed her up the grand staircase.

* * *

CHARLIE SAT ON THE COUCH IN HER LIVING ROOM WITH HER feet in Tom Sharon's lap. He gently ran his thumb along the curve of her arch, and she leaned back into one of the big fluffy pillows and closed her eyes.

"Oh my goddess, that feels so good." She moaned a little and relaxed into the pleasurable sensations. "You're a genius at foot massage. Did you know that?"

"Yes, I believe you've told me that before." Tom winked and gave her a wry smile. "So this spirit wouldn't talk to you at all?"

Charlie shifted and put her arm behind her head. She

stared up at the ceiling. "No. She sounded upset, though, and the way she cracked the mirror was unsettling."

"Are you still thinking it might be a Witch Finder then?"

"I don't know. Maybe. I mean, if this is the work of a Witch Finder, it wouldn't surprise me. I definitely pissed off their organization with that case in Florida a few months back."

A shadow of concern darkened Tom's face. "Promise me you'll take precautions. These Witch Finders are not magical, and they're not creatures. Your normal protections won't keep one of them from crossing any boundary you set. I don't like it one bit that these women died at the hands of a knife. It's all very... medieval."

"You've seen a lot of deaths. Have you seen people killed the way I described? Recently, I meant."

"I've seen slit throats, but through the back of the neck? No, I've never seen that. William might be a better person to ask," Tom said, referring to his brother. "He's been reaping much longer than I have."

"How long?" Charlie said, her ears pricking up. She'd tried to glean any bit of information Tom would share about being a reaper, which was very little.

"William became a reaper somewhere in the 1100s. You'd have to ask him about the date, though. I don't recall it."

"The 1100s? Like the Middle Ages 1100s?" Charlie said, sounding flabbergasted.

"Yes. Like I said, he's been at this much longer than me."

"And when did you become a reaper?" she asked for what seemed like the hundredth time in the past six months. Tom glanced away from her and dug his thumb deeper into her arch. She melted into the massage and then pulled her foot away. "If you think I'm going to drop it just because you exact some pleasure on my feet, you would be wrong."

Tom rolled his dark, amber-colored eyes and sat up straighter in his seat. "I guess there's no harm in it. I became a reaper in the year 1785 just outside of Arlington, Virginia."

"Oh, my stars," Charlie muttered. "Were you in the Revolutionary War?"

"Yes, but that's all I can say for now."

"Am I ever going to get the entire story?"

"Eventually, but until then," he said and crawled across the couch and over her body. "Could I interest you in a kiss?"

"Yes, I suppose a kiss will have to do." Charlie laughed. She kissed him squarely on the mouth and pulled him down on top of her, getting lost in his touch until the day's events drifted away.

CHAPTER 14

Lisa had been reviewing the estate documents for a client in her office at the law practice for almost an hour before her cell phone rang at 7:12 Wednesday morning. She picked it up. "This is Lisa Holloway," she said absently, closing a folder after checking a figure.

"Hey, Ms. Holloway, this is Adam Lane. I work for you at the garden center."

"Hi, Adam. Is everything okay?" Lisa leaned forward in her chair. Down the hall, she heard another early bird stirring around in their office. She raised her hand and pointed a finger at her open door. Swiping left, she mentally focused on repeating the phrase *Door Close* three times. When she finished, she held her breath as the door slowly closed. Once the door shut, she smiled, pleased with herself.

"I'm not sure."

Something about his dubious tone put Lisa on alert. "What's going on?"

"Maria's not here. And Maria is *always* here. She's the first one in every day, except Sundays, because, you know, she doesn't work on Sundays; but, when I got here, there's no sign of her."

"Did you try calling her?" Lisa said, unsure if she should be concerned or not. Maria seemed so dedicated and excited about working with her. Lisa couldn't imagine the woman being flakey.

"Yeah, I did. It went straight to her voicemail. I'm not sure if she has an emergency contact or not. Hang on just a sec, customer's here." In the background, Lisa heard keys jangling and the sound of the squeaking hinge on the gate when it opened. Adam's polite voice sounded far away as he greeted the customers and told them to look around. Adam came back to the phone and said, "I have a key, so I just let myself in and opened up."

"Thank you. I really appreciate you doing that. I'll see if I can get hold of Maria. Are you going to be okay there alone today?"

"Oh, yeah, no problem. I'll call the part-timers to see if any can come in to help. I just hope she's okay. I've never known her to even take a sick day. Okay, I've got to go. A customer has a question."

"Sure thing. Thank you again." Lisa ended the call. A cold rock of dread settled into her stomach while she thumbed through her contacts. When she dialed Maria's number, it only rang once before going straight to voicemail. She left a message and then called Peter Gannon. He had said if she needed anything, he'd be willing to help. Maybe he could give her some information about Maria. She could've kicked herself for not getting more than one emergency contact for Maria while they worked together during the past couple of weeks.

"I was wondering when you were going to call me," Peter said after answering the phone. "I knew I should've stayed on a little longer to help you transition in."

"I'm so sorry to bother you this early, but I have a bit of a situation."

"Okay, what's going on?"

"Maria didn't show up this morning."

"Maria? That's very odd. She's one of the best managers I've ever had. She started out on the floor. Rose through the ranks, and because she's so dependable, I made her manager."

"Yeah, I remember you mentioning something about that when we were in negotiations. That's why I'm a little worried. I tried calling her, and all I get is her voicemail. Does she have another phone number or another contact? I'm not at the garden center, so I can't check the files. I remember she mentioned her husband."

"I have her mother's number. Mrs. Lopez. She'll be able to give you the number for Maria's husband. Let me get my address book."

"Thank you, and again I'm so sorry to bother you."

"It's no bother. I didn't expect things to transition so smoothly. There're always a few bumps in the road."

A few minutes later, after writing down Maria's mother's phone number, Lisa gave the woman a call. The phone rang several times before a man finally answered.

"Hello, may I speak with Mrs. Lopez, please?" Lisa asked.

"I'm sorry, she's not here." His voice sounded full of gravel.

"Oh, I really need to speak to her. Are you her husband?"

"No, I'm her son."

"I'm so sorry to bother you, but I'm trying to get in touch with Maria. I'm her employer and…"

"Maria died yesterday afternoon." The man's voice shook.

The dread in Lisa's stomach grew colder, radiating through her torso like a dense fog.

"Oh, my gosh." Lisa's hand drifted to her neck. "I'm so sorry for your loss. My name is Lisa Holloway. I just purchased the garden center."

"Right, you're on my list to call," he muttered.

"I am so sorry for your loss. Is there anything I can do for your family?"

"I don't know…" He seemed to struggle to find words. "Maybe you could get her last paycheck to my brother-in-law. That would be really helpful."

"Absolutely. I'll make sure that gets done today." Lisa jotted down the request on a sticky note and put it inside the planner on her desk. "Would you mind if I asked what happened?"

"Somebody ran her off the road and then left her there to die. The cops don't know anything more than that."

"Oh my gosh, that's horrible. I'm so sorry." Lisa scrubbed her fingers through her hair. Goddess, she sounded so inane for saying the same thing repeatedly.

"Yeah, I gotta go."

"Of course. Again, please, if there's anything, anything at all, don't hesitate to call me."

"Sure," he said and hung up.

Lisa stared at her phone for a moment, the dread turning to a sick feeling. Hot bile rose in her throat and suddenly the urge to vomit hit her hard. She grabbed for her trash can, knowing she would never make it to the bathroom down the hall. When she finished, she wiped her mouth with the back of her hand.

"Those poor people," she whispered.

She rose from her desk and went to the bathroom to clean the trashcan, rinse her mouth and figure out what she should do next. The only thing she could think of was to call Jason. Maybe he could give her some information, or at least find out some more about what happened. The randomness of it hit her hard. Harder than she would've expected. That Maria could just be going along living her life, and then suddenly someone runs her off the road, and that's it. She could taste the salt on the back of her throat before she felt the tears spill onto her cheeks. She swiped at them quickly. And then rinsed her face. What was wrong with her? Still, to just die alone like that. Lisa shivered. Suddenly she wanted to talk to Jason, and she returned to her office to call him in private.

* * *

CHARLIE ARRIVED EARLY AT THE SHERIFF'S STATION THE next morning to set up her laptop. Once she settled in, she grabbed a marker and looked over the murder board while she waited for Jason and Billie to arrive. She added a few things beneath Evelyn's picture, including Brett Travis's name, and then wrote "green witch" with a question mark next to it. Since Evelyn's mother was a green witch, Charlie entertained the possibility Evelyn was, too. Sometimes such gifts ran in families.

Athena rounded the corner a few minutes later with a carrier holding four coffees and a paper bag. She set it down on the table. "Morning. I brought pastries."

"Morning." Charlie's face lit up at the breakfast offering. She grabbed a coffee and stirred in three sugar packets and two creamers. "How was your room?"

"Awesome." Athena opened her laptop and booted up her equipment. "Susan's really nice and the room was really comfortable. It's a shame I have to move to a regular hotel tonight."

"Why do you have to move?" Charlie peeked inside the paper bag and used her napkin to grab a bear claw. She took a seat and picked the slivered almonds from the top of the sweet confection before digging into it.

"It's kind of pricey." Athena reached for the bag and helped herself to a frosted scone and a coffee. "I might bring my girlfriend back for a weekend getaway sometime, though."

"Any sign of the ghost?"

Athena shook her head. She broke the scone into pieces and dunked it into her coffee. "Nope. But I warded my room pretty well."

Charlie finished eating her pastry and then brushed away the bits of icing that had scattered across the legal pad she'd set next to her laptop to take notes.

For a moment her mind drifted, and she couldn't fight the sudden torpor that overtook her body. When she finally shook it off, she stared down at her pad but saw little beyond the doodle she had drawn. Her mind kept drifting back to Nicole's room—the frosty mirror, the gibberish scrawl.

Charlie blinked, and when she looked down at her notepad again, a picture of a large black bird had appeared with the letters badbbadbbadb written over and over, taking up half the page. When had she done that?

"Daydreaming?" Jason asked.

Charlie startled and put her hand over her chest. "Good goddess, Jason. I didn't even hear you come in. You scared the life out of me."

"Sorry about that. You're here early." He peered over her shoulder. "What's that?"

Charlie touched her hand to the image and shook her head. "I don't know."

Jason picked up the pad and inspected it. "I didn't know you could draw like this."

Charlie shrugged. "I can't." She took the pad out of his hands. The detailed image of the bird looked as if someone with some talent had drawn it. "I don't remember doing this."

"Yeah, but…" He stared at her, confusion on his face. "That doesn't make any sense."

"Sure it does," Athena chirped from the end of the table. "She's psychic. It's probably automatic writing. Happens to me all the time."

"What's that? Automatic writing." Jason cocked his head, a curious look on his face.

"Basically, a spirit or some other entity sort of hijacks your brain, usually when you're daydreaming or doodling," Athena explained.

"Stars, I hadn't even thought of that. Maybe it's a message." Charlie studied the pad. The picture reminded her of Nicole's statue of the Morrigan. But the letters all seemed like gibberish to her.

"Really? That is just..." Jason scowled. "Weird, and a little terrifying. So, you can be possessed and not even know it?"

"It's not possession." Charlie rolled her eyes and laid her arms over the pad as if she were trying to hide it. "More like a communication from the spirit realm. Speaking of communication, I left Billie a message, but I haven't heard from her this morning."

Jason moved in front of the whiteboard. "She called a little while ago. She's stuck in traffic." He turned to Charlie. "I'm on my way to visit Evelyn's ex-boyfriend to check him out. Want to ride along?"

"Sure." Charlie tucked the pad into her bag. "Athena, can you stay here and help Billie?"

"Help Billie what?" Billie Taggart stood in the doorway holding a cardboard box with handles and a lid.

"Hi, Billie." Charlie gave the detective a smile. "Jason and I were about to go question a suspect in his case."

"So, I'm already forgotten, huh?"

"No, not at all." Jason reached for the box, but Billie held onto it.

"I've got it." Her curt voice stopped him, and he lifted his hands and stepped back so she could pass. Billie put the box on the end of the conference table.

"Billie, this is my partner, Athena Whitley." Charlie gestured to Athena.

"Hi." Athena grinned and gave Billie a quick wave.

"Hi." Billie nodded and looked over the board. "So, Tate, this is your case?"

"Yeah. There's plenty of room to add yours." Jason gestured to the extensive amount of white space.

"Sure." Billie turned to face Charlie. "I take it you won't be here to help make phone calls to my vic's coven?"

"I can help you." Athena straightened in her chair. Her green eyes flashed with excitement.

"Great. Thanks." Billie threw a glance over her shoulder at Jason, her tone a little icy. "Don't let me interrupt you two."

"My partner is just down the hall if you need anything." Jason jerked his thumb at the door.

"Beck, right?" Billie's dark eyes didn't leave his face.

"Yep." Jason rocked on his feet. "Charlie, you ready?"

"Sure." Charlie slung the strap of her bag across her body and gave Athena a smile. "Call me if you need anything."

"I will."

"Y'all have fun." Charlie tipped her head and gave Billie a brief nod before following Jason into the hall.

"You think she'll be, okay?" Jason asked.

"Who?" Charlie adjusted the hair caught beneath her purse strap.

"Athena. Billie's not the friendliest person."

"Oh, don't worry about Athena. She has skin as thick as a rhino's, and she can take care of herself." Charlie patted his arm. "She also has an infectious positivity, and it's really hard to dislike her. If you want to worry about someone, worry about Billie."

"I hope you're right." Jason chuckled. He grabbed the front door, opening it for Charlie, and they passed out into the bright morning light.

CHAPTER 15

Jason's phone rang a few times, and Lisa prepared herself to leave him a message. Finally, after the fourth ring, he picked up. "This is Tate."

"Hey, it's me." She kept her voice steady, focusing on the shelf of law books across from her desk to maintain control.

"Hey." He waited a beat. "What's wrong?"

Lisa let out a nervous chuckle. "Why do you ask that?"

"You sound funny. Are you okay?"

"I sound funny, huh? Has Charlie turned you into a psychic, now?" She teased, but it touched her heart that he sensed her distress from her voice.

"Nope. I just know you, that's all. What's going on? You at work?" His words warmed her.

"Yeah, I'm at work. The manager of the garden center died in a car accident yesterday."

"That's terrible. Did she have kids?" he asked.

"She has a son and a husband. I can't imagine how devastated they are. I talked to her brother, and he said it was a hit-and-run. Someone just left her on the side of the road to die." Lisa choked up and sniffled.

"Oh, honey. Is there anything I can do?" He asked so tenderly it made the tears she'd been holding back flood onto her cheeks.

"Her brother said something that struck me. He said the cops knew nothing about what happened, and I can't shake the feeling there's something deeper going on." She grabbed a tissue from her desk drawer and wiped her face.

"Now who's turning psychic?" Jason teased. "More than likely, they just can't release information to him yet. I'm sure they know something."

"I know. It's probably nothing." She collapsed against the back of her chair and let her shoulders slump.

"Why don't you give me her name, and I'll check into it. I can at least read the report."

"Really? You'd do that for me?"

"Yes. Since it's probably an ongoing investigation, there's not much I'll be able to share."

"No, that's okay. I just want to make sure something's being done."

"I'll dig around, see what I can find. Hold on a sec." She heard him speaking to someone else in a muffled tone. "Charlie's with me. We're on our way to question a person of interest. What's the name?"

"Maria Torres," Lisa said. Jason repeated the name for Charlie.

"Got it. Are you going to be okay?"

"Yeah. I wish Jen would hurry and get the café opened back up. I could really use one of her muffins," Lisa joked. Even though she rarely went for breakfast, she couldn't wait until The Kitchen Witch Café reopened after sustaining serious damage from a tornado last month.

"They're like crack," Jason agreed.

"Maybe I'll work from home today."

"All right. Do what you need to do to take care of yourself, okay?"

"Thanks. Love you. Tell Charlie I said, hey."

"Will do. I love you too. Stay safe."

The line went dead, and Lisa's arms and legs twitched. She shifted in her chair and opened her file folder but read the same line over again. Why couldn't she focus? She couldn't just take off to manage one of her businesses whenever someone quit or called in sick.

She didn't call in sick; she died.

Lisa buried her face in her hands. For the first time in her life, she didn't know what to do. Sure, she would have to hire a manager, but immediately running an ad or starting a search on a job-hunting website left a terrible taste in her mouth.

What would Evangeline do?

The words rang in her ears. There was only one way to find out. She picked up her cell phone and dialed her aunt.

"Hello?" Evangeline's soft voice put her at ease almost immediately.

"Hi, it's Lisa."

"Hi, I was just thinking about you."

"You were?"

"Yes. I was making my breakfast, and I had a funny image pop into my head."

"Really? What was that?"

"You, nine months pregnant, eating bacon like there's no tomorrow." Evangeline chuckled.

Lisa let out a nervous laugh. "That's not happening."

"Like I said, it was just a funny thought. Now, what can I do for you, sweetie?"

"I need to talk through a business situation. Are you busy this morning?"

"No. I told Jen I'd meet her this afternoon to walk through the café. Construction's finished. I'm hoping we'll be able to reopen here in the next few weeks."

"That's wonderful. It's ahead of schedule, isn't it?"

"Yes. I think Jen may have cast a little spell to help hurry things along."

Lisa smiled. "Sounds like something Jen would do."

"Why don't you come over. I'll make us some coffee, and we can have a nice, long chat," Evangeline said.

"I'll be there soon." Lisa pressed the end icon and

retrieved her purse. Arielle arrived at the reception desk just as Lisa passed through the lobby.

"Good morning, Ms. Holloway," Arielle said.

"Morning. I'm going to be out for a while."

"No problem." Arielle took a seat behind her desk.

"Thanks." Lisa gave the young woman a nod and headed to the parking lot.

Lisa knocked, and a moment later, Evangeline opened the door to her condo with a wide smile across her face. She wore her long, silver hair in a single braid that rested on one shoulder. Her bubble-gum pink toenails peeked from beneath the long chambray skirt that brushed the tops of her bare feet. Evangeline looked Lisa up and down. "My goodness, child, what's going on? You look as pale as a ghost."

Lisa pressed her hands to her cheeks. "I'm fine. I just had a bit of a shock, that's all."

"Come on in." Evangeline ushered Lisa into her condo. "Would you like some coffee?"

"My stomach's a little unsettled this morning." Lisa touched her hand to her belly. "Do you have any ginger tea?"

"Of course. Why don't you have a seat, and I'll put the kettle on." Evangeline gestured to the round dining table sitting between the small kitchen and the living room.

"Thank you." Lisa nodded, and a sense of calm settled around her shoulders. Had Evangeline cast a spell to make her guests feel at home and peaceful? If only she could hang out at her aunt's all day and not have to deal with reality.

"Jen just called and wanted to talk about colors," Evangeline said from the kitchen. Lisa could see her aunt milling around, gathering teacups and her special box of ginger tea.

"What sort of colors?" Lisa took a seat.

"As I said on the phone, they finished repairs and construction, but since the owner of the building is renovating to keep us as renters, Jen thinks we should do some updates to the décor."

"What updates? I like the Kitchen Witch the way it is. It's very homey."

"I know, honey. I feel the same way, but, you know Jen knows more about these things than I do. Anyway, she wants to show me a color combination she feels will really make people feel at home."

Lisa shifted in her chair. "Just tell her not to change too much."

"I will." Evangeline emerged from the kitchen and placed a wooden tray on the table, complete with a pink china teapot and matching teacups. She pulled out the tall, ladder-backed chair and took a seat, then poured Lisa a cup of what smelled like strong ginger tea mixed with lemon.

Lisa dosed her tea with a long squeeze of honey and took a sip. The warm, spicy tea soothed her throat. "Perfect."

After Evangeline poured herself a cup, she took hold of one of Lisa's hands and clasped it. "Now, what's going on? I don't think I've ever seen you so rattled before."

Lisa took a deep breath and let everything in her mind gush out.

"One of my employees died, and I know this sounds stupid, but I don't know what to do. I'm a grown woman. I've had employees. But I just feel overwhelmed. I may have bitten off more than I can chew by taking on this business. And I've never ..."

"But you've never had an employee die before." Evangeline let go of her hand and took a sip of her tea.

"No, I haven't, and I really liked her. She had all these great ideas, and now..." Lisa sniffled, shocked by the sudden urge to cry. "She's just gone. It seems so unfair. She's younger than me, and she has a four-year-old." Lisa closed her eyes and rubbed her temple. "Had a four-year-old."

Evangeline cocked her head, and a thoughtful expression crossed her aunt's face. "And you're wondering how you can help and be grieving even though you only knew for a short time."

"Yeah. I guess I am." Lisa blew out a heavy breath. "I could donate the flowers, but I feel like it's not enough."

"That's actually a lot. Flowers can be expensive. Are

you hungry? I made some blueberry lemon muffins this morning. Would you like one? They're not as fancy as Jen's, but ..."

"I would love one." Lisa sat up and gave her aunt a grateful look.

"Coming right up." Evangeline patted Lisa's hand and rose from her chair.

"It's so weird. I've been craving muffins lately." Lisa kept her eyes on Evangeline, suddenly ravenous for the sweet pastry.

A moment later, her aunt returned with a plate of four muffins, the butter dish, two small plates, and a clean knife.

Lisa grabbed one of the still warm confections, sliced it in half, and smeared one side with the soft butter before she scarfed it down.

"I guess your stomach is feeling better." Evangeline placed a muffin on a plate.

Lisa gave her a sheepish grin as she swallowed. "I guess so." She took another sip of her tea.

Evangeline narrowed her sharp blue eyes. "Is there anything else going on?"

"No. Why're you asking?" Lisa couldn't stop herself from reaching for another muffin.

"I don't know exactly what it is. But your energy seems... different. Not off, more like it's shifted. Almost radiating." Evangeline shook her head. "I've never seen your energy do that before. You're not pregnant, are you?"

Lisa coughed and practically spit out the muffin in her mouth. She reached for her tea to wash it down and coughed again.

"What? No. I..." Lisa's cheeks burned with indignity, but something in the back of her mind nagged at her. *You're late.*

Evangeline brought her cup to her lips and took another sip. Her gaze never wavered from Lisa's face. "Have you taken a pregnancy test?"

"No."

"When did you have your last period?"

"Are you my doctor now?" Lisa snapped and immediately regretted it.

Evangeline pursed her lips, and the scowl on her face deepened the lines on her forehead. "Is that the way you speak to me now?"

"No, ma'am. I'm sorry." Lisa blew out a heavy breath. "I feel so stressed and..." She clenched her jaw. "I might be a couple of weeks late. I've been trying not to think about it much because sometimes I'm irregular."

"Are you on birth control?" Evangeline asked.

"We use condoms. I used to get the worst headaches when I was on the pill, so..."

"Oh, honey." Evangeline reached across the table and put her hand on top of Lisa's. "You need to take a test."

"I know," Lisa whispered. "But I still don't know what to do about Maria."

"If I owned a flower shop, and one of my employees

died, I would donate the flowers. Then the first thing I would do as a business owner is hire a new manager."

Lisa leaned forward and put her head into her hands. "I was afraid you were going to say that. This has turned into such a time-suck."

Evangeline gave her an amused look. "Oh, bless your heart. What did you think it would be like? You're not running just your law practice anymore. Have you had any troubles at the florist?"

"No, thankfully, I haven't. I don't know what possessed me to say yes when Peter Gannon offered me the garden center." Lisa lifted her head, her expression woeful and a little lost.

"It was quite a surprise to all of us when you did, but now it's yours, and you have a responsibility not just to your business but to your employees. The people who work for you rely on their jobs to put a roof over their heads and feed their families. You need to buck up, buttercup. Do what needs to be done. Is there anyone you could promote?"

Lisa cocked her head. "Maybe. There's this young man. Adam. I don't know him very well, but he called me this morning to let me know Maria hadn't shown up yet. He opened the garden center on his own. I need to check in with him later this afternoon to see how things are going. Maybe he could step up. He's worked there for a while."

"Maybe you should offer him the job on a trial basis

and see how he does. He might like the responsibility, and the extra pay, of course." Wrinkles spread across Evangeline's cheeks when she smiled. "That's how Jen and I have always approached things at the café. People before profits."

"That's a good way to look at it." Lisa finished her tea and poured herself another cup.

"So, do you feel better or worse?" Evangeline asked.

Lisa added honey to her cup and stirred it with a spoon. The metal clinked against the fine china. "Better, and I appreciate your listening to me and your advice."

"That's what I'm here for, my love. I will always be here to help you girls through things."

It was on the tip of Lisa's tongue to ask, "Even if I'm pregnant?" She didn't know why she felt like she was seventeen again and had done something wrong. Some part of her dreaded learning the truth. The disappointed look on her father's face burned into her brain the day Jen returned home from San Francisco pregnant, out of wedlock.

Jack Holloway loved her and would love any baby of Lisa's that came along, but the last thing she wanted to do was disappoint him. Of course, Jen didn't have Jason. Her stomach flip-flopped. She took a sip of the ginger tea, letting it wash down her throat and calm her stomach. She would cross that bridge when she got to it.

Evangeline gave her a wink. "And don't forget to take that test."

Lisa bit her bottom lip and sank down in her chair. "Yes, ma'am."

"Whatever the results, we will love you. All right?"

"Thank you," Lisa said and reached for another muffin.

Lisa left her aunt's condo feeling slightly better and stopped home to change before she headed to the Palmetto Point Florist to order the flowers for Maria's funeral. Then she planned to go next door to the garden center to spend some time with Adam and get to know him better. She needed to hire a manager she could trust.

She parked in the employee section of the garden center, then walked across the parking lot to the small square building housing the florist. She opened the door to the florist and the cool air slapped her in the face. She took a deep breath, enjoying the thick floral aroma of mums and lilies. The shelves fairly groaned with plenty of houseplants—often as popular as bouquets. Peace lilies, golden pothos, anthurium, and snake plants. The displays looked a little dusty, but as the manager of the florist shop, Annette, had told her, they got little foot traffic.

A doorbell sound rang when she entered, announcing someone had come through the front door. A moment later, a woman with short silver hair and blue-framed glasses appeared from the back where the two floral arrangers worked.

Lisa approached the counter, offering her friendliest smile. "Hi, Annette."

"Ms. Holloway, I wasn't expecting to see you today." Annette returned the smile. "Is everything all right?"

"Yes, of course." Lisa's cheeks tightened. "I just wanted to talk about how I want us to handle a funeral spray and floral arrangements."

"Of course. Why don't we go to my office?" Annette waved Lisa back behind the counter. She grabbed an order pad and pen and then led Lisa to the small office just inside the back room. Lisa knew by now that this was where Annette handled orders that came in by the internet or phone.

The back warehouse area looked bigger on the inside than it did on the outside. Tall shelves stretched from floor to ceiling, holding a variety of vases and vessels for building flower arrangements. One shelf held the different foam—wet and dry. Boxes of card picks, cards and envelopes, and various tags took up space on another shelf.

Two women stood next to two long tables with buckets of flowers and greenery waiting on benches on either side of the tables. Vases and ceramic dishes of all different sizes and configurations formed lines on the table, stuffed with wet foam and various pieces of greenery, waiting to be selected and made into beautiful bouquets. Lisa smiled and waved at the two floral arrangers. One of them smiled at her, and the other gave her a brief nod and went back to working on her large arrangement of tropical flowers.

"Come on in." Annette closed the door behind them, and Lisa took a seat in the armless chair next to Annette's desk. "So, what can I do for you?"

"I'm not sure you've heard, but Maria Torres, the manager at the garden center, passed yesterday. I want us to provide the flowers for her funeral."

"Oh my, that's terrible. She was so young, too." Annette shook her head. "Her poor family."

"I know. It's horrible, which is why I don't want her family to worry about the expense."

"Of course." Annette jotted something down on the order pad. "What kind of flowers?"

"All of them. The casket spray, arrangements for the wake, whatever the family wants. Can you arrange that for me?" Lisa asked.

"Of course. We haven't gotten word from her family yet, but I'll reach out to them and let them know we're providing the flowers." Annette gave her a reassuring smile. "That's a very kind gesture. Flowers can be a big expense on top of a bunch of other big expenses."

"I agree." Lisa bit her lower lip. "I'm not sure what her favorite flowers were."

"Roses always make a lovely spray, but I'll check with the family."

"Can we say that they're from Palmetto Point Florist and Garden Center?"

"Absolutely. Is there anything else?" Annette touched her pen's tip to the pad and paused.

"No. That's all for now. Thank you. How are things going over here?"

"Same old, same old." Annette shrugged. "Nothing exciting to report."

"Thank goodness for that." Lisa let out a sigh of relief. "I'm going to leave that in your capable hands and head over to the garden center and see if I can pitch in."

"I'm sure they'll be happy to have your help," Annette said.

Lisa got to her feet and smoothed out her cargo shorts. She gave the floral arrangers a quick wave on her way out, then headed across the parking lot to the garden center.

CHAPTER 16

"We should've borrowed a four-wheel-drive from the sheriff's office." Charlie hung on to the grab bar of Jason's Dodge Charger, her body stiffening every time the car shifted and jolted. She could barely see the narrow strip of road stretching out before them, and what the tires gripped was mostly sand and gravel. Branches from bushes and palm fronds scratched along the sides of the vehicle.

"Dammit." Jason clutched the wheel until his knuckles whitened. "This is totally going to screw up the finish on this car."

"This isn't your personal vehicle, is it?"

"No. It's issued to me by the sheriff's department, but I still want it to stay in good condition."

"I'm sure the scratches aren't deep enough to cause any actual damage. A good detail place could probably buff them out." The road dipped, and her seatbelt locked, holding Charlie in place.

A beat-up, vintage travel trailer came into view. A dingy blue and white awning stretched out over the door, covering a couple of folding chairs and a rusty grill. Two vehicles blocked the rest of the view—a jacked-up Jeep with a bikini top parked nose–to–nose with an unpainted Camaro from the 80s. Dark energy emanated around the trailer, and the hair on Charlie's neck and arms stood up.

"I don't have a good feeling about this." Charlie pulled herself up on the grab bar and scanned what she could see of the property. Pathways into the woods trailed off behind the trailer.

"Don't worry," Jason said. "I'll call for backup if we need it."

"I should've brought Athena." Charlie reached into her bag and pulled out her wand.

"Why do you say that?"

"Because this guy's a witch." Charlie pointed to the silver pentacle sticker in the corner of one window. Wind chimes hung on both corners of the awning. A carved pentacle also hung from the wooden striker on the wind sail of each set of chimes.

"What makes you think he won't be helpful?" Jason gave her a skeptical look. "Lisa has wind chimes almost exactly like that hanging on our balcony."

"Yeah, but Lisa's condo doesn't give off a cloud of dark energy." She grabbed her phone and dialed Athena.

She picked up on the first ring "Hey. I think we're making excellent progress. We—"

"Hey." Charlie cut her off. "I need you and Billie to head out to Brett Travis's property."

"Sure thing." Athena's voice changed from cheerful to serious. "What's going on?"

"I'm sensing some dangerous energy."

"Got it. Do you think we need more help? I could call your cousins."

"No, I think you and I can handle it. Just make sure you bring your wand, and if you could enchant a pair of handcuffs, that would be helpful, too."

"Sure thing. How long did it take you to get there?"

"About thirty minutes. And if you can, procure a four-wheel-drive vehicle. This place is in the boonies, and the road is terrible."

"Four-wheel-drive. Got it."

"See you soon." Charlie ended the call and tucked her cellphone back into her bag.

"So, I'm going to assume you don't think this guy's one of your Witch Finders?" Jason said.

"Nope. But not all witches are good. If they were, I wouldn't have a job."

"Maybe we should just go talk to the guy." Jason shifted in his seat. "He may have some insight into what happened to her."

"He might. Are you wearing your vest?"

"No. Should I be?" He gave her a wary glance.

"I don't think he has a gun, but I'd feel better if you wore it."

"Okay, I won't argue with that." He reached into the back seat and grabbed the black Kevlar vest.

"Let me see it first." She held out her hand. Jason offered it to her with no arguments or questions. She reached into her bag and grabbed a black sharpie and quickly drew an encircled five-pointed star on the vest, then closed her eyes and whispered a spell.

"Protect the wearer from magic's might, protect the wearer both day and night." She repeated the spell twice more and handed the vest back to him. "It's safe now. You can put it on."

Without complaint, Jason opened the vest and brushed his hand over the place where she drew the star. "I don't see it."

"That's the point of a protective spell. You don't always see its protection. But it's there."

"Thanks." He slipped it over his head and adjusted the straps until it fit snugly against his chest and back. Jason looked up and jutted his chin at the trailer. "I see movement."

"Shouldn't we wait for Athena and Billie?"

"They're on their way." Jason hopped out of his car. "Come on."

Charlie scowled but, despite her instincts, refused to stay behind. She climbed out of the car, and the two of them approached the trailer with care.

"You hang back a second." Jason pointed to the edge of the canopy. "Keep your eyes and ears peeled."

Charlie nodded and held up her wand defensively. She scanned one end of the trailer and then the other.

Jason knocked on the door and stood back, waiting. Charlie cocked her head and tried to listen for any sounds inside.

"Brett Travis," Jason called. "This is the Sheriff's Department. We need to speak to you." He knocked again. A muffled thud came from inside, and then the sound of feet slapping against fallen leaves from outside.

"He's running." Charlie headed right around the side of the trailer.

"Dammit," Jason growled and headed left.

"He's here!" Charlie rushed toward the path leading into the woods. Cicadas screamed above her head. Palm fronds and skinny branches with teeth slapped against her arms and face, leaving welts and thin bloody trails. She really needed to run more often with Lisa.

Jason's heavy footfalls came up behind her, and he pushed past her. Charlie drove herself forward to catch up with him. They traveled deeper into the woods, and the dirt path disappeared beneath leaf litter and pine straw, becoming slick in places. Charlie's lungs burned, and she didn't know how much longer she could run at this pace.

The cracking sound of a tree limb breaking exploded overhead, and Charlie smelled a whiff of ozone. Jason startled at the noise and stopped, looking around to find the source. Charlie grabbed his vest and yanked him backward just in time to avoid being struck by the falling branch. They both slipped and fell on the slick leaves coating the dirt path. Jason landed hard on his backside, but Charlie broke her fall with her hands.

"Holy crap. Did he do that?" He pointed to the limb in front of them, blocking the path.

"Yep. I told you." She gulped big lungsful of air before she could speak again. "He's a witch."

"We just lost our best suspect." Jason wrapped his arms around his knees and hung his head, winded from the chase.

Charlie sat back on her haunches and brushed the sand and grit from her hands. She panted, trying to catch her breath. "Don't worry. He'll be back."

"How do you know?" Jason glanced over his shoulder, doubt in his hazel eyes.

"Well, not only are we blocking his vehicles, but we're also keeping him from accessing his stuff. When Athena gets here, we'll search the trailer and see what we can find."

"We've got to get a warrant first," Jason reminded her.

"We can start the search without one. Athena will take care of it." She stood up and rubbed the stitch in her side. "He's a witch. That means he's our jurisdiction."

"Right, different rules." Jason nodded and blew out a heavy breath.

"Yep." She held her hand out and helped him to his feet. "Let's head back."

* * *

Adam looked up from the checkout kiosk. "Hey, Ms. Holloway."

Lisa took off her sunglasses and stuck them in her purse, returning his wide smile. "Hey, Adam. I hope you don't mind, but I thought I'd come by this afternoon to see if I could help today."

"Sure." Adam kept smiling and nodding. "We can always use an extra pair of hands. Did you ever hear from Maria?"

Lisa frowned as she came under the shade of the kiosk. "I talked to her family, and I'm afraid I have some bad news."

Adam's dark eyebrows knitted together. "Is she okay?"

She'd practiced conveying the news in her head during her walk across the parking lot and decided to just come out with it. "Maria died yesterday in a hit-and-run."

Adam's blue eyes widened, and his cheeks turned ruddy with shock.

"Oh, my God, that's terrible. Her poor family." Adam covered his mouth with his hand and shook his head. "This is just... unbelievable. Do the police think it's an accident, or do they think somebody did it on purpose?"

"As far as I know, they think it's an accident," Lisa said, taken aback. "Why would they think otherwise?"

"It's nothing. Never mind." Adam held up his hands and shook his head.

"Adam, what do you know?"

He took a deep breath and blew it out. "Maria mentioned she thought somebody had been following her."

"Did she go to the police about that?" Lisa's voice rose in alarm.

"No. She didn't think they'd take her seriously. I mean, nothing happened. It was really just a feeling," Adam said.

"That's not a feeling people just get, Adam." Her stomach flip-flopped as her mind raced. "There had to be a reason."

"She said a black pickup truck followed her from here, twice. I used to walk her to her car, but I never saw it."

Lisa nodded. "I wish she'd gone to the police with it."

"Yeah." Adam sighed and looked around the garden center. "So, what are we going to do? I can't imagine this place without Maria."

"I wanted to talk to you about that. You've been here a while, right?"

"About eleven months." He tipped his head, curiosity in his blue eyes.

Lisa leveled her gaze. "How would you feel about managing this place on a trial basis?"

"Are you kidding?" A grin spread across his face and then faded. Uncertainty filled his pale blue eyes. "You know, I'm not sure I'd make a good manager. I'm not Maria."

"I know this is a hard way to get a promotion. But Maria had a lot of faith in you if that's any consolation."

"Thanks." He gave her a rueful smile.

"It's just a trial. If you hate it, you can go back to your regular duties, and I'll hire someone else. But if you do a good job, I'll make it permanent." She gave him a smile.

"Wow. Manager?" He scratched the back of his head. "I hadn't really thought about those kinds of aspirations."

"I know. But you seem like the kind of person who takes charge, and you know what needs to be done around here. And I can't manage this place. I have a job. Annette has a firm handle on the florist, so I don't have any worries about that."

He pursed his lips. "Could we hire a couple of new people?"

"Sure."

"I have someone in mind to help at least part-time. My friend, Nick. He's very responsible."

"Have him fill out an application. I'll interview him and run a background check."

"Cool. He's really awesome with plants."

"I used to think I was awesome with plants." Lisa

touched a silver satin pothos leaf, and the plant shivered. "I don't know what's going on with this one. It was fine a few days ago."

Adam shrugged. "It's kinda weird. I've never seen it wilt like this before. Maria just watered it the day before yesterday."

"Any chance we have a moisture meter back here?" Lisa leaned over the counter to scan the shelves for any obvious tools.

"Yeah, somewhere around here." Adam rummaged through drawers until he found the long metal pick with a meter attached to the top. He handed it to Lisa. "Here you go."

"Thanks." Lisa opened the pass-through and moved into the kiosk. She stuck the meter into the pot. The black needle moved slowly across the color-coded dial, which showed dry, moist, and wet before it stopped in the middle, showing the soil was moist but not overly so. She stared at the meter, puzzled.

"It's not dry." Lisa pinched the dirt between two fingers then sniffed it. Lisa removed the meter back into the drawer.

"Excuse me, could someone please help me over here?" A man in a baseball hat approached the kiosk.

Lisa gave Adam a nod. "You go ahead."

"Yes sir, I'll be right with you," Adam said.

* * *

THE GREEN WITCH

By the time Charlie and Jason beat their way back to the trailer, Billie and Athena were pulling in and parking a Chevy Tahoe marked with the sheriff's department insignia on the side. The two of them climbed out of the truck.

Billie quirked an eyebrow, a smirk on her face. "So, I take it you didn't catch him."

Jason scowled. "Nah. He went out the back window. Took off into the woods."

"I'll call in a BOLO." Billie unclipped her radio from her hip and waved Jason over. "This is Detective Billie Taggart. I need to issue a BOLO on a..."

Jason fed her the details. "White male, late 20s, black hair, on foot heading east toward Highway 17." Jason paused a moment and traded glances with Charlie. "Consider him armed and dangerous."

While Billie finished her call, Athena approached Charlie. "He had a gun?"

"No. A wand. He's a witch." Charlie swiped at the perspiration beading on her forehead and top lip. "He brought down a tree branch. It almost struck Jason. He's not screwing around."

"No. I gathered that." Athena put her hands on her hips and turned to face the trailer. "He warded this place up the wazoo."

"Yeah, I can feel that. Man, I'm sweating like a pig after that run."

"Oh, here." Athena unzipped her cross-body bag and handed Charlie a travel-sized package of tissues.

"Thanks." Charlie pulled several tissues out and mopped at the rivulets of sweat on her face and neck.

Billie clipped her radio on her belt and stepped up beside Athena. Her puzzled face showed her confusion at the conversation between the two witches. "What does warded mean?"

Athena gestured to the trailer. "Look over there," she said. "Wards are typically spells or sometimes sigils–special designs–put on a property to keep people out."

"I don't see anything." Billie squinted.

"They're not always discernible, but they're there. I can feel them. And Charlie and I can make them visible. I sense these mainly on his trailer."

"How does a ward work?" Billie folded her arms across her chest, her eyes narrowed, interested.

"Could be an overwhelming feeling to leave if you get too close. Or it could be something that hits you, or worse, mentally attacks you. Like your worst nightmare could come to life before your eyes," Athena explained.

"That's not terrifying at all." Billie backed up her sarcasm with a dark glare at the building on wheels. She pulled her arms tighter to her body.

"Don't worry." Athena faced Billie and chuckled at her concern. "We have magic of our own. We're masters at breaking through these things."

"Y'all stay here. We'll check it out." Charlie moved to

the metal steps leading to the door of the trailer. Athena pulled her wand from her bag. She motioned Billie to stay put before she followed closely behind Charlie.

Charlie lifted her own wand, and the tip glowed blue when she quietly chanted her spell three times.

"Wards reveal your boundary set, reveal your power for this test."

Charlie touched the wand to the door. A white-hot jolt shot through her arm, knocking her backward. Athena grabbed her before she fell to the ground. Her skin tingled as if she'd touched a live wire. Three electric white sigils, previously hidden, emerged on the trailer—one on each corner and one on the door.

Athena hurried around to the back of the building. "There are three more back here."

"You okay?" Jason sidled up next to her.

"I'm fine." Charlie massaged her hand, trying to make the prickling beneath her skin stop.

"Do you think y'all can crack it?" Jason's gaze met hers.

"Don't worry." Athena wore a confident grin as she returned from the other side of the trailer. "I haven't met a ward yet that I couldn't break. We just need a few things to make it happen. Charlie, can you help me?"

"Sure." Charlie followed Athena to the passenger side of the Tahoe.

Athena retrieved her bag and propped it on the hood of the SUV. She quickly dug out a rectangular box with a hinged lid. She lifted the lid to expose six large, clear quartz crystal pyramids. She handed three of the crystal pyramids to Charlie.

"Put one in front of each sigil on the rear of the trailer."

"Sure thing." Charlie nodded. After she set the last crystal in place, she returned to help Athena with the breaking ritual. "Do we need anything else? Candles?"

"Nope. Just our wands." Athena positioned the last crystal at the base of the steps. "I'll say the spell once, and then you can join in for the last two iterations. Ready?"

"Let's do this." Charlie lifted her wand and watched and listened for Athena's cues.

Athena raised her wand. The tip glowed bright blue.

"Wards of magic North, South, East, and West, break your bonds at my behest. Wards of magic, of protections spoken, now your bonds shall be broken."

She flourished her wand with a flick of her wrist, forming a light trail. For a moment, a four-petaled flower appeared. Then Athena slashed through the center of the petals, dividing them into four. The sliced flower separated; each piece spun 180-degrees before fading. Athena gave Charlie a nod, and their two voices and wands moved in unison. After the third iteration of the spell, Athena said, "So mote it be."

"So mote it be," Charlie echoed.

They pointed their wands at the crystal in front of the door. A jagged tendril of electric light stretched from the tips of their wands and connected with the clear quartz crystal. The energy flowed from the crystal, spreading to the other crystals, and encircled the trailer.

Every hair on Charlie's body stood straight up, including the hair on her head. Her skin tingled again, but not unpleasantly. The energy of her magic streamed through her hand to her wand. The surrounding air sizzled and popped. Each of the glowing sigils flickered out, leaving behind a black smudge in their place. The front doorknob turned, and the door creaked as it opened.

Athena lowered her wand, turned to Billie and Jason, and grinned. "Told you. There's not a ward I can't break."

Billie's forehead wrinkled and she pursed her lips. "If you say so."

"Great job." Charlie patted Athena on the shoulder.

"Thanks for the help, partner. You want to check it out?"

"Absolutely." Charlie nodded at Jason. "Do you have some gloves in your car?"

"Yep." A moment later, he handed each of them a pair. He grinned. "Let's see what Mr. Travis is hiding."

CHAPTER 17

Around 1pm, Lisa volunteered to pick up a lunch order for her staff from Sal's Sandwich Shop near downtown Palmetto Point. She parked her BMW in front of the small lunch counter-style restaurant and spotted a pharmacy sign two doors down. She glanced at her watch. She had just enough time to pick up a pregnancy test before their food would be ready. She glanced around the street, then ducked inside the drugstore.

It didn't take her long to find the family planning section, and she thought it ironic the pregnancy tests, condoms, and feminine hygiene products were all on the same aisle.

The sheer number of brands of tests nearly overwhelmed her. She grabbed the first box at eye level and skimmed the back. The package included three tests. Surely three tests would be plenty.

"Lisa?" The woman's voice came from behind her, and dread skittered down her back. "Lisa Holloway, is that you?"

Lisa put the box back on the shelf. She licked her lips and turned to find Mrs. Keene, her twelfth-grade English teacher, standing behind her. In the nearly twenty years since she had known her, the woman seemed to have shrunk. Her once raven black hair was now almost all a dull gray. Her warm brown eyes still glittered with keen intelligence, though, and she appeared to study Lisa.

"Mrs. Keene. What a surprise." Lisa's cheeks filled with heat. She turned her back on the shelf of tests, hoping Mrs. Keene wouldn't notice. "It's been a while."

"Yes, it has. I've heard so many good things about you over the years. A lawyer? I always knew you'd do great things. You were one of my best students," Mrs. Keene gushed.

"Well, I had an outstanding teacher."

"I heard you're getting married. Is that true?"

Lisa smiled widely. Gossip spread like a brushfire in a small town.

"Now, where did you hear that?"

"I believe I heard it from your cousin, Daphne. She cuts my hair and keeps me up on all the news about you and your sister."

"That sounds like Daphne, all right." Lisa smiled

through gritted teeth. "Are you still teaching, or have you retired?"

"I retired last year. My husband and I have done some traveling. Our oldest son moved to the West Coast, so we hopped in our car and drove across the country, stopping whenever and wherever we wanted. Free as birds. It was wonderful."

"That sounds like fun," Lisa said.

"Yes, it was." Mrs. Keene shifted her gaze beyond Lisa to the shelf behind her. One of her gray eyebrows quirked. Then she smiled. "Well, I won't keep you, dear. Looks like you're busy."

Lisa rocked on her heels. "Yes, ma'am. It was very good to see you."

"You too, honey. You take care." Mrs. Keene patted her on the arm, then traipsed down the aisle and disappeared around the corner. Lisa blew out a heavy breath, turned, and grabbed the box of pregnancy tests, then quickly headed to the checkout before she could run into anyone else she knew. The last thing she wanted was for this news to get back to Daphne. If it did, there would be no stopping the speculation and if there was anything she hated, it was speculation.

CHARLIE RUMMAGED THROUGH THE CABINETS OF THE trailer's tiny kitchen and dining booth. They'd each taken an area to search. Billie stayed outside to look through the outer storage compartments. Jason combed through the small bedroom, upending the mattress to check the storage compartments beneath it.

"You know what I wish?" Charlie opened the cabinets above the microwave and found dishes, glasses, and silverware.

"What's that?" Athena moved on to the tiny closet space above the drawers.

"I wish I could get Evelyn to talk to us. I thought I might dream about her or even Nicole. But no such luck."

"I know. That's been really frustrating." Athena twisted her lips and furrowed her brow as if she were thinking. "Maybe they just don't have the energy to do it yet."

"You're probably right." Charlie moved onto the dinette. She lifted the cushion from the bench seat and opened the storage compartment concealed beneath it. Inside were bags of herbs, a dish of various crystals, charcoal, chalk, and large bags of both black and white salt. "Looks like this is where he stores stuff for his spells."

"I have his spell books here." Athena pointed to the shelf above the hanging rod, holding his clothes. "You know, we could stake this place out and wait for him to come back."

"I guess we may have to," Charlie said.

"Could be kind of fun," Athena said, her voice chipper. "We could get snacks and pizza."

"I've staked out with Jason before. It's really boring. Just sitting around waiting."

Athena put her hands on her hips, and a sly grin spread across her face. "What if we set a trap for him? That way, we don't have to babysit this place."

"You can do that?" Jason peeked his head around the corner.

"Yeah. Sure." Athena shrugged. "It will save us some woman power."

Charlie chuckled. "I like the way you think. Let's do it."

* * *

LISA LOCKED THE DOOR TO THE SMALL BATHROOM NEXT TO her office in the garden center and opened the first of the three tests. She carefully read through the instructions. Her heart thundered in her throat while she unwrapped the stick and followed the steps.

When she finished, she set a timer on her smartwatch and stared at the small window in the long plastic stick. She read the instructions again. Two lines would appear for a positive result and one line for negative. She chewed on her bottom lip, wishing she had a spell to speed up time—without, of course, screwing up the whole space-time continuum. Her reflection in the mirror over the sink caught her eye, and she stared at herself. She couldn't be pregnant. She wasn't married.

Not yet. *That's not how things work, and you know it, Lisa Holloway.*

The last thing she wanted to do was start her marriage with a baby on the way. She'd been so careful and couldn't remember any problems with their birth control.

Maybe this is a good thing. You're not getting any younger.

"Shut up." She met her eyes in the mirror over the small, dingy vanity. Thirty-seven was on the older side of fertility. She knew that. When she was thirty, she'd even considered freezing her eggs, but then she met her second fiancé and thought there'd be no need. After he died, she just figured having kids wasn't in the cards for her. And to be honest, it had scared her so much, she never even checked the cards to see if she was right.

Jason wanted kids. He talked about it a lot. He even had names picked out and had tried them out on her.

"If it's a boy, what do you think about Tyler?" he'd asked.

"Tyler Tate?" She'd given him a dubious look.

"Yeah, I like the name Tyler. It works for a boy or girl."

"Tyler Ellen Tate. After my mother." She softened.

"Tyler Ellen Tate." Jason echoed. "I like that. Maybe Jack Tyler for your dad?"

"I could get behind that." It had warmed her heart that he'd taken to her family, and he loved kids. He was wonderful with Ruby and Evan. He would be a great dad.

"So, what's the problem?" she said to her reflection.

The problem was, she didn't think she'd be a good mother. Being an aunt was easy. But being knee-deep in diapers and sleepless nights, helping this baby grow into a decent human being, not to mention all the education that came with being a witch.

Motherhood totally suited Jen and Charlie. Even Daphne, who could be flaky in Lisa's opinion, would make a better mother than she would. Her watch timer dinged and vibrated on her wrist. Lisa dismissed the alarm and took a deep breath. She picked up the thin plastic handle and checked the test window. Her heart squeezed with panic.

A second line appeared next to the pink control line.

"Holy shit. I'm pregnant." She pressed her hand against her belly to quell the flutter of nerves. "Oh, Brigid, give me strength."

CHAPTER 18

"How does this work exactly?" Billie said, the look on her face full of doubt.

Charlie opened her mouth to answer, but Athena held her hand up, stopping her. Athena glanced around at the surrounding woods. She raised her wand and made a circle motion with the tip while she chanted three times, "Within the circle we four can hear, outside the circle no sound is clear." She ended with, "So mote it be," and lowered her wand. "Okay, you can talk now."

"What the hell was that?" Billie said.

Charlie explained. "She just made sure that no one can hear us. Which is smart." She gave Athena a nod. "We don't know if he's circled back and is watching us."

Billie scanned the surrounding trees. "Can't he just do what you did and break whatever spell you cast?"

"He's pretty seasoned, based on the wards he cast. But

no, he won't be able to break it." Charlie nodded to Athena. "Why don't you explain the trap to them."

"Sure. Basically, we're allowing him to come back. But he's on foot. If he tries to leave, his cars won't start. And if he goes inside the trailer, the doors will lock on him and won't let him back out until one of us breaks the ward."

"What about the windows?" Jason asked.

"He can't open them. He can't pull the toilet out and slip out underneath. I promise you. This spell will truly trap him." Athena folded her arms across her chest.

"Right. Because your magic wand is bigger than his?" Billie grinned, apparently pleased with herself.

"Something like that." Athena chuckled. "The wards we cast are master level. We can make any place a jail if we need to, and it will be unbreakable."

"And you have to be a DOL agent to break wards. They require a certain magic signature that can't be duplicated," Charlie chimed in.

"So it's biometric?" Billie asked.

"That's awfully close to what it is, yes." Athena grinned.

"Cool." Billie nodded.

Charlie grinned at Billie's response. Maybe Billie was letting go of some of her resistance to magic.

"So what happens, exactly? Do you have to check it every day like a rabbit snare?" Jason asked.

Athena shook her head. "No. As soon as he's locked inside, Charlie and I'll hear an alarm in our heads."

"Seriously?" Billie asked.

"Then Athena and I'll apprehend him," Charlie said.

"Will he know what's happening?" Jason asked.

Charlie and Athena exchanged glances.

"I took his spell books." Athena grinned.

Charlie shrugged and chuckled. "And all the stuff he needs for spellcraft. It won't take him long to figure it out."

The phone on Billie's hip rang, and she turned away to answer it.

"So we can take the stuff back and catalog it into evidence?" Jason said.

"Yeah. We'll need an interrogation room to use when we catch him," Charlie said.

"Sure," Jason said.

"Great, we'll ward the room before we use it and safeguard the cameras so he can't screw around with them," Athena said.

"How could he mess with the cameras?" Jason asked.

"Typically, witches and electronics don't mix well. Some witches can manipulate their energy to cause electronics to go on the fritz. But I have a spell for that." Athena beamed.

Jason grinned. "I bet you do."

Billie rejoined them. "That was Nicole's coven leader. You want to go with me to interview her?"

"Sure." Charlie looked at her watch.

"Actually, I was talking to Athena." Billie gestured to the tall, red-haired witch. "Unless you have objections."

"Oh." Charlie's cheeks flushed with heat. "No. I don't have any objections at all."

Athena's eyes grew wide. "I've never really interrogated people before."

Billie patted Athena on the arm, a reassuring gesture. "It's more like we're interviewing her. Just to see if she has any information that's useful."

"And Athena, you've watched plenty of interrogations," Charlie reminded her. "You'll be great."

"Thanks," Athena said, visibly relieved.

Charlie shifted her gaze to Jason. "We should get out of here so our trap can work."

"You got it." Athena quickly cleared the privacy spell and followed Billie to the Tahoe. Billie made a three-point turn, and the truck disappeared into the brush.

"You want to go check out Evelyn's apartment?" Jason asked Charlie.

"Sure, do you have an address?"

"Yep."

"Great. Let's do it," Charlie grinned, and she and Jason got into the Charger and made their way out to the highway.

CHAPTER 19

The super's keys rattled on a large ring when he unlocked the door to Evelyn's apartment.

"She was always a good tenant. Paid her rent on time. Never made any noise or had any complaints against her. She asked permission to install that video doorbell on the front. Said she wanted a little extra security. I didn't see any problem with it. I even had it installed for her. You know, for a fee, of course. It's a shame what happened to her."

He turned the knob and pushed the door open. Charlie and Jason followed him into the high-end modern apartment.

"Do you have security cameras around the property?" Jason asked.

"Yeah, but they're mostly pointed at the parking lots."

"I'd like to get that footage for the last thirty days, if possible," Jason said.

The super, a tall, lean man with a pinched face, shrugged his skinny shoulders. "We reuse our discs. I can give you fourteen days, but that's about it."

"I'll take what I can get. Thank you." Jason smiled.

"She had that doorbell thing set up to record. But I don't know where the digital recorder is." The super put his hands in his pockets.

"We'll find it." Charlie nodded reassuringly. "Thank you for letting us in."

"Yeah, sure. Just pull the door closed behind you. I'll come up and locked the deadbolt later. I called her mother, but she didn't want any of this stuff, so we'll just haul it out of here unless you need it for some sort of evidence."

"We might need some of it," Jason said. "We'll stop by the office when we're done."

The super stared at them for a moment more, gave them a brief nod, and then left them alone.

Jason made his way into the living room. "This is pretty swanky for somebody peddling psychic services."

"No kidding." Charlie scanned the space, which looked like a showroom display from a luxury furniture store. She brushed her hand over the supple, black leather of an Eames chair. "She has very expensive taste, that's for sure."

"Are you getting anything from that?" Jason pointed to her hand, still stroking the chair. A smirk twisted his lips.

"Just that she liked it. It made her feel good that she could afford these things." Charlie removed her hand. "The community's gated, though. We couldn't even get in until we talked to the super and got a code. If somebody's watching her, how did they get into the apartment complex?"

"They could've parked down the street and walked in."

"I don't know. That just seems more conspicuous than driving your car in and sitting and waiting."

"Yeah, it does."

Charlie noticed photos on a table tucked between the couch and a wall. She sat on the caramel leather couch to get a better look and studied a photo of Evelyn and her mother standing close together with their arms around each other, posing for the camera. Evelyn held her hand out, and one of the hanging plants appeared to reach for her.

"She was definitely a green witch." Charlie picked up another photo, this one of Evelyn with a scruffy man about her age and a woman with dark curly hair with a two-year-old on her lap, all sitting at a picnic table in a park. They grinned at the camera and made peace signs with their fingers.

"Do you think this is the ex-boyfriend, Brett?" She

glanced around and found herself talking to an empty room.

"Hey," Jason called from another room. "Come check this out."

Charlie put the picture back and followed the sound of his voice. She found him in what was supposed to be a bedroom but had been turned into a grow room.

"What the hell is this?" Jason gestured to the two two-foot by six-foot platforms sitting on top of wall-to-wall sheets of plastic stretched across the floor. A large 50-gallon drum rigged with a watering system and a pump sat between the platforms. Thin black tubing extended from the drum and wound through plants with tiny black stakes holding drip irrigation emitters into each pot. Large grow lights hung suspended from the ceiling over the setup.

"I'm no green witch." Charlie held her hand over a plant. Her fingers twitched and prickled. "But these plants are emanating magical energy."

"What would she use them for?" Jason asked.

"Magical potions, most likely. Possibly charms or curses."

"Would those be worth more than, say, a psychic reading?"

"Depends on the intended use, but charms and curses especially can be an expensive proposition. Most need highly specialized plants and incredible skill." Charlie glanced around the room for any other ingredients but found nothing.

"Any idea what kind of potion she could use these plants for?" Jason knelt next to a platform and held his hand above a plant. A long stem reached for him, and he jerked his hand away.

"Sorry. Potions are way out of my wheelhouse, but Lisa might know since she's a green witch. Or maybe Evangeline. She's a healer, and together, they have a pretty vast knowledge of plants and herbs."

"Do you have anybody at the DOL that could look at it for us? I already consulted with Lisa once, and I feel kind of weird about it. You know..." he shrugged, "...because she's a civilian."

"I was a civilian when I started consulting for you."

"Yeah, but you know how to take care of yourself."

Charlie chuckled. "I can't believe you just said that. I know she's going to be your wife and you're putting off a protective vibe, but don't underestimate Lisa. She'll kick your ass and hex you into next week if you cross her."

Jason laughed and rolled his eyes. "You're not wrong about the hex part. I've been on the other end of her temper. Never mention that time of the month to her because you'll definitely end up hexed then."

"I'd hex you for that too." Charlie grinned. "Let's take a plant with us. And the photos too."

"Sure thing."

Charlie picked up a plant and carried it to the breakfast bar separating the living room from the kitchen, where she set it down. "We still need to find where that doorbell security footage is being stored."

"The device stores the recordings in the cloud. I'll contact the company when get back." Jason unclipped his phone from the holder on his belt. "I'll call in a forensics team to go over this place. If it's here, they'll find it."

"Perfect." Charlie grabbed the three framed photos on the table behind the couch. "I think that's all we need for now. Let's stop by the super's office and see what he has for us."

"Yep." Jason picked up the plant and made his call while the two of them headed down to the superintendent's office.

* * *

"Are you sure this is the right address?" Billie parked her black Chevy Tahoe. The funky hand-painted sign on the overhang read Iona's Antiques and Collectibles.

Athena scanned the large window of the store and saw an antique sofa and chair, a tall cherry dresser, and a vintage Coca-Cola sign. Painted text on the window read "Pickers Welcome and All Offers Considered."

"This is the address Iona Waters gave. It looks kind of cool." Athena grabbed her purse and slung the long strap across her body, tucking the small pad of paper she'd brought into the back pocket. She'd noticed Jason and Billie kept a notebook with them that was much smaller than hers and made a mental note to pick up something easier to carry.

"I hate places like this." Billie made a face at the shop as she climbed out of the Tahoe. "They always wreak havoc with my allergies."

"I have some allergy herbs in my purse. They're my special blend, guaranteed to work." Athena patted her bag.

"Herbs?" Billie rolled her eyes and shook her head. "No, thanks. I appreciate it, but I'll just stick with my allergy medicine."

"No problem. Let me know if you change your mind," Athena said, unruffled by Billie's ornery demeanor. She sensed the detective had some sort of trauma buried deep inside the wall around her heart.

Billie met her on the sidewalk, an aggressive line around her mouth. Athena also sensed that no one got to see beyond that wall.

"You ready?" Athena kept her voice light so Billie would know she'd dropped the herbal advice.

"Yeah. I'll ask the questions. You can just observe, take notes."

"Fine by me. But if I have questions, I'm going to ask. After all, she *is* a witch." Athena met Billie's steady gaze, unwilling to back down if Billie put up a fight.

Billie's jaw tightened. "Fine. Do you have a badge, like

Charlie?"

"I do." Athena retrieved her credentials from her purse and showed them to the detective.

"Good. Let's go in."

The two of them headed inside the store. A wind chime tinkled above their heads, announcing their arrival. Athena quickly surveyed the energy of the place and immediately felt magic emanating from every corner of the overstuffed secondhand store.

They walked a good twenty-five feet around antique chairs, tables groaning with knickknacks, and various clutter for sale before they reached a long, glass-fronted counter. A cash register perched on one end of the counter, and on the opposite end sat a jewelry tree strung with wire-wrapped crystals of various sizes and colors on silver chains. A hand-printed sign taped to the front of the tree read "Free Cleansing with Every Purchase." Athena regarded the sign. Did this place only cater to witches? Or did the sentiment go over the head of ordinary shoppers?

"Good afternoon," a voice called from the rear of the store. A heavyset woman in her mid-fifties approached them from behind a standing lamp, a decorative screen, and an old-fashioned secretary. She wore a loose, flowery blouse over jeans, a salt-and-pepper bob framed her round face. She held a feather duster, which she'd been skimming over her goods. Upon seeing her prospective customers, she quickly stowed it behind the counter.

Billie let out three little sneezes in a row.

"Bless you," the woman said.

Athena reached in her purse and pulled out tissues. She handed the packet to Billie. "Here you go."

"Thanks." Billie yanked three tissues from the plastic holder and blew her runny nose. Athena eyed the detective and made a quick decision.

"Hi, I'm Athena Whitley, with the DOL. This is my colleague, Detective Taggart." She flashed her credentials for the woman. "Are you Iona Waters?"

"Yes." The woman's brown eyes filled with wariness.

"We called you this morning about Nicole Brewer. And you called us back." Billie sniffled and held her hand up. "I'm sorry, Athena. I have to..." She sneezed several times, turned, and hurried out of the shop.

"Oh my goodness. Is your friend all right?"

"She's just got terrible allergies. Sorry about that. About Nicole."

"Yes. Is Nicole in some sort of trouble?" The wrinkles around the woman's mouth deepened into a frown.

Athena threw a glance over her shoulder at the door. Billie had disappeared into the Tahoe. She sighed and turned her attention back to the woman. Charlie had been right. She'd watched a lot of interrogations in her time with the DOL. She could do this.

"No, ma'am. I'm sorry to say, but we found Nicole dead in her apartment yesterday. We're investigating her death, and it would be really helpful if you could answer some questions."

"Oh my goddess." Iona covered her mouth with her hand. "That's terrible. Poor Nicole."

"Do you know if she has any family we should contact? We haven't had much luck finding any next of kin."

Iona swiped a tear from her cheek and sniffled. "Nicole's estranged from her mother. She doesn't approve of Nicole's spiritual path. I believe she lives in Atlanta. Our coven is Nicole's family now."

Athena called up an image of Charlie putting people at ease in an interview and used it to try to channel her skills with Iona. "When was the last time you talked to her?" She heard her voice softening as she spoke and sent a mental thank you to Charlie.

"Monday night. She called for some advice about a spell."

Athena removed her pad and a pen from her purse to take notes. "What sort of spell?" She felt her excitement rising but kept her voice calm and neutral.

"She thought her ex-boyfriend was having problems letting her go." Iona leaned against the tall, metal stool behind the counter. She grabbed a tissue from a bottom shelf and blew her nose. "Are you sure it was Nicole?"

Athena finished writing and looked the woman in the eye. "I'm sorry, but we're very sure. Can you tell me more about the ex-boyfriend?"

"His name is Crow Bowman. He's a small-time drug dealer, from what I've gleaned. He's obsessed with her." Her jowls shook a little when she spoke of him.

"How so?" Athena wrote his name.

"He would show up uninvited at all hours of the night wanting to get high and hook up." The woman leaned forward on the counter as if she needed the extra support. "Nicole is a good girl... was... she was a good girl. And she wanted to stop the drugs."

"I know this is hard. I'm so sorry for your loss."

"Thank you," Iona whispered.

Athena glanced down at her notes and tried to remember the questions Charlie had asked during their last interview. "Are there any other people who might have had a problem with Nicole? Anyone who wanted to hurt her?"

"No. We all love her very much." Iona's cheeks glistened with tears, and she wiped them away with a clean tissue.

"Of course." Athena nodded and gave the woman a reassuring glance. "Did Nicole mention anything unusual that happened to her lately?"

"Nothing that really stands out, although..." Iona tipped her head as if she recalled something. "She told me she received some flowers a couple of weeks ago. There was no card, and she couldn't figure out who would have sent them."

"So, she didn't think it was her ex-boyfriend?"

"No. I think some part of her hoped it was from her mother. They were delivered close to her birthday," Iona explained. "But I'm sure it wasn't."

"How could you be so sure?" Athena asked.

"Nicole called her and left a message, but her mother never called her back. She was very sad about it."

"Hmmm." Athena nodded. "Has she ever mentioned feeling like someone was following her or watching her?"

Iona shook her head. "No." The thought seemed to bring on a fresh wave of sadness.

"Was the ex-boyfriend a witch?" Athena asked.

"Yes, but he's a solo practitioner. Although he came with Nicole to a few of our sabbats."

"Do you have Crow's number?"

"I don't. I'm sorry. He lives in Myrtle Beach, though. And I'm not sure if Crow is his real name or just a nickname."

The wind chimes rustled behind them as a customer wandered in.

"Is there anything else I can do for you?" Iona glanced at the customer and back to Athena.

"No, thank you. You've been incredibly helpful." Athena retrieved a business card from her purse and slid it across the glass counter. "This is my cell number. If you think of anything, please call me."

Iona picked up the card and looked it over. "Of course. What will happen to Nicole's body?"

"I'm not a hundred percent sure, but probably if no one claims her, the state will bury her."

"That's awful. I'd like to talk to my coven and see if there're some arrangements we could make."

"I think that'd be very nice." Athena felt a smile warm her face. "I appreciate your time."

"Of course." Iona opened the cash register and tucked the card inside before she headed off to find the customer wandering around the crowded aisles.

Athena walked out of the store, thinking about her interview. Had she asked enough questions? The right questions? She opened the passenger door to the Tahoe and found Billie leaning her head against the headrest with her eyes closed.

"Are you all right?" Athena removed her purse and climbed into the SUV.

"Yeah. I'm just waiting for these meds to kick in." Billie sniffed, and her voice sounded scratchy. "Sorry I left you. I could barely breathe in there."

Athena reached for her purse and dug around until she found her pillbox. She flipped open the top and took two capsules filled with herbs. "Take these. No arguing." She thrust the pills at Billie.

"I told you, I already took meds." Billie waved her off.

"And it will take them at least forty-five minutes to work. These won't interfere, and they'll start working immediately."

Billie made a scoffing noise. "Right. Nothing works immediately."

"Really? That's what you think after everything you've seen in the last couple of days?" Athena opened the cap of the bottle of water Billie had brought with her from the station. She tapped Billie on the arm with the bottle. "Take them. I promise you'll feel so much better."

"If you kill me with this, I'm going to come back and haunt you." Billie took the pills and swallowed them down with a gulp of water.

"So, you do believe in ghosts." Athena grinned.

Billie chuckled. "I do now. Did you get any information from her?"

"I got a name. Crow Bowman. But, not a number." Athena held up her pad of notes for Billie to see. "It wasn't as hard as I thought it would be."

"I see. Sounds like the girl's got her game on." Billie blinked and sniffed. "Hey, I can breathe."

"Told you." Athena chuckled. "Let's head back to the sheriff's station and see if we can figure out who this Crow Bowman really is and where we can find him."

"Sure. Maybe we stop and grab some dinner first? I'm starving." Billie turned the key, and the Tahoe roared to life.

"Sounds good. Do you know any good seafood restaurants? I'm really jonesing for some fish and chips."

"Yep. I know just the place." Billie put the Tahoe in gear and pulled out of the parking lot, heading south.

CHAPTER 20

Lisa closed her front door behind her as quietly as she could, then slipped off her shoes and placed them beneath the skinny table in her foyer. She dropped her purse on top of the table and plunked her keys next to Jason's in a blue porcelain bowl. The heavenly aroma of garlic and tomato sauce swirled through the air, and she breathed it in, her mouth watering.

"What is that divine smell?" Her stomach growled the closer she got to the kitchen.

Jason moved about the L-shaped space with ease. He'd already laid out pasta bowls on the breakfast bar. He'd used placemats and cloth napkins.

Impressed, a grin spread across her face. "What's all this?"

"I just thought my girl needed a little pampering

tonight. That's all. I even bought wine." He lifted a wineglass half-full of red wine to his lips and took a sip. "Can I pour you a glass?"

Lisa's grin widened. Dammit, a glass of wine sounded good. Then she remembered. "That's so sweet. But I don't think I should have any wine tonight. I've got to do some work after dinner. I have a couple of files that need my attention. Thanks, babe."

"Work?" Jason glanced at the clock on the microwave over the stove. "It's almost 8:30." He stepped back and looked her up and down. "You said you were going to work at home this morning. Why're you dressed like that?"

"After I hung up with you, I talked to Evangeline about what happened. She made some suggestions for the business, so, yes, I worked at the garden center this afternoon instead. I couldn't just ignore the fact that my manager died."

Luckily, she'd made a fresh batch of sweet tea that morning and just had to retrieve an iced tea glass and drop in a few ice cubes before she poured sweet tea to the rim.

"I'm not saying you need to ignore it, honey." The plastic chicken timer on the counter dinged, drawing Jason's attention. "Hold on a sec." He donned a pair of potholder gloves and opened the oven. The aroma of butter and garlic wafted out and followed the pan of garlic bread to the stovetop.

Lisa noticed two round aluminum containers with thick white paper covers on the counter. "Did you get takeout from Gambino's?"

"Yep." He slipped the potholders off his hands and pivoted to face her. "I got your favorite. Diablo shrimp. Yours is on top."

"Oh my goddess. You're so sweet." She kissed him on the cheek before grabbing the foil container. She bent back the foil holding the cover in place and leaned in to take a whiff of the large shrimp covered in a spicy tomato sauce artfully arranged on top of a bed of spaghetti. But instead of salivating, as usual, a wave of nausea crashed through her senses.

"Oh. My. Goddess." She dropped the container on the counter and backed away. She covered her mouth and nose with her hand, then bolted for the bathroom. She rounded the corner just in time and slid to her knees to empty the contents of her stomach.

"Honey?" Jason called after her, following her into the bathroom. "Are you okay?"

Her stomach heaved again, and she heard him open the cabinet, then turn on the water. He wet a washcloth and rung it out, then lifted her ponytail and placed the damp cloth on the back of her neck.

"Honey, I'm really worried about you. Maybe you need to see a doctor."

"I'm fine." She flushed the toilet, slipped the washcloth off the back of her neck, and scrubbed her face with the cool, wet fabric. "It must've been something I ate."

Jason helped her to her feet. "I can go get something different for you to eat. We can save the shrimp Diablo…"

"Oh goddess, don't even say it." She grimaced and threw her hand up. "There's some chicken noodle soup in the pantry. I'll just eat that. There's no reason you shouldn't enjoy yours."

Jason put his hand on her shoulder and gave it a gentle squeeze. "You sure you're okay?"

"I'm fine." She rinsed her mouth in the sink. "Let's just go eat dinner, okay?"

"Of course."

A few minutes later, after Jason had opened her can of soup and heated it in the microwave, the two of them sat enjoying their dinner. Lisa might not have been able to eat the shrimp, but the garlic bread comforted her.

"I got some more information about Maria." She tore the crust off a piece of garlic bread and nibbled on it.

Jason twirled his spaghetti on his fork and then stabbed a piece of one of the large meatballs. "What kind of information?"

"Evidently, she felt like she was being followed." Lisa scooped a generous spoonful of noodles into her mouth. "She told Adam it was someone in a black pickup truck."

"Okay. That's not a lot, but I'll see if the information's in her file."

"Thank you, babe."

Jason looked at her thoughtfully for a moment, then asked, "Do you know if she ever filed the report with the police?"

"Adam said she was afraid they wouldn't believe her. And since nothing had happened, she couldn't prove anything."

"Unfortunately, until something happens, there isn't much they could do except give her suggestions on how to protect herself." Jason stabbed a larger piece of meatball with his fork and shoveled it into his mouth.

"I need to do some catching up tonight on one of my cases. I'm thinking about taking the rest of the week off and spending it at the garden center."

"I thought you were saving your time off." Jason peered at her from beneath his long, dark lashes. Her heart melted a little. "You know, for the honeymoon."

"I'll accrue more, don't worry." She smiled and patted his hand to pacify him.

"All right. Go on, finish your soup before it gets cold." He lifted her hand to his mouth and kissed her palm. She moved her hand from his lips to his cheek and steadied her gaze on him. It was on the tip of her tongue to just tell him the truth. To tell him she'd taken three pregnancy tests during lunch, and every single one of them had come back positive. In her mind's eye, she could see the entire scene play out: he would be so elated he'd pick her up and spin her around before he kissed her deeply and told her how much he loved her.

A little voice inside her nagged. *Not yet. Not till you see a doctor.*

"I love you." She leaned in and kissed his cheek.

"I'm glad." He beamed. "Because I love you, too. More than anything in the world."

"Really? Do you love me enough to give me half a meatball?" She sat back and grinned.

He wrapped his arm around his plate and pulled it closer to him, "Now, that's where I draw the line."

Lisa crossed her arms and raised an eyebrow.

He swiftly cut a meatball in half, grinning as he speared it with his fork and handed it to her. "As you wish."

"Perfect." Lisa carefully laid the meatball on a piece of garlic toast, lifted it to her lips, and devoured it.

CHAPTER 21

Thursday morning, Charlie stopped at Flap's Coffee Shop close to the sheriff's station. The coffee was decent, and the muffins were good, but no one made baked goods like Jen. Charlie couldn't wait until The Kitchen Witch Café reopened. She really missed the atmosphere and her cousin's delicious food.

She walked into the conference room, balancing the coffee carrier and a bag of assorted muffins in her arms.

"Hey, early birds." Billie and Athena had beaten her to work, and they flashed their gazes her way when she placed breakfast on the conference room table.

Athena sat at one end, her fingers flying over the keyboard of her laptop. Billie stood in front of the whiteboard, shaking a dry-erase pen between her thumb and forefinger. She stared at all the information they'd gathered on Nicole Brewer. She stopped shaking the pen, uncapped it, and circled the name Crow Bowman, then added a question mark next to it.

"Crow Bowman?" Charlie grabbed a coffee and dosed it with two sugar packets and two creamers. "Who's he?"

"The ex-boyfriend." Billie tapped her lip with the end of the pen and continued to stare at the board as if it might offer some new information.

"Slash drug dealer," Athena added. She reached for a coffee and the paper bag of baked confections. She peered inside the bag before finally taking a banana chocolate chip muffin. "I've found two suspects with ties to Myrtle Beach. First, and most likely, is Carlton Crow Bowman."

"Is he in the witch database?" Charlie took a sip of her coffee and retrieved a blueberry streusel muffin from the bag.

"He's not self-registered. But he's definitely a witch." Athena shook her head and broke her muffin in half. "He had his magic bound once for selling illegal charms, so he has a file."

"What's a charm?" Billie's jaw tightened.

Charlie noticed new terms seemed to make her suspicious. Or was that how she expressed her curiosity? She wasn't sure, but gave Billie an explanation. "It's a spell on an object that attracts something or someone. Like a rabbit's foot for luck. Or, in my case, I charmed my keys. No matter where I put them down, I'll find them because they're drawing me to them." Charlie took a bite of her muffin.

"And that's illegal?" Billie tipped her head.

"It's not illegal to make charms for yourself or... like your kids or something. Intent is a factor. Making a charm that will draw harm to someone else is illegal."

Athena leaned in to read something on her screen. "I don't have all the details, but he was busted for selling revenge charms."

"Damn. Revenge charms? Really?" Billie's eyes widened.

"Yep. They can be nasty. Imagine a charm for an ex that makes everything they touch go to hell. Ruins their life. It sounds good at first, right?" Charlie balled up her napkin and took another sip of coffee.

"But the problem is, they often lead to physical harm, death..." Athena's brow crinkled. "Or even to suicide."

"Jesus," Billie muttered. "That's crazy."

"Billie?" Charlie held up the bag. "There are only two muffins left. You should grab one before Jason comes in."

"No, thanks. I don't eat breakfast. But I'll take a coffee." She reached for a cup, slipped off the plastic top, and took a sip.

"So, you said there were two Crows?" Charlie directed her gaze to Athena.

"Oh, yeah. John 'Crow' Bowman is a DJ based in North Myrtle Beach. But, I checked out his Facebook page, and he was at a show the night Nicole died. I doubt he could be in two places at once."

"What do you think, Billie?" Charlie spun her empty cup between her fingers.

Billie blew on her hot coffee. "I think it's a place to start."

"Sounds like we're taking a road trip. Has anybody heard from Jason this morning?" Charlie glanced at her watch. It wasn't even 7:30 yet.

Billie shook her head. "Nope."

Charlie turned to Athena. "Do you have an address for this Crow?"

"Yep." Athena closed her laptop and unplugged it, then slipped it into her bag.

"Cool. We'll head up the coast and text Jason to let him know where we're going."

"Sure thing." Athena slung the strap of her computer bag over her shoulder.

"Myrtle Beach isn't really my jurisdiction. We should probably check in with their police," Billie said.

"We'll call them if we need them. But we have jurisdiction over Mr. Bowman." Charlie tucked her blond hair behind her ears and grabbed her purse. "Ready?"

Billie nodded. "Sure thing."

CHAPTER 22

Jason parked in the lot next to the sheriff's station with Lisa's health on his mind. He stared at the squat brick building, not really seeing it, too focused on the events of last night replaying in his head. He'd never seen her take a sick day in the two years they'd been together. Not even with a cold. Every morning for the last few weeks, she'd woken with dark circles beneath her eyes.

He didn't dare mention how tired she looked or that he'd noticed that she'd stopped running every day. It was probably just all the stress she was under. A cold pang of anxiety wound through his heart. Maybe he'd bring up her fatigue in front of her aunt and sister tonight at Friday night dinner. It was a dirty trick, but he couldn't just sit by and let her be sick. What if something was seriously wrong, and she waited to find out?

His first instinct was to blame everything she'd taken on—the new businesses, her usual workload, plus all the wedding planning. If it were up to him, they'd just slip away someplace tropical to get married. He didn't really want all the fuss of a big wedding. Some part of him sensed she didn't really want it either, but she didn't want to admit it to her father. God, she was such a daddy's girl sometimes. Jason wondered what Jack Holloway really thought about having a big wedding. He'd have to ask his soon-to-be father-in-law without upsetting him or Lisa.

The sight of Charlie, Athena, and Billie leaving the building piqued his interest, and he stepped out of the Dodge Charger. He greeted them with a wave. "Hey."

Charlie grinned and walked toward him. "I was just getting ready to text you. We have a lead in the Nicole Brewer case. Want to come?"

"I have a couple things I need to follow up on here. Unless you want me to go?"

"No. It's fine." Charlie shook her head. "You stay here and get some work done."

"Thanks. So, where are you going?"

"Myrtle Beach." Billie joined them in front of Jason's car.

Jason cocked his head. "What's in Myrtle Beach?"

"Crow Bowman." Athena stepped up next to Charlie. "Hi, Jason."

"Hey, Athena." Jason chuckled. "Any alarm bells go off for Brett Travis yet?"

Athena grinned and shook her head. "Nope. Not yet. You'll be the first to know." She opened her mouth and made a face. "Or the third, really. You know what I mean."

"I do. Well, I won't keep you." He stepped up onto the walkway leading from the parking lot to the sheriff's station. "Call me if you need me."

"We will." Charlie turned, and the three women climbed into Billie's Tahoe.

THE APARTMENT BUILDING WHERE CROW BOWMAN LIVED was off the main strip of Myrtle Beach. The place looked like a throwback to the 60s, and Charlie guessed it hadn't had an update in at least twenty years.

A skinny, shirtless man opened the door, squinting against the bright morning light. The pair of dark board shorts he wore hit just above his knees. His long, platinum blond hair brushed the top of a pentacle tattoo on his left breast. Charlie could tell by the shade of his tanned face, he spent a lot of time in sun. She imagined him devoting his days surfing when he wasn't looking for customers down on the boardwalk.

"Hello, gorgeous." His gaze raked over Charlie, shifted to Athena, and then to Billie. He licked his bottom lip and grinned. "Three is my lucky number."

Billie's lips curled with disgust.

"Oh-kay," she drawled. "That's enough." She

unclipped her badge from her belt and flashed it in his face. "Are you Crow Bowman?"

The grin he wore faded, and he took a step back. "Who's asking?"

"Charleston County Sheriff's Department, that's who," Billie said.

"Not sure I can help you, seeing as this is Horry County." Crow folded his arms across his chest.

"Maybe you could help me?" Charlie opened her credentials and held them up. "I'm Charlie Payne, and this is my partner, Athena Whitley. We're with the DOL. Do you know what that is, Crow?"

He rolled his eyes and sighed. "Hey, I haven't done anything wrong."

Athena stared him in the eye, and his face went blank. "I'm sure you haven't, and I'm sure you'd be happy to let us look around, right? I bet you'd just love to answer our questions, wouldn't you?"

Crow swayed a little on his feet, and his blue eyes glazed over. "Right. I'd love to answer your questions."

"Thanks, Crow." Athena and Charlie exchanged a look before she pushed past him into the dimly lit apartment.

Billie's dark brows rose halfway up her forehead. She lowered her voice. "What just happened?"

"Huh." Charlie cocked her head and narrowed her eyes, trying to figure it out. "Looks like she used a compliance spell to make him more... well, compliant. Come on."

"You can do that?" Billie asked.

"Yep." Charlie gently took Crow by the elbow and led him inside. Billie followed them, astonishment written on her face.

Charlie guided Crow to a dingy upholstered recliner with dirty patches on the arms and a shiny spot on the seat where the gold velour had worn away. He sat with little coaxing. An end table piled high with empty food wrappers and a couple of prescription bottles with other people's names on them drew her attention.

"Billie, you wouldn't have any gloves on you, would you?" Charlie asked. Crow stared straight ahead, unflinching, as if he were daydreaming.

"Sure." Billie reached into her front pants pocket and produced a pair of black latex gloves.

Charlie slipped them over her hands and picked up a bottle, then popped the lid open. Inside, she found a curious mixture of loose herbs. She held it to her nose and sniffed. It smelled like freshly mown grass, and laundry that had dried in the sun, like Jen's fried chicken, and another scent she hadn't encountered in years—her mother's perfume.

For a second, she heard her mother's voice echo through her head. An image of her mother covering her eyes and counting filled her mind. "One, two, three... you girls better hide... four, five..." It took everything she had to pull the bottle away from her face and replace the lid. She shook her head to clear the long-ago memory. "This is not just an ordinary herbal supplement."

Athena turned away from the crudely-built entertainment center made of planks and cinderblocks. She took the pill bottle and read the label.

"What's pantoprazole?" Athena lifted the lid and took a deep breath.

"I don't know, but it's not what's inside the bottle," Charlie said.

For a second, Athena's eyes glazed over, and her lips curved up just a little. "Oh, goddess." Athena's voice softened, and her lids fluttered.

"Okay, that's enough." Charlie gently removed the cap and bottle from Athena's hand and closed it up tight.

Athena blinked hard a few times and her eyes cleared. She stared into Charlie's eyes. "A memory charm."

"Yeah. That's what it felt like."

"What?" Billie moved in closer with a curious expression. "What's a memory charm?"

"Common herbs that have been enchanted. They bring up your favorite memory or sometimes your worst memory." Athena sniffed and shook her head as if she hadn't quite freed herself of the charm's effects.

"They can be highly addictive, like heroin or crack. Are you okay?" Charlie touched Athena's arm.

Athena nodded and gave her a weak smile. "I'm fine. Sorry about that."

"No problem. Let me know if you need a break. Or a counter spell."

"I will. Thanks." Athena's eyes brightened.

"So, what's the legality of it? Is it enough to arrest him?" Billie stared down at Crow Bowman who was still in a muddled state.

"Definitely. It's illegal to possess them, and my guess is he's selling them. Is there more in the other bottle, Charlie?" Athena dug through her purse and pulled out her wand.

Charlie checked the second orange prescription bottle. This time she didn't open it but held it up to the light. A mix of herbs filled the bottle nearly to the top, but it felt heavier than it should have for the contents. She gave it a good shake and heard something rattle inside.

"There's something else in here. Looks like some crystals."

Charlie searched both sides of the end table, pressing against the sides. A panel clicked beneath her fingers, and she slid out a hidden drawer. Inside were squat tins of common herbs—rosemary, lavender, thyme, sage. She also found glass dishes holding different crystals—azurite, a bright blue iridescent stone; diaspore, a creamy opalescent stone; and hematite, a silvery stone that looked more like a metal than a crystal. She picked up a small black notebook tucked beneath the ingredients and thumbed through it.

"Bingo," she said, getting Athena and Billie's attention.

Billie pointed to the table. "How did you know to look for a secret compartment?"

Charlie answered without taking her gaze off the book. "Common trick of rogue witches."

Charlie held the book aloft, waving it at Athena. She'd recognized a variety of memory spells. "Oh yeah, I'd say he's selling these all right."

"Got him." Athena pointed her wand at Crow. A thin tendril of electric blue light appeared from the tip and wrapped around his wrists, then stretched down to wrap around his ankles, binding him so he couldn't run. "Crow, you need to come with us now. We need to ask you some questions about these charms."

"What?" Crow blinked hard and shook his head as if the compliance spell had worn off. "Hey! Those are mine." He tried to lunge and almost fell out of the chair.

Charlie held the book and prescription bottle up just out of his reach. "See these? Memory charms are illegal to make and sell. You know that."

"I'm not selling anything. Those are for my grandma. Her memory's failing," he grumbled.

"Um... right." Athena rolled her eyes and guided him to his feet with the flick of her wand. "And I'm the queen of the fairies."

"I didn't do anything wrong. It's a stupid law." His lips

curled into a snarl. "I swear to Freya they're for my grandma. I'm not selling them to her."

"Do you have any idea how addictive these things are?" Athena loosened the ankle bindings just enough for him to walk.

Charlie slipped off her glove and placed her hand on Crow's shoulder. Flashes of him delivering bottles to his grandma slipped into her mind… along with another image. Crow delivering bottles to several of his grandma's friends in her nursing home.

"Oh my goddess." Charlie shook her head with disgust. "You're selling them to your grandma's friends."

"Dammit. You didn't say you were psychic. Shouldn't you have to warn me about that or something?" His voice grew louder.

"Now, where would the fun in that be?" Charlie scoffed. "You know, we're not even here for this stuff. This is just a bonus."

"Why are you here then?" Crow asked.

"We're here because Nicole Brewer is dead, and you may have been the last person to see her alive, according to her coven leader. She said you were stalking Nicole?"

"What?" he whispered. Disbelief shadowed his face. "Nicole's dead?"

"Yeah. She was found two days ago."

"Oh shit." He let out a heavy breath and squeezed his eyes shut. "You think it was me."

"I don't know what to think yet," Charlie said. "You need to come with us and answer our questions."

"I didn't kill her." He fixed his frightened gaze on Charlie. "I swear to the mother goddess, I didn't. But I know who did."

"Good. Come on then, you can tell us all about it," Charlie said.

"If I help you guys out, do you think you might... overlook the memory charm thing. It really helps my grandma. She's demented."

Charlie and Athena traded looks of incredulity.

Billie rolled her eyes. "Do you mean she has dementia?"

"Yeah. That's it. Dementia."

"Holy crap," Charlie muttered. "We'll see. Billie, will you grab his t-shirt and those slip-on shoes by the door, please?"

"Sure." Billie nodded.

"All right, Crow. Move." Charlie grabbed him by the elbow and nudged him forward.

CHAPTER 23

Jason slumped over his desk to shut out the other investigators around him making calls and chatting. He'd become so used to the background noise typical of any busy workplace that it didn't usually bother him. Today, though, he needed his full concentration for the task ahead of him. He focused on the computer screen, clicked on the digital accident report for Maria Torres's hit-and-run, and studied the details. When his desk phone rang, he picked up the receiver without shifting his eyes from the screen. He gave his name to the unknown caller mindlessly. "Tate."

A man cleared his throat. "Yes, this is Deputy Matthew Blaise. You left me a message this morning?"

Jason sat up tall, his chair snapping up behind him. Finally. He'd been waiting all morning for this guy to return his call. "Yeah, thanks for getting back to me so fast. You're the crash scene investigator assigned to a hit-and-run out on Highway 165 on August seventeenth, is that correct?" Jason propped an elbow on his desk and held the phone to his ear.

"Yeah. That's correct," Blaise said.

"Would you mind answering a couple of questions for me?"

"Sure. I don't mind, but it's all in the report." Blaise sounded unsure about what other details Jason needed. "Unfortunately, it's going to be a tough one to solve."

"Right, I was looking through it, and you said it looked like somebody had run her off the road."

"Yep. You should find a witness statement to that effect. Basically, a witness said she was outside on her porch smoking when she saw a pickup truck speed alongside Ms. Torres's car and veer into it as if to run her off the road. She heard the crash, ran out, and saw Ms. Torres's car had flipped over into a ditch. Called 911. I figured whoever was driving the pickup truck was probably drunk."

"Sure. And I guess there're no traffic cams out that far."

"No, afraid not. That'd make our lives a lot easier, wouldn't it?"

Jason gripped the handset tighter. "Yeah, it would. Is her car still at the forensics impound lot?"

"Yep. I haven't heard from them, so it probably hasn't been processed yet."

"Sure. What about surveillance on any of the local businesses or private residences?"

"No. Mostly what you've got out there are farms, and any businesses with cameras have them pointed at their parking lot, not the street."

"Right." Jason rubbed his forehead.

"Do you mind me asking why the sudden interest, Lieutenant?" Deputy Blaise asked.

"A friend of her family brought an allegation to me that Mrs. Torres was being stalked."

Blaise lowered his voice. "I didn't see a report on that in the system."

"I know. She didn't report it. I wish she had." Jason clicked over to the witness statement. "So, the witness said the pickup truck was black?"

"Black or dark blue. It was early evening, so she couldn't be exact."

"Sure. And Ms. Torres drove a silver Nissan Altima, right?"

"Yeah. It's all there in my report, Lieutenant." Blaise let out an impatient sigh.

"Yeah, of course. I appreciate you calling me back."

"No problem." Blaise hung up before Jason could thank him further.

Jason put the receiver into its cradle and reached for his cell phone. He spun through his contacts until he found Charlie's name. He hesitated for a second. The other cases occupied her time this morning, and he really had no business dragging her into a separate investigation that had no bearing on either of the murders. Still... it couldn't hurt to take her out to the impound lot this weekend and have her use her psychic mojo on Maria Torres's vehicle. It might give him a lead he could pass on to Blaise, so the deputy could give the family some closure. And if it made Lisa feel better, that was just a bonus. He quickly jotted off a text.

I know you're wrapped up in the Brewer case right now, but could you make some time this afternoon to check out Maria Torres's car with me?

He pressed send. It didn't take long for Charlie to respond.

Probably. We're bringing Crow Bowman back to the station to interview him. Maybe after that.

Sounds good. See you then.

LISA PEELED THE BAND-AID FROM THE CENTER OF THE crook of her arm and inspected the tiny pinprick where the lab technician had drawn her blood. She'd made a call the first thing in the morning requesting a blood draw for a pregnancy test, and her doctor called it in right away. The tiny bruise shouldn't be noticeable by the time dinner rolled around. Or at least she hoped it wouldn't. She just hated that it was in such a conspicuous place. Lisa rubbed her hand over her arm and walked into the garden center, feeling lighter with each step.

She noticed Adam right away at the kiosk, checking out a customer. Two of the part-time employees she'd met—Jorge and Felicia—worked in different sections of the center. Jorge, a short, balding older man with a thick silver mustache, was helping a customer load up on potting soil.

Felicia, in her late 20s, wore her inky black hair short and natural. Her sepia skin glowed in the late morning light. She stretched her long arms, holding out a watering wand to douse the creative arrangements of different plants used to style some of the larger planters. Her dark eyes lit up when she saw Lisa, and she waved. Lisa couldn't help but smile and was grateful for how this place made her feel welcome every time she visited.

Her enthusiasm faded, though, as soon as she saw the state of the silver satin pothos. The plant Peter Gannon had sworn to her was a good luck charm had shriveled even more since yesterday. Of course, it was possible to drown any plant, but the only reason she'd ever seen a pothos wither this way was from lack of water. Some leaves had turned yellow and even brown in places in just one day. It appeared to be dying.

"Good morning, Ms. Holloway, or should I say good afternoon." Adam glanced at the old-fashioned analog watch on his wrist. He grinned.

"You're funny. Did your friend fill out an application?"

"Yeah, he did. I put it in your office."

"Thanks. Anything going on today I need to know about?"

"We've got a shipment of fall annuals. Maria ran an ad in *The Post and Courier* and in the *Palmetto Point Gazette* for a pre-Labor Day sale that starts today. I expect we'll be busy." He handed her a copy of the half-page ad from the Gazette.

"That's great. I hadn't even thought about sales and all that." Lisa looked over at the brightly colored ad. Marketing, she groaned internally. Just one more thing to add to her list. "Do you know if Maria kept a schedule somewhere?"

"There's a calendar in her office… well, your office, now I guess." His blue eyes filled with sadness.

"Right." Lisa put the newspaper on the counter and glanced around awkwardly. She pointed to the pothos. "She looks like she's not any better today, huh?"

"Yeah, I need to dig into what sort of pests could affect them." He shrugged. "But haven't had a chance yet."

"I just repotted it a couple of weeks ago, so it shouldn't be the soil." Lisa brought the plant down to the counter and took a pinch of dirt. Something sharp pricked her skin. "Ow."

"What happened?" Adam asked.

"I don't know. It's like I touched a piece of broken glass or something." Lisa inspected her fingertip and found it bleeding. A tiny, opaque white speck caught her attention.

"Glass? How would that have gotten into the potting mixture?"

"No idea." She dug through the pot again, this time taking care to see if she could find more of the little crystals. Without warning, the register dinged and the cash drawer opened. All the bill holders popped up allowing the cash inside to fly out. Money swirled around them as if caught in a tremendous gust of wind.

"What the heck?" Adam scurried to grab every single, five, ten, and twenty-dollar bill he could.

"Oh my gosh, what happened?" Lisa opened the pass-through and snatched up all the money floating around outside the kiosk.

Adam rushed to the drawer, slammed it shut, and turned the key. In one hand, he held a fistful of cash. He stared down at the machine as if he was unsure the register might open again. "I'll unplug it and plug it back in to see if that will solve whatever glitch is going on."

"Good idea." Lisa handed over the cash she'd retrieved to Adam. "That was totally weird."

"Yeah, it was. I've never seen it do anything like that before."

"I've been thinking about updating the entire system with a computer or tablet POS system, anyway. The old girl may just need to be put out to pasture."

Adam snorted. "Yep."

"Excuse me, miss. Can you help me?" A hand touched Lisa's shoulder softly, and she turned to find a woman smiling at her with shoulder-length silver hair and a pink visor shading her eyes.

"Yes, ma'am. I'd be happy to." Lisa wiped her grimy hands on her black cargo shorts.

"I was wondering if you could show me the bushes that you have on sale today." The woman held up a newspaper for Lisa to see.

"Sure thing." She turned to Adam. "Is everything marked for the sale?"

"Yeah. We have signs throughout the center. The bushes are located toward the back, ma'am. Just go to the end of this aisle..." He pointed her in the right direction. "Then turn right and head all the way back. If you get to a yellow loader, you've gone too far."

"Come on, I'll show you." Lisa smiled and gestured for the woman to follow her.

CHAPTER 24

Charlie and Athena led Crow into the sheriff's station. He wriggled against his restraints as if testing their boundaries.

"Stop it," Charlie ordered. She guided him through the building to Interview Room Two in the homicide division. Jason talked on the phone, but watched them pass his desk with keen interest in his eyes.

"What?" Crow protested. "I'm not doing anything." Charlie wasn't buying Crow's innocent act.

The wooden chair scraped against the floor when Charlie pulled it away from the table in the center of the room. She sat him down.

"Hey, you don't have to be so rough," Crow whined.

Athena slipped her wand from her bag and touched the pair of handcuffs restraining him. A slender tendril of energy emitted from the tip of her wand, giving the room an eerie blue glow. The cuffs unlocked, freeing Crow's hands.

"About time," he grumbled and rubbed his wrists.

Athena dropped the cuffs into her bag. "Don't get too comfortable." She pointed her wand at him and whispered, "Heavy as iron, immovable as stone, you shall not leave this chair until we're done. So mote it be."

"So mote it be," Charlie echoed. The two witches took a seat across from him. "So, Crow, I need you to state your name, please."

He scowled. "What? Why?"

Charlie gestured to the cameras pointed at the table. "For the record."

Crow scoffed. "No."

"Fine. Carlton Crow Bowman, you told us when we picked you up you knew who killed Nicole Brewer. Can you please elaborate on that for us?"

Crow shifted in his seat, leaning back in his chair as much as the restraining spell allowed. He narrowed his blue eyes and drew his mouth into a sneer.

"What about my deal? You said you'd drop the charges for the charms you found if I cooperated."

"No. I said we would talk about it." Charlie narrowed her eyes.

"Well, I'm not telling you anything till you give me a deal."

Charlie kept her face neutral. So he wanted to play games now?

Athena leaned forward. "You want a deal? Here's a deal for you. We charge you with Nicole's murder and with intent to distribute a class A magical charm. How's that for a deal?"

"Screw you." Crow crossed his arms and leaned hard against the back of his chair. He shifted his gaze to the corner of the room, not looking at either of them.

"What do you think we're going to find at your apartment, Crow?" Athena egged him on. "As we speak, a DOL team is combing through every hidey-hole you have."

Charlie turned her head slowly to look at Athena. For someone with doubts about dealing with criminals, she appeared to have a handle on how to give as good as she got from a lowlife like Crow.

Crow snorted. "Right. I was in the car with you. You didn't talk to anybody. And the DOL's in Charlotte. No way you'd get people there by now."

"The DOL has agents in almost every city in the US. Haven't you ever heard of texting? We've already got a warrant, and they've sent me updates. With photos. Want to see?" Athena took her phone from her bag and held it out for him. It took a moment for his curiosity to win out over his defiance, but he finally glanced at the screen. Crow scowled at what he saw.

"We move fast, Crow. What do you think we're going to find? Nicole's cell phone? Maybe the weapon you killed her with?" Athena leaned forward with her elbows on the table.

"I didn't kill her." Crow glared at them.

"Then tell us who did." Charlie met his angry gaze. A stray thought escaped his head. *You won't find shit at my apartment, bitches.*

"I think we'll find plenty," Charlie countered.

"You need to stay out of my head, bitch. Or you will be sorry." Crow lowered his voice and appeared to drop the hapless small-time charms dealer routine. For the first time, Charlie sensed the real Crow showing his face.

"That's my entire purpose here. To get inside your head and to get to the truth. You know what happened to her could happen to you, too."

"Not likely." His nostrils flared, and he folded his hands together before he blinked slow. Charlie felt a heavy wall go up inside his head, obfuscating every thought. He smirked, apparently pleased with himself for shutting her out.

"If you won't help me," he shrugged, "you can forget me helping you."

"No problem," Athena said. "We've got your charms and your spell book. You're on the hook for those, and we can hold you for 72 hours. I know we're going to find something on you. So, don't get too comfy."

"Screw that. I want a lawyer," he spewed.

"Fine. I'll call the Witch Defense League. In the meantime, you can sit here and wait," Athena said.

"No. I don't want some inept WDL lawyer. I get a phone call. I'll call my own. Thanks."

"No problem." Athena pushed her chair out and rose to her feet. She looked at her watch. "Wow, I can't believe it's already past two. I don't know about you, Charlie, but I'm starving. Do you want to go grab some food?"

"Time flies and all that...." Charlie stood up. "Sure. Do you want us to bring you something?"

"Yeah. Get me a burger and fries, and make sure everything is hot. I hate cold food," he ordered and tucked his hands into his armpits.

"I'll see what I can do, but I'm not making promises."

"I'll get you a phone, and then you can just sit here and wait." Athena retrieved her wand and a small ball of twine from her purse. She used her wand to cut a long piece of string and knelt next to him, tying it around his left ankle. When she finished, she pointed her wand at him and uttered a quick spell. "Heavy as iron no more, you're free to move about the floor. Unbreakable this string shall be. All your movements transmitted to me. So mote it be."

The string glowed bright white, then returned to its normal color. She made a circle with the tip of her wand and whispered another spell. A burst of energy rippled through the room, like a stone tossed in a still lake. "So mote it be," Athena said. "The room's warded, and that string around your ankle can't be cut or broken or burned. If you make any move to get free, I will know exactly where you are."

Crow's ominous glare sent a shiver down Charlie's

back. But she said nothing. She turned and left the interrogation room, glad to be free of Crow Bowman's energy. She practically ran into Billie, waiting outside the door with a confused look on her face.

"That's it? He just gets to lawyer up?" Billie threw her hands in the air. "I didn't even know there were witch lawyers."

"Yeah, he does. Our justice system isn't an exact mirror of the regular justice system, but there are a lot of similarities. He has rights. And because of things that happened to witches over the centuries, how they were treated by the law, you should prepare for him to walk out of here once his lawyer arrives. She'll have talked to a judge, and he'll be released under surveillance until his first hearing."

"Athena said 72 hours," Billie argued.

"That's only if he doesn't bring in a lawyer. Don't worry. If we make our case, and I'm sure we will, he'll be sent to lock up in Charlotte, or he'll be put under house arrest."

"Are you freaking kidding me?" Billie's voice rose a half-octave.

"It's okay, Billie. I know it's frustrating." Athena joined them outside the interview room. "We have a lot of leeway with how we conduct searches. We'll find the truth."

"I'm sorry. I want justice for Nicole too. Hopefully, the DOL agents doing the search will find something besides charms that point to him being our guy," Charlie added.

Billie scrubbed her hand through her thick, short hair, her brown eyes a little wild. "Do you think they'll find anything? "

"Maybe we'll get lucky and find more evidence of his illegal charm making. He closed his mind up tight in there. I couldn't probe his thoughts. Which makes me wonder how many run-ins he's had with the DOL where there wasn't enough to charge him."

"Yeah, I wondered that too. When his demeanor changed?" Athena shook her head. "It was almost like a glamour disappearing."

"Wait. You can probe people's thoughts?" Billie narrowed her eyes.

"Um..." Charlie traded an uncertain glance with Athena, then nodded. She lowered her voice. "Yes, to an extent. It's not always foolproof. I've learned how to listen to people's minds. The problem is people are good at lying to themselves. Although Crow seems exceptionally good at lying. I also think he's a lot smarter than I first thought."

"So what do we do now?" Billie asked.

"We wait to hear from the witches going through his apartment and hope they bring a boatload of evidence for us to comb through," Athena said.

"Shit," Billie muttered. "I hate this. He's going to get away with murdering her."

"We don't know that he actually killed her. That was just Athena trying to scare him, I think."

"I don't know. Just watching him react...my gut tells me otherwise," Billie said. "There's something we're missing, but I don't know what it is."

"Well, hopefully, we'll figure it out soon," Athena said.

"Hey." Jason approached from his desk with a cautious expression on his face. "Any chance you've got some time now to go do that thing I texted you about?"

Charlie glanced at her watch and sighed. "Will y'all be okay without me?"

"Yeah, no problem. We've got this," Athena said. "We'll grab some food and wait for his lawyer to show up."

"Great. Sure, we can go." Charlie simpered. "But, you're buying me lunch."

"No problem. I'm sure there's a McDonald's on the way." Jason grinned. Charlie rolled her eyes, and the two of them headed to the exit.

CHAPTER 25

"I really appreciate you doing this," Jason said for the fourth time and pulled into the parking lot for the forensic impound lot.

"It's no problem," Charlie said, trying to reassure him again.

"It's just, you know, in the past few weeks since Lisa took over the garden center, she's become close to this lady. I think the loss hit her harder than she expected."

"You don't have to explain."

"And she's been really emotional lately, so I want to do whatever I can to make her feel better."

"You're a good fiancé." Charlie sighed and patted his shoulder and stared out the window at the ten-foot chain-link fence surrounding the place.

Jason parked close to the entrance. The two of them

stepped out of the car and headed to the guard shack. When Jason flashed his badge, the officer signed them in, provided them with visitor passes and the location of Maria's Nissan Altima.

"Thanks," Jason said and handed Charlie her pass.

Charlie glanced around at all the cars waiting to be processed by a forensic team. "Is her car here because it's a criminal investigation? Or do they do this for all traffic accidents?"

"This place is mainly for criminal investigations. Since there're no witnesses or security footage, I'm hoping you'll see something the forensic team won't."

"Sure, but that won't be admissible, right?" Charlie asked.

"Probably not, but I might be able to nudge the deputy in the right direction, and maybe it'll give Lisa some comfort knowing we're doing something."

A chill crept around Charlie's shoulders, and she shivered despite the late afternoon heat. She glanced across the lot and saw a woman with shoulder-length brown hair walking the perimeter of the fence as if she couldn't figure out how to get out. Her translucent body revealed she was a spirit. Charlie's gaze flitted to the guard shack, where the officer appeared to be playing on his phone. A flurry of technicians worked a car in the garage structure at the opposite end of the lot, dusting for prints, vacuuming carpeting for fibers. Charlie suppressed the urge to call to the spirit out loud. Instead, she closed her eyes and inquired with her mind.

Maria? Maria Torres?

The spirit glanced around as if confused. Then she fixed her stare on Charlie. That's when Charlie saw the gaping wound in her face. Charlie recoiled a little at the sight.

"What is it?" Jason asked.

"She's here," Charlie whispered. "And she looks pissed."

Jason glanced around as if he hoped he might see her. He had come so far in the three short years they'd known each other. "What do you want to do?"

"Let me talk to her alone. So she doesn't get spooked."

He nodded and dug some gloves out of his pocket, and handed a pair to her. "Put these on."

"Thanks."

"I'll go distract the guard so he doesn't notice what you're doing." He gave the fence one more look, then walked away, raising his hand in the air. "Hey…"

Charlie turned and approached the spirit with caution. The gravel crunched beneath her feet, and the hair on her arms stood up. The spirit stopped pacing and glared at her.

"How the hell did I get here? I was just at work."

"You're Maria Torres?"

"Yeah. Who's asking?"

"My name's Charlie Payne."

"Great, Charlie Payne, how do I get out of here?" Maria sounded impatient. "I tried talking to those guys up there, but they ignored me. Assholes."

"I'm sorry that happened. I don't know if you remember, but we met once. I'm Lisa Holloway's cousin."

Maria stared at Charlie for a long moment, then tapped her bloody forehead. "Right. I'm sorry I didn't recognize you first. My head's a little muddled today."

"I'm sure it is. Do you know how long you've been here?"

The spirit gave her a confused look. She stared off into the distance. "I don't know. My watch doesn't seem to work." She glanced down at her arm. "I was just at work, but something happened."

"Do you remember what happened?" Charlie kept her voice calm. Telling a spirit about their own death could be tricky business. And she didn't want to risk Maria freaking out and disappearing before they could have a proper chat.

"What do you mean? What happened to me?"

"What's the last thing you remember?" Charlie asked.

Maria turned and faced her. "I was just at work then... I went to my friend's house. He asked me to get rid of something for him."

"Really? What?" Charlie asked.

"I don't remember," Maria snapped. "But, it was important."

The air around the spirit crackled and popped. Charlie had seen this many times, especially with an angry spirit. Charlie held her hands up to show she meant no harm. "All right. Can you tell me if someone was following you?"

"What? How do you know that?"

"Lisa told me. She was worried about you," Charlie lied.

"How did Lisa know? The only person who knows about that is my husband and Adam." She glowered and made a shooing motion with her hands. Then paced back and forth along the fence again, like a caged animal. "I have to get back to work. There's something I have to do."

"Things are probably confusing right now." Charlie used her most soothing voice. "Maybe if you talk to me, I can shed some light for you."

Maria stopped. She tapped her forehead with her hand. "They're just so many things I can't remember."

"I know. It's disorienting to have no sense of time anymore."

"Yeah." Maria's expression shifted, and her eyes filled with astonishment. "Yeah, that's it exactly."

"Do you remember a truck following you? Maybe chasing your car down Highway 165?"

Maria's brow furrowed and she closed her eyes. "It's kind of hazy. Like I said, I'd just left work."

"With the stuff your friend wanted you to get rid of?"

"Yeah. It was in my backseat." Maria nodded.

"Then what happened?"

"The headlights. This jacked-up black truck sped up behind me. I thought he was going to hit me, but he didn't. The only things I could see were those stupid bright lights and his grill in my rearview mirror."

"I hate that," Charlie said.

"Yeah, me too," Maria whispered. "I've got to get back to work. There's something I have to do."

"Okay. You can go back to work, but first, tell me what happened with the truck?"

Maria put her head in her hand. "He passed me, but he got so close. And he kept getting closer. I beeped my horn... Adam. There's something I have to tell Adam." Maria flickered. Her spirit's fear poured off her and washed through Charlie.

"It's okay, Maria. You're okay now."

"Oh God," Maria croaked. She fixed her gaze on Charlie. "He ran me off the road, didn't he?"

"Yes. He did."

"And my car flipped. Into the ditch. Into the water."

"What water?" Charlie asked.

"The standing water in the ditch. It never drains this time of year because of all the rain."

"Oh. Right." Charlie's stomach turned at the thought of Maria hanging upside down, half-submerged in dirty, stagnant water.

"I died, didn't I?"

"You did. I'm really sorry." Charlie remained

composed and hoped it would be enough to keep the spirit calm. "That's why I'm here. I'm searching for the man who did this to you. Can you think of anyone who would want to hurt you?"

"Too many people wanted to hurt us. He killed my best friend. I guess it shouldn't surprise me he wanted to kill me, too."

"Who wanted to kill you?" Charlie asked.

"Hey! What are you doing over there?" A harsh male voice came from behind her.

Charlie turned and found a man with a pair of keys in his hand. He wore a pair of gray coveralls with a sheriff's insignia patch sewn over the right breast. He glared at her. "You're not allowed back here."

Charlie blew out a breath and chanced a glance over her shoulder. Maria was gone.

"I'm here with Deputy Tate." She pointed to Jason standing at the guard shack.

"Then you need to stay with Deputy Tate. These vehicles are evidence. You can't be back here," he snapped.

"Sure. Sorry." Charlie held her hands up. "I just wanted to check something out."

Jason finally appeared to notice Charlie and the man. He cut off his conversation with the guard and jogged over to them, holding up his badge for the technician to see. "Hey, what's the problem?"

"You know what the problem is, deputy. You shouldn't be bringing civilians here."

"She's not a civilian. She's with another agency. We're working a case together, and I wanted her to look at the vehicle with me."

"Which vehicle?" The technician asked.

"A Nissan Altima. For the Torres case."

The technician frowned. "Do you have gloves?"

"Yes, we do." Charlie held up the pair Jason had given her and offered a contrite smile.

"Fine." The technician twisted his lips with disdain. "Just be careful out here."

"We will. Thank you," Jason said. They waited for the technician to move on before Jason led her away from the fence line. "What happened?"

"I talked to Maria. A little, at least. She didn't realize she was dead."

Jason shook his head and shivered. "I'll never get used to that part. If I die, please make sure I know I'm dead so I can just get to the other side."

"Good goddess, Jason, don't say things like that," she scolded. "And it doesn't happen all that often."

"Yeah, once is too often," he said. "So, what did you find out?"

"Someone killed her best friend, and another friend sent her on an errand to get rid of some stuff for him."

"What kind of stuff?" Jason asked.

"Not sure." Charlie pursed her lips. "She was confused and scared and angry."

"Can't blame her there."

"Me either. Do you know the cause of death?"

"I'd have to check. Why?"

"Her car flipped into a ditch. She said there was water. It probably doesn't matter."

"Okay. I'll check the M.E.'s preliminary report to see what it says."

"Can we look at her car? Maybe we'll find something more concrete."

"Sure. It's this way." Jason pointed away from the fence.

* * *

THE SIGHT OF THE CAR MADE CHARLIE'S HEART LURCH IN her chest, and she recoiled. Jason walked over to it with no hesitation, but Charlie couldn't get her feet to move. A dark aura enveloped the vehicle, from its partially crushed top to its wheels. If she touched that car, she would see everything that happened to Maria. Feel her fear and her pain, even experience her death. Her stomach turned.

Jason knelt next to the back wheel of the silver Nissan Altima. "Hey, there's some black paint here. Did Maria say if the truck struck her?" He paused for a beat as if waiting for her to answer him, then glanced over his shoulder. "What's wrong?"

She blew out a heavy breath. "She told me what happened to her, but this...."

"Why do you look so scared?"

"Because there's dark energy coming from that car. I don't think it flipped just because the truck ran her off the road."

"You think... what? They used magic?"

"Yep. With the intent to kill."

"You haven't even touched it yet. How do you know?"

Charlie held out her hand with her palm facing the car. Her fingertips prickled. "I feel it and I can see it radiating. Deadly magic like this sometimes leaves a signature. Whoever did this was a witch or maybe a sorcerer. This is not just a simple case of a hit-and-run by a drunk driver."

"Great. You're just racking up cases this week." Jason scratched the back of his head. "What do you want to do?"

"I want to check the inside of the car. Maybe we'll find something to explain it." Charlie drew closer to the vehicle, and a sense of tightness filled her chest. She wrapped her hand around her throat.

"What's wrong?" Jason put himself between her and the car. Alarm filled his hazel eyes.

"She remembered being submerged in water. It's..." She swallowed, and the taste of mud and decaying plants filled her mouth. "I can't breathe." Charlie backed away from the car several feet.

"It's okay. You're okay." Jason followed her. "I'll inspect

the car. You stay here. Are you okay? Do I need to call a medic?"

"No." Charlie took in a deep cleansing breath. The sense of choking on water disappeared. "I'm okay now. I'm sorry I scared you."

"Don't worry about it." Jason donned a pair of gloves and opened the car door. He bent down and peered inside the car's interior cabin. "I can see the waterline. If she couldn't get out of her seatbelt and panicked, or if she were barely conscious, I could see drowning as a real possibility. It doesn't take a lot of water."

"No, it doesn't." Charlie scrutinized his every move.

Jason sat in the driver's seat and ran his hands over the dashboard, checking every cubby and the center console before he opened the glove compartment. He rummaged through the few documents inside.

"Hey, this is weird."

"What is?"

"There's a plant in here that looks kind of like the one we took from Evelyn's apartment."

"Can you show me?" Charlie craned her neck but couldn't see the plant. "This is ridiculous," she muttered. She pulled her wand from her purse and pointed it at the car.

"Bad memories release, panic and fear be gone, leave this car now, you've stayed too long. So mote it be."

The car rocked a little, and a faint screaming filled her

head, then dissipated. Jason grabbed the steering wheel. He threw Charlie a look of surprise. "What was that?"

"Just making my work environment better."

She approached the car with caution but no longer felt the effects of Maria's death energy. Charlie walked around to the passenger side of the car and opened the door. A long tendril of a greenish-gray plant with heart-shaped leaves stretched upward between the center console and the passenger seat. She knelt next to the car and held out her hand. The tendril shivered and reached for her. Her mouth dropped open.

"Oh, my stars. That can't be a coincidence, right?"

"I don't believe in coincidence." Jason pulled a pocketknife from his front pocket.

"What are you doing?"

"It's hung up on something. I tried to pull it out and couldn't get it to budge." He flipped open the short, sharp blade.

"No. Don't do that." Charlie put her hand over the plant to protect it.

"It's just a plant, Charlie." Jason glared at her with disapproval.

"Yes. A magical plant. We don't know what cutting it will do to it. So just..." She scowled and let out a heavy sigh. " Hold your horses, dude. It's not hurting anything at the moment. Did you find anything else in here? Her purse, maybe?"

Jason closed the pocketknife. "No."

"Let's check under the seats. I need to think about the best way to deal with this plant."

"Fine."

Jason shook his head, unable to completely contain his irritation. He got out of the driver's seat and knelt next to the car, then positioned himself to see under the seat.

"Got something." He grabbed a small glass jar and put it on the center console.

Charlie donned her gloves before taking the jar into her hand. She held it up to get a better look inside.

"Herbs." She gave it a shake, and something inside rattled against the glass. "Crap."

"What is it?"

Charlie stood up and stepped away from the car. Jason watched her with keen interest. She twisted the metal lid and lifted it off. A dark gray wisp of smoke drifted up, and the scent of mums and death hit her nose.

Unlike the memories Crow's charm invoked, her head filled with screaming. For a moment, every painful event from her life flashed before her eyes so fast it made her dizzy; her parent's death, Bunny's stroke, the moment of her lowest despair when she sat in a tub of water and downed a bottle of pills.

She felt Jason snatch the jar away from her and close the lid. He took her hand in his and squeezed it tight. "Hey. You're okay. Whatever you're seeing, it's not real."

Charlie blinked away the visions and fogginess until

Jason's concerned face appeared. She sniffled and touched one hand to her cheek, now wet with tears.

"What just happened?" he asked.

"Did Lisa say if Maria was a witch?"

"No. Why?"

"That's a memory charm. And not the good kind." Charlie slipped her hand out of his and rubbed her face. "Not that there's really a good kind. They're all addictive as hell."

"What do you mean addictive?" Jason stared down at the small jar. "Like heroin addictive?"

"Worse. If you're exposed too often, you'll need them just to get through a day. And there's no 12-step program for it. Once you're addicted, there's no road back." She shuddered and pointed to the jar. "That one is more of a curse than a charm. Was there only one bottle?"

"Yep."

"Why didn't the deputy collect it at the scene?"

"Probably because it appeared to be an accident, and he's relying on the forensic techs to find anything to the contrary."

Charlie nodded. "Let's keep looking. Maybe there's more. Maria said her friend asked her to get rid of something. Wonder if this was it? Maybe he was making memory charms, too?"

"No telling." Jason stuck his hand between the driver seat and the center console. "I think I've got something." He stuck his tongue out a little as he poked his hands down further. A moment later, he yanked out a cell phone. He held it up like he had just won a prize.

"Oh, my goddess. Did it get wet?" Charlie asked.

Jason pressed the power button, and the screen lit up. "It still has juice, but it's locked."

"Maybe we can get it unlocked."

"Yeah, that's pretty tricky. Sometimes the cell phone carrier will have that information. Sometimes they won't. And the manufacturer is rarely cooperative when it comes to cracking open their tech."

"Even if it means finding a woman's murderer?" Charlie put her hands on her hips.

"Yep, we have to be able to tie other evidence that would prove opening the cell phone could lead to convicting a murderer."

"I bet Athena could get it open," Charlie said.

"What about Maria? Is she still over there?"

Charlie glanced at the fence line. There was no sign of Maria's spirit.

"No. Sorry."

"What if..." Jason started, wariness in his eyes, "you touch it? Maybe there's some of that residual energy you talk about."

"Yeah." She nodded and took the phone in her hand. After a couple of deep breaths, she closed her eyes. Electronic gadgets were her least favorite type of objects to connect with, but people spent so much time on their phones these days, she couldn't avoid it. She concentrated, pictured Maria in her mind. Maria's voice echoed through her head. Charlie homed in on it, listening to the conversation.

"What do you mean watch my back?" Maria said. "You said this wasn't dangerous."

"I know what I said. I'm sorry." The tinny voice of a woman came through the speakerphone. "B's already scared. He's hiding out."

Charlie focused her mind, trying to picture the conversation, but only Maria's voice came through clearly.

"What about you? Are you in danger?" Maria asked with real concern in her voice.

"Don't worry, I can take care of myself. He has his own fucking territory. I don't know why he thinks he can take mine."

"Evie, please be careful. It's just money. There are other ways to make it."

"It *is* just money. But you, of all people, know we can't live without it. If it weren't for money, Max could never have had his surgery. We both know how important it is."

"I know. But it's not worth dying over."

"Don't worry about me. You just take care of yourself and Max. He needs you. Hell, I need you."

"I need you too."

The voice stopped abruptly. Charlie strained, trying to find it again, but it was gone. She opened her eyes.

"Well? Did you get the passcode?"

"No. I got a conversation." She met Jason's expectant gaze.

"What did she say?"

"Someone was trying to take over her friend's territory. I wonder if it was the friend who died." Charlie stared at the fence line, wishing Maria would appear again.

"Okay. Do we have a name for the friend?"

"Evie and she mentioned someone named B. It sounded like she was working for this Evie." Charlie paused. Evie and B. "I need to look at the photos we took from Evelyn's apartment."

"I'm not following you."

"Evelyn is Evie," Charlie shifted her head back and forth slightly. "Maybe. And I think maybe B is Brett Travis. But we need to check those photos."

Charlie looked past him into the car, her gaze settling on the plant. The leaves shivered, and a pale-green energy glowed around it. "Do you see that?"

"See what?" Jason followed the direction of her eyes.

"The plant is glowing a little."

"Yeah. I don't see that."

"Figures," Charlie muttered. "We need to take it with us."

"Sure. But like I said, it doesn't want to budge." He knelt next to the passenger door and looked beneath the seat. "Holy crap, it's like it's growing under here. I see roots."

"We should call Lisa."

"Why?" Jason threw a glance over her shoulder as if she'd just lost her mind.

"Because she's a green witch, and if anybody can sweet talk that plant into letting go, it's her."

Jason sighed and pinched the bridge of his nose. "Can't I just cut it?"

"No," Charlie said.

Jason rolled his eyes and unclipped his cell phone from his belt. "I don't expect her to just drop everything and come running. She's been crazy busy lately."

"I know. Just tell her it's related to Maria's case. She'll come."

"I don't want her to have to see this. You're used to it. And she really liked Maria."

"Okay. Fine. Let me see if Athena has any advice. Maybe she can find a spell."

"Thanks," Jason said. "And if that doesn't work, then I'll call Lisa."

Charlie retrieved her phone from her bag and jotted off a quick text.

What do you know about magical plants?

Not a lot. Why?

Found one in Maria's car. Along with a memory charm. The whole scene reeks of dark magic too.

Interesting. What do you need?

A spell. Maybe. Plant's wrapped up around a car seat. I don't want to cut it.

Gotcha. Let me do some research and I'll head out that way. Billie left for the day already.

Cool. See you soon.

* * *

FORTY-FIVE MINUTES LATER, ATHENA ARRIVED. SHE PARKED her rental car next to Jason's Dodge Charger and hopped out with her large tote bag full of tricks. Charlie and Jason waited for her next to his car.

Charlie grinned in greeting when Athena walked up to them. "How's Crow?"

"His lawyer showed up and sprung him. It upset Billie so much she decided to head home." Athena shrugged. "But, I knew it was coming."

Charlie nodded, frowning. "Yeah. It totally sucks."

"The good thing is, I spoke to a judge and we have a tracking spell on Crow Bowman now." Athena grinned slyly.

"I love how you always find the bright side," Charlie said.

"So, where is this stubborn plant?" Athena glanced around the lot full of cars waiting to be processed. Her arms broke into goosebumps. "Wow. There's a lot of weird energy in this place."

"What are you sensing?" Charlie asked.

"Death and crime, mostly." Athena pursed her lips.

"There's a cheery combo." Charlie chuckled. "I tried

to talk to Maria. But, she didn't realize she was dead." Charlie shook her head. "I think those are the worst spirits to deal with."

"Oh my goddess, I can only imagine. I hope when I die, I'm not stuck in some fenced-in box like this."

"That would be a pretty horrible fate," Charlie said. "Although I'm not sure if she's stuck here. She kept talking about work."

""Come on, let's go look at this plant and get out of here," Jason said. "It's getting late, and they'll be closing up shop soon."

Athena and Charlie nodded and followed him inside the impound lot. Jason led them through the maze of cars to the Altima and opened the passenger side door.

Athena peered inside.

"Hey there," she said in the same voice she used for her cat Morty. She climbed inside and sat on the edge of the seat so she wouldn't crush the plant. One of the leaves brushed against her hand, and a faint green glow emanated from it.

"What happened to you?" She traced the stem down between the seats. "I can feel where it's wrapped around the metal of the seat springs." She gently let the plant go and scooted out of the seat onto the floorboard so she could get a better look underneath.

"It's not just a cutting. It has roots. There's a small pot down here with some dirt in it. It looks like it used to be planted in this."

Athena stuck her hand underneath the seat and pulled out a four-inch clear pot full of potting soil. Then took another peek. "She's wrapped pretty tightly. I don't want to cut it, but there may not be a way around it."

"So, you don't know some spell that would make her let go?" Jason asked.

"No, I checked all my green witch resources, and none of them cover a situation like this."

Charlie gave Jason a pointed look and pulled her cellphone from her bag. "I'm calling her."

Jason held his hands up as if in surrender. "Fine."

Charlie quickly thumbed through her contacts and pressed Lisa's name on the screen. The phone rang twice before her cousin picked up.

"Hey, Charlie. This is a surprise. Everything okay?"

"How busy are you?"

"Not too badly. Just doing some accounting at the garden center. Why?"

"I have a plant I need to salvage for a case, and it's being..." Charlie bit her bottom lip aware of how crazy what she was about to say sounded even to her. "Stubborn?"

"Define stubborn?" Lisa said, sounding amused.

"It wrapped itself around something and won't let go. It's giving off magical vibes, so I don't want to cut it."

"Why don't we video chat, and you can show me."

"Sure thing. I'll call you right back." Charlie pressed end on her screen and then opened her video chat app. A moment later, Lisa's face appeared. Charlie pointed her camera at the plant.

"Is this a car?" Lisa asked.

"Yes. It's for a case we're working. I have no idea how the plant got itself so tangled."

"Is this Maria's car?" Lisa asked.

Charlie glanced at Jason. "Does it matter?"

"Yeah. That looks like a silver satin pothos."

Charlie flipped the camera back to face herself. "So?"

"The former owner left me a plant. A lucky plant, that's what he called it. But really, this plant is imbued with magic. Maria took some cuttings from it a couple of weeks back. Said she was just trimming it up because it grows so fast."

"And you think this is part of that plant?"

"It sure looks like it. Does it respond to you?"

"Um...yes."

"Great. Hold your hand out to it and talk to it like you would a baby."

"Really? Charlie cocked her head.

"Yes, really," Lisa said impatiently.

Charlie sighed.

"I'll do it." Athena raised her hand and took the phone from Charlie. "Hi, Lisa."

"Hey, Athena. It's been a while."

"It's good to see you. Let me just turn the camera so you can see what I'm seeing." Athena pointed the phone's camera at the plant again.

"Just talk to it like you would a pet."

"Sure thing." Athena nodded and cooed, "Hey, baby." She held out her hand, and the long stem stretched toward her fingers. She moved her hand closer, caressing the leaves.

"I know you've been through so much. You're probably very thirsty." The plant's pale green aura glowed brighter, and silvery magic tendrils wrapped around Athena's hand and wrist.

"Oh my," Athena whispered, her voice full of wonder.

"I'm going to go out on a limb here and say that is a cutting from my plant," Lisa said.

"How do we get it unstuck?" Athena asked.

"Ask it," Lisa said.

"Are you kidding me?" Jason scoffed. "It can't be that simple."

"Of course it can. You just have to ask it the right way," Lisa said.

"Sure." Athena grinned. "Do I need to say an incantation?"

"Let's try asking it nicely first. If it doesn't work, then we can coerce it. But nature magic responds pretty well to kindness."

"Got it." Athena nodded. "Hey, baby. I can't imagine what you've been through. Why don't you come with me, and I'll get you back into your pot? We'll get you some water and some help."

Athena stroked one of the leaves.

"Oh my stars," Charlie muttered when the plant placed itself into Athena's palm. It shivered and shuddered for a moment before Athena was able to gently tug it from between the seats.

"Wow," Charlie mumbled. "That is just incredible."

"If you bring it to me, I'll take care of it," Lisa said.

"I'd love to hon, but it's evidence," Jason said.

"This is really our case now, sorry." Athena held the plant gingerly against her. "Since Lisa's offered, we'll let her care for it until we need it. Sort of like when you take an animal to the vet even though they're part of a case. It's easy to argue that without proper care, the plant would die. And nobody wants that."

"All right. I guess you're the bosses here." Jason threw his hands up in the air.

"Great," Lisa said. "I need to get back to work now."

"Sure thing. Thank you so much." Athena ended the call and handed the phone back to Charlie. She carefully placed the plant's root ball into the pot and tamped the soil.

"I cannot think for the life of me why Maria had a memory charm with her," Charlie said.

"That is super interesting. We should regroup and figure out how to approach this," Athena said. "Maria wasn't a witch, right?"

"Not that I know of. It sounded to me like Evie was the witch," Charlie said.

"Who's Evie?" Athena asked.

"I'm pretty sure Evie is Evelyn." Charlie said. "Why don't I ride with you, and I'll explain it on the way."

"Okay, great. I've got a water bottle in my car.

"Cool." Charlie said. "We'll meet you back at the station?"

"Yep." Jason said. "Sure. See you there."

CHAPTER 26

Lisa input the last entry and closed the accounting software on her computer. Then she sat back in her chair and let her gaze drift across the walls of the small office inside the garden center's main building.

Mostly it was a warehouse where they kept stock and fertilizers, potting soils, and bags of mulch. The rest of the building was a showroom for more delicate plants, specialized houseplants, orchids, and African violets. A whole section dedicated to ponds, including spitters, waterfall components, liners, pumps, and filters, took up nearly an entire corner. Anything that couldn't stand the weather, such as tools, lined the walls.

The office was tucked back in a corner behind a peg board display of hand tools and gardening gloves. The pretty brass clock on the wall caught her attention. It was nearly 6 o'clock. The day had flown by, and she couldn't get over how much she loved coming to work here this week, despite the tragic reason.

She stretched her back and shut down the computer, ready to head home for the day. She still needed to finish a couple of contracts before tomorrow. She grabbed her water bottle and slid it into her tote bag, then got to her feet. The air conditioning kicked on, and cool air rushed into the small space causing a chill to flutter across her shoulders. But it didn't explain why the hair on the back of her neck stood up.

The computer, which had gone dark, whirred to life, and she stared down at it. How the hell had that happened? She knew she turned it off. Standing, she leaned over and propped herself up with one hand on the desk and one hand on the mouse. She clicked the option to shut down again. The computer went through the motions, and again the screen went dark. Maybe it had been a faulty shutdown sequence. She slung her tote bag straps over her shoulder and headed for the door. Her hand was on the knob when the computer again came alive. A definite chill settled around her shoulders, and this time it wasn't the air conditioning. Lisa glanced over her shoulder and watched the computer boot itself up again. This time the cursor moved across the screen.

"What the hell?"

Lisa dropped her bag and returned to her desk. The cursor clicked through several folders until it found a document named "MTBizPlan." The mouse double-clicked, and the sound resounded through the space. Lisa's heart bounced against her ribs, her breath heavy in her ears.

The document opened on the screen. Lisa leaned in to get a better look. The title page read "Palmetto Point Landscaping Service. A business plan by Maria Torres."

"Maria?" Lisa whispered. That was ridiculous. Why on earth would Maria be here? Didn't she have family to haunt? The screen flickered to bright white, and Lisa blinked. For a second, on the backs of her eyelids, she could see her friend's form. When she opened her eyes, the article scrolled up the screen. "You want me to look at this?"

Lisa pulled out her chair and took a seat. She leaned in to read the document. Maria had outlined everything they needed to expand the business, including a budget, a list of contractors, sales goals for the first five years, and the expected ROI.

A thrill went through Lisa's chest, followed immediately by crushing sadness. Maria would never get the chance to be part of the expansion. Lisa wasn't even sure she could do it without her. She needed someone with Maria's vision and her drive. She scrolled to the end of the document.

"I'm so sorry, Maria." Lisa's voice broke. "I wish we could've made this dream come true for you."

Two words materialized across the bottom of the screen as if they had typed themselves.

He knows.

Or as if Maria had typed them.

Dread wound its way around her heart, and she watched the screen fill up with those two words. *He knows. He knows. He knows.*

"Who knows what?" Lisa said. Suddenly the document closed and the computer shut down on its own, leaving Lisa to stare into the dark monitor.

A knock on the door startled her and she jumped. She pressed her hand to her chest. The door opened, and Adam poked his head inside.

"I'm getting ready to take off for the night," he said. "Unless there's something else you need?"

Lisa let out a nervous laugh. "No. Maybe we can walk out together?"

He grinned at her. "Yeah, sure thing."

Lisa grabbed her bag and slung it over her shoulder. She shut the door tightly behind her and didn't look back.

CHAPTER 27

Friday morning, Charlie took the pictures from Evelyn's apartment out of their frames and taped them to the murder board. She didn't flash on any of them. She stared at the picture of Evelyn, an unknown man she assumed was Brett Travis, and a picture of Maria. She wrote the three names on the board and put a question mark next to Brett Travis's name. Questions swirled through her brain. Had he killed Maria? Had he killed Evelyn? Why did he run when they went to talk to him? Her mind went over the conversation Maria had with Evie. She had no doubt that Evie was Evelyn based on that conversation and the photo in front of her. What was she doing that was so dangerous? And why would someone want to move in on her territory? She wrote the word dangerous and territory on the board and underlined them.

"Looks like you've been busy." Athena walked in carrying a box in her arms, followed by two DOL agents Charlie had worked with before — Marigold and Sabine — both with boxes in their arms.

"Looks like y'all have too." Charlie capped the pen in her hands and dropped it in its tray. "What have we got here?"

"Just a little evidence to go through from Crow's apartment." Athena set her box down on the table next to her usual spot. She unloaded her laptop bag and purse from her shoulder. "There're four more boxes in Sabine's car."

"Wonderful. Can't wait to start combing through them." Charlie rubbed her hands together, her mood lifting a little at the thought of finding something that tied Crow to Nicole's murder.

Marigold set her box down and looked at the board. "My goodness. Are you working three murders?"

"Yes. Didn't start out that way, but it's been a crazy week. The one I picked up yesterday had been classified as a hit-and-run, but there's a magical signature attached to it." Charlie smiled at the brunette witch with olive skin and dark brown eyes. "It's good to see you, Marigold, it's been a while."

"You too," Marigold beamed.

"Are you stationed in Myrtle Beach?"

"I am, which is why I was excited to get in on this case. A lot of charms and curse dealings come across my desk."

"So you know Crow Bowman?"

"I sure do. I've been trying to tie him to another murder, but so far, he's been very slippery. I'm impressed that you got him into an interrogation room even though Athena said he didn't say much," Marigold said.

"Yeah, he clammed right up," Charlie said. "I'm planning to attempt contact with his victim again. Hoping she'll be able to tell me something."

"I hadn't even thought about that as a possibility. I guess I should have, though," Marigold said.

"Perhaps we should all remember we have different talents available to call on for assistance." Sabine gave Marigold a pointed look that Charlie recognized immediately. How many times had she flashed one similar at Jason?

Charlie looked from Marigold to Sabine. "I take it y'all are working as partners now?"

"Yes." Sabine nodded and pushed her lustrous black hair behind her ear.

Charlie gave them a thumbs up. "Well, we're lucky to have you two working with us today. Let's go get the rest of those boxes."

"Sure." Marigold headed for the door, Sabine and Charlie behind her.

Once they retrieved all the boxes, they began to sift through it all with meticulous care, cataloging everything, even if it seemed unimportant for now. After two hours, Marigold put her pen down on her cataloging sheet and scanned the table.

"I don't have anything relevant here. Nothing beyond the pill bottles and ingredients you found in the end table, Charlie."

Sabine sighed, a mix of frustration and fatigue. "Me either."

"Nothing here, either," Charlie admitted. She blew out a defeated breath and rubbed the back of her neck. She'd been so sure they'd find something on Crow. Her muscles tightened beneath her fingertips. "How about you, Athena?"

Athena looked up from her spot at the end of the table. She'd been doing what she did best, scouring databases on her laptop for information.

"I pulled Crow's phone records and Nicole's, then the data from the cell phone tower nearest Nicole's duplex. His phone was within range of her house the evening of her death. They talked a lot, so that jives with Iona's statement about him being her boyfriend, but that's all I've got."

"I guess that's a start. It's just very..." Charlie struggled for the right word.

"Circumstantial," Marigold said as if she had read Charlie's mind.

"Yeah," Athena's shoulders sagged. "There's no smoking wand, so to speak. Even him being in the vicinity doesn't mean much because I can't narrow it down further than the cell tower's range."

Charlie clicked her teeth together and stared at the whiteboard; her eyes fell on the three names she'd written earlier. Snippets of the conversation she'd 'listened' to when she touched Maria's phone echoed through her head.

He has his own fucking territory. I don't know why he thinks he can take mine.

Her mind grasped for connection. Charlie sat up straight. "Marigold, who did you suspect Crow murdered?"

Marigold tipped her head, and her dark brows furrowed. "Another charms dealer. Why?"

Charlie glanced at the murder board. "Maybe Evelyn was dealing in charms and curses. Maybe it was Crow who wanted her territory."

"Who's Evelyn?" Marigold asked.

"She's one of my other victims. As is her friend, Maria." Charlie rose from her desk and pointed to the DMV photos on the board. "Evelyn Turberville and Maria Torres. Evelyn had her throat slit and was found in her place of business. But, we found a room in her apartment dedicated to growing a magical plant. Which we suspect she may have been using in her charms."

"Maybe he knew that." Athena's eyes widened. She bounced in her chair a little. "About the plants, I mean.

Maybe it meant her product was superior to his. That plant we found yesterday was totally juiced with magic. I can only imagine what it would do if added to a memory charm."

"Exactly." Charlie's belly thrummed with excitement. "Having control over the ingredients would definitely be a motive for murder, wouldn't it?"

"Yes," Sabine and Marigold said in unison and then looked at each other and laughed.

Athena took a deep breath, her eyes narrowing. "What about Brett?"

"He's still a suspect until we rule him out." Charlie shrugged. "He ran when we went to question him. And according to Jason, only guilty people run."

"Let's put it on the board." Athena grinned. "I'll see if I can find any connection between Crow and Evelyn."

"Great." Charlie grinned, suddenly energized by their theories. She uncapped a marker and scribbled down their ideas. Now they just had to find some proof.

CHAPTER 28

The jacked-up black pickup truck came out of nowhere and sped up behind Lisa on her way home. She needed to change out of her grungy shorts and the blue polo shirt with the garden center's logo on it before heading to her father's house for Friday night dinner. All she could see in her rearview mirror was its grille and headlights. Her heart sped up a little when the truck flashed its lights at her.

Usually, when someone tailgated her, she took her foot off the pedal and slowed down just to piss them off or to make them pass. But some part of her wouldn't let her do that this time. She had more than just herself to think about now, didn't she? She rolled her eyes at herself. She didn't even know for sure she was pregnant. What was she doing?

Of course, you're pregnant. You took three home preg-

nancy tests, and they were all positive. Stop trying to fool yourself.

She pushed the thought away, and instead of slowing down, she sped up. As soon as she got to Market Street, the main business thoroughfare of Palmetto Point, she slowed down to the 25-mile-per-hour speed limit, and the truck seemed to synchronize with her. Her heart thudded in her throat. She pressed the phone button on her steering wheel, and the mechanical AI voice asked, "How can I help you?"

"Call Jason," Lisa instructed.

The phone rang once before he picked up.

"Hey, I was just thinking about you." He sounded almost cheerful.

"I think I'm being followed." The words gushed out in a stream.

"What?" His tone shifted.

"A black pickup truck's been following me since I left the garden center." She gulped in a deep breath. "I'm sure I'm just being paranoid, but...."

"No, it's okay. Where are you?" Jason asked.

"I just turned onto Market Street in Palmetto Point."

"All right. When you get a chance, take a right onto one of the side streets."

He had a calming effect on her, even through the phone, yet she didn't get his plan. "But..."

"Just trust me. Okay?"

Her voice shook a little. "Okay. I'm taking a right." She

flipped the signal lever at the next stoplight and turned right onto Benton Street. The pickup truck turned right, and her hands slid over her steering wheel from the sweat on her palms.

"Good. At the next stop sign, take another right."

"Are you just leading me in a circle?" she asked, not hiding her panic. A map of Palmetto Point flashed in her mind, a basic grid with three major streets running parallel to each other. Market Street, the location of most of the storefront's businesses; Church, and Alston Streets, largely the hub for law offices and insurance agencies, including hers.

Jason broke into her visualization. "Yes. Please just trust me."

"Fine." She gritted her teeth and came to a stop sign at the intersection of Benton and Church Streets where an old, white clapboard church sat on the corner. She turned right again.

"All right. I'm on Church Street now."

"Good. Now take the next right, and then let me know what happens. I'm not going anywhere."

She turned on her blinker and slowed down, then turned right onto Seaward Street. She slowed to a crawl and kept her eyes on her rearview mirror. Her heartbeat thrummed in her ears, and she held her breath. The pickup slowed for a second but kept straight on Church Street.

Jason asked, "What happened?"

"Pickup went straight." She let out a nervous laugh. "It went straight. Didn't even look at me. See, I'm just being ridiculous."

She stopped at the stop sign and pressed her head to the steering wheel. She took several deep breaths waiting for the adrenaline coursing through her to calm down.

"No, you're not. I'd much rather you be aware of stuff than not."

When her heartbeat returned to normal, she looked up and checked her rearview mirror again. There was still no sign of the pickup. She turned right onto Market Street and passed The Kitchen Witch Café, the windows still covered in brown paper and a colorful banner on the overhang reading, "Reopening Soon."

A strange pang filled her chest. She couldn't wait for the café to reopen and for things to get back to normal.

"Listen, I'm almost home. Are you coming by the condo, or are you going straight to Daddy's?"

"I'm just getting out of here, so I'll meet you at your dad's."

"All right. Drive safe."

"You too. Love you."

"Love you, too," she said and pressed the button on her steering wheel to end the call.

THE GREEN WITCH

LISA PULLED UP TO HER FATHER'S HOUSE, SURPRISED TO find him manning the grill. Her aunt Evangeline, her father's sister-in-law, bent over one of the long picnic tables and smoothed out a vinyl red and white checked tablecloth. When Evangeline straightened up, she stretched her back and put her hands on her hips. She looked comfortable in white thong sandals, a pair of pale, chambray, capri pants, and a pale pink, scoop neck tank top that complimented her tanned skin. Evangeline waved when Lisa got out of her car.

"Well, look at you." Evangeline grinned. "You're the first one here." She glanced at the silver watch on her wrist. "I don't know where everybody else is today."

"Jason's on his way. He'll be here soon." Lisa leaned in and kissed her aunt on the cheek.

"Jen went to Costco this afternoon and came back with these beautiful steaks." Evangeline gestured to her father standing by the grill near the large shed where he kept his lawn tractor. "And to be honest, I'm awfully glad she did. It is just too hot to turn on the stove."

Sweat gathered along Lisa's spine, and she nodded. "Couldn't agree more. Does Jen need help in the kitchen?"

"I'm sure she'll find something for you to do. She's making salad and deviled eggs. Jack's got baked potatoes on the grill."

Lisa's stomach rumbled. "Baked potatoes sound good."

Evangeline stepped closer, her gaze steady on Lisa's. She lowered her voice to a whisper. "So, did you take a test? Like we discussed?"

"I took three, actually."

"And?" Evangeline's thin silver eyebrows knitted together.

"I got my blood drawn, just to be safe. I'm still waiting on the results." Lisa shrugged. "The over-the-counter tests can give a false positive."

"So, they were positive?" Evangeline grinned.

Lisa sighed and rolled her eyes a little. "Don't say that out loud. I haven't told Jason, and it's not official. If I am...." She circled her hand as if to prompt her aunt into guessing the words she didn't want to say. "We should probably wait until the second...you know...." She circled her hand again. "To tell people. Right?"

Evangeline patted her arm. "That would be the safe thing to do." Evangeline let out an excited laugh and wrapped her arms around Lisa, pulling her into a hug. "I have a particularly good feeling about this. Oh honey, I'm so happy for you."

"What's going on? Why're you so happy for her?" Jack Holloway tipped his head, his sharp blue eyes full of suspicion. His lips disappeared into his thick silver beard.

"About her business, of course." Evangeline released Lisa from her embrace. Evangeline glared at him and clucked her tongue. "You know, eavesdropping is a terrible habit."

"Uh-huh." He stared down his nose at her, but his mouth drew up into a grin. "I think that might be the pot calling the kettle black."

"Oh, you go on." Evangeline shooed him away. "Don't you have steaks to cook?" Jack held up the tongs and clicked them together before he headed to the grill.

Lisa turned her back to her father and whispered, "And that is why we're not to talk about it anymore."

"Don't worry, your secret is safe with me." Evangeline winked. "Why don't you go help Jen."

"I think I will." Lisa cast a glance toward her father. "He's a nosy Nellie."

"Yes, m'dear. He is." Evangeline nodded and turned back to finish setting up the picnic tables.

CHAPTER 29

Lisa entered the cool house and braced herself. One deep breath put her at ease. None of the powerful aromas that usually hung in the air of the kitchen hit her this time. Just the faint scent of dish soap. Her stomach had been funny lately. Sometimes a certain food smelled so good she couldn't seem to control herself from scarfing it down. Other times, just a whiff made her stomach lurch, and she'd vow never to eat it again.

Her petite sister Jen stood at the counter with her back to the door. Her short, dark hair curled against her slim neck, and she hummed to herself as she chopped veggies on a wooden cutting board and placed them into a large wooden salad bowl filled with lettuce.

"Hey." Lisa hung her purse on a hook near the door

and surveyed Jen's kitchen, the hub for Friday night dinner.

Jen flashed a welcoming smile over her shoulder. "Hey, yourself. You're just in time. I boiled some eggs this morning for deviled eggs. Could you get them out of the fridge and peel them for me?" Jen wiped her knife on her dishtowel before she set it down, then spun around and met her sister's gaze. She cocked her head and grinned. "You sure look pretty today."

"Thank you." Lisa brushed her hands over the pale yellow sweater she wore, resting them on her stomach.

"Hmmm." Jen continued to gaze at her.

"What?" Lisa's eyebrows tugged together.

"Nothing." Jen shook her head and shrugged. "You just seem brighter today. That's all. Did you work at the garden center?"

"Are you psychic now?" Lisa teased and joined Jen at the counter. She stole a thinly sliced carrot from the salad bowl before her sister could swat her hand away.

"Funny." Jen made a face. "No. I'm serious. You look different. Happier. I think working with all those plants is affecting you. In a good way."

"Maybe so. I don't know why I'm so drawn to it. I mean, I've already found Maria's replacement, but I can't seem to stop myself from going in to work there." Lisa grabbed another carrot and leaned her backside against the counter. She sighed with contentment as she recalled her day for Jen.

"I can understand that." Jen grabbed a sweet red pepper from the pile of clean vegetables and began cutting it into bite-sized pieces. "Boiled eggs?"

"What? Oh, right. Sorry." Lisa popped the last bit of carrot into her mouth and retrieved the eggs from the refrigerator. She walked to the sink with the colander full of eggs in various colors—some blue, some green, some brown. "Gosh, these are almost too pretty to peel."

Jen scooped the chopped pepper into the bowl and grabbed a cucumber.

"So, you don't want me to make the deviled eggs, do you?" Lisa asked warily.

Jen snorted and threw a glance over her shoulder. "We want them to be edible, don't we?"

"You are so funny." Lisa chuckled and picked up the first egg. She cracked the shell against the counter, rolled it against the hard surface, and then peeled it. Before she could slip the egg into the colander, a sulfurous odor hit her nostrils. Her stomach gurgled, and hot bile rose in her throat. She quickly covered her nose with her hand, but the scent clung to her fingers, and she pulled it away. She bolted for the small half-bath just inside the hallway leading to the laundry room. She dropped to her knees in front of the toilet, and her stomach lurched.

"Lisa? Honey, are you all right?"

Jen's soft voice pierced through Lisa's thoughts, but her stomach heaved again, and she couldn't answer. The heavy weight of her hair lifted from her back, and she felt her sister's warmth next to her. Jen reached into the medicine cabinet with her free hand and pulled out a hair clip. She made quick work of twisting Lisa's hair off the back of her neck and trapping it into the clip.

"I'm okay." Lisa flushed the toilet.

"Obviously, you're not okay." Jen took a small paper cup from the dispenser on the vanity and filled it with water. She held it out for her sister. "Here. Rinse and spit."

Lisa did as she was told and then took the small hand towel Jen offered her. She wiped her mouth, closed the toilet, and flushed it again. If this morning sickness thing kept up (why they called it morning sickness, though, was a mystery—it seemed to happen whenever it wanted), she would need to carry a toothbrush with her. She hated the way her mouth felt after getting sick. "Any chance there's an extra toothbrush in that medicine cabinet?"

"No, sorry, sweetie. I have some mouthwash in my bathroom if you want it."

Lisa shook her head, filled the paper cup, and rinsed her mouth again. "I've got some mints in my purse."

"Maybe you need to go see a doctor."

Lisa tried to avoid Jen's stare of concern. "I went yesterday morning. I'm fine. It'll pass."

"Sweetie, I'm worried about you." Jen gently touched Lisa's upper arm.

"Please, don't worry. It's nothing." Lisa forced a weak smile. She hated lying to her sister. Even if Jen didn't see through her immediately, she couldn't hide her secret for long. Lying to a witch was nearly an impossible feat, especially in this family.

"Do you want some ginger mint tea? That always settles my stomach." The sympathetic look on Jen's face almost made Lisa blurt the truth.

"That would be great. Thanks." Lisa followed her sister into the kitchen.

CHAPTER 30

"Hey, y'all." Charlie grinned at Ben Sutton as she approached him chatting with her aunt Evangeline near the long picnic table. She'd seen him arrive as she left her cottage to walk across the yard to her uncle's house. "I wasn't sure if we were going to see you this weekend or not."

"I was only gone a week." Ben's blue eyes glinted, and he gave her a pleased grin. "Where's Tom?"

Charlie shrugged. "Duty called. So he has to work."

"That's too bad. I was just telling Evangeline how much I don't miss that weekly commute to Charlotte and back."

Evangeline grinned. "We like having you here all the time. I know Jen missed you this week, although she sure as heckfire kept me busy with stuff for reopening the restaurant."

"Any idea on when that will be, Evangeline?" Charlie asked.

Evangeline shrugged. "If all goes well, we'll be open by Labor Day."

"Thank the goddess for that," Charlie said.

"Hey, Charlie, we should probably get together and talk later. I've heard y'all have had a busy week." Ben took a few steps backward as if he were heading to the porch steps.

"Absolutely." Charlie nodded in agreement.

Ben jerked his thumb at the house. "I'm going to head in and give my girl a kiss."

Charlie nodded and focused on her aunt. "Is there anything I can help you with, Evangeline?"

"No, but thank you, honey. I've got everything covered." Evangeline touched Charlie's arm. "I'm going to see how Jack's coming along with those steaks and potatoes."

Charlie licked her lips. "Steaks and potatoes. Yum." She turned and caught up to Ben on the stairs. "I'm so glad you're back. I'm drowning in cases, and we could really use your help."

"Athena told me." Ben pursed his lips together. "Said there are some interesting coincidences between the cases too."

"Yeah, but we still have a lot of questions to answer."

"Sure. But not tonight." He grinned and sped up the stairs ahead of her.

A moment later, she entered the kitchen to find Lisa sitting at the table sipping hot tea and Jen wrapped in Ben's arms, near the sink and a tray of deviled eggs.

"Hey, y'all." Charlie let the energy of the room wash over her senses.

"Hey." Jen pulled out of Ben's arms.

Lisa took a sip of the tea and put the mug down on the table. She smiled. "Hey, it's good to see you."

The energy surrounding her cousin threw Charlie, and she studied Lisa for a moment. Her eyes widened. "Oh my goddess, you're pregnant."

"What?" Lisa gasped. Shock molded her delicate features. "Dammit, Charlie."

"Why are you damning Charlie?" Daphne walked in a little breathless, pushing her unnaturally red hair behind her ears. A strange smile spread across her lips. "Oh my goddess. You're pregnant."

"How the...." a stricken expression crossed Lisa's face. "You are definitely not psychic."

"No, but I can read an aura, and yours screams pregnancy." Daphne chuckled. "I figured you'd be careful not to get knocked up before the wedding."

"Oh, my goddess, please shut up. Just seriously, all y'all stop." Lisa shifted in her chair, her eyes darting around at the crowd. Panic spilled off Lisa, reminding Charlie of a caged animal.

Charlie pulled out the chair next to her, and sat down. She took Lisa's hand in hers. "I'm sorry, honey. I didn't mean to let the cat out of the bag. Does Jason know?"

Lisa squeezed her hand and shook her head. Her green eyes locked on Charlie's. "No. He'll want to get married, like, immediately."

"And what do you want?" Charlie asked. Daphne sat down in the chair across from Lisa.

"I don't know what I want yet. Other than to have the doctor confirm everything." She let out a heavy sigh. "I took a test yesterday morning, but I haven't gotten the results back yet."

"Why don't you just take an over-the-counter test?" Daphne asked.

"I did." The anguish in Lisa's voice matched the look in her eyes. "Three of them, actually."

"And they were all positive?" Charlie asked.

"Yes," Lisa mumbled.

"Well, honey, I hate to break it to you, but you're pregnant. And if I'm seeing it right, it's a boy." Charlie put both her hands around Lisa's and gave her a reassuring smile.

"Charlie!" Jen scolded. "Maybe she didn't want to know."

"No, I do." Lisa sat up straighter in her chair. "Although, I think I'll wait until they can do an ultrasound before I buy clothes and decorate a nursery."

"Good idea. But sweetie, you need to tell Jason," Charlie said.

"I know," Lisa whispered. "I just…"

"You don't want to marry him," Daphne teased.

"Of course, I want to marry him. But I already bought my dress and put down a deposit on a venue. Canceling the wedding will cost us so much money, and I just shelled out for a new business…." Lisa bit her lip and hung her head. "It's a lot to lose."

"How far along do you think you are?" Charlie asked.

"At least six weeks, maybe more."

"Oh honey, if I'm remembering your save the date cards correctly, you'll be nearly nine months pregnant on your wedding day," Charlie said. "Is that what you want?"

"No." Lisa put her head in her hands. "I just want things to work out the way I planned."

Jen placed a hand on Lisa's shoulder. "Maybe they are, in a way. Maybe this is how it's supposed to be."

Lisa looked up at her sister and made a disgusted sound. "I like my plans better. I've already bought the dress, and it's too tight now. I figured I'd just lose ten pounds, but…"

"Maybe you can still wear it." Charlie wrapped her hand around her cousin's wrist and closed her eyes. Seeing her family's future was often difficult for her. The visions were usually hazy if they came at all, and they were very changeable, based on any sort of decision. After a moment of trying, she gave up. "I'm sorry, honey, I can't see anything about you wearing the dress. It's all foggy."

"Wearing what dress?" Jason's distinct, intense tenor filtered through the room, announcing his arrival. He walked into the kitchen, and the screen door slammed behind him, and his gaze flitted around the kitchen before finally landing on Lisa. "You feeling okay, hon? Did you get sick again?"

Charlie let go of Lisa's arm and bit her lips together to stop herself from saying the wrong thing.

"Yeah, I did." Lisa looked up at him and gave him a weak smile. "But I'm fine now."

"Honey," Jason gave her a worried look. He moved closer and pressed the back of his hand to her forehead as if to measure her temperature.

"I'm fine." She reassured him.

He opened his mouth, but instead of arguing he changed the subject. "Did something happen to your dress?"

"Nothing, like that. I was just telling them I found another dress that I liked better, and I asked Charlie if she could see anything." Lisa reached for his hand and pulled it away from her face. Ben stared at the floor. The smile stretching across Jen's lips looked almost painful, and Charlie was afraid to turn around. Daphne sat next to her, wearing a smirk and a mischievous glint in her eyes. Charlie lightly kicked her cousin under the table. Daphne glared at her and mouthed, "Ow."

"That's up to you, babe, but I thought you bought it

already." Jason searched the faces of Lisa's cousins as if for confirmation.

"I did, but I can probably talk the dress shop into switching it to the other dress."

"Oh. Well, that's great then. See? It'll all work out." Jason grinned. "Hey, Charlie, you got a minute?"

"Sure. Are you going to be okay?" Charlie directed her words to Lisa.

"Of course. Y'all go talk shop. I'm going to finish my tea."

"Good idea." Charlie rose to her feet. "Hey, Ben, why don't you come with us so we can catch you up?"

"Sure." Ben leaned over and kissed Jen, and the three of them headed out of the kitchen.

CHAPTER 31

Charlie, Jason, and Ben stepped out on the back porch as a black Chevy Tahoe pulled into the driveway, parking behind Jason's Charger. Billie Taggart and Athena Whitley stepped out of the Tahoe. Athena waved at Evangeline. Charlie watched with some interest as Athena stepped across the yard and gave Evangeline a kiss on the cheek. Billie followed behind with a cautious expression on her face.

"Hold on a second, y'all." Charlie stopped on the top step and waved at Athena, gesturing for her and Billie to join them.

"Hey, Billie, I wasn't expecting to see you tonight." Charlie gave the detective a warm smile.

"Yeah, well, Jason said it was okay, and Athena insisted." Billie rambled on with a hard spark in her eyes, and Charlie sensed Billie's defenses go up.

"That's not what I meant. You are absolutely welcome here, and I'm glad you came." Charlie stepped aside and steered her attention to Ben. "Detective Billie Taggart, this is my commanding officer Ben Sutton."

"Hi." Ben offered his hand to shake. "I hear you've got a doozy of a case."

"Yeah, Tate and I both do." Billie gave him a nod and took his hand. "I'm just hoping together we can catch the killer."

"Me, too." Ben nodded.

"We were just catching Ben up on the cases. Why don't we sit for a few minutes before dinner gets started and discuss it?" Charlie put her hand on the back of one of the metal lawn chairs scattered across the long porch. They each took a seat, and she made herself comfortable on the porch swing.

"So, you set a trap for Brett Travis. Any movement on that?" Ben leaned forward in his chair with his elbows on his knees and a serious expression on his round babyface.

"So far, I haven't heard a peep, and I don't think Charlie has either, have you?" Athena crossed her long legs.

"Not yet. But eventually, he'll go back to that trailer. I can feel it in my bones." Charlie wrapped her hand around the chain suspending the swing from the rafter. "When he does, we'll catch him."

"So, do you think he killed his girlfriend? From a psychic perspective, I mean," Ben asked.

Charlie shrugged. "I hate to speculate because I've had no specific visions involving him. But he ran when we went to his property, and his trailer was warded up the wazoo. He also tried to drop a tree branch on Jason. So, there's something going on with him. Just not sure what until we question him."

"Right." Ben pursed his lips, and for a moment, his blue eyes became distant.

"We've got another theory we're working on, too, involving the suspect in Nicole Brewer's murder, but we're a little light on evidence for now. If Brett doesn't show up soon, or we don't find evidence on Crow Bowman, I'm going to depose the spirits. Whether or not they want it," Charlie said.

Ben snapped his attention back to the conversation. "I thought they weren't very cooperative."

"They're not. But, I've been thinking about ways to contact them without resorting to necromancy to get their cooperation. I need to run a test first," Charlie said.

"That sounds intriguing." A sly grin stretched across Ben's lips. "Do you care to share?"

"Not yet." Charlie shook her head. "Soon. I promise."

"Great. Keep me informed. And Charlie, if you must, don't hesitate to use necromancy. Okay?" Ben said.

"Sure thing, boss." Charlie smiled.

"So, I just wanted to say on behalf of the DOL... Jason, Billie, we really appreciate your cooperation in these two investigations. And all your support."

"Sure. Anytime, man, you know that." Jason grinned and held out his hand. The two men did an elaborate handshake that Charlie had never seen before.

Billie warily eyed Jason's handshake. "Sure. No problem, as long as we stick to the deal I made with Charlie. If he's not a witch, he's mine to arrest."

Ben nodded and quickly assured her. "Absolutely."

The kitchen door opened, and Daphne appeared with a large wooden bowl of salad greens and vegetables. She stepped out onto the porch with a grin on her face.

"Oh my goddess, Billie Taggart?" Daphne asked.

"Daphne?" Billie sat up straight in her chair and her dark eyes widened. "What are you doing here?"

"This is my uncle's house." Daphne grinned and glanced around. "Charlie's my cousin."

"Hi, Daphne," Athena held up her hand in a brief wave.

"Hi, Athena," Daphne's face lit up. "Wow, your hair looks great."

"Thanks. I tried that hair mask you told me about, and it's awesome." Athena leaned in as if she were about to spill a secret.

"I'm so happy to hear that," Daphne gushed.

"I really like the red hair on you, but of course, I'm partial to red hair." Athena chuckled.

"I better get this salad down to Mama before Jen comes out and has a hissy fit. If y'all will excuse me."

Daphne smiled wide and continued down the steps to the backyard cookout.

"We should probably go, too. I'm sure supper will be ready soon," Charlie rose from the swing, the chains creaking in protest.

Athena's stomach growled loudly. She gave them a sheepish grin. "Good idea. I'm starving."

"Come on, Billie, you can sit by me." Charlie tugged on the sleeve of the detective's pale blue t-shirt. "I can't wait to hear all about how you know my cousin, Daphne." Billie gave Jason a help-me look Charlie ignored.

"Sure. Okay," Billie said, sounding uncertain.

"So, Billie...." Charlie added some sour cream to her baked potato, then heaped on a couple of tablespoons of butter before adding salt and pepper. "Where did you meet Daphne?"

Billie shifted in her seat across from Charlie near the end of the picnic table. She sliced the New York strip into bite-sized pieces and appeared to concentrate hard on the meat, as if avoiding the question. "Um..."

"We have a mutual friend." Daphne, sitting next to Charlie, speared a piece of steak and a chunk of her baked potato onto her fork and shoved it into her mouth.

She shot Charlie a nonchalant look as she chewed her delectable combination.

"Who?" Charlie asked.

"You probably don't know her." Daphne shrugged and mashed up the potato on her plate, mixing in more butter. "She's a witch I went to beauty school with, Amanda Grimes."

"I see." Charlie gauged Billie, who still hadn't looked up from her plate. "So, you've known about the witch community?"

"Yeah, but that doesn't mean I believe. Although, it's kind of hard to ignore everything I've seen so far." Billie finally raised her head, but avoided Charlie's gaze. She pushed her salad around with her fork. "Y'all are the real deal. When I watched Amanda, it always seemed like her spells didn't really do much. Like, it was all make-believe and wanna-be mumbo jumbo."

"It can look like that sometimes. Some spells can take a long time to manifest." Charlie picked up a cherry tomato from her plate and popped it into her mouth.

"Right." Billie sipped her iced tea and still wouldn't meet Charlie's eyes. The walls around Billie's thoughts and emotions had locked tightly in place, and Charlie couldn't penetrate them. Whatever Billie didn't want to share, she'd evidently trained her mind so well that not even a stray thought could escape.

"Charlie," Athena said from her seat next to Ben.

Suddenly pale, she held her head in her hands. "Do you hear it?"

"Hear wha—" The blaring in Charlie's mind choked off her words, and she winced in pain. Instinctively she covered her ears, not that it would do much good since the sound obviously came from inside her head. Dizziness swirled through her, and for a second, she thought she might be sick. "Athena, how do we stop it?"

"Alarm be done. Hold tight our prisoner. Alarm be finished until we break the spell. So mote it be," Athena mumbled. The sound stopped, and Charlie slumped forward. She closed her eyes, hoping the nausea would pass. The spell to trap Brett Travis in his trailer worked, but Charlie wasn't sure she'd ever want to use it again. A warm hand touched her back.

"Are you okay?" Daphne asked.

"Just give me a second." Charlie swallowed hard and opened her eyes. The world stopped spinning, and she found Billie staring at her with curiosity.

"He's trapped. We've got Brett Travis. Do you want to go with us?" Charlie asked.

"Hell yeah, I do." Billie took one last bite of her steak and potatoes, then dropped her fork onto the plate. She nodded toward Jack and Evangeline sitting together. "Thank you for dinner. It really was delicious."

"Wait, a minute." Evangeline cast a confused look toward the end of the table. "What's happening?"

Charlie wiped her mouth with her napkin and rose

from her seat. "I'm sorry, Evangeline, but we need to apprehend a suspect."

"But, you're not finished with your supper," Evangeline said with genuine concern on her face.

"No, ma'am, and I'm sorry about that. But we need to strike while the iron is hot. Thank you for everything." Charlie reached for her bag.

"Of course, honey. I'll wrap up your dinners for you so you can eat them later if you'd like," Evangeline said.

"Thank you, Evangeline." Charlie grinned and blew her aunt a kiss.

"I hate to eat and run." Ben wiped his mouth and laid his napkin across his half-eaten dinner. "But I'd like in on this action."

"Me, too." Jason's fork clanked against his plate. He glanced at Lisa, his eyes full of contrition. "Sorry, honey. "

"It's your job, right?" Lisa shrugged. "Go. I'll wrap up your dinner and bring you a piece of whatever we have for dessert."

"You're the best." Jason leaned in and kissed Lisa on the cheek and got to his feet. Jason held up his keys and jingled them. "All right, who's riding with me?"

"I am," Charlie said

"Me, too," Ben said.

"I'll ride with Billie," Athena said.

"Great." Charlie rose to her feet. "We'll see you at Travis's place."

CHAPTER 32

"So, how's this going to work?" Jason put his car in park on the dirt road leading to Brett Travis's trailer.

"Athena will break the two sigils on the front of the trailer, and Charlie and I will subdue the guy," Ben explained as if Jason knew what that meant.

"I don't understand. How do you subdue this guy?" Jason asked. "He outran us last time. It's not like you guys can go in there, guns blazing. Not that I would suggest that even if you could."

"Right, sorry. We don't need guns for this." Ben shifted in the passenger seat as if to get a better look at Jason. "Charlie and I will use our wands to create streams of energy to penetrate the smallest hole in the exterior of the trailer. This thing is so old we shouldn't have a problem finding an opening. Our collaboration will capture and bind him. He won't get away from us. I promise."

"Wow. It's too bad we don't have something like that," Jason mused. "So, what can I do?"

"You and Billie should stand back." Charlie reached into her bag and retrieved her wand. When she found it, she met Jason's gaze in the rearview mirror. "I couldn't live with myself if either of you got hurt."

"I appreciate that." Jason nodded and then reached for the vest behind his seat. "Is this thing still protected?"

Charlie raised her eyes to the mirror and grinned at him again. "It will protect you as long as it's yours."

"Cool." He slipped his vest over his head and adjusted the Velcro straps on the sides so it fit him properly. "Are y'all gonna wear something?"

"Mine's around my neck?" Charlie held up a pentacle pendant with several crystals on it. "Don't worry, okay?"

"All right. Y'all are the experts here." Jason removed the keys from the ignition.

Ben took his wand from his bag and took a long, intense look at the trailer.

"Y'all ready?" Charlie asked.

"Yep." Ben nodded once and stepped out of the car. Charlie followed him.

Billie pulled her Chevy Tahoe next to Jason's Charger, and Athena hopped out, her wand at the ready. Jason got out of his car and walked around to the front of Billie's

Tahoe. A moment later, she joined him. Billie looked as antsy as he felt.

"Well, this is weird," Billie said, pursing her lips.

"Tell me about it." Jason folded his arms across his chest and leaned against the hood of Billie's SUV. The pair waited at a safe distance so the witches could work. It still amazed him every time he witnessed Charlie and Ben, and now Athena, literally working their magic.

Athena chanted a spell audible to the team but not loud enough to alert occupants of the trailer. Two symbols invisible a moment before burst into flames, becoming visible as they burned away, leaving only scorch marks on the trailer's dingy siding. Charlie and Ben raised their wands, and thin streams of blue light emitted from the tips. After a few seconds, the energy from their wands joined, shifting from blue to bright white. The door popped open and slammed against the trailer from the force of the energy. Brett Travis staggered to the doorway, his hands bound by a stream of white light.

"Goddess above. Is this really necessary?" He struggled against the pull of his bindings. "I swear I can explain everything."

Ben retrieved a pair of what looked like ordinary handcuffs from a leather holder on his hip. "I'm sure you can." Ben slapped the cuffs on Travis's wrists and released the energy binding.

Jason watched intently as a slender silvery thread

emerged from the tip of Charlie's wand. She aimed it at Travis's wrists. The wisp of glowing thread attached itself to the cuffs then wrapped around Travis's waist, keeping his arms at his side. Another silvery thread stretched from his waist, then down his legs before finally wrapping around his ankles, giving him just enough leeway to walk. Jason chuckled and shook his head at the magical equivalent of transport restraints.

Athena grabbed Brett Travis by the elbow and guided him to Billie's Tahoe before she loaded him into the back seat. Had she reinforced it with magic to hold him, or were the bindings on his wrists and ankles enough? Jason made a mental note to ask her later.

"It was way easier than I thought it was going to be." Jason directed his comment to Billie.

"Yeah, I was just going to say the same thing," Billie said. She pushed off from the front of her Tahoe and approached Charlie. "I know this is going to sound crazy, but what if it's not him?"

"What do you mean if it's not him?" Charlie asked.

"I know Daphne can do something to her face and hair to make her look different. Better, I guess. It's probably stupid to think so, but could he disguise himself as somebody else or, could he disguise somebody else to look like him?"

Charlie exchanged glances with Ben. "It's definitely possible. What makes you think that?" Ben asked.

Billie shrugged and shook her head. "I don't know. The whole thing just seemed too easy."

"The tools make it easy," Ben said. "But, we can verify his identity."

"Athena, can you confirm he's not wearing a glamour, please?"

"Sure," Athena said. "But I'm fairly sure it's him. I designed the spell to trap only him."

"Humor me," Ben said.

Athena pointed her wand at the prisoner. "Glamour be broken, reveal your true face. Glamour be broken across time and space. So mote it be." Little red sparks shot out from the end of her wand and rained down over the top of her prisoner's head.

"Ow," he complained, wincing away from the wand. "I'm not wearing a glamour. I was when I wanted to get back in my trailer, but as soon as I entered, the doors locked, so I figured you guys were coming back for me. Plus, I didn't kill her."

"We didn't mention killing anyone," Charlie said.

"Evelyn. I could never hurt her like that. I'm the one who called the cops."

"So, you found her, but you didn't stay around?" Jason scowled.

"I know what it looks like. But, I swear to the gods I didn't do it. I think whoever was after her is after me now."

Ben's eyes narrowed. "Fine. Well, then. You won't

mind giving us a statement and answering some questions for us."

"Not unless it means you'll protect me. I don't want to end up like Evelyn." Brett's dark eyes locked on Ben's face. "I'll even undergo a truth spell if it'll prove my case."

"All right." Ben closed the back door of the Tahoe on Brett and turned to Jason. "Do we have access to your interrogation rooms?"

Jason nodded with an affirmative smile. "Sure thing."

CHAPTER 33

Athena finished warding the interrogation room to secure it from prying eyes, but ensured the cameras could still record. It surprised her when Travis said he'd submit to a truth spell and made her think twice about whether he really was Evelyn's murderer. But of course, maybe that's what he wanted.

She opened the door and signaled to Jason. "We're good. Bring Brett Travis inside whenever y'all are ready."

Jason rolled in an extra chair so Ben could sit in on the interrogation, too. Charlie and Ben moved Travis into the interrogation room, sat him at the table, and released his bindings.

"I'm going to watch from the AV room," Athena said. Charlie gave her a quick nod and closed the door. Athena made her way to the small room where all the camera equipment for recording interviews lived.

Billie poked her head inside the AV room. "You want some company?"

"Sure, it'd be great to have an extra pair of eyes." Athena pointed to the chair next to her, and Billie took a seat. Two large monitors—one for each camera in the room—perched on movable arms in front of them. One camera, mounted near the ceiling, faced Brett. The second camera mounted above the door looked down at the room, showing the side view of the table. Athena noted that Ben stood in one corner, leaning against the wall, watching.

Athena retrieved a notebook and pen from her bag to take notes. Happily for her, the cameras here were as state of the art as the ones they had at the DOL, even picking up the sweat on Brett Travis's brow.

"So, Brett," Jason's voice sounded tinny but clear through the microphone on the table in front of the suspect. "Why did you run?"

Brett leaned back in his chair and crossed his arms. He wore a defiant look on his face. "I didn't know who you were. I thought you might be the guy who killed Evelyn."

"I'm fairly sure I identified myself." Jason cocked his head in disbelief.

"So what?" Brett shook his head. "You could've been wearing a glamour that made you look like a cop."

Charlie cleared her throat before she spoke. "Brett, where were you the day Evelyn died?"

Brett laced his fingers together and twiddled his thumbs. "I was at my trailer." Athena leaned in to study Brett's every move on the monitor.

Jason stared at Brett. "Can anybody corroborate that?"

"No. I'm there alone most of the time. Evelyn wasn't supposed to come over that night." Brett didn't look at Charlie or Jason.

"Her mother told us she broke up with you. She also said Evelyn told her she thought she was being followed. Were you following her, Brett?" Charlie asked.

"No. We broke up for like a week. We've been back together since April." Brett huffed and finally looked at Charlie.

"Why did you kill her?" Jason asked.

"You think I killed her?" An insulted expression molded the features of Brett's hound-dog face. "I loved her. Why would I kill her?"

"We have to ask the questions, Brett." Jason said, his voice steady. "Someone killed her. And when we came to talk to you about it, you ran. In my experience, that's pretty suspicious behavior." Jason's head rocked side to side. "Technically, you tried to kill me when you dropped that tree branch. I could charge you right now for attempted murder. Pretty serious charge, especially since I'm a deputy sheriff."

"No." Brett shook his head vehemently. "No. No. That's..." Brett's lips twisted with frustration. "That's not what happened. I wasn't trying to kill you. I thought you might be him."

"Him who?" Charlie asked.

"The guy who killed Evelyn. It wasn't me." Brett's eyes pleaded for someone to believe him. "Cast a truth spell. Then you'll see."

"How do you know who killed her?" Jason asked.

"I don't exactly, but when I hadn't heard from her since Saturday morning, I went by her Granny's old house. I'm the one who found her." He scrubbed his hand through his hair and hung his head. "It was the worst thing I've ever seen. I should've paid more attention to her schedule. She was worried that someone was following her. I told her we should cast a spell to catch him and then turn him over to the cops."

"But she didn't do that?" Charlie asked.

"No. She…" Brett paused. Athena could almost see him searching for some lie to tell. Hopefully, Charlie would pick up on it too. "She didn't have a business license, and she didn't want cops to shut her down."

"Right." The skepticism in Jason's voice put Athena at ease. Maybe it didn't take a psychic to see through Brett's BS after all.

"Yeah." Travis's lips curved into a grimace. "It was her livelihood. She wouldn't risk losing it. When I found her like that, I thought it was over the money."

"Sure. A business like that, doing readings, she probably gets paid in cash, right?" Charlie asked.

"Yeah. Exactly. And I thought maybe that's what somebody was after."

"We didn't find any cash, Brett," Charlie said.

"I know." Brett twitched and shifted in his chair.

"I don't know if he killed her, but he's sure as hell guilty of something." Billie scowled at the monitor.

Athena nodded knowingly. "Yeah. Definitely shady."

"That's because she hid it, and I'm the only other person who knew where it was."

"You took her cash. Didn't you?" Jason narrowed his eyes.

"Yeah, I did." Travis sounded put out. "She would've wanted me to take it. I know she would have."

Billie muttered, "Jesus," and sat back in her chair beside Athena. Disgust molded her lips. "This guy's a piece of work."

"Brett, was Evelyn making illegal charms and selling them?" Charlie asked.

Brett's eyes widened and he pressed his lips together. He shook his head and cleared his throat. "No. Of course not."

"Okay." Charlie nodded her head. "How well do you know Maria Torres?"

"Um." Brett glared at Charlie. "She's Evelyn's best friend. Has been since they were thirteen. They grew up together in North Charleston. Why?"

"Because she told us you gave her a bunch of charms to get rid of," Charlie shrugged. Athena couldn't stop a grin from spreading across her face. Billie leaned forward in her seat, glued to the monitor.

"I don't...I uh...." Brett swallowed hard. "I don't believe you. Why would she do that?"

"Probably because it got her killed," Charlie said.

Brett's jaw fell slack, and he slowly leaned back in his chair. "What?"

"Yeah. Tuesday night, two days after Evelyn died, and I'm guessing one day after you found her body, Maria was killed driving home, with your illegal charms in her back seat." Charlie put her elbows on the table and folded her hands together.

Brett's nose turned red, and terror filled his watery brown eyes. "Maria's dead," he whispered and shook his head.

"Yes, she is," Charlie said.

"If she's dead, how do you know about the charms?" Brett eyed her with disbelief.

"Like I said, she told me." Charlie rested her chin on her hands. "I'm a psychic medium. The dead tell me things all the time."

Brett's chest heaved. "I didn't kill Evelyn. I loved her. I loved Maria, too. And her son."

"You know who killed them, don't you?" Charlie asked.

Brett rocked back and forth and closed his eyes. Tears spilled onto his cheeks. When he spoke, it came out in a whisper. "He will kill me, too. He's ruthless and more powerful than we first thought. And if I tell you, he will hunt me down and kill me, too. And I don't want to die." Brett sniffled and swiped the tears from his face.

"Damn. He's good," Billie said.

"You don't believe him?"

"I don't know." Billie shook her head and shrugged. "He still hasn't given us a name. Or admitted to the charms dealing."

"Right." Athena bit her bottom lip and nodded. "Maybe we can help with that." She got to her feet and rounded the corner to the interrogation room. At the maple door, she took a deep breath and rapped her knuckles against the heavy wood. A moment later, she stuck her head inside.

"Hi, sorry to interrupt. Charlie, Ben. Can I talk to y'all, please?"

"Of course," Charlie's chair scraped across the floor as she stood up.

"We'll be right back." Ben's tone was more a warning than an announcement. Athena motioned for them to follow her to the AV room.

"I know I'm not a seasoned investigator like y'all, and he's definitely sleazy, and he's hiding something for sure, but I think he's telling the truth. I don't think he killed Evelyn."

"Why?" Charlie asked.

"Um, wait. Do you think he did?" Athena asked, her

cheeks burning. Maybe she was interpreting the whole thing wrong.

"No, honey, I don't actually." Charlie's lips stretched into a reassuring smile. "His thoughts are kind of chaotic, though. He's trying to hide something, and he's terrified for sure. I was curious how you came to that conclusion, that's all."

"Oh. He seemed really surprised about Maria. He said he'd submit to a truth spell." She shrugged. "It'll make him tell us what he's hiding."

"Yep." Ben scrubbed his chin and nodded. "That it will."

"I'm trained," Athena offered. "I can administer it safely."

"As long as he agrees, I'm okay with it," Ben said. "Charlie?"

"Sure. Can I sit in and watch?"

"Yes. Please." Athena gave her a grateful smile. "I just need to get a couple of things, and then we'll start."

CHAPTER 34

Butterbean yowled the minute Lisa walked through the door of her condo. She flipped on the light, juggling her bag and the two packages of leftovers Evangeline had sent home with her. As she maneuvered her way inside, she dropped her keys into the china bowl and her bag onto the table in the foyer.

"Okay, okay, I'm home," Lisa said in a reassuring voice.

The sturdy, flame point cat rushed to her, practically knocking her down as he wound himself around her legs. Lisa leaned over and scratched him behind his orange-tipped ears.

"Dude. What's going on with you?"

He yowled again, then growled, something he rarely did. The enormous cat put himself between Lisa and the rest of the condo. His fluffy blond tail swished back and forth. A shard of panic scratched through Lisa's chest, and she stood up straight and let her feelings of alarm stretch into the kitchen and beyond into the living room.

The sheer curtains in front of the sliding glass door rustled in the breeze. She'd locked the door when she'd left; she was sure of it. The hair on the back of her neck stood at attention, and she stepped sideways and reached into her purse. Her fingers found the smooth, slender wood of her wand. She drew it out, holding it in front of her.

A cloying floral scent wafted through the air, and she took a deep breath. Gardenias. Where the hell had that come from? She'd smelled it the other day, and it reminded her of her mother, which had filled her with love and nostalgia. Now, the atmosphere in her condo only filled her with dread.

"You can't stand here all night," she whispered to herself. "Move." Her feet obeyed, and she stepped forward just far enough to reach the kitchen light. When she flipped the switch, a shadow darted from beneath a barstool and across the living room floor. She let out a little scream, and her heart jumped into her throat.

The familiar gray striped tail of Jason's cat Watson disappeared behind a row of neatly alphabetized books on the media cabinet below the television. Her eyes grazed the room. Plants lay in smashed pots, including the pothos Jason brought home with him; the feet of the upended coffee table stuck into the air. The cabinet doors concealing her altar hung open, her statue of Brigid, her family photos, crystals, candles, gold pentacle, and the tarot cards Bunny had given her lay in broken pieces scattered across the living room floor. The thought of the black truck following her from the garden center popped into her head. A black shadow in her peripheral vision darted into the bedroom, and Lisa jumped.

Lisa's hand shook a little when she raised her wand, and the staccato beat of her heart sounded loud in her ears as she spoke.

"Show yourself."

She stilled her body and strained to listen to the sounds in the room. Silence filled her ears, but she couldn't shake the sense someone else was in the condo. She gritted her teeth and called up her bitchiest tone. "I know you're there."

Silence.

She continued, in the voice she usually reserved for men who thought she should be a "good girl" and do them some favor. Her tone usually made them regret saying such things.

"Show yourself, right this minute, or I will banish you to the deepest, darkest pit I can find."

A black mist formed directly in front of her, and her hands turned icy. The temperature dropped so much that she could almost see her breath. Her entire body broke into goosebumps. She held her wand up with resolve and took a step back.

"I don't know who you are or why you're here, and I don't care. You need to leave. This is my home. You have no right to be here."

Lisa whirled the tip of her wand, and it glowed green. The mist grew thicker and taller, stretching almost to the ceiling. It pulsed in time with her heartbeat. A heavy breeze blew her hair away from her face.

Butterbean hissed and arched his back, making him appear larger. As her familiar, the cat would do whatever it took to protect her, even give his own life if that's what it came down to. He growled and spit, putting himself between the mist and Lisa.

"Don't test me." Lisa scowled. "Spirit be gone, here you're not welcome. Spirit find the light—"

An empty decorative ceramic bowl lifted from the floor, hovered for a second before it sailed across the room directly at her head. Lisa's arms flew up to protect herself, and she barely had time to duck. The dish shattered against the granite counter of the breakfast bar. A whirling gust lifted the scattered debris–broken plants and planters, crystals, tarot cards––and spun it through the living room like a mini-tornado.

Lisa ran behind the counter for protection, Butterbean yowling loudly as he followed her. She peeked around the corner, helpless to stop the destruction of her living room. After a few minutes, the curtains settled back to gently fluttering in the breeze, the mist dissipated, and anything spinning in the air dropped to the ground. Lisa sat hard on her bottom and pulled her knees to her chest. Tremors waved through her, and her heart continued to pound. She closed her eyes and took deep breaths, counting in her head, one, two, three, four, until the adrenaline coursing through her calmed down. A soft, warm head bumping against her arm made her open her eyes.

Butterbean purred like a freight train and meowed at her.

"Good boy." She scratched along his cheek and behind one ear the way he liked. A soft mewling sound came from the dark recesses of the media cabinet.

"Watson? It's okay, sweetie, you can come out. The spirit's gone."

The gray tabby meowed again as if to ask, are you sure? Lisa made a kissy noise with her lips, and the small cat emerged but didn't move too far away from her hiding spot.

Lisa blew out a breath, finally feeling as if she could stand again. A moment later, she dug through her purse for her phone. She debated who to call first, Jason or her sister. Jason would be tied up for hours with his interrogation, and what could he really do? He wasn't equipped to deal with spirits. Charlie could help, but since she was working with Jason, it might be tomorrow before she called back. She opened her favorites and pressed Jen's name. After three rings, her sister answered.

She blurted out, "Hey, it's me. There was a spirit in my house when I got home, and it's pretty much wrecked my place."

"Oh my goddess, are you okay?"

"Yeah, I'm fine. It's gone for now. But, I'm scared it might come back."

"I thought your condo was warded."

"It is." She got to her feet and pick up some of the larger pieces of the porcelain bowl it had hurled at her. She opened the cabinet and threw them into the trash can beneath the sink.

"Did you call Charlie?"

"Not yet. She's in an interview, so I don't even know if she'll have her phone with her." Lisa grabbed the dustpan and broom to sweep up the small shards. She sighed and looked at the living room. "This place looks like a bomb went off."

Jen's voice shifted to mom mode. "Evangeline and Daphne have already gone home, so I'll come help you clean it up. You can stay here until we can all get together and clear the space."

"No. I can't do that. What about Jason?"

"He can come, too."

"He's not going to want to do that."

"Fine. I'll call Daphne and we'll help you clean up

and strengthen the wards. We can stay with you till Jason gets home."

"I appreciate that." Lisa swept the broom over the counter, gathering all the remnants of the bowl into a neat pile. She sighed. "I should text Jason and let him know what's happening, so he's not surprised when his keys don't work."

"Good idea. Now, ward the door. We'll be there soon."

"I will." Lisa smiled and softened her voice. "Hey, Jen. Thank you for being there."

"Anytime, sweetie."

Lisa hung up the phone and rinsed her hands before she grabbed her wand, fished out an empty trash bag, and headed to the bedroom to inspect the rest of the damage the spirit had done.

At the threshold, she flipped on the light. Her gut tightened as if someone had punched her. The bedroom looked almost as bad as the living room. Dresser drawers hung askew, and clothes had been tossed into messy piles. The small, pink jewelry box her mother had given her when she was seven years old lay on its side, with the lid broken off. Next to it, the little ballerina on a spring had tumbled upside-down.

Tears stung her eyes as she knelt to pick up the little plastic doll that used to pop up and spin to a short version of Swan Lake. She sniffled and gathered up her diamond earrings and the two gold chains—both graduation gifts from her father. A gold pendant monogrammed with LMH glimmered in the light. Another gift from her mother.

She picked up the broken satin-lined box and dropped the chains and earrings into it. After getting to her feet, she put the box on top of the dresser and slid the drawers back into place. It was almost as if the spirit had been looking for something, but what? The sheer mess of it all overwhelmed her, and she closed her eyes. She stifled a scream when the doorbell rang.

A moment later, a loud knock echoed through the condo, followed by Evangeline's anxious voice. "Lisa?"

Lisa rushed to the front door and stopped to peek through the peephole. Jen, her aunt, and cousin Daphne stood outside. She turned the deadbolt and opened the door.

"Hey, y'all got here fast." Lisa gestured for them to come inside.

Daphne shrugged and traipsed into the condo. "We're both close." Her clown red hair was gone, along with any trace of her usual glamour. She wore a pair of purple and green striped pajama shorts, a green tank, and a pair of flip-flops. Evangeline followed close behind Daphne carrying an oversize cotton canvas bag.

"Did you call Charlie?" Evangeline asked and put her oversized bag next to the table in the foyer.

"Not yet," Lisa said. "I'm sure she's busy right now."

The four of them moved into the living room. Evangeline's hand drifted to her mouth, and she walked to the built-in cabinet where Lisa kept her altar. "Oh, honey."

Lisa's shoulders sagged, and her eyes stung with tears at the sight of the ruined altar. She picked up the black velvet altar cloth. The gold pentacle in the center had been slashed. Her fist tightened around it, and she pressed it against her chest.

Jen's warm hand snaked around her waist. "I'm so sorry."

Lisa blinked back tears and sniffled. "It's just stuff, right? I can replace it."

Evangeline wrapped a warm arm around Lisa's shoulder. "Yes. Just stuff. You, on the other hand, are not replaceable."

Lisa leaned her head against her aunt's shoulder, and she kissed Lisa's forehead. Jen hurried to the foyer and returned with her phone in her hand.

"What are you doing?" Lisa asked.

"I'm calling Charlie."

"They're in the middle of an interrogation." Lisa reminded her sister.

Jen shook her head. "I don't care. She'll want to know about this." Jen put the phone to her ear. "Hey, Charlie, it's Jen. I'm at Lisa's. We've got an issue here. Lisa encountered a very destructive spirit when she got home."

Evangeline sighed and squeezed Lisa's shoulders. "We should get started on this mess. It'll make you feel a lot better once things are back in order."

"Okay, I left a message for her." Jen shoved her phone into her back pocket.

"Thanks for calling her." Lisa gave her sister a grateful smile.

"Anytime, honey," Jen said. "And don't you worry, we'll get this all cleaned up and make this place spirit proof with or without Charlie."

CHAPTER 35

The smell of burned sage and herbs hung on the air in the interrogation room. Athena blew on the ashes in a small wooden bowl until they no longer smoked. The ability to start a fire or put it out with a breath was a skill Charlie had never learned, but one she always admired whenever she saw another witch use it. Brett sat across from her at the interrogation table and stared at his hands while Athena prepared the spell.

Charlie focused on Brett's face while Athena cast the truth spell on him.

"Tell the truth, make it plain. Lie to us and feel only pain. So mote it be." Athena pressed her thumb into the bowl of ashes and made three dots with the soot on his forehead. She took a deep breath and cast a glance toward Charlie. "Okay. He's ready."

Brett fidgeted in his seat, and his eyes flitted between Charlie and Athena.

"All right, Brett, I'm going to ask you a few baseline questions. You can give me details, but that tends to get people in more trouble," Charlie explained.

"What kind of trouble?" Brett eyed her, his anxiety clear from the shift of his body.

"The spell may think you're lying if you misremember something," Athena clarified. "So, the fewer details you give us, the less likely you are to remember something wrong."

"It's better to just say yes or no. To avoid any unnecessary pain," Charlie said. She still grappled with the ethics of the truth spell and whether it was moral to force someone to tell the truth, especially under the threat of physical punishment. Maybe Ben and Athena had just been at this longer and had grown more comfortable with the idea, but the empath in her wondered if it was the right thing to do, even though he volunteered, even if it led to evidence that he was not Evelyn's murderer.

"You can still change your mind, you know. I'm very good at reading people's thoughts."

"No," Brett said a little too fast. "The only person I want inside my head is me."

"All right. Stick to yes and no answers if you can. Understand?"

Beads of sweat gathered on his forehead, and he held his breath a little after answering, "Yes."

Charlie gave him a reassuring smile. "Good job. Now. Is your name Brett Travis?"

"Yes." He swiped at his forehead.

"Do you live in a travel trailer?"

"Yes."

"Did you take cash from Evelyn Turberville's house the day you discovered her body?"

"Yes."

"Did you take anything else?" Charlie watched him carefully. She'd known the other answers, which was why she'd asked them.

Brett furrowed his brow. "No."

Charlie waited a beat, half expecting him to grab his head in pain. "Did you kill Evelyn Turberville?"

His expression morphed to one of disgust. "No."

"Very good." Charlie smiled reassuringly. "You're doing a great job. Do you know who killed Evelyn Turberville?"

Brett licked his lips. His eyes darted between Charlie and Athena again. "No." He screamed and grabbed his forehead, doubling over onto the table between them. His body tensed, and he blurted, "I don't know him exactly. I have an idea, but it's not certain."

Once he told the truth, the tautness in his upper body released as if a rubber band had been cut. He gulped in several deep breaths and sat up again. His face, now red, appeared strained and exhausted.

"So," Charlie drew out the word and eyed him with confusion, "you know who he is, but not his name?"

Brett sighed, and his expression told her that he knew they had him over a barrel. He shook his head. "Sort of. I know he's from Myrtle Beach."

Athena sat up straighter in her chair. Charlie kept calm and ignored her partner's excited energy. "Go on," Charlie prompted.

"I've never met him. Baldwin or Blanton. Something like that. Evelyn only knew about him because one of his goons tried to intimidate her and, like any good witch, she retaliated."

"How?" Charlie asked.

"I don't want to answer if the spell is going to shock me again. That hurt." He rubbed his forehead with his thumb.

"Fine. We'll come back to that. Let me finish my questions, and then you can tell us about the goons," Charlie said. "Was Evelyn selling memory charms?"

"Yes."

"Was she also selling memory curses?"

"Yes. But only to a few guys. It wasn't like..." He screamed again, and his hand flew to his head.

"Stop explaining or tell us the whole truth," Charlie said.

"Okay, okay. It was more than just a few guys. She had a distributor in Savannah she worked with. He liked her stuff because it was so potent."

"Were her charms more potent because of a magical plant?" Athena asked.

"Yeah, they were."

"Did Maria Torres give her the magical plant?" Charlie asked.

"Yes. A couple of years ago, when Maria went to work at the garden center, she took some cuttings home and rooted them. Evie noticed immediately the plants had magical properties."

"How did her competitor get the plant?"

"I don't know."

Charlie watched him carefully, but the pain didn't come this time.

Brett shrugged. "Maybe he bought one of her charms and figured it out."

"Maybe he did," Charlie said. "Thank you, Brett."

"Is that it?"

"Yes, it is."

"Can y'all protect me? I know he's going to come for me next."

"How do you know that?" Charlie asked.

"I've seen his truck a couple of times," he said. "He's got his goons following me, too. Just like he did Evie."

"We can apply protection sigils to your trailer and vehicle. I can also give you something to carry," Athena said. "It will act almost like a glamour. It won't make you completely invisible, but it will go a long way to him not finding you or even seeing you."

Brett let out a relieved breath. "That would be great. Am I in trouble about the money?"

"I don't think so," Charlie said. "We didn't find any money when we searched your trailer, so there's no real evidence you took it. We wouldn't even have your confession if you decided to recant."

Brett's eyes widened. "Right. I recant. I didn't take anything." He let out a scream and grabbed his forehead again doubling over. He banged his palm flat against the table. "I took it, I took it, I took it," he whispered. The spell released him again.

"Athena..." Charlie said.

"Right. Sorry. The truth's been told, release this hold. So mote it be."

Brett remained slumped over the table for a moment more, taking deep breaths.

"Are you all right?" Charlie asked.

He straightened up. "Yeah. I'm fine."

"Can you tell us about the guy who visited Evelyn? The goon?"

"Just that he's big. Like a body-builder kind of guy, and he told her that his boss was willing to share clients for a cut of her take. Evie laughed and put him off by giving him a free memory charm "to sample the goods." Only the longer you're exposed to it, the worse the memories become. More like a curse, I guess."

"Thank you for sharing that." Charlie gave him a mechanical smile. Now she knew how Crow had gotten hold of one of Evelyn's charms.

The interrogation room seemed warm. Charlie

rubbed her sweaty palms on her pants and pushed back from the table. "Athena's going to drive you home and install the protection sigils. We'll need you to wear a tracker spell as long as you're under our protection. Are you okay with that?"

"Why?" Brett said. "I've already told you I didn't kill her."

"It's really more for your protection," Athena said. "In case..."

Charlie noticed the long pause and added, "In case they somehow bypass our protections, and we have to find you."

"You mean find my body." Brett fixed his gaze on her.

"Not necessarily." Charlie's voice went up and she was thankful that she was not under a truth spell. "Do you have some objection?"

"No." Brett gave her a defeated shrug. "Track away, I guess."

"Thank you for cooperating." Charlie gave him a sympathetic look.

"Sure. I just hope you get the bastard."

"We're a whole lot closer now thanks to you," Charlie said. Brett gave her a look that said he wasn't so sure.

"Come on, I'll take you home," Athena said and rose to her feet.

The sound of Jason talking to the cats in the kitchen woke Lisa from her restless sleep. The black, shadowy mist filtered into her dreams, and she sat up several times during the night to check the bedroom, even after her sister, aunt, and cousin had performed a thorough cleansing.

The smell of bacon frying wafted through the condo tempting her to get out of bed despite the comfort of the soft duvet. She rose and dressed in a pair of dark blue cargo shorts and a green polo with the garden center's logo on it. She unplugged her phone and dropped it into the side pocket before stopping by the bathroom to brush her teeth. Her fingers made quick work of braiding her hair and pinning it away from her face. Her stomach grumbled, and she headed to the kitchen.

"Good morning, sunshine." Jason removed the cooked bacon from the pan and placed it on a plate covered with a paper towel that quickly darkened when the greasy, fragrant bacon hit it. Watson and Butterbean perched in the barstools at the counter and waited patiently for Jason to pinch off a piece of meat and place it in front of each of them.

"You're going to spoil them," Lisa warned and wrapped her arms around Jason's waist. She stood on her tiptoes and kissed the back of his neck.

"They're good cats. They deserve a little spoiling for taking care of you last night." Jason broke off the end of a crisp piece of bacon and split it in two. "Don't you?" He put the meat down, and Butterbean gobbled up his piece. Watson sniffed hers and touched her tongue to it before finally chewing it. "There's coffee if you want it," he said over his shoulder, using the spatula in his hand to point to the drip coffeemaker on the counter full of strong, dark, liquid energy.

Lisa glanced at the clean coffee mugs and stack of spoons on the counter. "Aren't you fancy this morning? I think I'll pass for now. You know, because of the acidity."

"Stomach still bothering you?"

"Just a little," she said. She pulled two plates from the cabinet and two forks from the drawer and put them on the breakfast bar. She turned her attention to the cats watching their every move. "Y'all are going to have to get out of here now."

Butterbean meowed in protest but jumped down from his stool, and Watson followed him without a sound.

"That looks good." Lisa peered around Jason at the stove.

Jason scooped some pancake batter into a pan. "Let's hope it tastes good."

"I'm sure it will be delicious." She retrieved the maple syrup and butter from the refrigerator and placed them on the counter with the plates. "I'm going to make some herbal tea. Want some?"

"Nah, I'm good." He flipped the pancake like an expert, and the image of him cooking Saturday morning breakfasts for their son flooded her mind. For the first time since she thought she might be pregnant, a thrill went through her. Maybe they could do this together. Would it be easy? No, but they'd have each other for support. And the image of a little boy with Jason's face and her green eyes warmed her heart.

"What are you staring at?" Jason chuckled.

She shook her head. "Nothing. You're just very handsome this morning. That's all."

"Thank you." He turned and winked at her. "You're pretty nice to look at too."

Lisa rolled her eyes and filled the electric kettle. It was time to know the truth and to tell him, no matter the outcome. She took a seat at the breakfast bar and removed her phone from her pocket. It didn't take long to open the app for her health care provider. Her stomach tightened once she logged in and saw a green flag marking new test results. She pressed the link, and the page opened. At the top, it simply read pregnancy test, and next to it, positive. A canned response to please contact her doctor for a follow-up appointment was printed below. Tears stung her eyes, and she let out a nervous laugh.

Jason grabbed the plate in front of her and slid two pancakes onto it. "Everything okay?"

Lisa sniffled and grinned. "Yeah, everything's fine."

Jason moved his attention back to the pan and added more batter. "Go ahead and eat up, before it gets cold."

THE GREEN WITCH

"That's okay. I can wait for you." Lisa cleared her throat and reached for the wooden box she kept on the counter for her favorite teas. She thumbed through the individually packaged bags until she settled on an orange mint. She unwrapped it and plopped it into the empty mug with a faded yellow shooting star on it. Her stomach flip-flopped. She needed to tell him. She'd been so wrapped up in the idea of not being pregnant it had given her no time to practice how she'd break the news. Like all things in her life, she wanted the moment to be perfect.

"Can you hand me the honey, honey." She grinned at her corny joke.

"Sure thing." He opened the cabinet above the stove and retrieved a small bottle of raw honey, then placed it on the counter in front of her.

"So, I've been thinking..." She squeezed out two long dollops of the thick honey and stirred it with a spoon. Jason's phone rang so loudly it startled her.

He grabbed it from the counter and answered it with one hand. "This is Tate."

Lisa bit her bottom lip, and listened to him talking to someone.

"Hey. What's going on?" He nodded his head. "Sure. When? We're just sitting down to breakfast. " He checked the divers watch on his wrist. She'd bought it for his birthday, and he'd gushed over it and scolded her over the cost all in one breath when she'd given it to him.

"Yeah, I can be there in an hour. Okay. I'll see you

then." He ended the call and put his phone on the counter again.

"Who was that?" Lisa brought her cup to her lips, and the tantalizing flavors of orange and mint washed across her tongue.

"That was my cousin Kenny. He asked me if I could help him move some stuff out of his boathouse. You're okay with that, right?"

"It's not a body, is it?" Lisa teased.

"No, sassy, it isn't." Jason slid two pancakes onto his plate.

Lisa shrugged and gave him a sly grin. "You never know with his clientele."

"What's wrong with his clientele? It's just people getting divorced." Jason took a seat next to her and snatched three pieces of bacon onto his plate.

"Exactly. There are so many emotions when people are dividing up their stuff. And that doesn't even count all the issues involving custody." She frowned and took another sip of her tea. "So, what are you helping him move?"

"He's got an old outboard motor he wants to sell, and he can't lift it by himself."

"Okay. Just be careful. Don't hurt yourself." She took a deep breath and blew it out. "Maybe later today, or tomorrow we can spend some time together. Talk about the wedding and other things."

"Sure, honey, whatever you want." He gave her a tight-lipped smile.

Lisa grabbed two pieces of bacon and smeared butter across the top of her pancakes. "This looks great, babe." Her mind raced. Maybe she should just blurt it out so they could talk about it. Although, she was supposed to be at the garden center at 8:00.

"Thanks. Let's dig in. Day's a-wasting." Jason said and drenched his pancakes in syrup.

CHAPTER 36

"Are you sure you want to do this?" Tom Sharon poured Charlie another cup of coffee and then topped off his cup. He put the pot back on the coffee maker before he sat down across from her at the small bistro table in her kitchen.

"I'm sure," Charlie said as she scooped up the last bite of her ham and cheese omelet, made to perfection by Tom. "This is so good. You could be a chef, you know that?"

Tom chuckled. "I'm flattered. But that's not my fate. It's Jen's."

"I can't wait for The Kitchen Witch to open back up. I miss her banana pecan pancakes." Charlie buttered the last bite of her toast and popped it into her mouth. "So, tell me why you're so worried about me doing some astral projection. You've never been concerned before." She lifted her cup to her lips and took a sip of the hot black liquid

"I'm not against astral projection, Charlie. I just wish I could be there. But, we've been so busy at the funeral home lately, it's hard for me to get away right now."

"I will be perfectly fine. Athena will be there."

"Just take care, all right? The astral plane is where most reapers live if they don't choose a human form like I do. An encounter could leave you detached from your body."

She deflected his serious tone by joking with him. "I'll just tell any reaper I meet not to mess with me because my boyfriend is a reaper, and he will beat their butt," she joked but wasn't sure he got it.

"It's not funny." He took a bite of his eggs.

"Sorry, you're right. I shouldn't make fun. I promise I'll be careful to avoid any reapers."

"So, what's your plan?" Tom asked.

"I've got some household stuff to do first; laundry, and a couple of errands I've been putting off. Then, I'm going to Susan Tate's B&B this evening. She's got a couple of vacancies and agreed to let me practice contacting her spirit butler via astral projection. If I'm successful, then I'll try to communicate with Nicole and Evelyn to see if I can get them to talk to me that way. They must have more information."

"All right." He finished the last of his eggs. He stared into space for a moment, his amber eyes distant. His eyelids fluttered, and he brought a contrite gaze back to her face. "I hate to eat and run, but duty calls."

"You go ahead. I'll clean up the dishes." She lifted her cup to her lips and took a long sip.

Tom rose from his chair, leaned over, and kissed her. He stepped to the middle of the room as the glamour he wore melted away, revealing his true reaper form. His black robes rustled, and he waved his bony hand at her before he disappeared.

Charlie shivered and got to her feet. She took another piece of bread from the loaf on the counter and popped it into the toaster. She would need her strength to deal with the day.

"It's so good to see you, Charlie," Susan Tate gushed. "And it was so sweet of you, Athena, to bring me dessert. Pecan chocolate chip cookies are my favorite."

The three women sat at the kitchen table, and Charlie glanced around. "It is amazing how much work you've done to this place. It doesn't even look like the same house anymore."

"I know. I kind of wanted it that way. We maintained historical accuracy in our restoration of the living room and front parlor. I wanted the kitchen to be as modern as possible, though, especially since I make breakfast here every morning."

"I love your stove," Charlie said, admiring the eight-burner restaurant-style stove. "That thing could turn somebody like me into a chef." Charlie chuckled. "Or at least somebody who likes to cook."

"The bedrooms are lovely, too," Athena said with a wistful look in her eyes. "At least mine was. I wish I could've stayed here for more than one night."

"I restored them back to the Edwardian style that my great-grandfather had picked when he redecorated. That was as far back as I wanted to go upstairs," Susan said.

"That's understandable," Charlie said, "considering the history of the house."

"Yes." Susan nodded and appeared to get lost in thought about the dark history of her family's home.

"Jason said you still have one spirit hanging around," Charlie said.

"We do. But, Henry's no trouble. In fact, I kind of like having him around because now I can say the place is haunted and charge a little more. It's crazy how many people come here hoping to have some sort of experience," Susan said.

"I can understand that," Charlie said. "There's something thrilling about connecting with the supernatural, especially in a relatively safe way."

Susan laughed. "We've had our share of skeptics too. But, they tend to leave in the middle of the night."

"I imagine so," Charlie said. "You haven't had any

more of the female spirits or your ancestor reappear, have you?"

"Not hide nor hair." Susan shook her head and gave Charlie a rueful glance. "Thankfully."

"Good. I'm glad to hear that," Charlie said. "I'd like to contact your butler ghost, if that's okay with you."

"You won't chase him off, will you?" Susan cocked an eyebrow, mock warning her.

"No. Not unless you want me to." Charlie shrugged. "By the sound of it, though, he likes it here. There's probably something of his in the house that's keeping him here. He'll move on when he's ready."

"So, what kind of experiment are you planning to do with Henry?" Susan lifted a glass of iced tea to her lips. She broke off a piece of the pecan and chocolate chip cookie and popped it into her mouth.

"Astral projection," Charlie said.

"Oh my word. You can do that?"

"I have projected my consciousness out to contact people before, or at least to their consciousness," Charlie clarified. "But, that's been with the living, not the dead."

"Oh my, that sounds so dangerous and exciting."

"Honestly, I just want to see if I can interact with him on the astral plane."

Susan took another bite of her cookie. "Fascinating."

"Jason's not a big believer," Charlie dropped her eyes.

"There's nothing new about that, is there?" Susan

patted her hand. "My son is certainly hardheaded sometimes with opening his mind."

"He is," Charlie teased. "But, we love him anyway."

Susan smiled. "Yes, we certainly do."

"So, do I have your blessing?"

"Of course," Susan picked up her iced tea. "I can't wait to hear the results. Can anyone do this astral projection?"

"Yes." Athena answered her. "Absolutely. It's a skill just like anything else. If you can meditate, you can learn astral projection. At least, that's my opinion."

"I'm reading a book on it now, and when I'm done with it, I'll be happy to lend it to you," Charlie said, thinking she should have brought it with her. "It will give me an excuse to come and visit with you again."

"Don't be silly. You're welcome here whether or not you bring a book."

"Maybe I'll even bring your ornery son with me."

"Now, that would be an absolute miracle. It seems these days he doesn't have time to come and see his old mother."

Charlie winked at her. "Let me see what I can do about that."

IT DIDN'T TAKE LONG FOR CHARLIE TO ENTER A DEEP, meditative state. She had been practicing meditation in one form or another for many years. What was more difficult was the idea that she could leave her body. She imagined a circle of light surrounding her and visualized a pair of hands glowing, sweeping away any negativity outside the circle, leaving her in a clean, positive space.

The book had told her to come up with a mantra to repeat to herself. *I float, I rise without fear,* drifted through her consciousness. She repeated the phrase to herself until a buzzing sound filled her ears. It grew louder and louder until she could barely stand it. Somewhere inside her mind, she saw her hands raise and cover her ears. Her body floated upward, and she found herself with her nose to the fancy tray ceiling. Without thinking, she flipped over. The sight of her body below her and a long, silver tether of energy attached to it caused a sudden pulling sensation. The next thing she knew, she bounced on the bed. Her eyes flew open.

"Dammit." She scrubbed her fingers along the crown of her head.

"What happened?" Athena sat down on the bed next to Charlie. "Did it work?"

"Yeah. Sort of. I made it to the ceiling, but I turned over and saw myself lying here."

"Did you see anything else?" Athena drew her legs onto the bed and into a half-lotus position.

"I saw a silver tether stretching from my body to me." Charlie stared at the ceiling. Could she have just passed through it if she wanted to?

"Do you want to try again? Or are you too mentally pooped? It has been a really long day."

"Let's try again." She closed her eyes and focused. *I float, I fly, I rise without fear,* she said to herself. After a while, her spirit lifted upward, passing through the ceiling, through the roof, until she found herself outside Susan's house. When she looked down at spirit body, she could make out her arms and legs, but they had no physicality, just a glowing shape she recognized as her limbs. A silvery thread coiled loosely around her and led down through the roof, binding her spirit to her physical body on the bed. Elation filled her, and yet it didn't overwhelm her. Instead, it paired with a sense of calm.

The book told her she could travel by using her thoughts. What exactly should she think? Where did she want to go first? *Living room.* In a blink of her third eye, Charlie stood in the center of Susan Tate's living room. It was a mix of contemporary furniture and antiques. A beautiful crystal chandelier sparkled with warm light, and Susan sat in a chaise lounge next to one window, reading a book.

Charlie watched Susan only for a moment. A sense of guilt filled her at the idea of creeping around without Susan realizing it. She noted Susan's book title so she could check once she rejoined her body. Some part of her wasn't sure if this was real or if she was imagining it. But knowing the title was an easy enough test of this new ability.

A thought popped into her head. What would the house look like from 300 feet in the air? A second later, she hovered above Talmadge House. The sprawling old mansion, bathed in the full moon's light, glowed like a beacon. *I'm floating, I'm flying, I'm rising.* Could she leave and come back? The image of Tom filled her mind, and a buzzing reverberated through her entire body. A moment later, she floated through a hospital corridor. A machine beeped loudly from a nearby room, and a couple of nurses and a doctor rushed past. Charlie floated closer to get a better look. Tom materialized, his reaper form unseen by the nurses and doctors working hard to resuscitate a young woman. The spirit of the woman suddenly appeared beside her body, looking down.

Tom reached out his hand. "Don't be afraid." His silky voice slid through Charlie's mind and echoed through the room.

"I'm not scared." The young woman looked up at him without a trace of fear on her face. "I'm glad it's done. Am I going to hell? Is that why you're here?"

"No, child. I'm here to guide you, that's all." The warmth of his voice soothed Charlie, and her admiration for him grew. This was how she wanted to be when she became a reaper. Gentle. Loving. Warm. The spirit slipped her hand into Tom's.

"And for the record," he told her, "there is no hell."

A sense of relief flowed from the young woman and

the slight shadow hanging over her spirit lifted, revealing her brightly glowing soul.

Tom looked up, his golden-brown eyes locking with Charlie's for just a second. "Charlie?"

Charlie grinned and waved, then quickly she thought of Talmadge House. A split second later, she stood in the grand foyer.

"Who are you?" A sharp, nasally, southern voice said from behind her. She turned to find a short, portly spirit floating in the doorway to the parlor. His dark waistcoat, gray trousers, and gray vest, and the stiffly starched collar with a black tie reminded Charlie of old photos from the turn of the 20th century.

"Are you Henry?" she said.

"You're a reaper," he hissed. He grimaced, and his jowls jiggled a bit before he disappeared.

"What? No, I'm not." She pictured him, and suddenly she appeared in front of him.

"How did you do that?" He snapped and held up his hands in front of his face as if to shield himself from her. "I'm not ready to go." He backed into a corner and disappeared through the wall.

Charlie rolled her eyes. "Dammit, Henry, I'm just here to say hello, to see if this works."

Half of his body emerged from the wall. He stared at her, his gaze wary. "You promise?"

"Yes, I do. Why do you think I'm a reaper?"

"You look like one of them."

"I do?" She held up her hands and could see nothing reaper-like about them. They appeared to be like her physical hands, only translucent.

"There is a minor difference." He cocked his head and held his chin between his thumb and forefinger. "Your robes. They're white instead of black, and I can see your pretty face. But you reek of reaper."

"Can you show me?"

"Of course, Madame. Come with me. There's a mirror in Mistress's room. She's exceedingly kind, so she won't mind if we use it." His body drifted out of the wall, passing her. Charlie followed him across the hall. She paused for a moment before she heard Athena call her name and ask her a question.

"Hold on just one second for me, please." Charlie held up a finger.

Charlie pictured Athena. In a flash, she appeared in front of her co-conspirator, sitting on the end of a bed with the digital recorder in one hand. She averted her gaze from her own body to avoid the earlier mishap and focused on Athena's face.

"Charlie, if you can hear me, please say something to this little light." Athena tapped a red light on the digital recorder. "Say something as loud as you can."

Charlie leaned in. "I don't know if the recorder will pick this up, but I'm here. I've contacted Henry. He's a little afraid of me, but he's going to help me. I can't wait to tell you all about it."

"So intriguing," Henry said. Charlie found him floating next to her, staring at the recorder. "Perhaps you can tell me about the little things people hold in their hands. They're very curious. And people seem to be mesmerized by them. They hardly look away."

Charlie laughed. "Very true. Do you know what a telephone is?"

"Of course I do." Henry sniffed and jutted his chin.

"It's a telephone." She left her explanation at that because how did she explain, it was really a minicomputer and portal to the world now?

His eyes widened. "Extraordinary."

"Yes. It is. Now, where is this mirror?"

"Right this way," he said and disappeared.

Charlie envisioned him and transported herself to a large bedroom. A carved four-poster bed with deep purple and gold bedding took up one side of the room.

The hardwood floors gleamed, and a large alpaca rug covered part of the floor. Henry moved in front of a large dresser facing the bed. Above it hung a mirror. Charlie drifted in front of it and faced her reflection. The clothes she'd worn were gone, replaced by luminous white robes. Her hair appeared longer and blonder, and it curled about her shoulders, rustling as if a breeze blew through the room. Her face was her own, only translucent, as if she were a spirit. Her blue eyes glittered. Everything about her appearance felt right to her, and all doubts about becoming a reaper in the future washed away.

"This is so strange," she said, leaning in to get a better look.

"Mmm. Yes," Henry agreed. "Now, you see why I thought you were a reaper. Apart from the color of your robe, you look just like one of them."

Charlie nodded. "Eventually, I'll become a reaper when I die."

"I didn't realize it was a choice one could make."

"I didn't choose it. Death chose me because I accidentally picked up a reaper's scythe," she said.

"How remarkable," Henry said.

"That's certainly one way to look at it." She gazed at herself a little longer. Was this what Tom saw? It excited her to ask him. "Do you think I'm scary looking?"

"Startling, certainly. And I immediately sensed you might try to make me crossover," he said.

Charlie turned away from the mirror and faced the spirit. "You know, I'm a psychic medium when I'm in my body, and I cleaned this house over three years ago. You shouldn't be here."

"Yes, I remember you. All those women." He shook his head and made a tsking sound.

"Why didn't you go with them? It's so much nicer on the other side."

"I wasn't ready. This is where I was born, where I was raised, where I worked, and where I died. Is that not enough?" He looked wistfully around the room. "I love this old house. And I decided the day I died, I would stay here as long as any Talmadge would have me. Since Mistress has no objections, here is where I remain."

"I won't force you to move on if you don't want to," she said.

"Thank you." He bowed his head. "Your friend is a bit panicked."

"How do you know that?"

"I can hear her calling for you. Can you not?"

Charlie strained to listen. Athena's voice seemed like a distant echo. "A little."

"This house is in my care, and I know everything that happens here," he said.

"Indeed. I should go to her." Charlie smiled. "Thank you for everything. Meeting you was very enlightening."

"Glad to be of assistance. Take care, ma'am." He floated through the mirror on the wall and disappeared.

Charlie imagined her body. Within seconds, her eyes fluttered open. She stared at the fancy moldings of the tray ceiling. A smile stretched across her lips, and she laughed.

"Charlie? Are you okay?" Athena hopped to her feet. "You scared me there for a minute. You wouldn't wake up."

"I'm sorry I scared you." Charlie's eyes widened, and she bolted upright. "Quick, play back the recording."

"What?" Athena said.

"You were asking me questions. Let's see if the recorder heard my voice."

"Sure thing." Athena hit rewind and then play. They heard Athena saying "as loud as you can." A second later, a very faint but distinguishable voice answered her.

"Oh my goddess, it totally worked." Athena breathed.

"Indeed it did," Charlie said. "You will not believe what I saw."

CHAPTER 37

Charlie drifted up the steps to Nicole Brewer's duplex. When she passed through the door and entered the apartment, she knew immediately it was a dream. An awfully familiar dream. She scanned the room, noticing how neat and clean everything was despite being secondhand. All the plants near the front window thrived in the bright indirect light. A blue velvet couch beckoned in a cozy way. Nicole rushed down, her feet heavy on the steps. Charlie recognized the outfit she wore from the first dream she'd had of her; ripped black jeans and a black tank top. Although now she wore a gauzy, floral, kimono-style blouse, too. Her bare feet showed off her purple-painted toes. Nicole breezed through the living room, heading to the back of the house and into the kitchen. Charlie followed her, trying to pay attention to every detail. When a spirit communicated this way, she knew everything meant something.

Nicole's phone chirped on the kitchen counter. She ignored it. The electric kettle came to a boil and automatically shut off. Nicole opened a small cabinet next to the sink and retrieved a box of herbal tea, a shiny black mug with a flower skull on the front, a bottle of Stevia drops, and a small jar, like the one they'd found in Maria's car.

She unwrapped a teabag and dropped it into her mug, then poured boiling water over it. While the tea steeped, she leaned against the counter facing away from the cabinets and gently unscrewed the jar's top. She brought it to her nose and inhaled several times. Her eyelids fluttered, her eyes rolled back in her head, and she sank to the floor.

Charlie knelt beside her. "Oh, Nicole. He got you hooked on those memory charms, didn't he?"

Nicole took another deep breath of the jar's contents. She rested her head against the cabinet. After a few minutes of drifting in and out of consciousness, a loud banging startled them both. Nicole blinked slowly as if struggling to pull herself out of a haze. Somehow, she had the presence of mind to close the jar. She battled her way to her feet, almost falling over twice. Once she was up, she shoved the small jar behind the mugs in the cabinet before trying to shake off her stupor.

"I'm coming," she called to the house.

Charlie followed Nicole to the front of the apartment.

Nicole peered through the peephole then pressed her forehead to the door. She sighed, and her shoulders slumped a little as if she didn't want to see whoever was there. Finally, she unlocked the deadbolt and opened the door.

"What do you want, Crow?" Nicole asked.

Crow Bowman pushed his way past her into the apartment. "You know exactly what I want. I want my money. Or you can give me back the product, and I'll find somebody else to sell it."

Nicole bit her bottom lip, bowed her head, and stared at her feet. "I don't have either of those things."

"You used it all, didn't you?" His hand snapped to her neck. He seized her throat and yanked her toward him. "You bitch. Do you know how much money all that product was worth?"

"I'm sorry, I just—"

"Shut up. I don't give a shit about your excuses. You're such a fucking junkie." He squeezed his fingers tighter around her throat. Nicole clawed at his hand.

"Crow, stop," she choked out. "Can't breathe."

He gripped her a little tighter for a second, released her, and pushed her down. She fell hard against the stairs.

"I should fucking kill you." Crow slipped a large hunting knife from a sheath attached to his belt. He wrapped his hands around the hilt. The glint of the metal reminded Charlie of the first time she dreamed of Nicole.

Nicole sniffled back tears and crawled across the floor. "You don't want to do that. You know that, somewhere in that icy heart of yours, you love me."

"I certainly love that thing you do." He softened and patted her on the head. She gazed up at him with watery eyes.

Nausea rippled through Charlie's gut, watching the scene play out. Nicole unbuckled Crow's belt and unzipped his baggy jeans. Crow held the knife to her throat as she reached into his pants and took hold of him. Death or sex. It was an impossible situation. Charlie closed her eyes, unwilling to bear witness to this power play. She turned away and drifted to the kitchen.

"Wait! Don't go." Nicole's voice resounded through Charlie's head. Her spirit appeared, blocking her way.

Charlie glared at Nicole. "I don't want to see this. You deserve so much better."

"No, I don't." Nicole shook her head.

"Yes, you do. You may have had a problem, but that doesn't mean you deserve to be treated like this."

A strange little smile crept across Nicole's lips. "I wish I'd met you when I was alive."

"I wish you had, too," Charlie said. "Why did you bring me here?"

"To show you something."

"What? That Crow's your killer? I know that now. It doesn't mean anything if I can't prove it. I need evidence. Real, concrete evidence."

"Please, come with me." Nicole held out her hand.

"Where are we going?" Charlie asked.

"You'll see." Nicole drifted through the kitchen and out the back door leading to a tiny, fenced-in yard. Charlie sighed and followed the spirit.

A thick gray fog wrapped around them, making everything hazy. When it finally cleared, Charlie realized they were in the middle of a small warehouse. "What is this place?" Charlie turned in a full circle.

"Shh..." Nicole put her finger to her lips, and she waved Charlie over to a staircase. She pointed to a door at the top. Light shined from the square window. Charlie blinked, and the fog returned. They were inside the office now. Shelves lined three sides of the room from floor to ceiling. A dozen potted plants with heart-shaped leaves, silver satin pothoses, filled three shelves, with a bottle of organic fertilizer and a gallon-sized watering can perched on another. Grow lights suspended above each shelf gave the plants all the light they needed. Another shelving unit held clear shoe boxes formed in neat stacks, each labeled with masking tape and hand-printed letters; Azurite, Diaspore, Blue Apatite, Bloodstone, and Hematite. All crystals used for memory, focus, or dreams.

Crow and two assistants sat around a table.

"I know this plant." Charlie moved at the speed of thought. "This is in the memory charm. Have you ever heard of Evelyn Turberville?"

Nicole appeared behind Crow who was working with

a black marble mortar and pestle on the table in front of him. She pointed at it.

Charlie moved in to get a better look. Several small bowls filled with crystals glistened in the overhead light. Crow took a few pothos leaves, put them into the mortar and began to grind them up. He gathered a generous amount of herbs Charlie didn't recognize, and sprinkled them into the pothos paste.

"This should be some good shit right here. Small batch will always be the way to get top dollar." Crow's chest puffed up. "Imagine remembering things you didn't even do."

"You're a genius, boss," the thick-necked guy sitting next to him said. "You'll go down in the history books for this."

"Dumbass, I don't want to be in anybody's history books. I just want to sell my shit and make my money. And I don't want anybody else getting in my way."

"Sure thing, boss. What do you want me to do?"

"You need to make sure Travis takes the fall for Madame Turberville's death. You got that? I've already got my people moving into her old territory," Crow said.

"Travis?" Charlie said. "Does he mean Brett Travis?"

"Yes," Nicole's voice whispered across Charlie's senses. She pointed back to the conversation happening between the men.

"Sure, boss. How do we do that?"

"We need to make him confess, and one whiff of this will make that happen. That's where you come in."

Charlie drifted around the office. On one of the shelves, she spotted a black cell phone case with a flower skull printed on it and a hunting knife in a sheath like the one Crow had held to Nicole's throat.

"That's my phone. Is it enough?" Nicole asked.

"Maybe," Charlie said. Nicole's face crumpled, and she put her hands into her wild, dark hair, rocking her head from side to side as if she was experiencing a terrible headache. A loud cry gushed from Nicole, washing through Charlie. All Nicole's pain, frustration, and fears stung Charlie's senses, wrapping around her like a jellyfish, leaving welts all over her body.

"Please stop, Nicole. I'll make it work. I'll find a way to get a warrant and arrest him so you don't have to worry about it anymore, okay? Please, you're hurting me."

Nicole drew her hands out of her hair and dropped them. Ghostly tears glimmered on her translucent cheeks. "I'm sorry. I didn't mean to."

"I know." Charlie took a deep breath and blew it out. "I'll make him pay, I promise."

"Thank you," Nicole whispered. A sense of peace flowed from Nicole now, and a wonderous expression crossed her face. She lifted her hand and pressed it against her breastbone. "So weird."

"What is?" Charlie asked.

"This tugging in my chest." Nicole's wonder morphed into fear. "It wants me."

"What wants you?" Charlie peered into Nicole's watery eyes. The thought *hell* drifted through her head. "You think hell wants you?"

"That's where I deserve to be."

"Honey. You were already in hell. What you deserve now is peace and healing. And love." Everything swirled around them, shifting like sand caught in a dust storm. When it settled down, they stood together in the middle of a forest clearing.

"What's happening?" Nicole asked, her voice small and fearful.

"I don't know." Charlie scanned the circular space around them. A bright moon shone above, casting light over the tops of the trees. A loud clicking sound drew her attention to her right, where an intense light appeared, blinding her for a second. She held her hand over her eyes until her vision adjusted. The light stretched in bright rays across the field toward them.

Nicole recoiled. "Oh my goddess, are you a reaper?"

Charlie glanced down at her hands and saw the white robes she'd worn during her astral projection had returned. Her heartbeat thrummed in her chest. "Not yet."

The light expanded, reaching for Nicole. Charlie could feel its warmth. A sweet hum of music or maybe it was voices all joined together, calling to them.

"You're supposed to go in there," Charlie said. "Can't you feel that?"

"Will you go with me?" Nicole said in a small voice.

"Sorry. I can only take you this far," Charlie said, unsure how she knew that. "Just be brave and step into it. Trust that you will be surrounded by love."

"Nicole?" A voice drifted from inside the light, and a shadowy figure of a woman appeared.

"Granny?" Nicole whispered.

"Oh, honey. I've been waiting for you." The shadowy woman held out her hand and beckoned Nicole forward.

"It's okay, Nicole. I'll take care of Crow," Charlie said. "You go on. Be with your granny."

"Thank you," Nicole said. A moment later, Nicole took the shadowy woman's hand, and the two of them disappeared.

* * *

CHARLIE'S EYES FLEW OPEN, AND SHE SAT UP IN BED, surprised to find Tom sitting next to her reading.

"Are you all right, my love?" Tom turned his book upside down on his lap.

"Yeah. I know how to get Crow."

"That's wonderful. But, it's a little early for you to go hunting." Tom stretched his arm out and pointed to the clock on her bedside stand, which read 2:30 am. "Why don't you come over here. You can lay your head on my shoulder until you fall asleep again."

Charlie snuggled up next to him and breathed him in. She wrapped her hands around his waist. "I had the weirdest dream. I was a reaper, but I wasn't dressed like you. I wore white robes like I did when I astral projected, and I helped Nicole cross over after she showed me everything she needed to."

Tom stroked her hair. "You were wearing white robes when I saw you in the hospital a few hours ago."

Charlie pushed up on her elbow and looked him in the face. "I almost forgot. So, you saw me?"

"Yes, I did."

"What do the white robes mean?"

He coaxed her to lie against him again. "Mmm. I'm not sure. It's intriguing, though."

"Yes. I thought so too." Charlie breathed slower, and her lids grew heavier. "I wonder if I can help other spirits like Nicole."

"Shh. You rest now. It's not time to know all the things yet."

A warmth spread across her shoulders, drifting down through her torso, and her entire body relaxed against him until she could no longer stay awake.

CHARLIE PULLED INTO THE DRIVEWAY OF HER EX-HUSBAND'S house and put her car into park. Evan was supposed to be waiting out on the front porch. It was close to 96 degrees, so she cut him a little slack. She considered using the horn, but if she did, Scott might dig in and be stubborn. He hated when people beeped. She opened the door, ready to step out when Evan came flying down the steps of his father's front porch with his backpack and duffel bag in tow. She rolled down the window.

"Hi, sweetheart. How was your first week of school?"

"Fine," he grunted. He opened the back driver's side door and tossed his things inside. Then he got in on the passenger's side, fastened his seatbelt, and didn't say another word.

Oh, the joys of raising a teenager. Charlie rolled her eyes.

"I see you're in a good mood," she said. "You want to get some supper? I'm starving."

"Is The Kitchen Witch open again?" He lifted his foot and put it on the dashboard.

"No, it's not. And I would appreciate it if you'd get your feet off the dash." She put the keys in the ignition, and the engine roared to life. A moment later she headed back toward the highway.

"I was thinking maybe we could go to Shem Creek and have some seafood to celebrate your first week of school."

"There's not much to celebrate. It's just school."

"I know, but it's high school. You're not a little kid anymore."

"Yeah, I know," he huffed.

"Hey, what's going on?" she asked.

"Nothing." Evan fidgeted with his seatbelt.

"Evan Michael, I know a lie when I hear it."

"Nothing's wrong, Mom, I swear. I'm just," he grumbled, "a freshman. I may as well be invisible."

"I don't believe that. First, it's private school, and it's not that big. So, what's really bugging you?"

"Nothing. I mean, I like my classes, I guess. It's just..." His shoulders sagged. "Rachel broke up with me."

"What?" Charlie said. "Why?"

"Some junior guys think she's pretty. And she likes all the attention. Forget it. It doesn't matter."

"I'm sorry, honey. That totally sucks. Maybe we could go to Shem Creek for seafood *and* we could have dessert? Would that make you feel better?"

"Maybe. What's the name of that place that's on the water that has that gigantic sundae?"

"Mickey's?"

"Yeah, I think that's it. Can we get calamari too?"

"We can get whatever you want." Charlie turned her attention back to the road.

"You know, my birthday is almost here."

"It's still a couple of months away, but I'm aware." Charlie grinned. She took the ramp onto the highway heading to Mount Pleasant. "Did you have a request?"

"Yeah," he said. "I'm going to be fourteen, and I think I'm a pretty responsible guy."

"You do?" Charlie said, trying not to sound amused.

"Yeah. I do. And I think it's time I had my own wand." He snuck a furtive glance in her direction. "You said you got your first wand when you were thirteen, and I'll be a whole year older."

Charlie nodded and suppressed a smile. "Having such a powerful object means you need to take lessons on how to use it."

"Right." Evan glanced at her, his voice cautious. "Does that mean you'll let me have one?"

"Possibly. But there will be conditions."

Evan bounced in his seat. "I'll do anything. Whatever you say."

"First, you can't take it to your father's house. It has to stay with me. Your dad would absolutely lose his mind if he thought you had a magical weapon at your disposal."

"No problem," Evan said.

"Second, you're not allowed to use it without supervision. At least for the first year. And you have to show me you know how to use it responsibly."

"I can do that. I'm very responsible. You can ask any of my teachers. I'm probably the most responsible student they have."

"I'll remember that next time you show me your report card." Charlie gave him a sly grin. "Third, and probably the most important condition, you can't show it to anyone, or tell any of your friends you've got this cool new toy." She sighed. "I hate to force you into the broom closet, but for now, it's the safest place for you to be. We don't live in a place that's always one hundred percent accepting of us. Do you understand?"

"Sure." Evan looked at her thoughtfully. "Could I show it to another witch?"

"Maybe. Let's cross that bridge when we get to it. Until then, it's a secret."

"Got it." He banged his fist lightly against the armrest on his door. "I'm going to have my own wand."

"Yes, you are. But you have to follow all the rules."

"Yes, ma'am. I will. When can we pick it out?"

"Let's think about that when we get closer to your birthday. Right now, the only thing I want you to think about picking out is what you want to eat tonight."

Evan rolled his eyes. "Geez, Mom, you're as bad as Jen when it comes to food."

Charlie laughed. "I guess I am."

CHAPTER 38

Lisa arrived at the garden center before anyone else Monday morning. She intended to repot the lucky plant and then head to her law office. She'd wanted to repot it over the weekend, but it had been too hectic, and she was so tired by the end of each day, she fell asleep on the couch while Jason made dinner.

She let herself into the kiosk and stood in front of the plant on its shelf. The poor thing appeared so wilted. She stroked the plant, unsure how to help it. It seemed like everything she tried only made it worse. She could feel its magic diminishing, draining away. Ever since Maria died, the plant seemed cursed.

"I need you to help me." She spoke to it in a quiet voice. "I don't know what's wrong with you. I've done everything I know, short of repotting you again."

One of the tendrils struggled to lift itself, and when it finally gathered enough energy to make a move, it partially wrapped a tendril around her wrist as if to answer her. She took it as a yes, maybe even a plea for help.

"All right. That's what I'm going to do then." She glanced around the empty garden center. The milky morning light of the early hour gave the place an eerie feeling.

She gently removed the stem, then set about gathering supplies from the main building. Once she'd found everything she needed—a new terra-cotta pot, a fresh bag of potting soil, an apron, gloves, and clean tools—she set them on a potting bench used for making displays. She unstrapped the plant from its shelf and moved it to the bench. Then she retrieved a watering can full of fresh water and a jar of organic fertilizer.

She donned her apron and gloves and carefully loosened the soil before she lifted the plant from its pot onto the table to inspect the roots. Why had so many of them withered and turned mushy? A blue crystalline speck in the soil drew her attention. She picked up the tiny nugget and held it up so she could see it better.

"What the hell?" she muttered. She brought it to her nose and sniffed it. "What are you doing in the soil?"

She sifted through the rest of the potting soil and found enough of the culprit to recognize copper sulfate algaecide when she saw it.

"Who did this to you, baby?" She grabbed a nearby hose and gently rinsed away all the soil still clinging to the roots. When she finished, she laid the plant on its side, allowing it to rest while she retrieved her fine clippers and some alcohol pads. Carefully, she sterilized the sharp steel blades and trimmed away all the dead roots. She filled the new pot halfway full of fresh soil and placed the plant on top of it while she whispered an incantation.

"Build new roots, strong and fast. I protect you against those who would attack. By the elements; earth, water, air, and fire, your life be restored despite those who conspire. So mote it be."

She covered the roots with more soil and gave the plant a good drink of water. By the time she carried it back to the kiosk, the leaves no longer appeared wilted. It had already begun to perk up.

"You're going to be all right. I'm not going to let anything bad happen to you." She brushed her fingers against a leaf, and the plant shuddered beneath her touch. A spark of green magic appeared and wound through her fingers. A sense of calm and peace went through her.

Before she lifted the plant to its shelf, she added one more layer of protection. She grabbed a Sharpie from the penholder next to the register and drew a protection sigil. She retrieved her wand from her purse and touched the tip to the sigil. It glowed bright green, and she pressed her hand against it, charging it with her energy. When she lifted her hand, the sigil became invisible.

She smiled down at the plant, pleased with herself. "That should take care of you."

She carefully lifted the plant to its shelf, refastened the strapping, and headed out before Adam showed up to open the center.

CHAPTER 39

"Any luck?" Charlie sat down next to Athena at the table in the conference room.

"Nothing yet. Searching through all of Mr. Carlton Crow Bowman's known aliases at the moment. Then I'll check any possible aliases he may have used."

"Sure," Charlie glanced up at the murder board, where she'd finished adding details about her dream.

Billie walked in carrying four coffees and a bag from a bakery in West Ashley called Daily Bread. "Morning. I brought breakfast today."

"Morning, Billie. Thanks." Charlie reached for two of the coffees, for herself and Athena, along with sugar packets and creamers.

"So, what're y'all working on?" Billie took a coffee and pulled out the empty chair across from Athena.

"I dreamt about Nicole this weekend. She showed me

some very interesting things." Charlie added sugar and creamer to her coffee then helped herself to a bear claw.

Billie's lips stretched into an uneasy grin, and she shook her head. "I can't believe I'm actually going to say this, but what did Nicole show you?"

Charlie took a moment and went through the dream with Billie but left out the reaper details. Billie was nowhere ready for knowledge about reapers.

"So, she's gone? You can't talk to her anymore?" Billie asked.

"I could summon her, but I'd rather not. I think she gave us plenty to go on. She's better off where she is now."

Charlie sipped her coffee, and waited for Billie to argue. Instead, Billie stared down at the cup in her hand, her expression pensive. She sensed Billie's questions building but wasn't ready to lay herself out like an encyclopedia of witchcraft and the occult.

Charlie shifted her attention to Athena. "So, how hard do you think it will be to find this warehouse if it exists?"

"Not too hard. I didn't sense Crow was some sort of criminal genius, did you?"

Charlie laughed. "No. Not really. He's shrewd, ambitious, and definitely well versed in charm making, but I have to believe he's going to screw up."

"Agreed. The thing I find interesting is a lot of criminals use variations of their own name. It's probably a whole lot easier to remember your own first name and give yourself a new last name than it is to—"

"Or," Athena's fingers slowed down on her keyboard, "to use your first name as your last name." She leaned forward, almost pressing her nose to the laptop screen. "I just found records for a CB Carlton on a lease for a warehouse on 13th Street in North Myrtle Beach. I'm cross-referencing utility bills and comparing it to the average usage of other warehouses in the same district."

"You can do that?" Charlie asked.

"Yes, I can." Athena gave Charlie a side-eyed glance. "Although it's not exactly something I would share with anybody."

"Sure." Charlie nodded and glanced to see if Billie was still lost in her thoughts.

"Interesting. Mr. Carlton's power bill is 50% higher than just about everybody else's in the same area."

"What does that mean?" Charlie asked.

Billie perked up. "Pot growers have high power bills. That's one way we find them."

"Exactly." Athena beamed.

"He wasn't growing pot, but he was definitely growing plants in my dream," Charlie said.

"I think we've found the son of a bitch," Athena chirped. "We should check it out before we head into a full-on raid, though, so we don't go in blind."

"Okay. You want to head up there now?" Charlie finished up the last bite of her pastry and crumpled her napkin, ready for anything.

"I was actually thinking something a little more high-tech." Athena cocked her head. "But, I need to make a call first. You have Evan this week, right?"

"Yes, I do. But I'm sure I could get my uncle and Jen to watch him if we need to head up to the beach."

"Who's Evan?" Billie asked.

"He's my son," Charlie said. Billie nodded in understanding.

Athena reached for her phone. "Let's see what Ben says first. Then we'll decide next steps."

"Great." Charlie rubbed her hands together. "I can't wait till we catch this guy."

"Me, too," Billie said.

* * *

THREE HOURS LATER, BEN ARRIVED WITH THE MOST crucial part of their reconnaissance mission. Charlie held the door open for him, and he lugged a large black box into the conference room. Charlie, Billie, and Jason all looked on with great curiosity.

Ben unlocked the box and lifted the lid. "I had to borrow this from another DOL office. Sorry it took so long to get it here.

"A drone?" Charlie asked.

"Yep," Athena chirped and peered into the box, her face beaming like a child with a new toy.

"Won't we still have to get pretty close to the building?" Jason asked.

"We have to be within five miles," Athena said.

"What about the North Myrtle Beach Police Department? Do we need to let them know?" Billie asked.

"Only as a courtesy. And I've already done that," Athena said.

Charlie peered into the box. "These things are kind of noisy, won't they hear it?"

"This thing is warded up the kazoo." Athena spoke with the confidence of an expert user. "It won't show up on any radar, and it's silent. It won't be invisible, obviously. But one of the wards does make anyone who looks up forget about it as soon as they see it."

"Very clever," Charlie said.

Ben began unpacking the device. "Charlie, you and Athena are going to North Myrtle Beach tonight to scope it out. If you get proof it is Crow's place, I'll have reinforcements come from Charlotte, and we'll conduct the raid."

"Sure thing," Athena said.

"No problem. I just need to make a couple of calls," Charlie said.

"I'd like to tag along, if that's okay," Billie asked.

Jason raised a finger. "Me too."

"Great." Athena clapped her hands together. "Let's get to it."

CHAPTER 40

The four of them arrived in North Myrtle Beach after rush hour with Billie driving the black Chevy Tahoe. Once the sun had set, Charlie and Athena set up two blocks down the street from CB Carlton's warehouse. Athena unlatched the Tahoe's tailgate and unboxed the drone and monitoring station. Charlie watched in awe as Athena fired up her laptop and connected wirelessly to the drone to get a live-action feed.

"It's so amazing we have this," Charlie said.

"I know. Some witches don't like technology and wouldn't touch this with a ten-foot pole, but it's going to make our life a whole lot easier." Athena typed a command into the computer, then grinned. "There we go."

She picked up the joystick and pressed the power

button on the drone. "Charlie, can you keep an eye on the monitor? Let me know what the camera sees?"

"Sure thing." Charlie seated herself on the tailgate and pulled the computer onto her lap. Jason and Billie gathered behind Athena to peek over her shoulder. Athena stepped back and looked at the coordinates she fed into the drone's controller. Then, with some gentle maneuvering of the joystick, the drone lifted into the air and buzzed out of sight.

"I should've thought to bring some chairs," Jason said.

Athena pointed at the vehicle. "I packed a couple in the cargo section."

"Of course you did," Billie rolled her eyes. "You think of everything."

Athena grinned. "Yeah," she teased, "that's kinda my job. Charlie, do you have eyes on the warehouse yet? I'm showing we're at the coordinates."

Charlie stared at the laptop's monitor. "Yeah, it's Crow's place. I see two armed witches on the roof. Can you zoom in closer?"

"Yep, sure thing." Athena pressed a couple of buttons on the controller, adjusting the camera lens.

"Can you do a perimeter sweep?" Charlie asked.

"Yep." Athena maneuvered the drone a little closer and swept the streets surrounding the building.

"All right. I see two more witches armed with wands," Charlie said.

"I'm going to do a preliminary search for sigils and

wards." Athena pressed a button on the controller with her thumb. "Switching to infrared now. The sigils or wards should emanate at a higher temp than the walls where they're written. That should make them visible."

"Got it." Charlie leaned in closer to the screen. A circular sigil appeared, glowing bright red.

"Holy shit. What is that?" Jason rested his arm on the tailgate and stared at the screen alongside Charlie.

"It's a protection sigil. We'll have to cast to get rid of it. Athena, can you go slower along the wall? I think I see more."

"Sure." Athena made an adjustment with the controller, and the camera panned along the perimeter walls.

Charlie's stomach dropped like a cold rock. "I've got sigils set up at cardinal points all the way around the building. We're going to need as many witches as we can get to break them."

"Damn," Athena said.

"And in my dream, there were two goons with him in the office," Charlie reminded her.

"What does 'cardinal points' mean?" Billie whispered to Jason.

"It means north, south, east and west. He's got sigils on each side of the building," Charlie explained. "Plus, he's sealed the sigils using the elements to make his protections stronger."

"Does that mean we can't get to him?" Worry filled Billie's brown eyes.

"It makes it harder, but not impossible." Charlie painted a reassuring smile across her face. "We'll get him."

"Good." Billie set her jaw.

"What's our guard count so far?" Athena asked.

"Four. Plus goons," Charlie said.

"We should probably assume it's at least double, maybe even triple that." Athena's lips twisted with displeasure. "I'm bringing the drone back. Then we'll call Ben and let him know how many reinforcements we need."

"Cool. Let's pack it up." Charlie blew out a heavy breath. "Tomorrow's going to be a long day."

"I guess we need to find a hotel," Billie said.

"It's already done. I booked three rooms at the Holiday Inn Express on the highway," Athena said. "I know it's not beachfront…"

Charlie shrugged. "As long as it's clean, that's all I care about. I brought some salt and sage just in case."

"Good thinking," Athena said.

CHAPTER 41

Ben showed up the next morning in what appeared to be a food truck selling crepes, with twenty-five witches in tow. He parked in the same spot Charlie and Athena had used the night before. In daylight they saw an added advantage of two disreputable buildings on the site with space to park the cars used by Ben's army of witches. Charlie had met some of them before, but most she hadn't. Each of them wore a vest that reminded Charlie of Jason's Kevlar vest. Only these vests had protective symbols stitched into them and crystals fastened in various places. The letters DOL were printed in white on the back. Ben stepped out of the truck, emanating an excited energy she rarely saw.

"Crepes?" Charlie pointed to the artful signage on the side of the truck with an amused expression on her face. "Are you competing with Jen, now?"

"Very funny," he said. "Why don't you come in and take a look at the command center."

Charlie followed him into the truck, which somehow looked larger on the inside than it did on the outside. She wasn't sure if it was a spell or an optical illusion, but there was enough room for her to stand in the center and turn in a circle to take it all in. Above a long desk on one side were mounted what seemed like a wall of computer monitors. Charlie noticed that a few of the monitors showed split screens with three, four, and five camera angles. She leaned in for a closer look.

"Are these body cams?" Charlie asked.

"Yeah," Ben said. "It's a better way for us to collect evidence and to see what we're facing on the ground here. If you look closely, you can see we're also monitoring bio signs, just in case somebody's exposed to something." Ben shrugged. "After all, he's making memory charms and curses. We can't be too careful."

"This is fantastic," Charlie didn't hold back her excitement. "Do I get one of those fancy vests?"

"Of course, you do. I got one for Athena, Billie, and Jason as well."

"It might be trickier to get Billie and Jason to wear them," Charlie said.

"They have to wear one if they want to join in the raid," Ben said firmly.

"I don't have a problem with that. Your operation," Charlie said.

"Our operation," Ben corrected.

Charlie nodded. Athena and Billie arrived a few minutes later carrying the drone.

"Oooh, are these the new vests?" Athena picked one up and inspected it.

"Yep." Ben nodded at the protective vest she held. "That one's yours if you want it."

"Cool beans." Athena slipped it over her head and adjusted the Velcro straps until the vest fit snugly against her body. "So, where do you want me, boss?"

"I'm thinking your talents may best serve us on aerial surveillance since you're the one who's used the drone the most."

"Cool." Athena beamed. "I can do that."

"Great." Ben clapped his hands. "I've got a spot down toward the door for you with a dual monitor setup.

"Yes, sir." Athena, clearly enjoying herself, slid down to her place and pulled her laptop from her bag. "Is it okay if Billie stays with me? It'll take two of us to monitor everything and make sure all the controls are working properly."

"Whatever you need," Ben said.

Billie peered inside the truck. "Wow. This is pretty cool." She walked the length of the desk, studying all the monitors.

"Athena wants you to work with her, if that's okay," Charlie said.

"Sure. Wherever you need me."

Ben handed a vest to Billie. "Here you go,"

"What's this for?" Billie accepted it warily, turning it over in her hands. Her fingers brushed over the crystals and the symbols on the back surrounding the letters DOL.

"That's for you to wear. Sorry, but it's non-negotiable," Charlie said.

"Even if I'm working in here with Athena?" she asked.

"Yeah," Ben said. "We don't know if Crow's men will make their way over to us. It's for your own protection against any stray magic that might come your way."

"Okay," Billie said reluctantly. "I take it these guys are going to be using guns?"

"No. Witches rarely use firearms. Most use wands," Charlie explained.

"Or their hands," Ben chimed in. Charlie knew he rarely carried a wand with him and preferred using the tools the goddess gave him. Charlie smiled.

Ben's voice dropped a register, respectful but no longer casually chatty. "We should get this show on the road."

"Yes, sir," Charlie said, responding to his authority and experience. "We should set up a perimeter."

"How are you going to do that?" Billie asked. "It's not like people are going to just stop because they see witches standing in the road."

"We don't need actual people to keep the perimeter. Our perimeter will be a series of charms and wards that will make people naturally turn away if they come too close," Charlie clarified.

Billie's eyebrows rose halfway up her forehead in surprise. For a second, Charlie thought she saw admiration in her eyes. "That's different."

"Yep," Charlie said. "And highly effective. I can get everyone started casting the perimeter wards."

"That'd be great, Charlie," Ben said. "Thanks."

"Wait!" Athena stopped Charlie before she could step outside. She handed a small box to Charlie. "It's an earpiece. So we can hear each other." Athena quickly showed Charlie how to put it in and slipped a wire over her ear and down her collar.

"Great."

"Don't forget the lingo we practiced," Athena said.

Charlie grinned and nodded. "Roger that."

Athena snorted, and Charlie left her to finish setting up.

When she stepped outside the truck, Charlie crossed to Jason who was talking with a witch name Marigold. He wore a smile on his face, and the two chatted easily. Charlie handed Jason a vest.

"Hey, Marigold," Charlie said.

"Hey, Charlie. Jason here was just telling me that he's getting married next spring." Marigold beamed.

"Yes, he is," Charlie said. "You remember my cousin, Lisa? She worked with us on the Keeley Moore case."

"Yes, of course. She's your bride-to-be?"

"Yep, she is." Jason nodded.

"Interesting." Marigold cocked her head and gave him a curious look.

Jason tucked his chin and an awkward energy rippled through him, spreading out toward Charlie. "Yeah, why's that?"

"I don't know. I just don't see it happening in the spring."

"I didn't think you were psychic, Marigold," Charlie said.

"Oh, I'm not. But I don't sense springtime for the wedding, that's all. I could totally be wrong, of course."

"What are you sensing?" Jason asked.

"I'm sensing the ocean. Are you planning on getting married at the beach?"

"No, we plan to get married at my mother's bed and breakfast." A look of confusion spread across Jason's face.

"It's on a marsh," Charlie said. Charlie gave Jason a side-eyed glance. He really hadn't had a moment to spend with Lisa thanks to this case. And from the way he acted, she didn't think Lisa had told him about the baby yet. And if she were honest, she didn't sense a wedding for next spring either.

"Oh, well, that totally must be it." Marigold tapped her forehead with two fingers.

"We should really get everybody moving," Charlie said.

"Sure thing," Marigold said.

Charlie stepped up on the back step of the command post truck. "If I can get everyone's attention, please."

The witches chatting and milling about stopped and directed their attention to Charlie.

"Thank you for coming today. When I first encountered the target, he appeared to be a small-time charms dealer. Unfortunately, I seem to have underestimated him. We're not sure exactly how large his operation is, but he's rather wily, so let's just everyone be careful out there today. Keep on your toes. And wands at the ready. I need nine witches to cast a perimeter ward around a four-block radius of the target's warehouse. Do I have volunteers?"

Hands went up into the air quickly, and Charlie chose the first nine. She gave them a map so they could easily home in on where they needed the boundaries to be. Then she handed out diagrams to everyone of the warehouse entrances and offices based on property records Athena had found.

"During our recon yesterday, we found that there were four exterior guards. We don't know how many interior guards they have. The property is also marked with protection sigils on each side of the building. We'll need to break those first before we can breach the warehouse. I don't know the strength of the sigils, so I propose we use as large a casting circle as we can to burn them away. I expect there will be some sort of alarm mechanism, so, as soon as the sigils are gone, we need to move in fast. Any questions?"

Charlie looked out over the crowd of serious faces, awed by their dedication. She could tell they had no idea what they were walking into.

"Great. Thank you so much. Let's get started."

CHAPTER 42

As soon as the perimeter wards were in place, Charlie and the twenty-six witches split into two groups. Half moved in on the building, while the other half formed a large casting circle to break the protections. Once they had burned the sigils away, group two would join the rest in descending on the warehouse.

Charlie and Jason moved to the head of the first group and waited. Charlie's heart pounded so hard against her ribs, she thought surely it would leave a bruise. She worried about Jason. Quietly, she said, "Maybe you should go back and wait at the command post."

"No," he said flatly. "I want this guy as much as you do. Three people are dead because of him. I can't let that slide."

"Nobody's asking you to. It's just I can't protect you. And it's not like you have a wand to protect yourself."

"I'll be all right," he said. "But I appreciate the sentiment. I think I've been around these things enough to know when to keep my head down, and I'm pretty good in a physical fight."

Charlie rolled her eyes but couldn't help herself from turning to grin at him. "Yeah, I guess you are."

For the first time that day, she really looked at Jason. There was something odd about him. His torso looked huge. "What are you wearing?"

"I've got my vest on, too, the one you drew the pentacle on. It's my talisman in this dogfight."

The first collection of sigils on the side of the warehouse caught fire and burned away, leaving just a black smudge on the wall.

"Get ready," Charlie whispered.

Jason nodded. "Yes, ma'am."

"Charlie, this is Athena. Do you read me?"

"Loud and clear. Do you have eyes on the sigils? Over," Charlie said.

"Roger that. The last mark is on fire. Everyone stand-by."

"Roger that," Charlie said. The radio lingo had not been completely new to Charlie, but she made Athena practice with her last night when Athena had first shown her the earpiece.

"Engage," Athena said. It didn't take long for Crow's guards to start firing.

"Cover me," Jason said. Despite the crossfire of blue, red, and green shots of energy firing across the empty street between the DOL witches and Crow's guards, Jason charged toward a door next to a closed drive-in bay on the side of the building. Charlie followed him, firing at any unfriendly witch that aimed a wand his way. She stunned the first two guards, and two more emerged. Jason grabbed one of them by the collar and slammed him against the wall knocking him out. He grabbed the wand from the stunned man's hand.

"What should I do with it?" he said.

"Toss it across the street." Charlie flattened herself against the wall and landed a stunning spell in the back of the next guard through the door. She and Jason slipped inside, and an alarm echoed through the space. She pressed one hand against her ear and searched along the wall for a way to open the drive-in bay door. After a moment, she found a garage door button and pressed it. As soon as she did, the DOL witches flooded inside. Streaks of red, blue, and green energy filled the space between Crow's men and the DOL witches.

"Freezing spells," Charlie called. The DOL witches aimed their wands at the hiding spots of the guards still shooting at them. In a concentrated effort, they all shot the same spell at the guards, and one by one, they fell to the ground. Charlie took a moment to finally look around.

The space looked to be about five thousand square feet, most of it dedicated to a grow operation with a watering system, powerful grow lights, and waist-high platforms holding dozens of large pots. The majority of the containers held silver satin pothoses like the one in Maria's car, but there were also other plants used for memory charms and curses.

It was hard to miss the large black truck on jacked-up axles with, by Charlie's estimation, 35-inch tires. It was parked near a bay door opposite the one where she and Jason had entered.

Charlie continued to scan the space. She spotted Crow and the two men who'd been with him in her dream, watching the chaos from a large office window overlooking the warehouse,. For a second, her eyes locked with Crow's, and he cocked his head and smirked. An explosion overhead startled everyone, and they ducked for cover. A black and green powdery substance rained down from above, making it hard to breathe.

Charlie quickly covered her nose and mouth with her hand. Her eyes watered, and she stumbled backward. She grabbed Jason by the back of his vest and dragged him out through the open bay door, both coughing and wheezing. When the screaming started, it took her a moment to figure out what was happening. She watched as the witches trapped inside the building fell to their knees. Some of them screamed and struck out at some unseen foe.

Charlie started back inside the building, but something grabbed her by the bottom of her vest and yanked her.

"No," Jason said. "I think it's that memory charm thing you were talking about. It started to affect me before you got me out."

"What do we do?" Charlie watched helplessly.

"Charlie? Charlie, do you read me?" Athena sounded strangely distant even though she was right in Charlie's ear.

Charlie couldn't take her eyes off Crow sauntering down the steps of the office with a duffel bag and wearing a gas mask. He turned to give her a two-fingered salute.

Charlie aimed her wand, sending a stunning spell at him. He quickly grabbed one of his crony's arms and pushed him between them, using the poor man as a shield. Charlie's spell struck the thick-necked man, and he fell to the ground. Crow and his other minion climbed into the truck. A drive-in bay door on the other side of the building opened, and the truck drove away.

Panic filled Charlie's chest. "Athena, are you seeing this? Crow's getting away."

"Roger that. I've got eyes on him."

"Come on." Jason tugged her vest. "My car's not far from here."

Charlie threw her hands up in the air. "How on earth are we going to find him?"

"Ask Athena if she can direct us to him." Jason remained calm, and his energy helped ground her. She nodded.

"Athena, if we follow him, can you direct us to him?"

"Roger that," Billie said.

"Hi, Billie," Charlie said. "Thanks. Over."

"Come on. Every second we wait is a second he gets farther away." Jason took her arm and pointed her in the direction of his car.

CHAPTER 43

Athena's heart raced as she tried to get a lock on Crow's truck.

Billie sat next to Athena inside the command post truck with the laptop and the monitor in front of her. "There he is." Billie pointed to the thirty-two-inch monitor in front of them. "Let me see if I can figure out what street he's on." Her hands moved almost as deftly as Athena's across the keyboard. "He just turned onto Harrison. It looks like he's headed toward the highway."

"Got it." Athena pushed the joystick forward, and the drone obeyed.

"Charlie, do you read me?" Billie asked.

"Loud and clear," Charlie said. "We just got to Jason's car. Do we know where we're going?"

"Yes. Head for Harrison Street. He's moving toward Highway 17."

"Roger that," Charlie said. Athena heard Charlie and Jason speaking in muffled tones but didn't have time to listen closely. She was too busy watching Crow escape.

"You have eyes on him yet?" Athena asked.

"Negative. Wait." Charlie's tone shifted. "I see him. I guess it's kind of hard to miss him in that damned truck."

"That's what I'm counting on," Athena said. "Stay with him if you can. But proceed with caution."

"Roger that," Charlie said.

"He's on the on-ramp," Billie said.

"I see him." Athena zoomed the camera lens out to get a better idea of where Charlie and Jason were in relation to the truck. Cars jammed the four-lane road. Jason's Dodge Charger was pinned in by cars on three sides and the shoulder on the other. It was almost as if the universe was conspiring against them. She tipped her head at an intriguing thought. Or a spell. A sinking feeling filled her chest. What if she'd underestimated Crow?

"If you can get behind him, that would be very helpful," Athena said.

"We're doing our best," Charlie said. "Every time we make a move, we get blocked."

"That's what I was afraid of." Athena clicked her teeth together, trying to think of a counter spell.

"Dammit," Athena heard Jason say in the background.

"He just got on the highway. Looks like he's going north," Charlie said.

"Roger that," Athena said. "I'm gonna have to go with him."

"Sure. We'll get there as soon as we can."

Athena shifted the joystick away from Harrison Street, lifting it far above the highway. Even though the drone was heavily warded, the last thing she needed was for him to get wind of it. The truck weaved in and out of traffic.

"Geez," Athena said to her monitor. "It's almost like you know we're following you."

The truck disappeared beneath an overpass. Athena waited a beat, expecting it to reappear. It didn't.

Billie leaned forward with her hands flat on the desk. "Where the hell did it go?"

"I don't know." Athena paused the drone for a moment, letting it hover, still waiting for some sign of the truck to appear. But all she saw were several sedans and SUVs, all of which had been on the highway with him.

"What's happening?" Ben asked.

"I don't know," Athena said. "All of a sudden, he's just gone."

"How could that be?" Ben asked. "I don't know anybody who can do an invisibility spell that's worth a damn. Especially not for something the size of that truck."

"Charlie, do you read me?" Athena asked.

"Loud and clear."

"Do you have eyes on him?"

"We're on the highway now, but there's no sign of him. You don't see him?"

"No, I don't. He seems to have disappeared."

"What? How?" Charlie's voice sounded strained.

"I don't know. I'm going to follow the highway for a couple more miles. Maybe I'll be able to pick him up there. He went under the 501 overpass. Can you please check it out on the ground?"

"Roger that."

Athena stared intently at the monitor but the sinking feeling from before worsened. She hated to admit defeat. Failure was not an option. She gritted her teeth, and her cheeks burned. "Come on, you son of a bitch. Where the hell are you?"

A soft hand touched her shoulder. "Athena, I think he's gone."

"No. He can't be. Trucks just don't disappear into thin air, even if he is a witch."

Billie patted her shoulder. "I'm sorry, honey,"

"Shit," Athena muttered. Tears stung her eyes, but she refused to let them fall. She turned to Ben. "I'm sorry. It looks like I lost him."

Ben scrubbed his face with his hand and stared at the monitor. "You did your best. Why don't you bring the drone back in so we can review the footage? Maybe something will become more apparent then."

"Yes sir," she said. "Charlie, do you read me?"

"Roger that," Charlie said. "There's still no sign of him. We're under the overpass, now, and there doesn't seem to be any indication of what could've happened."

"Don't worry about it. Y'all just come on back to command, okay?"

"Roger that," Charlie said.

* * *

CHARLIE JUMPED OUT OF JASON'S CAR AS SOON AS HE PUT IT in park, and headed to the crowd of witches congregating around the crêpe truck. Two healer witches worked to counteract the curse that had rained down on them inside the building. Most of the witches had recovered, but there were still a few who seemed trapped in terrifying memories of their past, screaming and striking out or rocking back and forth, whimpering to themselves.

Charlie could feel their pain. If she tried, she knew she could probably hear their thoughts, but she knew it wouldn't serve her to do that now. A wave of guilt washed over her. Why had the effects spared her?

Ben and Athena stood near the open door of the command truck. As soon as Ben saw her, he raised his hand in a wave.

"I'm so sorry, Ben," Charlie said as she approached.

"Hey, there's nothing to be sorry for," Ben said.

"Everybody did a great job today. We just didn't anticipate a few things."

"Right. Like Crow being smarter than I first thought. His whole operation is actually pretty sophisticated," Charlie said.

"Yeah," Ben said. "I've got a team in there clearing out the air now, so we can confiscate everything."

"That's going to make him very edgy," Charlie said.

"That's what I'm hoping for," Ben said.

"I really hope we can find something to tie him to Nicole and Evelyn's murders. Maybe even Maria's."

"Maria's death may be a long shot," Ben mused. "Maybe you should try to talk to Evelyn again. See if she can lead you to physical evidence."

"I can try astral projection. If that doesn't work, I guess we could summon her. But, I've dealt with hostile spirits before, and I don't have anything to leverage. I doubt she's going to be assuaged by guilt. She's dead. Her best friend is dead."

"What about the boyfriend?" Ben asked. "Can you use him as leverage?"

"Maybe." Charlie rubbed the back of her neck.

"Charlie," Jason called. He half-jogged to her with an intense look on his face. He held his phone in his hand. "Beck just called me. Brett Travis walked into the Sheriff's department and confessed to Evelyn's murder."

"What the hell?" Ben said.

"They got to him." Charlie clenched her jaw. "I saw

Crow making a memory charm that I'd never heard of. The sigils weren't enough. We should've brought Brett into protective custody."

"Based on a dream?" Jason asked.

Charlie rolled her eyes. "Yes."

"You guys head back to Palmetto Point. See if you can straighten this out." Ben looked out over the crowd of witches, some still suffering from the effects of Crow's booby trap.

Charlie followed his gaze, and a pang of guilt filled her chest. "You sure?"

"Yeah. I'll stay here for a while. I called in more reinforcements to process the warehouse. We'll be fine."

Charlie sighed. "I'm sorry."

"For what?" Ben gave her a curious look.

"For not seeing through Crow better. I should've anticipated him pulling something like this."

"You're psychic, not omniscient. Give yourself a break. We now have everything we need to charge him and put him away for a long, long time."

"I know, but...." Charlie sighed. "Some of these witches may be permanently affected by that stupid curse."

"We've got the best healers in the country. They're in good hands. We just need to get him off the street now, so no one else is ever affected by his charms again." Ben touched her arm and gave it a gentle squeeze.

"Okay." Charlie nodded. "I'll see if Evelyn can lead me to him."

"Good. Keep me updated."

"I will," Charlie said.

CHAPTER 44

"So, he just walked in?" Charlie folded her arms across her chest and stared at one of the monitors in the AV room at the sheriff's station. Jason and Beck watched with her.

Brett Travis hunched over the table in the center of Interview Room Two with a yellow legal pad and a pen, scribbling away. After a moment, he suddenly stopped, ripped the page off, crumpled it up, and tossed it on the table next to dozens of sheets of paper.

"Yep." Beck pointed to the screen. "If he keeps doing that, he's going to run out of pages."

"I get the sense he can't form coherent enough thoughts to finish writing the statement," Charlie said. Brett stopped and his eyes glazed over. "See that? He's confused."

"Or," Beck put his hand on his hips, "he was lying the first time."

"I promise you. He wasn't lying." All the weight from the day settled on Charlie's shoulders. She'd been up since 5 am, and it was nearly 4 pm by the time they got back to the sheriff's station from Myrtle Beach. "I know for a fact he didn't kill her."

Jason said, "We need to trip him up."

"Agreed." Charlie took a deep breath.

"Are you sure he's not the murderer?" Beck cocked his head. "I mean, he is the boyfriend."

"No, Beck. He's not the murderer. I know you and Jason always think it's the husband or the boyfriend, but I promise you this isn't about love, or passion or any of the reasons a man kills a woman. Evelyn was murdered because Crow Bowman wanted her territory."

"You still have to prove that, right?"

"Yeah," Charlie rubbed the back of her neck, digging her fingers in to try to loosen up the tightness that stretched into her shoulders. "Come on. Let's get in there and talk to him."

"You got it," Jason said. He turned to Beck. "You going to stay here?"

"Oh, yeah," Beck chuckled. "This should be interesting."

Jason nodded. A moment later, Charlie and Jason walked into the room and sat down in the two metal folding chairs across from Brett Travis. He glanced up from his notepad with a glazed look in his eyes. He might've been a weasel and a thief, but Charlie knew he wasn't a murderer. She just had to convince him of that now.

"Hey, Brett," Charlie said. Brett didn't seem to see her, even though he looked right at her. "Are you having a hard time writing down your confession?"

Brett blinked, and his eyes cleared. He stared at the papers crumpled all over the table and the pieces that had fallen on the floor. "Yeah. Sorry about the mess. It was so clear when I came in here."

"But, it's not now?" Charlie asked.

He closed his eyes. A shiver went through him. "Parts of it are clear."

"Tell me about the parts that are clear," Jason said.

"Blood. Evelyn's blood on my hands." Deep purple circles rimmed his hound-dog eyes as if he hadn't slept.

"Do you remember our first interview, Brett?" Charlie asked.

"It's…" His eyes glazed over again, "hazy."

Whatever was in the charm Crow had used on him held on tight. The image of the witches doubled over during the raid flashed through Charlie's head. What if this happened to them? What if the charm he used on them lingered like this? What if Ben was wrong and the healers couldn't help them recover? Anger shot through her. Crow would pay for this.

"Do you remember Friday night?" she asked. "When

you told me you found Evelyn and called it in. Do you remember that?"

"No. I remember lying to you."

"Okay. Do you remember the truth spell? Or Athena taking you home and putting sigils on your trailer? She gave you a bracelet to wear, to protect you. Do you remember that?"

Brett's thick eyebrows drew closer together as if he were thinking hard, trying to remember. A deep line formed. He shook his head. "No."

"Can I see your arms?" Charlie asked. Brett's gaze moved slowly to his arms. A second later, he held them both up. There was no sign of the protective tracker Athena had put on him. Charlie studied him for a moment more. "So, you killed Evelyn?"

"Yes."

"All right, tell me about it. How did you do it?"

"I came up behind her and slashed her throat."

"What'd you do with the knife?"

"I...." He squeezed his eyes shut again and tapped on his forehead. "I don't know. But I know I killed her." His voice broke, and tears seeped from the corners of his eyes.

Charlie reached across the table and put her hand over his. A vision jolted through her mind—Brett in his tiny bedroom, unwashed and stinking with fear and uncertainty. The door to his trailer blasting open and one of Crow's goons marching in, a wand in one hand and a charm bag in the other. Brett screaming and fighting to get away. The thick-necked goon stunning Brett, holding a linen bag to his nose and mouth, forcing him to breathe in. Brett's body, limp and twitching on the floor of the trailer. The goon slipping the bag into an air vent and leaving as if nothing happened. Charlie blinked away the vision and gave Brett's hand a squeeze before she let it go.

"Brett, when you killed her, at what point did you steal her money?"

Brett cocked his head. "I..."

"You previously told us that you called the police because you found her dead and that you took her cash because you needed it. Remember?"

"I took her cash." He said aloud as if he were mulling it over. "I took her cash."

"Yes, you did. Did you take anything else?"

"No. Everything else had been cleaned out," Brett said automatically.

"How could it have been cleaned out if you killed her?" Charlie asked.

Brett's eyes cleared and widened. He straightened in his chair. "It couldn't."

"Because?"

"I didn't kill her," he whispered. His entire body sagged with the realization as if a great weight had just rolled off him. His dark brown eyes glistened with tears. "I didn't kill her."

"No, you didn't. Do you know what the killer took from her house?"

"Yeah." He nodded as if eager to answer. "He cleaned out her potions room, where she experimented with her charms, where she first grew the plants."

"So, he didn't know about the grow room in her apartment." Charlie sat back in her chair and studied him.

"I don't think so. He took all the other ingredients, too; the crystals, the other herbs she was growing or that she'd dried."

"That's why you went into hiding. Because you were afraid he was going to come after you, too?" Charlie asked.

"Yeah. After what happened to Maria, I knew I was next."

"I have a source that showed me how he was going to get to you. He wanted you to confess to everything and take the fall. And he almost succeeded."

"I remember now. The big dude broke into my trailer and did something to me. I don't remember that part very well, though. It's still hazy."

Charlie nodded encouragingly. "It might take some time. You need to stay away from memory charms. He put the charm in the ventilation of your trailer. And I bet if we searched your car, we'd find something there, too. He thinks he's smarter than us."

"What's going to happen to me?" he asked.

"I don't know. I think that's up to you and the choices you make from here on out," Charlie said.

Brett stared at Charlie with a helpless look in his eyes

and blew out a breath. "For what it's worth, I loved Evie and Maria. They were my family. I hate what he did to them."

"Me too. Now, I just have to find him so we can make him pay for it." Charlie pulled the yellow legal pad away from him. "I don't think you need this anymore. There's nothing to confess, right?"

"Right." Brett gathered all the crumpled papers. Charlie grabbed the trashcan by the door and helped him toss the mess inside.

CHAPTER 45

"Jesus, Charlie, I don't know about this." Jason paced the floor in front of the whiteboard in the conference room. The room was a mess from all the time they'd spent there, trying to track down Evelyn and Nicole's killers.

"Shouldn't you do this someplace more...I don't know, peaceful?"

"No. Everybody knows we're working a case here. The door locks, I can ward it to keep people from disturbing me, and you're here to help. It's as good a place as any, and we're running out of time." Charlie scrutinized the room they'd been using for almost two weeks. All the pictures and notes written on the murder board pointed back to Crow. If this were the only way to find him, she'd had to try it.

Jason stared at her. His hair was ruffled from scrubbing his hands along his scalp, and he locked his uncertain eyes with hers. "Maybe you should wait for Athena. She's really good at this kind of stuff."

"Don't be ridiculous. You can do this, and you should get used to this stuff if you're going to be part of the family." A wry grin spread across her lips.

Jason scoffed. "I doubt Lisa's going to let me stand in a casting circle with you."

"You might be surprised what Lisa will want you to do."

"Wouldn't it be better just to go to Evelyn's house?" Jason's eyes pleaded. "Maybe she's there."

"It would take too much time, and I don't have to be there to contact her. I'll find her faster in the astral plane."

"I can't believe I'm about to say this, but maybe we should call Tom. He can go into this astral plane with you, right? As back up?"

"Tom's busy, but if I need him, all I have to do is call his name and he'll come. Even if I'm not in my body."

Jason made a worried face.

"What?"

"I don't like to think about you leaving your body. It's like you're dead or something."

"I won't be dead. And you'll be fine." She patted him on the shoulder. "Now, let's get started."

"Okay. I'm going to tell Beck not to disturb us."

"Great." Charlie dug through her bag until she found

the kit that Jen had helped her put together for times like this. She untied the string and unrolled a velvet storage bag with an embroidered pentagram in the center. Then she retrieved four white candles and their holders, and placed them in a cardinal formation on the conference room table. A zippered compartment contained her favorite crystals for meditation. She withdrew several and placed them in between the candles. Charlie drew out a nag champa incense stick along with a box of matches, and placed it in a wooden holder.

A moment later, Jason returned. He quickly closed the door and turned the lock. "Don't burn that."

"It helps me slip into a trance state faster. Is it a problem?"

Jason pointed to the ceiling and the two large sprinkler heads.

"Oh. Gotcha." She frowned and bit her bottom lip. Then she remembered something else Jen had made for her. She held up one finger. "I know what will work."

She quickly dug into her purse and pulled out a 10ml roll-on bottle. She uncapped it, rolled it across the pulse points on her temples and wrists, then rolled it across her forehead and solar plexus. She took a deep breath, and the mix of aromas—frankincense, lavender, clary sage, and sandalwood—relaxed her. She recapped the bottle and tucked it into the velvet bag. "That should do it."

She climbed onto the table, placing herself in the center of the candles and crystals.

"I need you to take that box of matches on the chair and light the candles for me. The wicks are smokeless. No worry about setting off sprinklers."

Jason nodded and lit the first candle. "Do I need to say anything?"

"No. Just approach it with reverence."

Jason met her gaze and gave her a nod. After he'd lit the last candle, he said, "Are you comfortable like that?"

"I'm fine."

Jason took a seat in one of the chairs. "I'll be here if you need me."

"Thank you." She closed her eyes. The relaxing aromas of the essential oils wafted around her. She took long deep breaths and focused on the mantra I float, I fly, I rise without fear.

It didn't take long for her to hear the familiar buzzing in her ears. She sensed Jason sitting at the end of the table, standing guard over her. The sensation of floating drifted through her, and she rose out of her body. She thought of the sky and found herself outside.

The sun hung low, painting the sky pink and orange. The beauty of the scene stunned her, but the sound transfixed her. The harmony she heard all around sounded as if the universe were singing. She reveled in it a moment more before starting her journey.

She pictured Evelyn's face and the room where Evelyn died. And, with the speed of thought, she was there.

"Oh no!" Evelyn screeched. A large marble paperweight rocketed at Charlie. She ducked out of habit, but not fast enough. Still, the object passed right through her.

"I'm not going with you. No matter what you say."

"Why are you so scared of me?" Charlie asked. Then she remembered Henry and his reaction. "Evelyn, wait. I'm not a reaper."

Evelyn held an old beer stein over her head. She stopped herself mid-throw. "Then why do you look like one?"

"Take a good look at me. Do I really look like a reaper?"

Evelyn dropped the beer stein on the concrete floor. It smashed into a broken heap. She cocked her head. "Your robes are different. And I can see your face. But you have that same rustling sound they do and—"

"I don't have a scythe. I couldn't capture you if I wanted to."

"Maybe you're just trying to trick me. There's a reaper here, skulking around."

"I'm not trying to trick you. I swear." Charlie held up her hands. She scanned the room for any signs of a reaper. Tom had said they wouldn't take too kindly to her being in their space, dealing with souls. "I'm not one of them."

"Then, why are you here?"

"I need your help. The man who killed you, Crow Bowman, he's gotten away from me."

A snarl twisted Evelyn's lips. "Boone."

"Who?"

"He's Crow's right-hand man. He's the one who killed me. He's a dufus, but he's really strong and can cast a stunning spell like I've never seen before."

"Crow set up Brett to take the fall for your murder."

"Brett? No." The spirit shook her head. "How did he do that?"

"He created a new charm to implant memories. Brett walked into the sheriff's station this afternoon and confessed."

"Brett wouldn't hurt a fly. He hated the curses, wouldn't deliver them for me, even though they paid the best."

"Is that what he gave Maria to deliver?"

"Maria? Maria has nothing to do with delivering product."

"I'm sorry to tell you this, but Crow had Maria killed, too."

"What?" Evelyn gritted her teeth and snatched up a bowl filled with potpourri. She tossed it against the wall where it shattered. She let out a frustrated screech. "I swear to Diana, I am going to kill him."

"I know you're mad." Charlie proceeded cautiously. "You should be mad. Maybe you can use that energy to help me find him. Before he kills someone else you love."

"Crow's in Myrtle Beach."

"Maybe, but I can't find him."

"You found me," Evelyn stilled.

"Because I knew exactly where to look. I don't know where to look for him. He gave us the slip earlier today when we raided his warehouse."

"You took down his operation?" A look of glee spread across Evelyn's nearly translucent face.

"We did. And that worries me. Because if he disappears, he's just going to go back to making these terrible charms, and Brett will never be safe."

"They're not all terrible," Evelyn said. "They helped my grandmother when she was dying. She was lost in happy memories for the last few weeks of her life. Which isn't a bad place to be."

"Is that how you got into it? When we first met Crow, we found that he was selling memory charms to nursing home residents. He claimed it was for his grandmother."

Evelyn scoffed. "I doubt that. From what I know of him, he doesn't have any family."

"I see," Charlie said. "He had me fooled, and I'll tell you right now, that's not an easy thing to do."

"Well, he is a sociopath."

"That I can see," Charlie said. "Where would he go, Evelyn? If he were desperate?"

"You know his memory charms were pretty bad before he got hold of one of mine."

"Because you had different ingredients in yours."

"Yeah. It was a plant that I've only seen one place. Maria got clippings from the plant and gave them to me.

She was convinced there was something magical about them because they brought her so much luck. And the owner of the business where she worked just gave them to her. I never did figure out exactly how it was magical. It was just a pothos, which is a pretty common house plant."

"You took the cuttings and rooted them," Charlie said.

"Yes. And Maria would bring me new cuttings all the time. Even though I grew new plants from the cuttings, they lost potency over time. Don't get me wrong. I still made a superior product to Crow's garbage." She sighed. "But the fresh cuttings helped with charms that need a little extra oomph, if you know what I mean."

"We found the grow room in your apartment," Charlie said. "We've already confiscated all those plants. And right now the DOL is confiscating all the plants from Crow's warehouse. If I were Crow and I knew that my livelihood hung on this plant, I'd go right to the source."

"Yeah. Me too," Evelyn said.

"Please. Can you take me to the source?"

Evelyn's eyes widened, and she held up her hand. "No! I am not going with you."

A hissing noise filled Charlie's head. It grew so loud she could barely stand it. She covered her ears with her hands, even though she had no true physical form.

"What are you doing here?" a raspy male voice hissed. "This is not your territory."

Charlie turned toward the voice. A reaper loomed

over her. His green eyes glittered inside the void of his hood and fixed on her. All Charlie could see was his size and the gleaming blade of his scythe. How many times had she seen Tom's scythe? Too many to count, and never had it gleamed like this one. She put herself between the reaper and Evelyn.

"There's been some sort of misunderstanding—"

"You are trying to take her away from me! I see no misunderstanding." He raised the scythe as if to cut her down.

"This can't be your territory. Tom Sharon and his family..."

The reaper hissed again. Charlie recoiled at the horrid sound. "Tom Sharon is a sorry excuse for a reaper. Masquerading as a human. Loving a human."

"Tom Sharon, I don't know if you can hear me, but I need you," Charlie whispered. In less than a second, Tom materialized. He took in the situation at the speed of thought.

Joy and William, Tom's reaper brother and sister, materialized, too, with scythes in hand. Charlie drifted backward toward Evelyn. The poor spirit froze in place, unable to move.

"So, you are a reaper," Evelyn whispered.

"No. Not yet. Not for many years to come. But, these reapers are my family," Charlie said. "They'll protect us."

The three reapers circled the intruder. Their robes blurred with the speed of their movement.

"You do not belong here." Tom's silky voice burned with a fury Charlie had never heard before.

"How dare you try to steal a soul from my book." Joy's usually sultry voice hissed with accusation.

"You have been warned, Ben Azrael, many times," William said in his strangely lilted southern voice. "Again, you appear without permission. You are not welcome here."

The circle of reapers drew closer to the intruder.

"Evelyn, we need to get out of here," Charlie said.

"What's going to happen to him?"

"It doesn't matter. Take me to the source of the plant. Now."

Charlie reached for Evelyn's hand and, instead of arguing, Evelyn took it. The two of them disappeared from the room just as the screaming began.

CHAPTER 46

Charlie waited a beat to get her bearings. Evelyn had taken her to a parking lot, and she needed to scan the space before they made another move. Long shadows bathed Palmetto Point Garden Center, Lisa's new business. Was she there today, or at her law office?

A green minivan turned into the parking lot and pulled into a space near the front gate. Evelyn moved closer to the vehicle. Charlie followed her to get a better look at the driver. She peered in through the window. Crow and the man she'd seen escape with him leaned into the windshield, studying the building.

Charlie imagined herself inside the van and was immediately transported to the second row of seats behind the driver.

"So, what's the plan, boss?" Boone asked.

"We're going to wait until five minutes before they close, then we'll slip inside and hide until everyone leaves," Crow said.

"Why don't we just break in?" Boone stared at Crow, his mouth hanging open as if he didn't understand the plan.

"I don't want to leave a trail. The DOL is already hot on our ass. They'd investigate a break-in. We wait 'til they close, take the plant, and get out through the back loading dock. Nobody will ever know we've been here."

"Then what happens?" Boone sounded a little sad. "They probably took everything. You should've just let me blast them with a fire spell."

"Yeah, well, I didn't want you burning us alive, too. We'll start over. It ain't my first time, and it probably won't be my last. We'll go to Florida. There's lots of old people in Florida who would love to remember better times in their lives. And if we go to Miami, I'm sure we'll find plenty of customers for curses. Don't worry, dude. Haven't I always taken care of you?"

"They got Cory," Boone said.

"Yeah, that was a great loss." Crow hung his head a little. "None of this would've happened if that bitch, Evelyn, had just agreed to a deal."

"Screw you," Evelyn said from the third row of seats. A plastic bottle cap sailed through the air and struck Crow on the back of the head.

"Hey!" He rubbed the place where it had hit him. "What was that for?"

"What was what for?" Boone gave him a puzzled look.

Crow bent down and picked up the bottle cap. He glanced over his shoulder into the back of the minivan. For a second, Charlie felt their eyes connect, but if he saw her, he didn't show it. He tossed the bottlecap out the window and shook his head. "That was weird."

"Oh my goddess." Evelyn pointed past Charlie. "It's Maria."

"Evelyn, wait," Charlie said, but the spirit disappeared. "Dammit." Through the front window, she saw the two spirits come face to face. They appeared to talk for a moment before throwing their arms around each other.

Crow leaned forward and tapped the digital clock built into the dashboard. "It's time."

Boone nodded, and the two of them hopped out of the van and headed into the garden center.

It was time to find out if Lisa was here. Charlie pictured Lisa's face, and, in an instant, she appeared beside her, standing near a shed inside the garden center. A loud beeping noise startled Charlie, and she jumped out of the way. A pallet loader forklift drove past her so quickly she could have sworn she felt a breeze from it. Lisa waited patiently as the driver of the forklift backed it into the shed. A young man in his twenties with sandy brown hair and a slight green glow around him climbed off the forklift, closed the shed door, and fastened the padlock.

"Great job today, Adam," Lisa said.

"I guess you won't be around much after this, will you?" he asked. The two of them headed toward the kiosk in the middle of the garden center.

"I won't be in every day anymore, no. I'm afraid I've let my law practice slide too much. I've got a lot of catching up to do, and with everything else on my plate, it's just too much to come here more than the odd weekend. But, I totally trust you can handle it. You're a great manager, Adam. And I know you can run this place."

"Thanks. I appreciate your faith in me." He smiled shyly. "And I appreciate your hiring my friend, Nick. I promise you, he won't let you down."

"I'm sure he'll be great." Lisa cocked her head. A slight grin played on her lips. "And since you're the manager now, if he doesn't work out, you get to fire him."

Adam chuckled. "Don't worry. I'll make sure he's great."

"I'm sure you will."

"You want me to stick around while you close up? I totally don't mind."

"I thought you had a date."

"Yeah." He shrugged. "I can be a little late."

"No, you can't. First impressions matter. You don't want her to think that you're always going to be late for things."

Adam blinked at his boss giving him dating advice, then grinned. "Yes, ma'am."

"Now, go on. I'll close up. Just turn the sign over on your way out."

"Sure thing."

Charlie spotted Crow crouching along the far aisle, hiding behind a display of bushes.

"Evelyn, where are you?" Charlie called.

"What? I brought you here, just like you asked." Evelyn appeared beside her. Maria materialized on her other side.

"I remember you," Maria said. "You were the one nosing around my car."

"Yes. I was trying to help you."

"I know." Maria rolled her eyes.

"You've been haunting this place and Lisa's condo. Haven't you?" Charlie asked.

"I was trying to kill that stupid pothos. I knew they'd come after it, and I didn't want Lisa to get hurt. But, she repotted it and now I can't get close."

"She probably put a spell on it. We need to find a way to protect that plant and my cousin from Crow." Charlie floated past them toward the hiding man.

Crow signaled Boone, and he returned a thumbs up in silent acknowledgment. Boone headed for the kiosk, where Lisa was counting out the drawer and filling out a deposit slip.

"Excuse me," Boone said. "I was wondering if I could get your help."

Lisa glanced at her watch. Charlie could see exhaustion on her face, the dark circles under her eyes.

"Yes, of course. I didn't see you there," she said to the tall, beefy man with spiky hair. "We were just about to close."

Boone nodded. "I promise it won't take long. I just need to pick out some sort of garden ornament for my wife."

"Sure." Lisa closed the cash drawer and opened the pass through. The pothos sitting on a shelf inside the kiosk suddenly sprouted a pair of long tendrils. If Charlie had not seen it for herself, she wouldn't have believed it. One of the tendrils wove through the lattice, as if bracing itself. The other brushed across Lisa's shoulder and curled around her arm . Lisa's eyes widened, full of surprise.

"What the..." Lisa muttered.

Charlie had no physical body, but it didn't stop her from feeling a sudden sense of urgency. She spotted Crow creeping closer.

"Oh my goddess, Lisa, you need to get out of here," Charlie yelled, even though she knew Lisa couldn't hear her. "Evelyn, I know you can do something. Can you throw something at him?"

"Sure," Evelyn said.

"I can too." Maria held her hand out, and a pen lying on the countertop rose up and flew at Boone's face.

The man stumbled backwards and swiped at the air. The fright startled him into dropping the pretense. He looked over at Crow, who stood from his hiding place.

Lisa looked in Crow's direction and realized their true intentions. She backed into the cash register, turned, and quickly opened the drawer. "Take the cash. It's all here. I haven't deposited anything yet. Just take it and go. I don't want any trouble."

"We're not looking for your cash, lady," Boone spat.

Crow smirked and approached the counter. "But, we won't say no since you're offering."

"What do you want?" Lisa asked. The pothos withdrew from Lisa's arm at Crow's approach. It's heart-shaped leaves trembled.

"We need your little friend here." Crow pointed to the pothos.

"What? Why? It's just a plant."

"It's also an important part of our business." Crow reached into his pocket and pulled out a small sachet. "Grab her!"

Boone seized Lisa by the arms. Another pen pelted him. "Hey!" He glanced around.

Lisa brought the heel of her hiking boot down hard on his toes. He yowled in pain, and she slid past him, taking off toward the office.

Maria slammed the pass-through down, blocking Crow from entering. "Hurry. Go get help. We'll keep them busy."

To my body, I must awake. Charlie chanted the mantra through her mind, and the world grayed. Dizziness swirled through her, disorienting her. The sensation of falling from a great distance rushed upon her, then she landed and opened her eyes in the conference room.

"Lisa!" Charlie jerked up and scrambled off the table. But, her body didn't respond as she expected and she fell to the ground on all fours. It took a moment for the spinning to stop.

When she felt a warm hand in the center of her back, she looked up to find Jason kneeling next to her. "What's wrong with Lisa?"

"She's in danger. Crow went after a plant at the garden center. We have to get to her."

"Can you walk?"

"I think so." Charlie pushed herself to her feet to prove it. Jason was right there when she stumbled.

He smirked, "I'll drive." He grabbed her bag for her and helped her to the door before stopping to ask. "Are you going to be able to do this alone? I mean, I'll be there. But, like you said, all I've got is a gun, and they have magic."

"You bring your gun and your vest, too. For once, I don't care if you shoot. I'll call Jen. The family will back me up."

"Let's go," Jason said and helped Charlie out the door.

* * *

"OF COURSE WE'LL COME," JEN SAID THROUGH THE SPEAKER on Charlie's phone. Charlie could hear hammering in the background. "Evangeline and I are at the café doing some last-minute things. We'll grab Daphne and head that way."

"Thanks, Jen. We'll meet you there. Make sure you bring your wand."

"Sure thing," Jen said. "And, Charlie, it will be okay. Lisa is a fighter. And the baby will actually add a layer of protection for her."

"Right. I forgot about that," Charlie said. "I wish it made me feel better."

"I know. We'll see you soon."

The line went dead, and Charlie held her phone to her chest for a moment. She wished with all her might she could just close her eyes and move to the garden center at the same speed she could on the astral plane. Her stomach wound into a tight knot.

"Hey, Charlie," Jason said.

She noticed his knuckles, tightly wrapped around his steering wheel, had gone white.

"It's going to be okay, Jason. We're going to get to her in time."

"Yeah. Sure." Jason nodded and swallowed hard. "It's just... what baby?"

"What?" Charlie asked.

"Jen said 'the baby will protect her.' What baby?"

"Oh crap," Charlie muttered. "She hasn't told you yet."

"Told me what?" Jason asked.

CHAPTER 47

Lisa slammed the office door and turned the deadbolt. If her assailants were witches, and she had a strong suspicion they were, the lock wouldn't hold them for long. She switched her monitor over to the split screen that showed the views from the six cameras spaced throughout the garden center. The cameras didn't pick up sound, so she couldn't hear what they were saying. She zoomed in on the view of the kiosk, trying to at least see what they were doing.

The two men did their best to loosen the straps she'd used to affix the lucky plant's pot to the kiosk shelf. As they did, the pothos shot out new tendrils that wove tightly through the lattice. Lisa had cut it back severely only a couple of days ago. She had thought it would take weeks for the plant to recover. As strange as it sounded, she felt it didn't want to leave her, and that it would do anything to stay in the garden center.

Regardless, she couldn't just let these men accost her place of business. She grabbed her cell phone from her purse and called Jason.

He picked up on the first ring. "I'm on my way."

Lisa's eyes popped wide. "What?"

"I already know what's happening," he said.

"How?"

"How do you think?"

She didn't need to think. "Charlie."

"Hey Lisa," Charlie said. "Crow, the dude we raided this morning in Myrtle Beach, is after a plant you have."

"Yeah, I know."

"Is he there now?" Jason's voice was tight.

"Yeah. He and his friend are trying to get the pothos loose from its holder. But there's a spell holding it in place, and unless they figure out how to break it, it's not happening."

"Where are you?"

"I'm in my office. I've got the door locked, but if they decide to come after me...." Her voice trailed off.

"We'll be there before then," Jason said.

"Do you think these are the guys that followed me in that truck?"

"Yep," Jason said.

"Listen. Y'all be careful approaching these guys, okay?"

Charlie broke into the conversation. "Do you have your wand?".

"I do. And I'm not afraid to use it."

"You just stay put until we get there, "Jason growled, "because we have a lot to talk about once all this is done." A strange flash of anger in his voice confused her.

"What's wrong? You sound mad."

"I'm not mad. I'm disappointed."

"You sound mad," Lisa argued.

Charlie asked, "Jason, is this really the best time?"

"This may be the only time," he snapped.

"Why are you yelling at Charlie?" Lisa asked, completely dumbfounded.

"Why didn't you tell me you were pregnant?"

Lisa sighed and covered her face with her hand. "Dammit, who told you?"

"It doesn't matter who told me. It should've been you."

"Really? You're going to be mad at me about this right now, when I have criminals breaking into my place of business?" she yelled. "It was Daphne, wasn't it?"

"It wasn't Daphne," Charlie said. "Jen accidentally let it slip on the phone just now. She thought you'd told him. You said you were going to tell him."

"It doesn't matter now who told me. What matters now is you staying safe 'til we get there and lock this guy up. Then we're going to have a long talk."

"Listen, I've got to go. The bad guys are heading toward my office."

"You be careful," Charlie said.

"Don't worry about me." Lisa hung up and stuck the phone in a pocket of her cargo shorts. She pushed the argument out of her mind as best she could as she slipped out of the office into the darkened hallway. If she turned left, she'd end up in the showroom. Right, and she'd end up in the loading area where they kept mulch, river rock, small pebbles, and groundcover sold by the square yard. It wouldn't offer much cover, but if she could get into the shadow of the building and slip between some of the aisles, she might be able to make her way toward the kiosk. She would have to take them out one at a time, though.

"There she is." The big, meaty witch pointed at her. A shot of red energy sailed past her, and she could smell the electric ions. She took off fast, zig-zagging behind the tall piles of decorative rocks. Her hiking boots weighed heavy on her feet, and her thighs burned as she pushed to move faster. Several shots flew past her, causing mini-explosions of small rocks to explode around her. She managed to get off a couple of defensive shots before pointing her wand at the closed chain-link gate between the showroom and the bulk supplies. Open. The gate swung inward on its squealing hinges.

Once she passed through it, she flicked her wrist and thought close and lock. The gate slammed shut, and the padlock slid itself into place and clicked shut. She dashed behind a selection of potted trees and bent over, hands on knees, taking a moment to catch her breath. If she could hold them off until Jason and Charlie got there, it would be okay.

"Hey, cut it out."

Lisa peeked out of her hiding spot to see the big goon on the other side of the fence, defending himself against rocks sailing through the air and pelting him. Out of nowhere, a travertine paver slammed into the side of the guy's head. He dropped like a stone.

"Maria?" Lisa whispered.

"Maria's dead."

A chill skittered down Lisa's back. She spun to face the platinum-haired thug who held his hand up, palm facing her. Magic sparked between his fingers. He had to be the boss. "Crow? You killed Maria?"

"I ran her off the road myself. Made sure that bitch wasn't going to make it out alive."

Lisa held her wand out in a shaking hand. Jason was on his way. She just had to keep herself safe until he got there. Herself and the baby.

"You're not going to make it out of this alive, either," Crow snarled. "You put some sort of binding spell on that plant, didn't you?"

"Something like that." She stepped away from the trees, into the aisle where she had more room to maneuver. "I'm not going to tell you how to break it, if that's what you're getting at."

"You don't have to do anything." Crow followed her. "I'll just kill you. That's the easiest way to break a witch's spell."

Lisa scoffed. "I see somebody's been reading you fairytales. Killing me won't break my spells."

Movement on the ground caught her eye. She stumbled away from the gate in surprise and tried to refocus her gaze on Crow instead of on the half dozen pothos tendrils wriggling through the chain-link. They were growing at an impossible rate as it continued to creep along the concrete behind Crow.

Bind him. Feeling silly, she thought at the pothos, Bind him.

Crow frowned at her. Lisa realized she hadn't hidden her shock fast enough. He turned to see what had caught her attention.

Bind him! Like Charlie, Lisa repeated the plea a third time and sealed her intention with a yell. "So mote it be!"

Crow turned back to face her and raised his sparking hand. But, he was too slow. The tendrils shivered and rushed at Crow's ankles, coiling around his legs like a dozen boa constrictors. "What the hell?"

Suddenly the pothos drew back, yanking his feet out from under him. Crow fell forward, breaking his fall with his arms.

In the distance, a siren wailed. Lisa shifted the aim of

her wand to Crow's head as the pothos wriggled around his body. "That's for Maria."

Jason cut his siren as he turned into the parking lot of the garden center, leaving his lights flashing. Jen's truck and Daphne's Chevy Tahoe squealed in behind him. The five of them, Charlie, Jason, Jen, Daphne, and Evangeline, leapt out of their vehicles with wands and weapons in hand. The sign had been turned to Closed, but the front gate was unlocked. As quietly as she could, Charlie opened the gate just wide enough for the five of them to slip inside.

"We should fan out," Charlie said. "Daphne, you and Evangeline go that way." Charlie pointed to the right where the pottery and statuary were. "Jen, you're with me. Jason, you go left and be careful."

Jason nodded. Charlie and Jen held their wands in front of them, heading up the center aisle toward the register kiosk. When they arrived, Charlie stood in awe of what she saw. Crow Bowman lay on his side next to the kiosk, hogtied by thick tendrils of the pothos. With every twitch, the plant tightened, and Crow cried out in pain.

"Oh my goddess," Crow's face lit up when he saw Charlie. "You've got to get me out of here. The bitch is crazy. I can't feel my hands, man."

"Lisa! Lisa, where are you?" Jason called.

"I'm here," Lisa said.

"Can you watch him?" Charlie asked Jen.

Jen pointed her wand at Crow's head. "He's not going anywhere."

Charlie wound her way through the aisles to where she heard Lisa's voice. She found her cousin approaching with a slow-moving Boone. He had some trouble walking with his hands secured behind his back. Charlie wondered if the blood trickling from a wound on the side of his head might also have something to do with his balance issues.

"Move it." Lisa barked. A stream of blue energy emitted from the tip of her wand and wrapped around Boone's wrists.

Boone tripped again when a rock flew out of thin air and struck his shoulder.

"Come on!" he called out, his face reddened with frustration. "I'm not trying to escape. You can stop now."

Charlie saw Maria and Evelyn following close behind Boone, each carrying a handful of rocks.

Jason threw his arms around Lisa and pulled her close.

"I'll take him from here," Charlie took Lisa's wand as her cousin wrapped her arms fully around Jason.

"I can't believe you're safe. How did you do this?" Jason asked. He pulled out of the embrace and stroked her cheek.

"I had a little help," Lisa said. "Maria's here."

"So is her best friend, Evelyn," Charlie said. "But that doesn't explain the plant."

"It was pretty close to death, and I saved it. We bonded. I think it wanted to protect me." Lisa shrugged.

"It's amazing," Charlie said. "Jason, can I see your handcuffs?"

"Sure thing." Jason unclipped the cuffs from his belt and handed them to her.

Charlie enchanted the cuffs to prevent Boone from unlocking them with a spell, then snapped them onto his wrists. "You are under arrest by the authority of the DOL."

Evelyn pegged Boone's face with a pebble, and he jerked. "I'm going. Please just get me out of here. Freaking ghosts."

"Don't worry." Charlie nodded at Evelyn and Maria. "Where you and your buddy Crow are going, you won't ever have to worry about ghosts again."

CHAPTER 48

The chains of the porch swing creaked with every push of Jason's feet. Lisa snuggled up next to him with her legs across his lap and her head on his shoulder. Jason and Charlie had taken Crow and Boone to the sheriff's station and put them in a specially warded holding cell where they didn't spend much time. Ben and Athena arrived hard on their heels with two DOL officers to transport the murderers to Charlotte for their arraignment. Then Lisa gave her statement to Ben, and, at Jen's insistence, everyone headed back to her father's house.

"I can feel you stewing," Lisa said. "Do you want to talk about it?"

"Here?" Jason asked.

"It's as good a place as any."

Jason looked to the back door and the kitchen light

shining out onto the darkened porch. The crickets in the yard chirped, and the air smelled like rain.

"What about your family? You really want to air this out in front of them?"

"I thought you knew by now, there are no secrets in this family. They will end up knowing one way or another. If that's not enough to send you running, I don't know what is."

He squeezed his arm around her tighter. "I'm not running anywhere."

"Thank goddess for that because I don't want to do this by myself."

"Let's get one thing straight. You are not going to have to raise this baby alone. You hear me?" He tipped her chin up and stared into her green eyes. "If it were up to me, we'd get married tomorrow."

"I knew that's what you'd say. But I don't want this to be like a shotgun wedding. And I don't want to be standing in front of the altar nine months pregnant either."

"Okay, we know how I feel. I'm not interested in a wedding. I'm interested in a marriage."

Lisa peered into Jason's face. He brushed a loose piece of hair behind her ear. He was the only person who ever made her feel this safe, except for her father. "Well, we have a conundrum, then, don't we?"

"Why is this wedding so important to you?"

"I don't know. I guess because I grew up looking at my

parent's wedding photos. They had this huge wedding, and they were so happy."

"Do you think it made them love each other more?"

"No, of course not." Lisa laid her head on his shoulder again. "But my mom's not here. I thought a big wedding would make me feel closer to her. That's all."

"What if we found a way to include her? Would you be open to that?"

"Possibly." A curious smile stretched across her face. He leaned in and kissed her soft, warm lips.

"I will take possibly," he whispered. "Jen whispered in my ear earlier that she has some ideas. Maybe we should hear her out."

Lisa sighed, but there wasn't a trace of defeat on her face, only peace. "All right, Jason Tate, I'll marry you. Sooner rather than later in a ceremony smaller rather than larger."

"I mean, as long as our family is with us, that's all that matters, right?"

"Right," she whispered. "That's all that matters."

"Oh my goddess," Jen gushed. "You look so beautiful."

The quiet thrumming in Lisa's chest grew stronger. She sat at a dressing table in a bedroom at Talmadge House. An array of hair styling tools and a tackle box full of make-up covered most of it, along with a box holding a crown made of grapevine twigs, greenery, and her favorite flowers. Lily of the valley, orange roses, and a few stems of her silver satin pothos filled out the rustic headpiece.

Daphne put finishing touches on Lisa's long, strawberry blond hair, then she placed the flower crown on her head. "I agree. You are gorgeous. The dress is perfect, and so is your choice of flowers."

"Thanks," Lisa said. A small bouquet of the same flowers from the crown sat on the table, wrapped with a long, gossamer ribbon they would use for the handfasting part of the ceremony. It had thrilled her when Jason didn't argue about the pagan ritual.

Lisa rose to look at herself in the large, oval mirror in the corner. "You don't think the dress looks too dated?"

"Not with the changes Mama and I made." Daphne sidled up next to her, a grin on her face.

Lisa smoothed the short, silk taffeta skirt and admired how her aunt and Daphne transformed her mother's dress from a lace-covered, puffy-sleeved, and slightly overly-sequined wedding dress to something more fairy-like. Evangeline had ripped out all the lace, sequins, and the high collar but left the sweet-heart neckline that accentuated Lisa's long swan-like neck and dropped the puffy sleeves off her shoulders so they floated like clouds. Then Daphne applied a glamour to the dress giving it a dreamy quality that enhanced Lisa's skin and hair.

A knock on the door drew Lisa's attention away from her reflection. "Come in."

The door opened, and an older man with thick, white hair and black-rimmed glasses poked his head inside the room.

"Oh, my goodness. Aren't you just the most beautiful thing I've ever seen." A wide smile stretched across his lips, causing his face to wrinkle. The black robe he wore over a gray, pinstriped suit hung to just above his ankles.

Lisa grinned. "Judge McKenzie, thank you so much for coming on such short notice."

He shook his head. "How could I not come for my favorite student?"

"I know you're retired now, and my request to officiate a pagan ceremony isn't typical," Lisa said.

"Don't you worry about a thing. I am happy to do it. Your aunt and I will ensure you have the ceremony you want."

"Thank you, sir. It means so much that you're here. "

He smiled again and patted her arm. "I won't keep you any longer. I just wanted to say hello before I headed down."

"I appreciate it," Lisa said. "I'll see you downstairs."

"Yes, ma'am. I'll be the one standing next to that fiancé of yours."

"How does he look?" Lisa's stomach fluttered.

"Very calm." Judge Mackenzie chuckled.

Lisa laughed and fidgeted with her dress. "Well, that makes one of us."

"You'll be fine." The judge turned and disappeared through the door just as her father and Charlie entered the room.

Sudden tears threatened to fall, and Lisa sniffled.

"No, no, no, no." Daphne waggled a finger. "No tears. I did not apply waterproof mascara." Daphne fussed over Lisa again, this time whispering a spell to set her make-up until after the ceremony was over.

"Charlie, can you help me out?" Jen asked, trying to reach the zipper on the back of her dark periwinkle silk dress.

"Sure thing." Charlie zipped her up. "I love that color. It really brings out your eyes."

"Me, too." Jen held out the short skirt and then let it fall.

"It's time to start." Charlie glanced at her watch. She grabbed the bouquet from the table and placed it in Lisa's hands. "Are you ready?"

"I am." Lisa nodded and blew out a breath. She turned to her father.

Jack Holloway's lips had disappeared into his thick, silvery beard. He sniffled, and looked as if he might cry at any moment. Lisa tucked her arm into the crook of his elbow. "I have already been scolded once about crying. If you start, there will be no stopping me no matter what kind of spell Daphne cast."

"You just look so much like your mama." He sniffed and kissed her on the cheek.

"Oh, Daddy." Lisa swiped at the tear that fell to her cheek.

He whispered in her ear, his voice raspy with emotion. "She would be so proud of you,"

"Thank you," she mouthed.

"I love you, sweetie."

"I love you too, Daddy. Now, let's go get me married before I completely fall apart." She chuckled. Jack covered her hand with his and nodded.

BEHIND TALMADGE HOUSE, A LARGE LAWN STRETCHED TO the marsh. The sun sat low in the sky, bathing everything in a golden light, and a gentle breeze blew off the water, keeping the gnats and no-see-ums at bay. Jen had cast a spell on the candles so not even a gale force wind could blow them out and ruin the joining of Lisa and Jason's lives and energy together.

The judge stood inside a circle of flickering candles, a serene smile on his face. Jason waited outside the circle. He was dressed in his best navy blue suit and matching tie. The rest of the guests, mainly family and a few friends, all stood outside the circle watching with awe on their faces as Jack Holloway led Lisa across the lawn.

When they reached Jason, Jack kissed Lisa on her

cheek and took his place in the circle of loved ones; Charlie, Evan, Tom, Daphne, her boyfriend Darius, Evangeline, Ruby, Jen and Ben, Susan Tate, and Jason's grandmother Sugar Blackburn.

"You ready?" Jason asked and held out his hand.

Lisa took a deep breath and intertwined her fingers with his. Her stomach fluttered, full of the butterflies of anticipation, excitement, and a little fear if she was honest with herself. She nodded. "Yes."

"Thank you all for coming this lovely evening to witness the joining of this couple, Lisa Marie Holloway and Jason David Tate, as they embark on a wonderful new adventure together."

The judge glanced at a notecard Lisa had given him at the rehearsal. "Lisa, Jason, please step into the circle."

Lisa handed her bouquet to Jen. Her sister slipped the ribbon from it and passed the silk fabric to Lisa. Jason helped her step over the candles, taking care not to knock any over, and they stood, side by side, in front of the judge. Lisa handed the ribbon to him. He took it with a smile.

"Now, please, everyone, join hands and complete the circle," the judge instructed.

Lisa felt the strong, loving energy of her family envelop them, protecting and holding space for them. Every doubt and fear she'd harbored melted away.

"Jason, Lisa, please join hands," the judge said.

Jason and Lisa faced each other and took each other's hands. Jason beamed. Lisa couldn't help but mirror him.

The judge wrapped the long ribbon around their hands. "Today we are gathered to celebrate the handfasting of this couple, Jason David Tate and Lisa Marie Holloway. Jason, Lisa, with this ribbon I entwine, your bodies, and your hearts, from now until the end of time."

* * *

THE FAIRY LIGHTS STRUNG AROUND THE LARGE FRONT PORCH of Talmadge House twinkled, giving the space a warm glow. The buffet set up on one end of the porch had been picked nearly clean with only the wedding cake left, a simple two-tiered confection iced in smooth chocolate buttercream and decorated with orange ombre rosettes on top.

Everyone surrounded two long tables, their plates empty of the delicious shrimp and grits Jen had prepared. Lisa and Jason sat in the center, and she couldn't help but let the joy of the day wash through her.

Ben stood up and grabbed a bottle chilling in a nearby bucket. The cork popped, and champagne overflowed onto the porch. Jen hopped up and gathered the champagne glasses from a tray, including special crystal goblets that her parents used at their wedding.

Lisa watched Jen and Ben pour the bubbling liquid and pass it around to all the adults at the table.

Ben cleared his throat and held up his glass. "As best man, I guess it's up to me to toast the happy couple." He grinned, his gaze locked on Lisa and Jason.

"Jason, you've become a good friend to me, and all I can say is I'm glad you and Lisa went first."

Laughter traveled across the small crowd. Jen rolled her eyes but continued grinning, unshaken by her boyfriend's comments. Lisa grabbed her bouquet from beside her empty plate and tossed it to her sister. Jen caught it with a laugh and a warning glare.

Ben blanched. "All jokes aside, I wish you and Lisa all the happiness in the world. I know you're going to be a great dad. I'm sure you've got your kid's bulletproof vest all picked out."

"Sure, but Lisa's already got a wand picked out, so, we're even," Jason chided.

"That just means this baby will be doubly protected, and as part of this family, exponentially loved." Ben lifted his glass. "To love and babies."

"To love and babies," the crowd echoed and sipped their champagne.

Lisa put her glass on the table and slipped her hand into Jason's. Her family continued to eat, tell tales on each other, and laugh. The warmth and intimacy of this small party overflowed with love making her aware, if she'd stuck to her guns, and insisted on getting married next spring, this moment, would never have been so satisfying, so full of joy.

Jason entwined his fingers with hers and met her gaze. He brought her hand to his lips. "Are you okay with this imperfect wedding?"

"Who said it wasn't perfect?" She gave him a knowing grin and shrugged. "Maybe it's not what I originally planned but it's exactly what I wanted."

Jason grinned and pressed his warm lips against hers. She melted into it. "Good, Mrs. Tate."

Lisa pulled back and her eyebrow went up. "Who said I'm changing my name?"

Thank you for reading *The Green Witch*. When I started this book, I thought I'd put the worst behind me, but man was I wrong. I am what they call a discovery writer, which means I listen to my characters and they help guide me to discover/uncover the story along the way.

I "knew" what was supposed to happen, but none of the characters agreed. It led to a lot of writing/revising/writing some more to get it right. I also let a comment from a review get in my head, and almost had myself convinced that no one but me wanted to hear Lisa's story. Anyway I pushed through, and finally Lisa and Charlie started talking, and I started taking dictation. The result is this book, which is the longest book I've written in the series so far. Hopefully you'll find it entertaining and worth the wait.

In the next book, *The Glamour Witch*, Daphne is accused of murder and goes on the run to prove her innocence when Charlie and the DOL are presented with iron-clad evidence. Now Daphne must figure out who the real killer is before she's caught and put away in DOL jail forever. There's lots of mystery, intrigue, ghostly encounters, and family time to keep you entertained. And of course Daphne's irrepressible spirit to carry us through.

Click here to preorder: The Glamour Witch.

· · ·

Or you can signup for my newsletter and to be informed when *The Glamour Witch* is available for purchase. htttps://wendy-wang-books.ck.page/482af1c7a3

Connect with me

One of the things I love most about writing is building a relationship with my readers. We can connect in several different ways.

Join my reader's newsletter.

By signing up for my newsletter, you will get information on preorders, new releases and exclusive content just for my reader's newsletter. You can join by clicking here: http://wendy-wang-books.ck.page/482af1c7a3

You can also follow me on my Amazon page if you prefer not to get another email in your inbox. Follow me here.

Connect with me on Facebook

Want to comment on your favorite scene? Or make suggestions for a funny ghostly encounter for Charlie? Or tell me what sort of magic you'd like to see Jen, Daphne and Lisa perform? Like my Facebook page and let me know. I post content there regularly and talk with my readers every day.

. . .

FACEBOOK: https://www.facebook.com/wendywangauthor

Let's talk about our favorite books in my readers group on Facebook.
Readers Group: https://www.facebook.com/groups/1287348628022940/

You can always drop me an email. I love to hear from my readers
Email: wendy@wendywangbooks.com

Thank you again for reading!

Printed in Great Britain
by Amazon